LagOOnieville

Volume I

by

B.R. Emrick

LAGOONIEVILLE™ – Volume 1
BR Emrick

www.lagoonieville.com

ISBN: 0-9770869-0-9
Printed in the United States of America by
roguepublications™

Lagoonieville™ is a new version of Big Eye Bertha ISBN 1-932560-72-6

Dedicated to
Baer de Barkalot, D/T *Barracouta*
The best boat dog in the Caribbean

With appreciation to

Brion Sausser, Diane Mendez,

Jasmine Brown, Jim Wilkinson,

and my wife, Julie,

for their contributions

to the first novel of the

LagOOnieville™ Collection.

1

The Lagoonies

A BEER JOINT TWELVE HUNDRED MILES SOUTHEAST of Miami and only five feet from a little backwater lagoon was, like most Caribbean waterfront bars, an open-air and authentically grubby little place. It was a notorious bar, known by most sailors on the underbelly of a lower-latitude maritime society, as Dirty's Beer Joint. It was a unique piece of paradise that attracted well-worn people, mostly men. They were boatfolks, ordinary boat-bums who hung out spending time, which was about all they had to spend. Most were veterans from some jungle or desert war, or an unreasonable courtroom battle, and were left with various mental and/or physical wounds. They called themselves Lagoonies.

Dick "Dirty" Farrar, the owner, had been a dirty professional boxer and wrestler before being forced to retire and move to a community not easily found by stateside authorities. His bar was intentionally well off the tourist trail, as they only asked questions and snapped pictures of the salty old place. And pictures increased Dirty's exposure to past fans who might remember why Great Walking Eagle, his ring name, had suddenly disappeared.

Most of the boating community were asleep as dawn brought its first light to the peaceful little lagoon; the only movement was a squadron of four pelicans soaring silently a foot over the silky-smooth water. Then, as if commanded by some unheard order, they simultaneously rose without a single flap of their wings to a height of thirty feet, where they rolled 180 degrees and fell straight down, splashing head first in the still saltwater, happily sacrificing the morning's tranquility for their breakfast.

Painter Pete Morgan was one of eight men sitting at Dirty's bar watching the pelicans. He was believed to be one of the exceptions, who had not come to the islands from the battlegrounds to drink himself to death. Instead, he claimed that he came from the business world of Houston, and, when the oil business took a big dive, he did too. Pete cashed in his chips, bought a forty-foot sailboat, and left Houston and his ex-wife behind to find a friendlier face and a better place.

A year later, he sailed into Miami. Six months later, he had reached the bottom limits of his cruising kitty. He had enjoyed life fully and spent his money freely, knowing he was going broke much faster than planned. He had

had too much fun to care until the day arrived when he had to make a choice: pay the dock rent—or eat.

Reality had finally caught up with him; he would have to go back to work or rob a bank. While he was basically honest, the idea of turning to crime wasn't as appalling as going back to a nine-to-five existence. Pete had tasted the freedom that a cruising life offered in exchange for financial security, and it appealed to him. He could never force himself back into the daily ritual of employment and conforming to society's notion of what was acceptable.

Instead of working, or robbing banks, he left the glitter of Miami and sailed east to the Bahamas where he discovered a new world. Pete had entered the Lagoonieville Nation. It wasn't a place defined by borders, but by a state of mind. He met people just like himself while sailing from one tiny island to the next. He was totally at home in the islands and comfortable with the other penniless-by-choice sailors. It was the lifestyle he had been searching for since dropping out.

For the next few years, he explored all the islands of the Caribbean and easily adjusted to his new financial status; it was not all that bad. He lived by catching fish, selling some to restaurants and eating the rest. The sale of a three-foot Wahoo to a restaurant could keep him in food and beer for a week.

His fishing career ended one day when he caught a spirited young lady named Sadie June. She was an island girl in Trinidad who took him in for a while and taught him the art of painting signs, which was her business. Pete loved her and his new work. All went well until things started getting uncomfortable for Sadie, and, one night, she politely asked Pete for her paintbrushes back, after he suggested they get hitched.

He managed to buy his own brushes and continued sailing south, touching up signs on bars, restaurants, and boat transoms. If they did not want to pay, he swapped his brushwork for booze and food. He no longer had to fish to stay alive. Fortunately, Pete did not require much money, so very little of his time was spent painting. Most of it was used for drinking, chasing the ladies, swimming, fishing, and watching the local sports of cricket and soccer, which he enjoyed, but didn't understand any more than the women in his life.

He sailed up and down the Lesser Antilles and South America's Atlantic coast, revisiting his sign customers for touch-ups and treats. That was his lifestyle and he was content; the days of a big income, new cars, a huge home, and fine clothes had forever passed. His world now revolved around doing enough work to support his needs and keep his sailboat, *Gypsy Bitch*, in seaworthy condition. There was a spiritual bond between *Gypsy* and Pete; she was not as pretty as she had been, but she took damn good care of him.

He had found Dirty's Beer Joint by accident one day, and liked the place and the people. Since then, he had not made another trip to South America and was happy where he was for awhile. His painting business seemed to be able to keep up with his bar tab, so things were good in the Virgin Islands.

Four thousand, two hundred and three miles due east of Dirty's was a much different scene. A small band of the Awwakies, an African desert tribe, had correctly read the signs Mother Nature provided for those who understood, but none could imagine how bad the storm was going to be. The camels were brought into the tribe's largest tent, and placed around its perimeter. Everyone brought their water bags, meager food supplies, and the bundles of yucca fibers they had spent the last three weeks collecting from the desert plants, which was a major part of the tribe's income.

The twenty men, women, and children huddled together, each covering their possessions with their bodies to keep them from blowing away, should the worst happen and they lose the tent to the wind. The men were concerned about what was to come, but had done this many times. Sandstorms developed frequently in their world. The tribe was prepared for the coming onslaught, but this time the children cried as they felt the fear in their mothers' souls. The animals were unusually restless, sensing winds from some unseen evil were approaching.

Two days later, if anyone was alive in the region, they would have found the tribe and their animals scattered all over the area with every orifice, lung, and stomach packed full with the beauty of the desert. Sadly, the same thing had happened all over North Africa as a massive weather system developed and began its journey toward the Atlantic Ocean.

Pete and the other guys in Dirty's bar were suffering from various degrees of hangover, and to each, Dirty's breakfast with a cold beer was the cure. Only six items were on the never-changing breakfast menu that hung crookedly on the wall: Dirty Egg, coffee, Bloody Mary, beer, booze, and Dirty's Pipe cooler (four Alka-Seltzers in cold club soda with a shot of tequila).

Dirty Egg was a big plate covered with eggs as-you-get-'em covered with a gooey layer of cheese, Tabasco sauce, a thick slice of fried Spam covered in over-used grease, and a couple of chunky slices of French loaf made a few days before and smeared with a bulky layer of butter. Dirty's breakfast filled you up and the beer was always cold.

Pete, with both elbows on the bar, nonchalantly chewed on stale bread while watching a man rowing a dinghy. He said to the others, "Why doesn't Tom take that damn outboard off? I've never seen him use it."

The guy next to him, Rigger Grady, answered, through a mouthful of food, "Probably ain't got enough money to buy gas."

"What's new?" snapped Dirty. "He's the poorest of you bunch of shitheads. None of you fuckers got any room to talk when it comes to being broke. I'm carrying tabs on all you lazy bastards."

The lazy bastards sat in silence, munching on whatever was on their plates, while watching Tom pull on mismatched oars he had salvaged some time ago from some other misfortunate soul.

A guy across the bar, Captain Murphy, said, "You'd think he'd make an effort to get longer oars. He works twice as hard to make way than if they were the proper length."

Grady said, "Seems I've heard a phrase about people whose oars don't quite reach the water."

As Salvage Tom tied the frizzy painter to a mangrove limb, he looked up at the bar, grinned, and said, "*Lulu* sank last night."

"Again!" Grady said in disbelief. "Damn, man, pull *Lulu* out of the water until you can fix the damn thing."

Tom plopped on a barstool, as Dirty said, "Okay shithead, save your breath. I'll buy you a beer," and he slammed a Heineken, known as a greenie at Dirty's bar, down in front of Tom, who showed his appreciation with a big smile of yellowed teeth. He gulped half of it down, saving the rest to sip with breakfast. "What're my chances of getting a Dirty Egg?"

In his usual irritated manner, Dirty growled, "Sometimes, Tom, I think you sink that fucking boat just so you don't have to pay your tab. Come to think of it, it always seems to happen about the time I'm ready to cut your skinny ass off."

"Sorry, Dirty. I'll get something to you pretty soon. I'm working on a deal now and—" A howl erupted from the other crows, as Dirty called his clientele, interrupting Tom.

Grady hooted, "Another big deal, a golden horizon in the works?" Salvage Tom always had a big project just over the horizon that was going to make him financially well. It never happened, but his faith that something would never faltered.

"Good thing you're in the salvage business, Tom; you're the best customer you got," came another zing from the gathering of crows. Tom was used to it and expected to be the brunt of their morning hangovers until the next guy with some rotten luck came along.

Tom grinned and responded, "A good saltwater bath once in a while is good for *Lulu's* dry rot." He was willing to take crap from the other Lagoonies, but anxiously wanted it over so he could have a serious talk with Pete. He was excited about his newest project and needed Pete's help to pull it off, but had to hold his eagerness in check. This was not the time; his pals were having too much fun razzing him about his newest golden horizon and about his beloved *Lulu* that was resting on bottom.

Everyone had a good time at Tom's expense, not out of unkindness or to have a cheap laugh, but only because it was a way of life for them, and nobody would have changed a damn thing.

Grady bought breakfast beers for everyone; it was the start of another day for the Lagoonies of Barracuda Bay.

Carl Snow, Ph.D., lived for his job. He went to work early, stayed late every day, and usually put in seven days a week, depending on the time of year.

When he wasn't on the job, he studied various satellite images from around the world on his personal computer at home. His apartment was off Collins Avenue in Miami with a view of the barrier island of Miami Beach and its surrounding beautiful blue water. However, the view had no special appeal to him; in fact, the draperies remained closed except when his landlady came up once a week to clean the place.

Carl was twenty-eight years old, and a classic egghead. His physical appearance was okay, but he dressed funny. Even though he drove to work every day in his ancient, albeit air-conditioned, 1972 Mercedes, and worked in the air-conditioned environment of an ultra-modern building, he wore field clothes: high-top boots, Levi's®, a T-shirt, and a khaki safari jacket. Every pocket in his jacket was full of pencils, pens, note pads, handheld anemometer, mints, sunglasses, spare reading glasses, magnifying glass, mini-flashlight, folding knife, pocket-sized telescope, sun block with an SPF of 30, and a squeeze tube of Repel® for the bugs. He dressed this way to mimic his favorite professor: Abe Tate, professor of Tornado Technology, in Amarillo, Texas.

Weather fascinated Carl for as long as he could remember. His specialty, tropical systems, had progressed beyond fascination and had been his only love since high school, maybe longer. Whatever anyone might say about Carl's peculiarities, he was not stupid; he had been first in his class since kindergarten. His mind was a sponge when it came to science, but it was like a tough old leather shoe in the area of social graces. He would rather chase cars down Biscayne Boulevard like a dog than go partying with his co-workers. Dating was not important and he only did so when someone forced him to meet a neighborhood girl.

His only other interests revolved around traveling to weather seminars and listening, in the middle of the night, to AM talk shows about extraterrestrials and doomsday science.

Finally, September 1 arrived. It was opening day for Carl's favorite time of the year: the peak month for Atlantic hurricanes. He knew it was going to be a busy month and had been watching unusual weather patterns over the African Sahel region. They had been experiencing horrific *haboobs* since May, and they were not tapering off, as they should. The *haboobs* were dry storms that formed over the vast desert after days of rising temperatures and low barometric pressures. Oddly, a large concentration of moisture-laden air was growing, but stationary, off Africa's east coast.

He was not sure what was creating the phenomenon and had no intention of asking; the last thing he wanted was interference from his supervisor or co-workers. It was vitally important to understand why the thing was developing before he made its presence known. Only then, would he present it to the staff and emerge as the smartest of the bunch—and then, maybe, they would stop making fun of him.

Other things were happening, too, that were setting the stage for severe weather in the Caribbean and United States. *La Niña* had developed in the Pacific Ocean and was swelling to gigantic proportions. He believed this was causing the moisture increase waiting to pounce on Africa, but didn't understand why it wasn't moving. The eastward-flowing tropical jet stream was weaker because of *La Niña* and should not be stopping the westward-moving rain clouds.

In addition, there was an unusual flow of very warm water flowing down from Europe via the Portugal and the Canary Currents, which would certainly transform any passing low-pressure system to a dangerous Cape Verde hurricane.

The people of the Caribbean dreaded Cape Verde-spawned hurricanes, as they were severely intense storms and had a tendency to track right over the Windward and Leeward Islands rather than turning north early to miss the islands. The worst part of the scenario was that the center of the North Atlantic high-pressure systems had shifted more than usual. All were sure signs that something in nature was brewing and was going to be troublesome for somebody.

Carl felt guilty for not pointing out the forming system's deadly potential, but he was on top of it. He had plenty of time before it blew out over the open sea of the Atlantic Ocean to spawn a whopper hurricane or two. He prayed that no one else would discover the system before it hit the Atlantic, as he would lose the chance of getting a phenomenon named after him. And this one, he had already named: *Snow's Massive Storm Accumulation Event.*

Everything unusual or nautical that floated into Barracuda Lagoon eventually found its way onto the walls and ceiling of Dirty's place. The bar itself was an old, battered, fifty-foot sailboat that had floated up during a hurricane years ago. Its bottom had been torn apart on the rocks, so Dirty and a few other Lagoonies dragged it up on land and made a bar out of it for their own use. It became the place for sailors, and Dirty even put up some money to buy kitchen equipment and commercial beer coolers, but the floor was still just dirt.

Once or twice a year, the trade wind blew hard enough to blow the dust off everything and, occasionally, a hurricane pushed enough water on land to reclaim, temporarily, the once stately sailing vessel, *Anna May Jones*.

Dirty loved the old bar, but never admitted to liking anything. He was a grouchy old fart in his 60s, and delighted in busting the balls of anyone new to his establishment, especially tourists. The average tourist usually did not finish his or her first beer before having enough of his rough, burly behavior. Some would not even make it to a barstool.

That roughness, however, was what everyone who knew Dirty liked about him. It was all an act, like his wrestling career, and his ring name. He swore an old Indian chief named him Great Walking Eagle the day he turned twenty-one and became a man. He didn't learn until he was forty why the chief had chosen such a proud name and was delighted to learn it was an Indian expression for a man who thinks of himself as an eagle, but was too full of shit to fly.

Two other crows who were also full of shit crashed a dinghy's bow onto the little beach between mangroves. As they stepped ashore, Zachary Taylor yelled, "Beer! Dirty, we need beer!" Zach, at forty, was a mysterious man. He would be gone for days, or months at a time, researching stories for his next novel. Zach had money, but you would never know it by the way he lived. He claimed to be a novelist, but no one had ever seen his name or books on a shelf. No one had read his work, but if pressed, he would show you single copies of ten books, all with his picture on the back cover. Zach's delight in life was raising hell and pissing off people with his overly-long shaggy-dog stories.

Zach's pal, Baer McNaasti was also a mystery. He had lived in the mangroves for twenty years, and it was rumored that he used to be a badass paramilitary tied to the CIA. He denied it, saying he was just a drunk living on disability from some fire department.

Most of the Lagoonies could guard a secret or two, so Zach and Baer fit in well. As Zach took a bar stool, he said to Dirty, "Man, have I got a story for you. Have you heard the one about the woman who loved dogs?"

Dirty leaned down and looked into Zach's eyes. "One fucking peep out of you about the woman who loved dogs and I'm coming over the bar with my bat."

Zach snorted, and said, "You old grouch, you need to listen to my jokes, they might help you develop a sense of humor." Dirty held up and pointed his baseball bat at Zach.

The captain of *Laughing Molly*, the oldest charter schooner in the Caribbean arrived and sat down. Dirty pointed the bat at Captain Murphy. "Tell me you got paid."

Murphy sneered, "The owner said check's in the mail. I'm taking *Molly* out for ten days and don't have enough money to buy fuel. Sorry, Dirty, I'll get caught up when I get back."

"Why don't you leave old *Splinter Queen* and her tight-ass owner and get a real job, like pumping gas, so you can pay your bar tab?"

Pete leaned over to Grady and said, "Wonder what'd happen to Salvage Tom and Murphy's crew if Dirty wasn't here? Tom gets shitfaced every day and without Dirty's tab, he'd never eat."

"Don't talk about drinking, my friend; you drink more than he does," quipped Grady.

"Yeah, but I eat a lot, too. It's different when you pour cheap rum into an empty stomach."

"Don't feel sorry for Tom, Pete; he's living the life he wants, just like the rest of us."

"I'm just trying to say something nice about Dirty for a change. Without Dirty's food, a lot of guys would be a lot skinnier."

Tom and a handful of other men in his tax-bracket were aware of Dirty's generosity, but never acknowledged it, and Dirty appreciated that they didn't.

To show compassion was not in his character. Besides, Dirty was in line for some serious payback when his time came to face God, and if he could soften the punishment, all the better.

Grady asked, "Does Tom have any family?"

"Naw, the closest thing he has to a family is us, the Lagoonies. I don't think I've ever even seen him with a woman."

Grady laughed and said, "You got to be kidding. Who do you think he named his boat for?"

After a moment of thought, Pete said, "Not Whorehouse Lou?"

"Yep. In exchange for labor, Tom gets to spend his two and a half minutes crawling over 300-pound Mama Lou, whenever she needs something done."

Tom, like most of the Caribbean rebels, had a hidden past. A nasty war wound, booze, and a bad wife had gotten the best of him. He lost his job as the number-three systems engineer for NASA and opted for a less painful way of life when his ex-wife chose a happier life with her new hubby, Tom's old boss. That had happened many years ago and the hurt had faded, but the memory of his pain was always nearby, unless he was drunk.

Murphy yelled, "Turn on the Weather Channel, Dirty. Let's see if we have any storms heading our way."

Dirty yelled back, "You wanna watch TV, go the fuck home."

The crows moaned and whined. No one had a television on their boat and depended on the local bars to keep them up-to-date, especially during this time of year. Finally, Dirty turned on the set in time to catch the satellite view of the Atlantic and Caribbean. It was unusually clear for September.

"Why don't you so-called sailors learn to read the weather like the true sailormen of yesteryear?" yelled Dirty with his usual sarcastic grin.

Murphy yelled back, "Too much work and, besides that, they wouldn't have done it either if they had had televisions."

One of the other crows, Chuck, one of Murphy's crew, yelled, "Hey Dirty! Let's have a storm-naming party!"

"Who the fuck said that?" Dirty asked, while glaring at Chuck.

"Me, Deano, Dean Martin. Let's party!" Chuck had a personality disorder, and assumed movie star identities to suit any circumstance, be it Boris Karloff, Fred Astaire, or Lassie.

"You know the rules, whoever you are, asshole. It's bad luck to name a storm until a tropical storm develops."

Grady said, "I can't believe it's so clear. There isn't even a tropical wave brewing. Must be something really disruptive over Africa."

"You can bet your ass there's something going on over there." Pete added. It's been over a week since we've had blue sky. The African dust was so thick the other day you couldn't see Big Hatch from Red Hook."

Pete took the hurricane season seriously. He had ridden out seven major hurricanes since he became a member of the Caribbean community and knew what they did to people and places. Moreover, not only during the storm, but for months and years afterwards, people would have to adjust to hardships, both material and psychological. That hardship was not taken lightly, nor was the death the boating community faced with every storm. He had lost friends to the storms; many disappearing forever.

Pete feared, but harbored no ill feelings toward the storms and respected them for what they were: A natural way to keep the tropics in balance. Heat from the intense summer sun accumulated in the waters and atmosphere, and occasionally the water needed stirring and cooling. Mama Nature definitely knew how to stir things up. Occasionally, the shoreline's thick overgrowth needed thinning to allow for new growth. Mama was very good at reducing foliage. Rocks had to be smashed to make new soils for future generations and Mama had been smashing them ever since there was a rock. The same happened for the waterfront communities; what better way to remove old buildings and make room for the new? Hurricanes were a required tool of nature.

"I don't think we'll be lucky this year. The more rain we get reduces the chance of one of the monster hurricanes forming," offered Murphy.

"You better be wrong. We haven't had any rain and it's bloody hot. Even the trade winds have been uncommonly weak this year. Is this an ozone thing?"

"Don't know, but I was down in Frenchtown yesterday and all the Frenchies are uneasy about it. It's kind of spooky, like the quiet before the storm. They're worried about the thick layers of African dust that are covering the islands. They say it's never been this bad, but years when it was almost as bad, they had a run of Cape Verde storms."

Grady, bored with the doom and gloom of hurricanes, said, "Well, as long as it stays nice and quiet today. I've got to go up *Wind Dancer's* main mast, and that's not my favorite job. The last time I was up there, it was a clear day and I could see Miami Beach."

All of the crows heard the remark, but no one said anything; they ignored the overused statement. Grady was the local rigger and there were few sailboats in the area that he hadn't been hoisted up to inspect or repair mastheads, anchor lights, or rigging; and he said the same thing about every mast he went up.

Heights did not bother Grady, and if they did, nobody would ever know. He was a tough son of a bitch, a stand-alone guy. He admitted that he spent three combat tours in Vietnam and the Middle East before he decided to quit killing people and kill a little time instead. He had been living the life of a sailor since he was discharged from the Green Berets.

Everyone liked Grady; he was a solid man with a great sense of humor and deep pockets for anyone who needed a little help. He and Pete had become friends and they ended most every day trying to empty Dirty's rum supply. They got along well together because both respected the other's privacy.

When Grady took off to climb the tallest mast in the Virgins, Salvage Tom slid over next to Pete. "Hey, Pete," he said in a hushed voice, "I need to talk to you in private. You got a little time?"

Pete winced at the thought: *Tom's going to hit me for money again.* He did not mind helping Tom out occasionally, but certainly not on a regular basis. About a year ago, he stopped loaning Tom money, even though he was always repaid, eventually. Shortly after the payback, however, Tom would be broke again and borrow it back. Instead of loaning him money, Pete started exchanging money for work on the *Gypsy Bitch,* or by letting him help with the signs.

"Yeah, Tom. What you need?"

"This isn't about a loan, Pete; I need to talk to you. I've got something going on and I need your help. It's confidential, and I don't want to talk around here. How about coming over to *Lulu* tonight?"

Pete looked at him suspiciously and asked, "Are you trying to trick me into helping you raise *Lulu* again?"

"No, man. I'll have her up and halfway dry by three this afternoon. I've got something really important to talk to you about."

"Okay Tom, but why don't you dinghy over to my boat about seven. We'll have a couple of martinis and I'll grill us a steak. How does that sound?"

"Sounds like I'll be there about seven."

As always, one by one, the early crows left, but were replaced by the next flock, and then the next. "New crow, same old bird shit," Dirty often said.

2

The First of September

THE FAMILIES OF THE JAMAL TRIBE in Chad's Ennedi Plateau had reached their breaking point after experiencing the worst possible weather for two weeks straight. Dust storms had never been as severe in the village's two-hundred years of recorded history. Their goats and camels had been moved into tents and the few houses that existed, to keep them from being skinned alive by the never-ending blast of sand. Things were not getting any better; all they could do was pray that Mohammad would provide rain and give them strength to outlast the storms.

At four o'clock that afternoon, Pete was back in the bar for a well-deserved cold beer. He complained to Dirty, "I've been standing in my dinghy for three hours painting a new name on Zach's old boat. Now *Mermaids Folly* has a shiny new name painted in passionate fucking pink. The sweetie pies named it *Tinker Balls* and are tickled silly."

Dirty, completely uninterested, turned his attention to a cigarette that had fallen out of a rusted old ashtray and onto the bar top that was already covered with butt-burns and peeling varnish. He yelled, "You fuckers ain't got no upbringing. Give you a nice place to go and you leave your fucking butts burning while you hose down the bushes."

Then he yelled to a very black man who had just stepped over to a hole in the mangroves to add to the tide.

"Willie! Damn you! Stop pissing all over my fucking trees. Go to the head; get cultured; you fucking shithead." Willie, another of Captain Murphy's crew, was from Trinidad, and didn't give a shit about anything, as long as he had a tad or two for his corncob pipe. He ignored Dirty.

Grady came in and sat next to Pete. "Hey Pete, on top of *Wind Dancer's* mast, I could see Venezuela today. Lots of beautiful women were on the beach and that made me think that we should go chase some lovelies tonight."

"Can't tonight, my bullshitting friend. I have a dinner guest coming over."

"You dog!" Grady said. "While the cat is away, eh...Would she have a friend?"

"Might have a friend, but *her* name is Salvage Tom. You want to date a woman who's a friend of Tom's?"

"You've been hanging around those guys on *Tinker Balls* too much."

"Screw you. Tom wanted to talk, so I invited him over for a steak. It looks like he could use a big chunk of meat, anyway."

"Okay, sounds good to me, too. I have to meet someone at five, but that won't take long. What time should I be there?" asked Grady.

"Not tonight, old buddy; he has something hot on the fire and wants to talk to me about it in private."

Grady said with interest. "Think he found another yacht to salvage and is looking for backers?"

Pete shrugged his shoulders. "Don't have a clue, but I doubt that it's another yacht. He'd be putting the touch on everyone right now if that were the case. I'm sure it's just another one of his golden horizons, but what the hell, won't hurt to listen."

Grady looked at Pete and said in a serious tone, "For some reason I'm curious about this one. Let me know what he has on his mind."

"Sure, but it'll cost you a bottle of rum, one shot at a time and right here at Dirty's."

"I don't know what it is about you Pete, but you seem to be everybody's best buddy when it's raining shit. It's certainly not because you're a good listener and honest about your opinions. I know you; you don't give a shit. Maybe it's because you've got good sense . . . when you're sober. Whatever it is, I'm glad you've got it and not me. You'll sit up all night talking to Tom, get drunk, and, tomorrow, you won't have any idea what you talked about, and Tom won't either."

"Well at least we'll get to empty a bottle and have a few laughs."

Abby and Jerome Savage leisurely lounged on the main deck of the *Star Wind*, the newest addition to the Caribbean's fleet of cruise ships. They had lived on one ship or another for the last three years, but this was the first time the young couple had been aboard *Star Wind*.

Abby and her mother were the sole heiresses of a major newspaper tycoon who had died a few years ago. Mom stayed close to the business, but Abby and her new husband loved to travel. Their world was the ports-of-call that ringed the Caribbean Basin.

That afternoon they sipped chilled and tangy rum swizzles while lounging poolside under the hot tropical sun, even though it was somewhat blotted by the African dust. Abby loved the sun; over the years, it had turned her skin to dark amber. Her husband was darker, but he had inherited his color from his African ancestors. They were a happy couple and were always the center of attention on whatever ship they traveled. Everyone instantly liked Jerome; his big white smile brightened even the foulest mood. Abby's was as friendly, but her beauty and her sexy body eclipsed her personality. All who met them realized the two were born with golden spoons firmly in place.

Finishing her drink, Abby looked at her watch, and said, "Jerome, it's almost time to leave."

Jerome jumped up, kissed his wife with a loving peck, and answered, "Let's get going, slowpoke." They retired to their luxury suite, and, forty minutes later, disembarked the ship. She wore a thin but tasteful white dress with an open collar. Her jewelry was strands of black plastic beads that hung loosely around her neck and a colorful plastic bracelet circling a wrist. She had been in the Caribbean long enough to know how to dress and look good without inviting a street thief to steal her expensive jewelry.

Jerome had the kind of body fashion designers hired to show their clothes. His muscular physique was perfect in every dimension; he had been a model, and a few other things, before Abby had found him. He wore long white slacks, off-white open-laced shoes, and a light beige tropical shirt open at the neck. His only jewelry was a Timex diver's wristwatch.

The handsome couple walked through the colorful shops that were spread everywhere around Charlotte Amalie Harbor. They browsed and bought the usual tourist fare, a few T-shirts and postcards, and then hailed a taxi. It was time to go to Captain Bean's.

As they entered Captain Bean's open-air bar, the spectacular view of the islands, stretching eastward, captured Abby's attention. Each island was covered in vivid shades of green and served as a picturesque background for sailboats' snow-white sails, slowly drifting down Pillsbury Sound.

Jerome spotted his contact and led his charming wife over to a stool that had been saved by the man wearing a black Hawaiian shirt. They nodded hello but said nothing.

After one drink and halfway into the second one, Jerome muttered, "It's under this stool. See you on the next sailing of the *Norseman*."

While looking away from Jerome, Grady quietly answered, "Take care, and kiss Abby for me." Abby heard him and gave him a smile that broke his heart. She was the most beautiful woman he had ever known, and, if anything ever happened to Jerome, he would damn sure pursue her. But many men had the same thought.

Grady and Jerome had worked together for years and were friends, if such a thing were possible for either man. Since Jerome married Abby, their old partying days were over, but now Grady enjoyed the company of both. St. Thomas, however, was not a place they could socialize; that would have to wait until their next rendezvous, which Jerome described in the note he had covertly stuck under the barstool. The chic couple finished their drinks and made a show of putting their packages on the bar in preparation to leave. Jerome got the bartender's attention by leaving a twenty-dollar tip, as Grady reached under Jerome's stool and slipped the note into his pocket.

An unattached tourist took the stool Jerome had been sitting on and Grady was happy; it was a woman, and she was by herself. Her blonde hair, recently braided, indicated this was her first trip to the islands and she would love talking to a veteran islander. As usual, Grady was right; the woman from Chicago was fascinated.

As always, Salvage Tom was late. He rowed his beat-up little dinghy to Pete's boat and boarded, carrying a tattered file folder in his well-used briefcase, a cardboard Priority Mail envelope. He had swapped his tattered wetsuit for tattered cut-off shorts and a wrinkled T-shirt that was not quite dry from the sinking. His footwear was the same as usual: none.

Pete asked, "What'll it be, a gin or vodka martini?"

"Either or both, whatever you're drinking."

"I put a piece of garlic in mine; it makes cheap vodka taste better. You want one?"

"That's weird, but sure."

After a sip or two from the chilled glass, Pete asked, "So what's up? Sounds like you have something important on your mind."

"You're right. I've had something important on my mind for a long while. I just recently decided what to do about it and that's why I need to talk to you."

"Why me?"

"Because you're the only one I can trust around here."

"Just don't turn your back. I'll steal *Lulu* before you can turn around."

"You're not that stupid."

"So what can I do?"

"Pete, last year I found the wreck of a big sailboat in a hundred feet of water off Martinique. Remember me telling you about it?"

"You made a few bucks from the insurance company, didn't you?"

"Yeah, three thousand bucks for locating the wreck and another ten grand for putting her on a barge. Took about two weeks to find it and haul it in."

"Thirteen grand, not bad pay. You find another one of those?"

"Nope; but I did find something possibly related to that yacht that could be worth a lot more than the salvage deal."

"If you found a sealed South American bundle, I don't want to know about it, Tom. Sell it if you want to, or burn it, smoke it, snort it, but don't get me involved."

"It wasn't dope. It was a treasure map."

"A treasure map? Like an ancient treasure map?"

"Yeah, but—"

Pete interrupted, "Shit, Tom, you have to quit chasing rainbows. You've been down the pirate treasure map route twice that I know of, and lost your ass both times. You know there's a million phonies floating around."

"Yeah, but this one is real and I know it's valuable."

"What makes you think so?"

"I found it in a sealed briefcase near the sunken yacht and it was the only thing in the case."

"That doesn't mean shit. The guy probably bought it thinking it was real, or was going to have it framed for an office wall."

"That isn't the case Pete. There's more to it than that." He hesitated a moment: *did he really want Pete to know?* Then he calmly said, "The briefcase was handcuffed to a dead man."

Pete was silent for a moment. "I didn't know you recovered bodies."

"I don't. I cut the chain off and stuffed the body in a reef for the critters to finish off. I figured that if anyone wanted the briefcase, they'd think the guy took it to his grave, or he sank the boat to cover his tracks and took the treasure for himself."

"That's stupid . . . and illegal."

"I don't care; I did it. Why give it to an insurance company? The insurance company had me do several more dives to look for any other bits and pieces, but nothing was said about the briefcase, a map, or a missing man. The guy could have fallen off one of a hundred cruise ships or yachts. The owner even hired three other divers to go down with me. They weren't locals, and were damn sure looking for something, but never let on. I found out the owner of the yacht was some super-rich guy from France. His hobby is Caribbean history and he has a respectable but private museum in Paris to show the artifacts he has found."

"This is getting interesting. Did you try to sell the map back to him?"

"I'm not a crook," Tom said, as he held his Nixon fingers to the sky. "How would I know if it belonged to him or the guy who had it chained on his wrist? As far as I'm concerned, I was paid to find and raise the wreck; nothing else was stipulated, so anything else I found is mine by rights of international salvage laws. Just because it was connected to a dead guy that nobody knew about doesn't change a thing."

"I have a feeling the map is in that file folder. Are you going to show it to me?"

"That depends on you. Are you going to help me find it?"

"Shit yes, I'm going to help you...unless it's buried under the governor's bedroom."

"Good! Now, how about another one of those garlic things dipped in vodka to celebrate?"

"Before I fix drinks, Tom, I have to tell you that I'll help, but only if I feel right by doing it. I will not commit until I know the details. If something is wrong or seriously illegal, I'm not getting involved. I will not go to the slammer over money. Fair enough?"

Tom agreed while Pete made another batch of icy martinis. When he returned, Tom had several papers scattered about the table. Most noticeable was a very old hand-drawn map. Handwriting covered the map's borders, but was unreadable.

Pete, with a touch of sarcasm, said, "Too bad you can't read that shit. It probably says that this map is a phony and the guy who drew it was hallucinating on bad drugs."

"I can read it. It's in French and many words are archaic and even modern scholars don't know some of them. And that's what I've been doing for the last year. I have translated it myself by going through the library in San Juan."

"I'm impressed. So what does it say?"

Tom pointed to the words with his index finger as he read, "Seaman Andre Phuckewe's bones are guarding this gift to the King of the Seas. God bless this seaman's sacrifice. This bounty is a contribution from the Spanish dogs of San Juan as I, and my stout crew, forcibly acquired it. I now claim it belongs to me and mine. I've selected the place as described to keep my retirement safe from roaming eyes and thieving hands until we chase the Spanish curs from our port in St. Martin."

Tom explained. "These are names of the seamen killed taking the bounty. And this is the date and the captain's signature; it's Captain Newl. I checked him out and he and his crew were killed two days later in a battle off St. Martin."

"Where'd the map come from? Who found it? How many copies have been made? Shit, you might get to the site and find an army camped out and digging."

"Nope. The yacht had just left the area where Captain's Newl's ship went down. It was loaded with diving and light salvage gear. I think they were looking for the wreck, hoping the treasure was aboard. It wasn't, but the map was, and even if they were well-educated Frenchmen, I doubt that they could have translated the old language to get the directions."

"Well, they wouldn't have to translate too much. All they have to do is find the island shown and start looking."

"It's not an island; it's a small cay off an island. They'd never find it unless they picked the right place to look and found the small cove shown here."

"You know where it is?"

"Of course. But that doesn't mean it's going to be easy pickings."

"Let's have another drink, my friend."

Carl Snow stared at the time-lapse images of the giant dust storm over Africa. It had finally started its move off to the west, and Carl was running out of time. When it got closer to the Atlantic, alarm bells and whistles would be heard everywhere, and he would lose the chance to own the phenomena. He wanted to tell the boss, Dr. Lewis, about it, but knew Lewis would leave it to his favorites to explain the monster storm. They would get all the credit, again.

3

September Second

PETE STUMBLED OUT OF HIS BERTH, MOVING and thinking as if only half his brain were working. The functioning part knew he had a transom name to touch up before the boat was splashed, and there was something else to do that he could not quite remember. Thoughts of the grand treasure they were so eager to find in their drunkenness last night were well hidden by the vodka-fog in his brain. He stood in the galley, leaning against the sink for support while having his usual breakfast, two Alka Seltzers, which he chewed, rather than dissolved, and then washed the pieces down with cold club soda.

Memories of last night began to fade in, and as the salty tablet began foaming in his mouth, he swallowed, letting the fizzing liquid slide down his dry throat. His burning stomach showed its appreciation of anticipated relief by sending gas downward that emerged as a hearty fart.

Then he remembered what he had been struggling to recall; he had committed to sail off to Martinique on one of Tom's golden horizons. He angrily uttered, "Oh shit. What have I gotten myself into? Another stupid treasure map. . . . If it's authentic, then someone lost it and could be watching. And whom would they watch? The diver who salvaged the wreck, of course."

He lit the burner under an old scarred and stained coffee pot; dumped some water in the pot, added some grounds to yesterday's, and dug out a mug buried under a sink full of dishes. "It'd be fun to go treasure hunting, but a lot of work—find it, dig it up, try to sell it. And all on the quiet."

He looked in a locker: the cupboard was bare. He looked in the refrigerator and rummaged around until he pulled out an almost empty bag of rye bread. "Then there's the possibility of having it stolen by those watching or the government, which they will if they find out about it. Maybe we can go, after I think this thing out."

He lit another burner, stuck a somewhat dirty fork into a slice of bread and held it over the open burner to make toast.

Carl Snow was at work earlier than usual; he needed to use the ultra-fast AA Wilson computer to plot the storm, based on the latest weather systems between East Africa and the United States. He worked up several possibilities and they all produced nearly the same results.

The huge sandstorm had turned out not to be a single storm, but several individual low-pressure systems grouped together and rotating around central lower pressure. They were moving off the parched land and over the Atlantic. The ocean, already warmer than usual because of the hot weather, along with the warmer than normal southbound current, would stimulate the storm's need for more energy. Clouds, clearly visible on satellite pictures, had started their counter-clockwise movement around each low and the lows began to move counterclockwise around the extremely low-pressure center. Tons of heat and moisture were sucked into the storm each second, fueling the super-massive disturbance.

The accumulation of moisture that had been sitting off Africa had started moving during the night and appeared to be drawn into the low-pressure system, as well. In addition, another low-pressure system that had been north-west of the forming storm was showing indications that it was being pulled into the bigger system.

Carl's excitement was not the only thing building. When Carl's boss arrived, the over-eager employee met him at the door. "Mister Lewis, Mister Lewis, we got a big one coming. A storm you're not going to believe," said Carl with his usual nerd twitter.

"You mean that dust storm over Africa?"

"That's no dust storm, sir. It is a series of full-blown low-pressure systems; they're hurricanes over sand."

"Let's not get carried away, Carl. The winds are high, but not unusual for this time of year. Sure, it might pick up strength when it moves over water, and it might even develop into a tropical storm, but let's be patient and watch for a few days."

"That's not a good idea. Rotation has already started around a central area. But there are areas within the mass that have been circulating for over a day now. I don't know what the winds are, but they are at least tropical storm intensity. We want to put out an early warning on this one. It's going to develop into a massive hurricane, so shipping and the Caribbean islands need time to prepare for this monster."

"Carl, stop overreacting. Everything that comes off Africa that's stronger than a sparrow's fart in September makes you go ballistic. Relax; I'll take a look at it later."

"But Mister Lewis—"

Lewis interrupted Carl's argument by saying, "Carl, I have three systems out west that are surely going to produce tornadoes, and a volcano in Colombia that may start puking at any moment. Wildfires in California, Wyoming, and Utah, and everyone wants to know when it's going to rain. Moreover, there is a depression in the Atlantic that's probably going to develop before your African dust bowl takes off. I don't have time to look at a dust storm that is just leaving a populated area and going out to sea where it can't hurt anybody for several days, at best. So stop bugging me." Lewis turned away, pissed. He hated being met at the door by the excited little pest. As he walked into the kitchen to get his first cup of coffee, he said to Mary, who was pouring milk into her coffee, "One of these days I'm going to fire his ass."

"Sounds like Carl's nervous again," Mary said as she sipped her coffee.

He nodded affirmative. "Or I'll transfer him to another department . . . yeah, I'll send him to Ms. Clark, that'd piss them both off."

"Boy, he did piss you off."

Carl came into the kitchen, which only made Lewis madder. "But Mister Lewis, remember 1970 when 500,000 lives were lost in a storm? This one will match that number, or exceed it, if we aren't totally prepared. The power in a hurricane is equal to hundreds of A-bombs, you know."

Lewis walked out without speaking to Carl. Carl stayed on his heels until Lewis reached his office. He deliberately closed the door in Carl's face. Carl walked away feeling dejected, his shoulders slumped.

Mary met him on the way. "You knew he'd act that way. He never pays any attention until wind speed and circulation can be verified by one of the monitors floating in the Atlantic or reports from passing ships."

"Or from one of his favorites around here," Carl added. "He doesn't make judgments based on personal intuition and knowledge. The data he wants may not happen for two more days. And he'll continue to ignore me."

"Well, Carl, stop meeting him at the door. Let him get coffee, sit down, and review the new data himself. It's like you want to be first in line, teacher's pet. You need to grow some cool, buddy."

"Wait until he works for me; he'll be required to meet me at the door every morning. Heck with it, I'm going to do something."

At his desk, Carl called the Coast Guard in San Juan. "Commander Snyder, this is Doctor Carl Snow at National Hurricane Center. I have a major storm brewing and suggest you post preliminary marine warnings to the islands in the Caribbean."

"Snow, is this a directive from Doctor Lewis?"

"Lewis is not aware of what is developing. This is my discovery."

"Well then, we don't spook island folks by threatening them with a possible storm. When your boss thinks there's danger, he'll call me."

Carl winced at the loud click from the commander's abrupt hang-up. It was not a surprise; Snyder did the same thing every time Carl called.

He muttered, "Stupid people. They only have four days to get ready for this monster, and they don't care. If Lewis decides to name it tomorrow, they'll only have three days. By the time the word gets around to all the people in the Windwards, the darn thing will be on them."

Rigger Grady showed up for breakfast just as Pete was about to leave. Grady's red eyes and rumpled demeanor clearly indicated that he had not been home. Pete had tried to bring Grady in on the deal, but Tom gave him an emphatic, "No". He had his reasons, and it was security, not greed. The fewer people who knew, the better. The days of traditional pirates had passed in the Caribbean, but there was no shortage of the modern version.

If word got out about the treasure, somebody would try to steal it, and the worst of the pirates were the governments. It would not matter which government might lay claim to the treasure, corrupt officials would seize the map and that would be the end of the story. Local governments, protected by their own police forces, were not honest when big bucks were at stake. The greedy officials were usually connected to drug lords, and if anyone made noise outside of their control, the druggies would make sure the accuser would be found dead or never found at all. The incident would be another unsolved crime added to a very long list. Other than modern-day communications and transportation, the Caribbean had not changed much since the days of the buccaneer.

Pete said, "See ya later Grady, got to go. By the way, you really look like shit. If you survive the morning, I'll buy this afternoon."

"I'm not waiting for the afternoon," Grady said, as he motioned Dirty to slide a greenie to him.

"Have you seen Tom this morning, Grady?"

"Naw." Grady picked up the cold beer and took a big drink. He was somewhat beat up from the rough handling by the tourist from Chicago and drinking until the sun rose. He decided to take the day off. Dirty's cold beers made him think he felt better.

Tom was in none of the usual places and Pete knew why: he was hiding in case Pete woke up more sober minded. Fantasies were an easier sell with vodka reasoning. And Tom was right; Pete wanted out, but his sense of honor wouldn't allow it; a deal was a deal, drunk or sober.

Later that morning, with beer number three in front of him, Grady watched Pete pull his boat into the fuel dock across the lagoon and was puzzled. Usually when Pete went sailing, he would ask Grady to join him, unless Emily, his on-again-off-again girlfriend, went along. But a couple of months ago, she swore that she'd never sail with him again. She was afraid of the water and Pete only sailed when it was windy and rough and always pushed the boat to the extreme.

Grady asked Dirty, "Where's Pete going?"

Dirty looked at Grady with contempt; "Now how the fuck would I know? Do I look like his fucking secretary? You're shit-faced, Grady; go home and get some sleep."

Grady slurred, "Maybe Emily changed her mind. I bet he's taking her out today."

"Your brain is saturated, Grady. You know she went to see her parents in the States."

"Oh yeah, three weeks ago. She went to see her folks, I know that." Grady took another drink, as he watched Pete get into an old Jeep and drive away.

Two hours later, Grady was on his fourth-wind and nearly coherent again when Pete returned to his boat with several bags of groceries. Several large bags from the hardware store followed. The last bundle was a piece of canvas wrapped around something. Before he reached the boat, while struggling to carry everything in one trip, a shovel fell out of the canvas.

Grady's curiosity was mounting, and his memory of yesterday returned. He muttered, "Must be that thing that Tom wanted to talk about."

As Pete took *Gypsy Bitch* from the dock and back to her mooring, Salvage Tom walked into Dirty's joint; he had been drinking somewhere else. Apparently, he had scored a few bucks from Pete. Grady encouraged Tom to sit next to him by tempting him with a cold beer. Tom never turned down a free drink; besides, he liked Grady.

"Hey Tom, you and Pete going sailing?"

Surprised, Tom asked, "Did Pete say something?"

"Naw, but he has been out there loading the *Bitch* with all kinds of stuff, so I thought you guys might be going out on a salvage job. If you are, I've got some free time right now, and a few extra bucks that I could put into your venture."

Tom did not know how to respond; he knew that Pete and Grady were buddies. If Pete told Grady, he did not want to be caught in a lie to a guy who had never refused him a loan. He took a big gulp from his beer while he thought how to answer. "Grady, Pete's taking me to a job. It's no big deal, but I can't discuss it with anybody."

Grady let the conversation drop and told a few jokes while they both drank more beer. He was not in the best of shape, but he was a skilled drinker. An hour later, Tom was wasted and became more talkative.

"You know, Grady, I might have room for you, but I've got to think it over, okay?"

Acting as though the earlier conversation was forgotten, Grady responded, "What kind of room?"

"On my treasure salvage. What you were asking me about when I came in."

"Oh, forgot about that. You mean the deal you and Pete are working on?"

"Yeah, but I gotta think about it."

"No problem, Tom. What kind a deal is it? You find another big yacht?"

"Nope; can't tell you."

"Too bad; it'd be fun to do some serious diving for a change."

"There may be some diving involved, but I hope not."

"How long you guys going to be gone?"

"Maybe ten days."

"Wow, the treasure sure as hell ain't anywhere around here. You must be going to Venezuela."

"No, I'm figuring five days on site in case we run into problems."

Then he stood and said, "Got to hit the head," and he ambled off to the mangroves.

Grady quickly pulled out Jerome's rumpled-up note and jotted down everything he learned from Tom. He was drunk enough that he might forget something before the next sunrise.

1 - Apparently some kind of treasure, not a wreck.
2 - On or near land, not offshore, hoped no diving would be involved.
3 - Allowing five days at the treasure site leaves two and a half days to get there. Pete's boat at six knots for sixty hours is three hundred sixty miles.
4 - Will be going down-island.

Grady turned around to see Pete come in. He sat next to Grady, and the rest of the afternoon was spent drinking beer, telling jokes, and generally acting irresponsibly.

Dirty added to the folly when he unexpectedly rang the hurricane bell as hard as he could and a bit too long, then announced, "Season's here, you fucking swabs. We got a tropical storm and a big bloomer sneaking off Africa. The hurricane naming bash is officially on!"

Everyone cheered, not because a storm was on the horizon, but according to tradition, Dirty bought everyone a couple of rounds; it was party-time.

The official Dirty's Damn-Hurricane Board was hung on the wall covering an old, yellowed poster of Doris Day. Dirty claimed she was his mother.

Hurricane names used by the rest of the world were disregarded in the lagoon; they were too wimpy. Names had to represent personalities of a real person or event, and could only be female for the same and obvious reasons the ancient mariners used the unpredictable gender for the honor.

The process of selecting a storm's name took place after it reached tropical storm status and had a disposition of its own. An hour was allowed to entertain names, and, of course, there was laughter, lots of screaming and yelling, and an occasional fistfight. Everyone had a good time.

At the conclusion of their discussion, those still standing would vote on the best name for the first storm. Fat Ass Alice won the event because of its pear shape, which reminded the crows of Dive Shop Alice, who had the biggest ass in the Caribbean.

Dirty opened the gates to insanity again to name the second storm, but everyone seemed to regard it more seriously. One name kept resurfacing and for good reason.

The survivors of Chad's Jamal tribe got their wish. Mohammad had given them rain, but apparently did not understand the meaning of overkill. The cherished water ran freely off the land, forming puddles, then ponds, and then lakes—and still it rained.

Grady had a nose for sniffing out opportunities, and he had a feeling a lot of money was involved in Tom's newest scheme. He wanted in. Grady was known as a good-time guy, but nobody knew much about him, and nobody ever would.

Pete sometimes suspected something in Grady's past was shady, but so what; most of them had a problem here or there. He had noticed that Grady was leery of the police and avoided all contact with them. Grady justified his actions by telling Pete that his ex-wife wanted him in court to collect more alimony. Pete believed him, as he had his own experiences to remind him how serious ex-wife problems could be. What he didn't know was Grady had never been married.

Most everyone knew Grady had been a Green Beret, but they did not know he had been dishonorably discharged. He had a long police record that started when he was fourteen years old. The last entry on his record was doing time in Leavenworth, Kansas, in the federal penitentiary. He had been convicted of stealing hundreds of land mines. The government knew he was selling them to the enemy, but unfortunately, could not prove it.

Leavenworth was not a place to meet nice people, and that was where he had met Jerome Savage. They shared a common philosophy: criminal activity was not a crime, it was opportunity seized before someone else could. Shortly after they were released, Jerome had followed up on a plan he had devised and brought Grady into the business. Jerome had shared a cell with a major player in the drug smuggling world, and used that connection to set up the operation with the world's largest smugglers, the Ortega Cartel. They liked his ideas; it was a slick operation and almost impossible for the government snoops to smell them out.

Jerome's orders for product went through one of the cartel's top men, who personally made the arrangements on the supply side. No one would warn the authorities of an impending shipment. Grady handled the Caribbean purchases, and Jerome had similar managers in Mexico, Central America, and the United States. He moved tons of cartel merchandise every week and seldom became personally involved, leaving his time free to cruise with his beautiful wife.

Four times a year, Grady and Jerome met to discuss business, make plans for the future, take care of deadbeat accounts, and divvy up the profit. Grady made brief contacts with his six wholesalers in the Caribbean every two months. Each would give him a sealed-in-the-pack CD featuring a popular artist.

Jerome provided a sophisticated computer that would read the disk for an encoded series of beeps. Those beeps turned into orders for the next two months. A coded summary would be emailed to Jackson Julian, Jerome's comptroller, whose computer would generate another code that was sent to the respective wholesalers with instructions on where to wire the money. Jackson's computer made certain that no bank account was ever used more than once.

The cartel took care of the politicians and police to keep their routes protected, and they made the dope deliveries, so there was never a transaction where money and dope changed hands. The merchandise was top of the line; there were no hassles over money or distrust, and there were no paper trails. Business was good and everybody involved was making more money than they could spend, except the users who worked themselves to death or stole everything they could to support their addiction.

Grady was not as intoxicated as he appeared; his mind was working, scheming to get closer to his god, the all-mighty greenback. He was to meet Jerome in St. Lucia next week and was sure Jerome would love to go on a treasure hunt.

At midnight, Tom had enough and was getting sleepy at the bar. Grady and Pete helped him into his dinghy and towed it to *Lulu*. Tom fell overboard trying to get aboard his boat, and his laughing and drunk companions fell overboard, too, while trying to fish him out.

On their way back to Dirty's, Grady asked, "Where are you guys off to tomorrow?"

"Tom won't tell me. All he said was to get the boat ready for a three-day sail. I tried to get you in on this, Grady, but Tom said he had too much time already invested in the thing and apparently it only needs two men. Sorry old buddy; it looks like this one's a full boat."

"No problem. I hope you guys find the wreck or whatever you're looking for."

"Me too. We need money."

"Lots of money?"

"Don't know. Tom found an old treasure map supposedly drawn by a Frenchman. It's so old that it took a lot of time to translate it."

They got back to the bar in time to have one more, then another, before going their separate ways.

Pete, back aboard the *Gypsy Bitch*, leaned his head on a bulkhead while taking a leak. He muttered, "Too bad she doesn't like boats. Too bad I don't like houses. Why's she so stubborn? She could go with me tomorrow. We should be living together."

Instead of going to his schooner, Grady, a hardened criminal, smart, conniving, and a ruthless son of a bitch, went to see his only full-time employee. He was a man no one associated with Grady.

Bill Graves had the image of a successful investor and maintained a beautiful cover for Grady's assets: a big house overlooking the down-islands, local bank accounts, and a twin engine Learjet. He was a dangerous man without a conscience, and was the muscle behind Grady. Bill was a borderline psychopath and was in awe of Grady's ability to pull off everything he wanted, including his boat-bum facade, and his rigging business as a front to cover the money he spent locally.

Bill had been a hit man for the Cuban Mafia, the only Anglo to reach that status, which proved to Grady's satisfaction that Bill had the right stuff. He brought him to St. Thomas, set him up with a millionaire's lifestyle, and treated him well. The workload was light, and the way Grady operated was reasonably safe.

When Grady arrived, Bill was in the computer room looking at a map of the Atlantic. He pointed to a massive group of clouds off the African coast. He said, "I can't figure out why no one has said anything about this system. Shit, if this thing keeps developing we're going to have a hell of a storm."

"The weather boys probably see some high-level winds that are going to rip it apart. Something that size would certainly get their attention."

Grady walked away from the screen and sat at his desk. "Listen, Bill, early tomorrow I want you to go down to the lagoon. Take your binoculars and a camera with a telephoto lens. Find the sailboat *Gypsy Bitch* and get a picture you can use to spot her from the air. About three o'clock take the Lear and see which way they're going. I don't want the people on board to know we're tracking them, okay?"

"You got it, boss."

"Find them every morning and evening and chart their course. I'm pretty sure they're going to the Windwards. When we know where they're going, you, maybe Jerome, and I are going to take something away from them."

"They're competing for one of our clients?"

"Nope. They may have found an old treasure and I want it."

"You got it, boss."

"Okay, I'm going to use my room tonight; shit, I'm drunk and tired. Been going like this for two days."

Bill did not drink or do drugs, and could not understand why Grady would do so much damage to his body. He was a health freak; his highs came from his own body and sexual marathons with a string of young women he had cultivated. The only thing he liked more than sex was violence; he enjoyed fighting, especially over serious matters. A fight to the death was the ultimate high. Resolving problems with people in Grady's business-world appealed to Bill's sadistic nature. The person would be lured onto the Lear with a pretense of making a big deal. Then, while Grady was flying at ten thousand feet, Bill would dig out an anchor chain from the rear compartment in full view of the impending victim.

A switch activated a concealed door near the floor. As it opened, the combination of wind howling through the cabin, the chain laid out on the floor, Bill's nasty smile and the fire in his eyes, and the problem guy quickly understood what was about to happen. Usually, a savage fight would take place and it was never an even match; Bill was too skillful and sinfully ruthless.

The victim would be revived after he was chain-wrapped. Bill would sit next to the man and tell him that Grady said he could live if he had any worthy information. The victims were eager to tell him anything. The promise was a lie, and when Grady was certain no boats or other air traffic were in sight, he would give Bill the signal and the man would be rolled out of the bomb bay.

The terrifying free fall was not a pleasant way to die, but Bill would lie in the doorway and watch until he saw the splash. He thoroughly enjoyed the show. Grady's system worked; the dead—and there were many—had never surfaced to offer evidence that needed to be explained.

The wind howled over the Cape Verde Islands and it had come with little warning. Everyone, except the four men operating the weather station, was surprised. An hour after the storm hit, the weathermen were also stunned; it was the first time they had seen real sand, hail, and rain in a storm in the middle of an ocean.

The folks aboard the motor yacht *Good Times* were surprised that night, too. They were 200 miles away from the Cape Verde Islands, and the yacht was on autopilot. The crewman on watch was asleep and nobody saw the offshore weather monitor's flashing beacon. The collision with the floating beacon knocked a six-foot hole in the yacht's starboard bow. In less than ten minutes the beautiful yacht slid below the sea's surface. The ten persons on board barely had enough time to get the life rafts in the water and climb aboard.

The captain assumed the helmsman had sent out a mayday, but instead, he had made a dash for the first raft that hit the water. If a mayday had been sent, a rescue mission would have been launched and the rescuers could have reported that the storm was much stronger than it appeared from outer space. Unfortunately, the damaged weather station would not be able to relay the rapidly dropping barometer, the escalating wind speeds, or the rain and hail quickly developing in the towering storm system.

4

September Third

THROUGH THE PORTHOLE OVER HIS BUNK, PETE OPENED one eye to see a sunrise that was just starting to paint the morning. He muttered in a dry, cracked voice, "Shit... should've called it off... Emily, why aren't you here to stop me?" Reluctantly, he crawled out of his berth and scratched his ass while trying to figure out what to do.

He looked at the ship's clock on the bulkhead. Tom was late. "Good, maybe he won't show and I can go back to bed." After his usual Alka-Seltzer breakfast, shower, and perked coffee, Tom still had not arrived. He called for *Lulu* on the VHF. Another boat, *Chicken Coop* answered. "Tom's on McNaasti's boat. *Lulu* sank again."

As Pete pulled up to McNaasti's boat, he shook his head in mock shame and said, "Tom, you're going to have to fix that damn thing or run her up on a sandbar to keep her from going under every time you forget to turn the bilge pump on."

"Fuck it! The pump was on; *Lulu* just had enough. I couldn't pump enough, even with the crash pump. I think a plank must've sprung."

By nine-thirty, they were aboard *Gypsy Bitch* and sailing out of the little harbor. Tom sighed, "Sorry for the delay. I guess this will make for a night arrival at our destination."

"That's not good news unless it's an easy harbor. Don't you think it's time to tell me where we're going?"

"Martinique. Do you know how to get into Marin?"

"I've been there, seems there was shallow stuff around the edges and inside the harbor."

"You got that right. I bought a new chart, in case you don't have one."

"I hope you aren't going to tell me we're going to be digging holes in Marin; that could create a little curiosity. And Tom, that treasure map you have is not of Martinique."

"Relax, the treasure isn't on the main island; it's an uninhabited island off the East Side. You wouldn't believe how many maps I have scoured to match islands. That took a full week at the geographic office in San Juan."

"You're sure it's the same one."

"I feel positive that it is."

"Good enough. Hang on to the wheel while I plug the coordinates into the autopilot and then we'll sit back and have a beer."

"I like the way you sail. The wind is better today; this ten to fifteen from the northeast is perfect." Tom looked at the surroundings and added, "I think the gods are with us on this venture, Pete."

Carl Snow knew better, but could not help it; he met his boss at the door again that morning. It produced the expected results. Lewis was pissed, but he promised to take a serious look later that morning. Feeling put off again, Carl returned to his desk, but he was not concerned with Lewis, only the storm. Something was screwy; the weather monitor off the Cape Verde Islands was not transmitting and that was crucial for monitoring weather coming off Africa. The last report from Cape Verde confirmed that they were being affected by a big sand storm. The satellite image looked bad; there was circulation, its circumference was spreading, and cloud heights were climbing. It had to be a hurricane. Hurricane Bunny—what a cute little name for such a whopper of a storm.

Carl muttered, "Allen, you better look out, or you'll be eaten by a Bunny before this day is over."

The survivors of the motor yacht, *Good Times*, were experiencing harsh conditions. Only one raft, of the two deployed, survived. Heavy seas had swamped the raft with the yacht's owners and captain aboard. The emergency locator beacon, EPRIB, went overboard with the captain; it would continue sending its mayday message to passing aircraft and satellites as long as its batteries held.

Rescue Operations Center in Utah picked up several distress signals from the African coast; the EPRIB, floating and firmly tied to the dead captain, was one of them. Cape Verde Search and Rescue would have been quick to respond; however, the island did not receive any calls or emails. It appeared that Cape Verde was in the middle of a strong storm and Operations Center blamed communications failure on abnormal electrical conditions.

The U.S. Navy's Mediterranean Fleet was informed of the coordinates of the distress signals. Within minutes, a sub-chaser was dispatched to fly over. The last-ever transmission the carrier received from the sub-chaser was, "Damn, you better wake somebody up in Storm Center. This is not a disturbance; it is a full-blown hurricane. We're altering our search pattern to take some of the punch out of the wind."

Carl received a call from Naval Operations that afternoon. They wanted to know what was going on in the Atlantic, west of Cape Verde. Carl could only tell them what his official position was, since his boss had not bothered to look at the developing system; it was classified as a tropical disturbance. The Navy fleet commander suggested Carl pull his head out of his ass and take a look around. They had distress signals and a lost aircraft in that same area.

Further efforts to contact Cape Verde were useless; the connection could not be made. The lines were down on the island from a bad storm, the microwave system was out, and there was too much interference for satellite systems to work.

This only added to Carl's already agitated state; he knew he was about to piss off the boss again. He stomped in to Lewis's office, even though there were two other people in conference with him. "Sorry Lewis, but your time is up. You must give me authorization to issue warnings on this storm. Navy called and they have missing aircraft. We have lost contact with Cape Verde, and the east Atlantic weather monitor isn't transmitting. Satellite photos show cloud heights approaching six miles and the damn thing is huge and getting bigger. Bunny is its name, but it's going to be a brute to anything that happens to be in its path."

"Damn it, Carl! Are you nuts? Can't you see these people sitting here? Can't you understand that I'm busy? I told you I'd look at it as soon as I can get a free minute. Now get the hell out of my office, and if you like working here, don't ever do this again."

Carl had been correct, his boss was pissed, but he held his ground and he got angry, too. "That's bullshit! I've been trying to get you to give the okay on this for two days. There's a monster storm brewing and you've been playing games with me. Well, too many people are going to get hurt unless we get early warnings out, and, get them out right now! And not whenever you get a free minute!"

He threw the charts on Lewis's desk, folded his arms over his chest and refused to budge.

Lewis was shocked at Carl's aggressiveness; he had never heard him say a cuss word. Then he realized that he had ignored the nerd a little too long, but he was too angry to give in, and yelled back, "That's it! You're fired! I'll mail you your last paycheck."

"I expected to be fired when I came in here, but I'm not leaving until you acknowledge what's out there." He sat down next to the visitors, signifying his stubbornness. The two visitors looked terribly uncomfortable.

Lewis was so angry; he looked like he was going to pop. Carl was afraid his ex-boss was going to beat him up, but he still did not move. The room was deadly quiet; tension seemed to shake the windows.

Finally, Lewis grabbed the charts, sat down, and looked at each of them several times. The scowl on his face turned into a frown as he cooled down. Then he stood up and said, "It appears you did the right thing, Snow. This is incredible; it could develop into the worst storm modern man has ever experienced. I want all the data you have."

Carl was stunned, but very pleased. He asked, "Didn't you just fire me?"

"I already apologized, Carl. I said you did the right thing, now get out there and do your job. Or do you want me to get on my knees and beg for forgiveness?"

Carl dearly wanted just that, and in front of his co-workers, but said, "No sir. I've got everything all set, including your notification statement... if you approve, of course."

Back at his desk, Carl reread the prepared statement on the official status of the storm to be sent to every station in the world.

> Tropical Depression 2 has been upgraded to hurricane. Hurricane Bunny is located over the Cape Verde Islands and is moving toward the west-southwest at 20 miles per hour. Hurricane Hunters are en route to investigate the storm's strength and movement. Updates will be broadcast as new information becomes available. As of 1500 hours, September 3, the center of Hurricane Bunny is located at 25 degrees west longitude, 16 degrees north latitude. Winds exceed 80 miles per hour. The eye is well formed and extends 30 miles from the center. Hurricane force winds extend out 60 miles and are expected to increase. Tropical storm winds extend out 285 miles from the center. All islands in the Caribbean should take appropriate measures to prepare for a potentially dangerous hurricane. At its current heading and speed, tropical storm winds will start affecting the Windward Islands in 93 hours. Hurricane force winds will develop in 108 hours.

He hit the computer's send-key and the message instantly transmitted to the Broadcast Division's computer for distribution. He leaned back in his chair, feeling victorious. All he had to do was sit back and wait for information to come in from the hurricane chasers and watch what happened on each pass of the satellite. He entertained the delicious idea of calling the dummies that he spoke to in the Caribbean about the early warnings, but decided not to jeopardize his first-time success. The storm could go north instead of west, but he was willing to bet his Jungle Jim jacket that it was going to slam directly into the islands.

Carl waited until nine that night for the hurricane chaser's report. It should have been in the storm a half-hour ago, and the data uploaded into the computers already. Finally, he called to see why nothing was happening. Communications said there had been no contact, so they suspected bad conditions disturbed the transmission of radio and IWRS signals.

Carl hung up and muttered, "Baloney, the weather officer turned off the automatic send on the weather reconnaissance system to hog all the data and glory for himself."

An hour later, nothing had changed, and Carl assumed the plane had radio problems and would call in when it landed at El Aalun International, where it was expected to arrive in two hours. Two and one-half hours later, he called again. The plane had not arrived; there was nothing on radar. If the plane had gone down, they should have picked up the emergency locator beacon that automatically activates on impact. The Air Force was concerned and another aircraft was scheduled to be sent out at dawn to investigate.

Carl fell asleep in his chair and stayed there until the morning cleaning crew came in at five-thirty. When he awoke, he scurried to see the latest satellite view of the storm, and was not surprised. Several other people were standing around looking at the image. It had indeed grown. In fifteen hours, it was now three hundred miles wide. He needed the aircraft information on wind speeds to know more about what it was going to do. It was obvious that the wind had increased, as evidenced by the clouds; they were now seven miles high and the storm's eye was three hundred miles closer to the Windwards.

Hurricane Allen was no more. It was in the Bunny's belly. A call to Keesler Air Force Base, the hurricane hunter's operation center, confirmed what he had suspected last night: the first aircraft had not returned. As soon as the storm passed, they would have planes in the area looking for survivors. Carl prepared his next advisory.

> Hurricane Bunny, advisory number 2: Sept. 4, 0600 AST. At 0600, the eye of Bunny is 15.5 degrees north latitude, 30 degrees west longitude. Movement continues at west-southwest at 20 miles per hour. No change in direction anticipated. Storm winds extend out to 300 miles from the center. The center of Bunny is 1860 miles due east of the Windward Islands. If conditions do not change, the eye will be over the islands in 93 hours, Sept. 8 at 0300 hours.

At eleven that morning, Carl got a call from Keesler Air Force Base. "Flight 556 just reported in. They only made one pass because it's too rough inside. But I do have some news for you that you're not going to like."

"It's a lot stronger isn't it?" asked an excited Carl.

"How about 120-miles-per-hour winds, 80 miles from the eye wall."

"Is that as far as they penetrated?"

"No, they made one full pass, but don't expect another. A military fighter could do it, but not our equipment. They got readings of constant 200-miles-per-hour winds near the wall and turbulence they couldn't believe. The eye wall is now thirty miles out from the center. Barometric pressure is down to a whopping twenty-six point six. We have one giant Category Five storm and it's going to get worse by the looks of things. I've just sent the data to your computers; the aircraft was having trouble transmitting directly to you. Take a good look at it."

"What am I supposed to do now? I need data that only your aircraft can give me."

"According to the pilot you'll have to do without eye-wall readings. It's too dangerous. They'll make passes at it, but no full insertions, unless it starts to weaken. Rely on the satellites."

```
Hurricane Bunny, advisory number 3: Sept. 4, noon. The center of Bunny is 15.3 degrees north latitude, 32 degrees west longitude. Direction continues at west-southwest. Movement is at 20 miles per hour. No change in direction anticipated. Hurricane force winds extend out to 110 miles from the center. Wind speeds are 120 miles per hour near the outer edge building to 200 near the eye wall. Tropical storm winds extend out 180 miles from the center on the west side of the storm and 290 miles on the southeast sector. The center of Bunny is 1740 miles due east of the Windward Islands. If conditions do not change, the eye will be over the islands in 87 hours, Sept. 8 at 0300 hours. Bunny is a category 5 hurricane and is extremely dangerous. All marine and aviation activities should stay well clear of the area.
```

Like most Caribbean sailors, Tom had tuned in to the offshore weather broadcast, a part of his daily ritual during the hurricane season. As Tom turned the SSB radio off, he asked, "Did you hear that? Where'd that mother come from? Yesterday it looked like just a glob of clouds on television. Shit, that's spooky. I've never seen one form that big so far out, have you?"

"Nope. They start getting nasty around forty-five degrees. If the son-of-a-bitch is that big that far out, what's going to happen when it gets over the warm waters of the Caribbean?"

"Who cares, Pete? It can't get any worse than 200-miles-per-hour wind. Shit, anything stronger is overkill. It's like being shot to death by twenty bullets."

"And the damn thing is heading west-southwest. That's odd."

"I guess naming the storm after Big Eye Bertha was pretty much appropriate. She's big, she's crazy, she'll scare the shit out of you, and she's definitely an oddity in nature."

Big Eye Bertha was the moniker of a woman who hung out around the little community of Red Hook. She stood over six feet tall, weighed over 250 pounds, and had been on the receiving end of too many dull heroin needles and bottles of cheap rum. She walked the streets around the little shops waiting for some fool to come close. When it happened, she stood fully erect, usually towering over the person, and looked down on them. She would squint one eye and open the other one wider than should be possible, and stare, as if she could see the thoughts inside their heads. Normal people were easily frightened away, no matter how macho they were. Moreover, as they hastily skirted away, she'd bellow out in a maniacal laughter with a voice so deep you'd swear it came from a man. The laughter was not meant to scare; she was truly laughing with glee.

Everybody on the island knew she was crazy, including Bertha herself, but the police stopped throwing her in jail years ago and there were no crazy houses in the Virgins; they would only overflow.

If Pete and Tom had seen the latest satellite image, they would have turned south and found a hiding place in South America. The deep crimson red of the eye wall had gone off the scale, the white of its eye a deadly contrast. Pete went below to plot the storm on a chart, and when he returned, he was worried.

Tom was sucking on the open end of a Budweiser. Not hiding his concern, Pete said, "I think we might be smart to turn back to St. Thomas. If we do it now, I can find a place in the mangroves for *Gypsy* and we will have time to get *Lulu* up and on the hard before the weather turns to shit. If we keep going, we'll make it to Martinique before the storm, but I don't know if there will be a safe place for the boat by the time we get there. With that monster on the horizon, everybody's going to get into the hurricane holes early."

"That's good logic, Pete, except you forgot something. That storm has to turn to the northwest, then the north and then the northeast. It's just a matter of time. The chance of it going to the northwest is much better than it continuing its westward track. I think our chances are much better being there."

"That's true, but we may be talking about survival."

"There's another reason to continue, Pete, and a damn important one. Our treasure is on a small cay, east of Martinique. It's surrounded by reefs and will be an extremely dangerous place to be during a hurricane. The treasure is buried under a big rock and three or four feet of sand. If a kick-ass storm like Big Eye hits, I'm sure everything on that island that isn't rock is going to go away."

"What's the elevation of the island? Is the treasure buried above the surge and wave action?"

"The tallest point is less than fifty feet and I won't know where the treasure is until I see the island. Even if it were buried at fifty feet, there's a chance it wouldn't survive. What the winds don't blow away, the surge created by twenty-six inches of mercury is going to be incredibly high. Add the waves created by the long fetch of the Atlantic, and we're looking at fifty footers breaking over our tiny island."

Tom stood and stretched. "Under those circumstances, I vote for getting there as fast as we can, finding the treasure, and heading for high ground."

"Tom, if the treasure can be dislodged by a hurricane, then I'm sure it must have happened already. In 300 years, that island certainly had some bad hits."

"Not like Big Eye. After I identified the island, I had the same thought. A normal category three, which would be big considering the location, would only have a pressure of nine-hundred-forty-five millibars. That would generate thirty footers and a surge of twelve feet."

"Okay, Tom, convince me that you know what you're doing with this treasure map and I'll go along. Otherwise we're going back to the hurricane hole."

Tom went below and motioned Pete to follow. With the map spread out on the table, he translated, while pointing to different parts of faded print. "This says, 'line up the southernmost peak of the main island with Sailrock. Walk fifty long paces in line. Eggrock guards the bones of my loyal seaman, Andre Phuckewe, and his bones lie under waist-high sand to faithfully guard my treasure.' This part over here says, 'My chests hold the gold the Spaniards need to defend El Morro.'"

Pete asked, "El Morro, the big fort in San Juan?"

"It could be, or it could be El Morro in Havana, or it could be any or all of the El Morros. There were plenty of them in the New World. Whichever, it definitely states, *chests*, meaning there's more than one. It could be a huge pile of gold and damn sure too much to let Big Eye take it. She'll just blow it."

"Some humor you have. Okay, I'm convinced." Tom went back outside while Pete calculated their estimated arrival time. He was not happy at putting his boat at risk, but he had always managed to find a secure hiding place wherever a storm happened to find him. Besides, Tom was probably right; the storm would be more likely to hit St. Thomas than Martinique.

He went out to the cockpit; Tom was emptying another beer can. "We're about 340 miles out of Martinique. That'll put us on the island the afternoon of the sixth. Tropical storm winds will start on the seventh around 1800 hours. That gives us one full day to find, dig, and get out of the way. Around 2200 hours, we'll get hurricane force winds. We have to be secure by nine on the night of the seventh. You agree?"

"You'll be eating my dust to get there. I've been through too many hurricanes; they scare me. Besides, I plan on being around for a long time to spend my untold wealth on really fun stuff. Shit, I'll bet I can even afford to get a dick transplant."

Pete spit out a mouth full of beer with a sudden laugh. "A what? A dick transplant? Where'd you come up with that?"

"Why not? They do livers, hearts, lungs, and those are complicated organs. All I want is a weenie. I'll just browse around the morgues until I find the biggest one in the Caribbean and tell 'em to sew it on. If it doesn't work, then I'll use one of the little air pumps they have for soft noodles."

"A dick transplant?"

"Yeah. . . . I don't have one. Uncle Sam took it away."

"You're shitting me." Tom was not smiling, which bothered Pete. Pete added, "Your *uncle* took it away? This sounds better than one of Zach's tales. Tell me all about it, I need a good laugh."

Tom looked at him and then went below for another beer. When he returned, he sat down, sighed, and sighed again, as he released a barrier that separated his secret from the world. He looked at his feet, and said, "Why not. I'm not crying over spilled milk, Pete; but I've never talked to another guy about this. It rather bothers me that absolutely nobody in the world gives the slightest shit about my life. Does that sound wimpy to you?"

"No. We all want to be appreciated, but what's that got to do with a dick transplant?"

"If this ever gets out to the Lagoonies, you can expect to wake up one morning tied to an anchor."

"I'm not going to say shit. What happened?"

Tom looked at the sea, away from Pete. "All my life I wanted to be a champion. I wanted to contribute something to others. Wanted to be noticed. I've gone through life at the back of the pack, eating the dust from everyone else. I've never been first at anything; have never had the first taste of life's offerings, only the leftovers."

"You're sounding pretty fucking corny, Tom."

"It's not corny to me. That has been my life's pattern since I was a kid. I didn't even get laid in high school. In fact, I didn't get laid until I was in the Army and that was by a Mexican whore in Tijuana just a few days before shipping out."

"So welcome to the planet. You've got lots of company, and no one got laid enough at that age."

"Not really. My wish to make a difference and be respected was only a stroke of luck away since I was in a war. I did a good job, took my chances, ever eager to make that difference to the guys I served with. My opportunity ended suddenly, however, by shrapnel from a mortar shell. Fortunately, the blast didn't take off my legs or an arm, hands or even a finger. It did put a few holes in my body... and it blew my entire manhood off."

"They shot your dick off?" Pete asked, while fighting back the need to laugh.

"Pecker, balls, asshole, and part of my lower belly. I got scars that would make Frankenstein cry."

"No shit? Can I see?"

"Fuck no, you insensitive bastard."

"Just kidding. I wouldn't look at something that fucked up. And if you don't have a pecker, what the hell do you do with Mama Lou?" Before Tom could answer, Pete asked, "And if you don't mind me asking, how do you shit without an asshole?"

The questions earned him another dirty look. Tom answered, "Lulu and I are just friends."

Pete smiled, and then said, "So you want a dick transplant. You'd probably pick one on a big black guy who has a whacker that hangs down to his knees. A big black cock sewn on your lily-white belly. I'm sure that will turn the ladies on and if that doesn't, then surely being screwed with a dead man's dick will."

"Fuck 'em—I'll be happy."

Pete and Tom laughed; then Tom continued; he had gone too far already, but this was the one time he had talked about it and it made him feel good to share his misery with another person who might give him something he desperately wanted, but could never ask for: respect, with maybe a touch of sympathy.

"Uncle Sam, whom I was ready to die for, discharged me as a substandard human. My contribution, my sacrifice to the war effort was forgotten in the mangle of other bodies. My thanks were a Purple Heart and ugly red scars where my private parts used to be. Throngs of soldier-hating Americans, who would be delighted that I was so horribly maimed, greeted me when I returned to the civilized world. That was the lowest point in my life, Pete. My moment of glory had passed and unlimited pussy lasted one night."

Pete felt bad for Tom, but was not sure if he was just bullshitting.

Tom continued his tale of woe. "I was fooled a few months later by one of the girls in my hometown. She had heard about what happened to me. The thought of having no sexual contact with me but getting the security of a husband's disability pension from the Army sparked true love. Her love lasted long enough for me to adopt her three children. I was happy, but boy what a mistake that turned out to be."

"I hear it coming, Tom. She divorced you and gets most of your pension for child support, right?"

"Not yet. The Army put me through college and I got dual master degrees from MIT in electrical and mechanical engineering."

Pete interrupted, "You what? You're an engineer?"

"Actually, I went on to get my doctorate. I was a rocket scientist, Pete, but don't tell anyone. Since sex and women didn't clutter my thoughts or time, I became more receptive to learning. I took a very good job with NASA working on the space shuttle, and was happy. But once again, hard luck grabbed me. My happiness ended abruptly when I came home early one day and found my boss making up for my sexual shortcomings. I understood my wife's needs, but it still hurt. I also accepted this sort of thing happening to disabled husbands and decided to forgive and forget. My wife and my boss were not ready to forget their pleasure, however; they divorced me from my family and my job. *That's* when she took a big share of my disability pension, when the judge ordered a whopping share for child support for the adopted kids. And then, even the kids didn't want anything to do with their mother's spent-husband."

Pete said, "You didn't need a dick. You got a royal fucking without it."

"That part of my life was actually harder than losing my seldom-used penis and his pals. I was as alone as any man in his twenties could be, but there was always that expectation on the horizon to keep my spirits up. The hope of something or someone wonderful in the future played a huge part in keeping me from swallowing a lead pill."

"Damn, Tom, you've had a lot of fun. I hope you punched the bitch in her chops before you left."

"I never even hinted at being violent, but she put a court order on me to stay away and to never call her or the kids. It was a clean break, only her lawyers had free shots at me."

"Welcome to Divorce City, but you've got a lot of company. How did you end up down here?"

"One day I answered the calling I've had since I was just a kid; I moved to the tropics to live the life of Bogart and seek out adventures as a marine salvager. I had no knowledge of boats and water, but I was a damn good engineer and that's what salvaging is really about. I taught myself everything about the business from deep-water diving to the legal aspects of Admiralty

Law. I did well, considering my experience, for the first few years, then the dreaded Caribbean disease of limin' got hold of me."

"Well you sure got a good dose of it, didn't you? Your aggressive salvaging slowed down to work-only-when hungry," Pete said with a smile.

"Yep, and I likes it!"

At five that evening, Grady's telephone rang. It was the anticipated report from Bill. "Spotted them, boss. At four, they were about forty miles southeast of St. Thomas just off St. Croix. They turned more to the south, and if they continue their present heading, it will take them to one of the islands between Redonda and Guadeloupe. I'll take another swing out in the morning."

"Good. Don't lose them."

"No problem. Hey, are you monitoring that storm?"

"What storm?" Grady thought it was going to go north and had not been concerned. Most people on St. Thomas had not been officially warned that a major storm was lurking in the Atlantic, and neither had the bulk of the population on all of the islands. The only people who knew were those who relied on the Internet for weather information, and a few concerned sailors.

Hurricane hunter Captain McCory walked around his Hercules WC-130 doing his final inspection before flying into the jaws of a giant Bunny. As the senior pilot for the National Oceanic and Atmospheric Administration's Aircraft Operations Center, he had flown into over 160 hurricanes and had learned how to survive.

He had company on his inspection that day, aerial reconnaissance weather officer Jerry Mittee. The crew called him One-eye Frenchy because he was a New Orleans coon-ass and his right eye squinted shut when excited and he got excited over the smallest things.

McCory sat on his haunches to inspect the landing gear, and said, "Today is not just another penetration, One-eye. Category five storms are never ordinary hurricanes, even if being ordinary is ever a possibility with any hurricane. Hurricanes, like every other living thing on earth, have their own personalities. Some are just windy, some full of rain, and others are just plain full of nasty. Then there are the Cape Verde category fives, with obscene winds, tornadoes, and even kitchen sinks flying throughout the system. You get rain at the lower altitudes, so thick, it's like being underwater. Towering clouds twelve miles high penetrate the troposphere; the hail at the higher altitudes is enough to smash windscreens and physically destroy aircraft."

One-eye squinted and said, "What you think, Captain? You think I don't know that? I'm a weatherman; remember? You just get me there, and then follow my instructions. I'll know everything about this little Bunny. Why you try to make me think this is going to be like trying to lick a pit bull's balls? It's no big t'ing, just a storm, and I been in a few. Been in George when it was a Cat Five."

McCory smiled and knew it would do no good to argue. Nobody could win an argument with that stubborn son of a bitch. Mac smiled; he would take One Eye to the storm but he was not going to let him direct the path Mac would steer. The damn Bunny had already killed two airplanes and it was not going to munch on Mac's Hercules. "You're in for a new experience today, One-eye, and don't get excited when I don't skim the surface or circle up the eye wall so you can get some pretty pictures. You stay on that machine of yours and tell me what you'd like to see. If I think we can do it, I'll get you there. You young bucks all think you're invincible, but I know better. I know what fear is all about and I know some things about being stupid, too. Today's storm is not a personal challenge against nature; we're here to safely get data and then get back home. Yesterday, we lost George Schlitz, his crew, and his airplane because he challenged Bunny."

"But, my friend, he didn't have One-eye for his weatherman. I'm the best there is. I know storms like the soft places between my woman's legs."

"Well, you screwy little Frenchman, just be sure you don't insert us in the wrong hole. What happened to Schlitz is not going to happen to me. I'm going to be gentle with Bunny. I'll take my time and look for the right signs, fly around and over if possible. Your equipment will get your data, but it'll be slow going. This won't be a balls-to-the-wall assault on Mother Nature, as I did in my youth. And, as you would have me do today."

"Captain Mac, you hurt my feelings," One-eye said with a mock-pout.

Fifteen minutes later, they were airborne and McCory said to his co-pilot, "That crazy Frenchman doesn't understand this storm. He thinks it's just another hurricane with stronger winds. That's why I delayed taking off so long; I want to give him some time in Bunny to get a feel for it, but no more than about fifteen minutes. Then it'll be getting dark and we'll land in Africa for the night. That'll be enough information for the fat-ass desk jockeys. There's no need in flying through something like Bunny every six hours."

"You get a big Roger on that, Mac. Flying through that thing to satisfy some egghead's need for data is no reason to take this kind of risk. Hell, fat-ass paper pushers sit in their big air-conditioned buildings, well removed from harm's way, and think up more stupid tricks for us to do. Any fool knows that if a storm like Bunny moves over you, you're going to get the shit kicked out of you. It doesn't matter a twit what the wind speed is, or the direction, or what the barometer reading is when it's on you. All that matters then is whether the structure you happen to be in will stand up to it, crumble, crash, or blow away."

From thirty-five thousand feet Mac could see the storm hundreds of miles away. The white spirals of feeder bands that continuously got higher, thicker, and darker led to a deep blue that darkened to a black mass on the horizon. "That black mass is where we'll be in an hour or so. That's where the monster lives," he mumbled.

The co-pilot added, "The Bunny's hutch in hell."

5

September Fourth

```
Hurricane Bunny Advisory Number 4: Sept. 4, 2000 hours
Atlantic Standard Time. The center of Bunny is 15.6
degrees north latitude, 34.8 degrees west longitude.
Direction shifted to west, west-northwest and may
continue this shift with movement at 20 miles per hour.
Hurricane force winds extend out to 110 miles from the
center. Wind speeds are 120 miles per hour near the outer
edge building to 220 near eye wall. Tropical storm winds
extend out 180 miles west from the storm's center and 390
on the southeast sector. The center of Bunny is 1,560
miles due east of the Windward Islands. If conditions do
not change, the center of the eye will be over these
islands in 78 hours. Bunny is a category 5 hurricane and
is extremely dangerous. All marine and aviation
activities should stay well clear of the area.
```

"What the hell are you talking about?" yelled Carl Snow into the telephone. Weather Reconnaissance Squadron at Keesler Air Force Base had called to inform him no insertion flights would happen until tomorrow afternoon. That idiotic approach to gathering data on Bunny angered Carl; the only thing that angered him more was that the caller refused to call him by name. They talked several times a day when the squadron was tracking storms, but the airman always called him Miami.

The caller continued, "Captain McCory is not authorizing flights into the storm. It's too big and too dangerous to risk men and equipment for multi-penetrations. He'll fly the storm himself, but one time a day is all you are going to get. You'll have to rely on satellite data for anything else."

"That simply is unacceptable. It won't do! I need data. These storms just don't happen every day, you know. You can't see the little changes on satellite images. You got to be there, to look at things with a three-dimensional view."

"Captain McCory said the keys to his WC-130 are on his desk. Come by anytime you need more data and go get it yourself. He also said to bring your own crew; his boys stay on the ground."

"You better tell him he can't talk that way to us. He's nothing more than a freaking military pilot. Give him an order to get his heinie up there. We need information and it's his job to get it. Let me talk to this Captain Cory."

"He's a reserve officer, Miami, and flies commercial for a living. I'm not going to give him an order he'll just laugh at. And his name isn't Cory; it's Captain McCory. Mac is sitting right across from me and just told me to tell you to go fuck yourself, Miami."

Carl responded, "Well, Captain McCory, or McChicken, or whatever his name is, better get on the program," and slammed the phone down. He made a beeline for Lewis's office, but this time he knocked, and waited for an invitation to enter.

"The Weather Squadron pilots are refusing to fly Bunny and we need the data. They can't refuse our needs, can they?"

"It appears they are. What are you going to do about it? You could go yourself....Maybe you have an instruction manual stuffed in your jungle jacket on how to fly through hurricanes," Lewis said, obviously enjoying Carl's frustration. "Other than that, Carl, what are your options? I suppose you could take them to court, but the storm will have been a thing of past decades before the courtroom doors actually open. We might offer a bonus to the pilots to risk their lives going through dangerous storms. But, Carl, this storm has swallowed up two other airplanes already and on our budget, I doubt that you'll get any takers."

"Doctor Lewis, this is a very unusual storm. We need data."

"Fake it, Carl. What difference is it going to make anyway? The storm is a killer and it'll demolish everything it happens to float over. That's all that counts with a storm this intense. Get the warnings out; scare the hell out of the people to make them get out of the thing's path. That is all we can do."

"What about all those people? They live on islands; there's nowhere to run."

"Well, what difference is all that data you want so badly going to make to those poor souls?"

"Don't you think we ought to recommend they start flying people off the islands? Should we get our military transport involved to get these people out of the way?"

"You got to be shitting me, Carl. In the first place, the storm has already started its move to the north. It will continue and may miss the Caribbean entirely; then do you know what you'll have? Islands looted by all the people who didn't evacuate, lawsuits against us from every single person who moved, for scaring them, and from those who didn't. Then we'll get more lawsuits from the airlines and hotels. Carl, this is just a storm, an act of nature. The people in its path know about storms; they're not stupid and they've been through hurricanes before. Hell, they expect to get hit by these killers once in a while. They have the freedom to go or stay."

"That's baloney. If Bunny were headed for the States, every cop and national guardsman within miles would be out on the beaches herding the masses out of the area and using force if necessary."

"That may be true, but down there is not the United States, Carl. Down there is...down there. It's somebody else's responsibility. At least we give them warnings; don't expect more."

On the island of Martinique, the weather was hot and still; a slight breeze helped cool things off in the hilly areas, but at sea level it was almost unbearably still. Only ten percent of the population had listened to a television or radio that day. All of the wealthy were very much aware of the Atlantic storm. To most of the locals, it was doing the same thing all storms do: getting bigger, getting stronger, and turning-north soon-or-later, mon. It was better to wait and see if it turned before getting too concerned, as getting ready for a hurricane was a lot of work.

The locals had the music of their favorite dance hall, bar, or boom box to keep them entertained. That was the only thing on their minds after working in the heat of the sun all day.

Tom was below, sleeping off a dozen beers, while Pete had helmsman duty from eight to midnight. All he had to do was be sure the autopilot stayed on course and dodge floating objects like big ships or other boats in the middle of the Caribbean. The light wind did cause him a little apprehension, as the weather always went slack before a big storm. Nevertheless, Big Eye was too far away for it to be affecting the area. The weather report said it started its move to the north and if that continued, he couldn't care less about the slack wind. He had five more cases of beer, three hundred gallons of water, two hundred gallons of fuel, and lots of food aboard. They could stay in the slick glassy calm for days and love every minute.

Looking up into the star-filled night, it was hard to believe that only a few days away, a hell and brimstone machine was raging. A colossal blender fueled by more energy than a bunch of atomic bombs stirred the air, seas, and landmasses to get rid of the old, and bring in new life. Mama Nature was housekeeping.

Grady received his call from Bill. The boys had maintained a heading directly to Martinique, which made Grady happy. If the storm made it to the Windwards, he would show up and announce to his pals that he was worried and had called Customs, until he learned where they had checked in. They would be impressed that he chartered a plane to come get them. "My, what a nice guy I am."

After gaining altitude, and if the unsuspecting idiots had the goodies, he would let old Bill find out if crows can fly with a little chain on their tails. If they did not have the treasure, then they would have the map on them. Grady would play along and, surely, they would cut him in after rescuing them. Either way, it would be like taking money from a sidewalk drunk.

Carl Snow sat in front of his keyboard for the longest time. He desperately needed data to put out reliable bulletins, not to do so was against his rules of being a topnotch meteorologist. He had already fudged once on his first advisory, but upgrading the storm to a hurricane without aircraft confirmation had been a safe bet. However, if he stated that winds were 200 miles per hour and they were actually 250, this would make a great deal of difference to Carl.

Someone had to be disappointed, and since he had done nothing to deserve it, he did not care what the pilot thought; he was expected to fly airplanes for the taxpayers' protection. That applied to Carl, too; every weather forecast was supposed to be completely reliable. Therefore, he typed an accurate weather bulletin and desperately wanted to send it.

> Attention all stations: Hurricane Hunter pilots of the 403rd Wing Weather Squadron are too chicken to do their jobs. So use the last report and your imagination to assess the current conditions of Mega-Storm Bunny. All of you in its path will die, but nobody cares or knows where it is going, so don't worry—be happy.

However, he tempered his feelings and wrote an advisory that would hint at the truth, but would not get him fired.

> Hurricane Bunny, advisory number 5: Sept. 5, 0600 hours, AST. The center of Bunny may be SOMEWHERE near 15.8 degrees north latitude, 38.2 degrees west longitude. Movement SHOULD be west-northwest and MIGHT continue in this direction at MAYBE 20 miles per hour. Hurricane force winds MIGHT extend out to 110 miles from the center. Wind speeds MIGHT be 120 miles per hour near the outer edge and COULD build to 220 near the eye wall. Tropical storm winds PROBABLY extend out 180 miles west from the center and POSSIBLY 390 miles on the southeast sector. The center of Bunny is between 1350 and 1100 miles due east of the Windward Islands. If conditions do not change, the center of the eye MAY OR MAY NOT pass over these islands in 67 to 85 hours. Bunny is a category 5 hurricane and is extremely dangerous. All marine and aircraft, OTHER THAN WEATHER RECONNAISSANCE SQUADRON HURRICANE HUNTER AIRCRAFT, WHICH ARE DESIGNED TO FLY THROUGH HURRICANES, should stay well clear of the area. Next satellite advisory will be at noon. MAYBE we will have ACCURATE wind conditions from the United States Air Forces' 403rd Wing, Weather Reconnaissance Squadron—IF aircraft are made to fly.

He read the bulletin. "There, it's done, and no lies. It's a politically correct weather forecast and one thing is for sure: if Doctor Carl Snow's name is on a weather report, they can leave the umbrellas home, if I say so."

It took fifteen minutes to be summoned to Director Lewis's office. "Damn it Carl, couldn't you have kept it simple. Now we're getting calls about why our aircraft aren't tracking that fucking storm."

"That's not my concern. The taxpayers pay me to be as accurate as possible. I didn't say the pilots were chicken like I wanted to. I just said we didn't have any data because no aircraft were flying."

"Screw that. You knew they were going up this afternoon; you could have faked it once or twice until the next report came in."

"It's never been suggested to me by any of my instructors in college or in the field to fake reports because someone else doesn't do their job. Maybe those pilots will see the need in obtaining our data in the future. And if they get enough phone calls from irate taxpayers, maybe they will better understand my position."

"Well, understanding everyone's position in the tricky business of storm tracking certainly would offer more intelligence to our group. I guess you're right in your assessment once again, Carl."

"I thought you would appreciate my position after giving it some thought, sir."

"You're right. I want you to leave right now, Carl. Miss Stein will assume your responsibilities while you're away."

Carl was perplexed. "Why am I being pulled off? You agreed with me."

Lewis punched a key on his intercom and said, "Oh, Miss Stein, you will handle Carl Snow's position until he returns in a few days. He's joining Aircraft Operations to enlighten the flight crews on his needs, and to get a better understanding of their position in storm tracking during Bunny's rampage."

Carl felt a physical jolt hit him. The words had come as a complete and unpleasant surprise. "Wait sir! Just wait a minute, sir; I didn't say I wanted to be a part of their operation. All I wanted was for them to do a better job."

"I thought you did, and it was a good idea, too. Maybe after a week of Bunny, you'll have shown them the error of their ways. You're lucky; you get a chance to see what a once-in-three-centuries hurricane really looks like. To the rest of us, the storm is just pretty little pictures with pleasing colors."

Carl was worried and said in his defense, "I've seen plenty of storms, Doctor Lewis. Don't forget that I tracked tornadoes as a grad student."

"Tornadoes ain't shit, kid, and you didn't see what they had to offer inside where all the action is. Now you will, you lucky guy."

As Carl tried to think of something to say that would be meaningful and decline the offer, his boss helped him out of his chair and said, "Go downstairs to the travel office. Get your ticket and be on the next flight. Oh, and by the way, you might want to pack some upchuck bags in your jungle suit."

It was a little past six o'clock when Tom and Pete cheered the news about the storm's continued drift to the northwest.

"Keep going Big Eye...just a few more degrees, and we'll be okay." Tom said. "The worst we can expect is a tropical storm, and I eat them for breakfast."

Pete looked at the glassy seas and said, "Good thing Big Eye isn't coming our way. We're sitting ducks out here without any wind."

While drinking their breakfast beers, an airplane flew overhead. "That sounds like the same plane that flew over yesterday. It must be one of those contract operations hopping freight down island."

Pete tossed a yellow and red rubber tube with triple hooks over the side, and let the slow speed pull fishing line off his hand-line. "Fishing contest!" he challenged.

Tom grabbed his fishing line and responded, "Bet you a pound of pirate gold that I catch a bigger one."

Both shifted positions to get more comfortable after Tom opened the cooler and took out two more beers. A few minutes of silence passed before Tom said, "I hope the noon weather report will be a little more exact than this morning's. There were a lot of maybes. I thought that was odd, didn't you?"

Carl landed at St. Croix's Henry E. Rohlsen Airport, and walked across the airfield to the Weather Operations Center. Flying through a hurricane, especially a super hurricane, was not his idea of a grand adventure, it was frightening—no—horrifying! As he entered the squadron's office, he bolstered his attitude. He was the scientist and was not going to show fear to military types. It was up to him to set a good example. Up to him to show the spirit of leadership in getting a good job done every single time.

Inside, several people were behind a long counter, but nobody noticed him. He stood at the counter, waiting, until he lost patience and said loudly, "Excuse me, but I'm Doctor Carl Snow with the National Hurricane Center in Miami. Can you please tell Mister …"

A worker, without looking up, interrupted him and said sarcastically, "I know who you are, Miami. What's with the jungle suit? Going on a safari?"

"This isn't a jungle suit; it's my *travel* jacket. As a severe weather professional, I'm always ready for the field."

"That's good. Well, Miami, take all the sharp pointed objects out of your *travel* jacket or you are going to have a lot of holes in your hide."

"What do you mean?"

"You're not exactly going to be flying first class on a jumbo jet with a glass of chardonnay at your side and a cup full of warm mixed nuts to munch on. You're going to be strapped into a hard chair with hard belts, and you're going to be shaking like you never thought possible. If you try to open your mouth to speak, you could be breaking teeth. You'll be pissing in your britches, and more, unless you empty your bowels before the shit hits. If you have false teeth, take them out, or risk losing them in the vomit bag. All metal objects are to be left behind. That includes rings, watches, chains around your neck, rings pierced in your belly button or other body parts that I don't want to hear about."

"Why?"

"In case the aircraft gets hit by lightning. Any questions?"

Any questions? Carl thought. *Is he serious? Holy smoley! What have I gotten myself into?*

He did not express his feelings verbally, but the staff found it hard not to laugh, as he telegraphed those feelings though the wide-eyed expression on his face.

A woman behind the counter said, "Miami, go into the third door down there. He's waiting to meet you."

"Tom Dennis, the squadron commander?"

"No, Colonel Dennis is stationed at Keesler. It's, as you call him, Captain McChicken."

That stopped Carl in his tracks. Field hands were just voices on a telephone; he never thought that he would actually come face-to-face with them. In the corridor, he hesitated for a moment, and then uttered, "To heck with it, it's better out in the open anyway. Time for the pilot to be a man and do the job expected of him."

Carl's macho attitude was only momentary. As he walked into the small office, he saw McCory sitting in a metal folding chair. A smoking cigarette hung from the corner of his mouth; he was leaning back in the chair with his feet crossed on the desktop, which wrinkled and dirtied the weather maps. His hands crossed behind his head, he looked completely at ease, and he looked very familiar.

The captain got to his feet, all six feet, five inches of him and he looked exactly like John Wayne. The appearance of the big man startled Carl; he was speechless. He was also hoping the bigger man would not pound him into the bare concrete floor he was standing on for his insulting remarks.

"Relax, little pilgrim," said the big man in a pretty good impersonation of the Duke. "Ready to saddle up and go play in the rain, partner?"

Carl, still nervous, did not respond. The thought foremost in his mind was McCory was smoking in a federal building. He did not know if he should mention it.

The pilot offered a handshake and said, "Sorry about the John Wayne business, but I've been doing it for years. Everybody says I look like him so I have a little fun with it. My name is Sam McCory. I know your name from the many weather sheets that come out of Miami, but it's a lot different meeting face-to-face. I'm glad you wanted to come down here to give us a hand with old Bunny. She's certainly a handful."

"Well, Mister McCory, to be honest, it wasn't my idea. My boss sent me to see if I might offer any inspiration to you folks on this end of the business."

"Well, little pilgrim, we're sure happy as hell he did." The Duke was back. "And by the way, Miami, it's captain, not mister. I'm in the Air Force when I hang around here. Anytime you feel up to inspiring us, go right ahead. When you meet the rest of the crew, you'll see we damn sure could use some inspiration."

Mac picked up his empty coffee cup, put an arm on Carl's shoulder and led him back to the main office. "Let's get some coffee."

Carl felt better. "I'm glad to hear that; I was afraid there might be some resentment against an outsider trying to offer improvements." Mac gave him a big smile while Carl was thinking: *Mom always told me, everything happens for the best. The next time I want data, I won't have to resort to playing hardball with these fly-boy characters.*

"Oh, by the way, Miami, you'll be pleased to know that the public at large wasn't too happy about us only flying into Bunny once a day so we are back on two flights a day."

"Well, I'm glad to hear that. It's sure going to make my job easier."

The big pilot and everyone else in the office smiled at the young man's ignorance. Some smiled at the thought of smart-ass Miami painfully puking his guts out while trying to contain the contents of his airsick bag that would be swinging wildly in the cabin of the WC-130 when Mac decided it was payback time.

Mac led him back to his office and resumed his position on his chair, put his feet back up on the desk, wrinkling the charts even more, and said, "Miami, you have to be here at O-three-hundred hours and we leave as soon as everything is checked out. Do you know what time that is in civilian time?"

"Of course, I'm a scientist, you know."

"That's right, you're a scientist. Sometimes I forget things." Mac wanted to tell Carl that he had the credentials to be a scientist; but he was only a pain in the ass. Nevertheless, Mac had been around, Carl was not unique. "Well Miami, listen up and do as you're instructed for your own protection. The crew is going to be too busy to baby-sit, so you'll be on your own. You're solely responsible for gathering and recording data and I suggest you use the time between takeoff and storm insertion to study the equipment manuals. Since you are a scientist, if you want to visit a part of the storm I might miss, then let me know. Feel free to do anything you want, but stay out of the flight crew's way."

Carl said, "No problem. I'm pretty much up on all types of weather equipment..."

Mac cut him off. "Bring plenty of spare batteries for any equipment you're bringing with you. We don't have a power source to recharge batteries on the airplane. If you are recording sound, you need to use a small remote peanut microphone placed inside your headset. You must wear the headset, which we provide, at all times. It's noisy inside *Bouncing Betty*, about 110 decibels, and it gets worse in the storm. The headset is the only way to be heard." Carl nodded his head that he understood.

"You are going to fly into a very well-formed canyon-wall eye. If you're prone to acrophobia, you may not want to look outside while in the eye. The stadium effect inside Bunny is terrifying. The walls rise up from the sea to about ten miles in a sheer vertical mass. If you have a camera tucked in your jungle jacket and want pictures, a wide-angle lens works well. A suction cup lens to a window adapter will do a good job. If you use polarizing lenses, you may have problems. They pick up interference from our windows, so expect to see rainbows on your prints."

Carl said. "I don't need a camera." He pointed to his head, and continued, "Total recall."

"Good. Don't leave your coffee pot on in your room in the morning; there's no guarantee that we'll be back here at the end of a very long day. If we land at a different base and you're not happy about it, then you'll need to arrange for your return trip from there. Be sure you bring plenty of money. You don't have a head cold, do you?"

"Me? No."

"I had to ask, sorry, but you can't fly on these missions if you have a cold. We change altitudes instantly as we pass through the lower pressure zones and the minus-fifty-degree temperatures make sinuses go crazy. We don't carry any medications on the aircraft—not aspirin, decongestants, or air sickness pills. If you need 'em, bring 'em....Don't be embarrassed when you start spewing your guts out. Just aim it away from the equipment. I repeat, do not puke on the equipment. It's runny and seeps into the electronic circuits. It not only shuts down our data gathering but also starts fires that could cause us to be blown out of the sky. In addition, Miami, the ground crew will not clean it up, so you'll have to do it when we get back. That means taking the equipment apart and cleaning inside the cabinets. You can't believe how foul old puke can smell, and it stinks for days."

Carl was devastated. His brief stint as a macho scientist had turned him into a wide-eyed egghead who had never been subjected to dangerous, uncomfortable, or uncontrollable situations before. Mac was delighted, as he continued, "I recommend you have a meal prior to flying. Stomachs seem to do better with something in 'em. We have in-flight box lunches, which include a couple of sandwiches, usually sardine or cow tongue, as those are Texas Charlie's favorites, and he's the meal maker. A couple of sodas and snacks will be thrown in, too. Sometimes Charlie will bring fried chicken that his kid makes. Unfortunately, it's cold and the greasiest shit you can imagine. Unless you have a strong stomach, don't eat it. This is about a twelve-hour flight and that's a long time to have the shits if Texas Charlie's chicken is bad. We also provide coffee and water."

Carl was looking less comfortable with his new role as Hurricane Hunter Scientist and was thinking of a way to miss the morning flight. However, he knew it would only delay the inevitable. Lewis was going to make sure he flew up the Bunny's butt-hole every day. He needed data—but not nearly as badly as he had needed it yesterday.

"Miami, it's warm and toasty here, and on your favorite airliner at thirty thousand feet. However, thanks to budget considerations, *Bouncing Betty* isn't insulated very well. It gets colder than Hillary's shoulder the day after Monica. In addition, we'll be flying at very low and high altitudes, so bring clothes to dress in layers and a change of clothes, in case we don't get back here for a few days. I recommend that you buy a couple pair of thick, warm socks. The floor is metal and very cold. Buy some long underwear, too, if you didn't bring any with you."

"I live in Miami, why would I have long underwear?"

"I don't know. Why would you wear a jungle jacket when you live in a big city? Why would you wear camouflage combat boots to work in an office?"

Carl winced at the zing, and thought: *Why do they pick on me? What's wrong with me wearing what I want to?*

"If you don't have any questions, Miami, why don't you take off, get the things you'll need, get lots of rest, and be here, on this very spot, at O-three hundred, okay?"

"Err, that's three in the morning, right?"

"Err, that correct. By the way, there's one more thing. We have an outstanding safety record, but you're certainly aware that two aircraft have been lost in this beast. You have to sign a release form before boarding the flight tomorrow. The form states that you fully understand that we will be flying through unbelievable thunderstorms with severe turbulence, hail, and dangerous lightning, and nothing, including your safe return, is guaranteed. You look like the sort of adventurous spirit who loves excitement, but be careful what you wish for!"

Texas Charlie, meal maker and flight mechanic, yelled in his conspicuous Fort Worth accent, "Hey Mac, the weather is on." As they all gathered around the radio, Mac asked, "What's for chow tomorrow?"

"I got a hankering for fried chicken, Charlie answered with a straight face."

> Hurricane Bunny, advisory 6: Sept. 5, 1800 hours AST. The center of Bunny is at 16.4 degrees north latitude, 41.7 degrees west longitude. Movement is west-northwest and should continue in this direction for the next 24 hours. Movement is at 20 miles per hour. Hurricane-force winds extend out 180 miles from the center. Wind speeds are at 140 miles per hour near the outer edge and building to 250 miles per hour near the eye wall. Tropical storm winds extend out to 240 miles from the center to the west of the storm and 450 miles on the southeast sector. The center of Bunny is 1,170 miles due east of the Windward Islands. If conditions do not change, the center of the eye will be over those islands in 58 hours. Bunny is a category 5 hurricane and is extremely dangerous. All marine and aviation activities should stay well clear of the area. Next advisory will be issued at 0600 hours Sept. 6.

Meatball, the co-pilot, yelled out, "Hey Miami! Which one of you yo-yos named this mooncalf after a cuddly little rabbit?"

"Bye-bye Bunny," Pete said with joy. "Just keep on going out into the open Atlantic and blow the crap out of anything you want to." Both men were happy about the more northward turn. Everybody in the Windwards was happy, but some were still concerned. The old-timers knew not to count a storm out until it was far to the north of their position, and even that was not a guarantee. Storms had reversed directions before.

6

September Sixth

BY THREE IN THE MORNING, CARL HAD already been awake for three hours; he was too nervous to sleep. Warm winds blew gently across the dimly lit tarmac, but Carl was shivering. He felt cold, but knew it was only apprehension. He was forced into doing something that made him physically ill and there was no need for it; he was paid to use his brains for the betterment of man, not to wait in the dark for a wannabe John Wayne to take him for a ride into hell.

"Where are McCory and crew?" Carl stood alone with alternating thoughts. *Was McCory fooling around with him and the flight was actually scheduled for a normal hour? Or, did they cancel and not inform him?* At three-fifteen, a car, with another following, pulled into the parking lot. Headlights were turned off and four doors slammed shut in the darkness. He heard murmured conversations and an occasional laugh as four men walked into a circle of light by the gate. One of them said, "Hey! Who's that?"

A voice Carl easily recognized as Texas Charlie's, answered, "He's God's gift to hurricane hunters. He's going to show us how to do it today." The others laughed. One of the other men remarked, "Another fat-ass hotshot, eh?"

The remark irritated Carl, he thought: *Go ahead and make fun. I'll show you what difference real knowledge makes today.* He pretended not to hear the crew's remarks as the four men walked by and barely acknowledged his presence. Three of them headed directly to the waiting WC-130 sitting well away from the circle of light. It was invisible in the dark, with only the shape of its tail sticking up over the slightly lighter horizon. Charlie unlocked the office and went in; Carl followed him.

Carl asked, "Where's everyone else? Mac told me to be here at three this morning. Did they cancel the flight and forget to call me?"

"Nobody cancelled the flight. It might piss off some fat-ass paper shuffler in Miami. We wouldn't want to do that," he answered with a smirk. "Mac will be here when he gets here."

Carl resented Charlie's attitude: *Whom was he calling a fat ass? He's the type of person who is ruining the weather service. The stupid cluck should be excited that I'm going with him.* He took a deep breath to relax, as mom had always told him to do in unhappy situations. It worked. *Rather than fight ignorance with anger, I'll make an effort to fit in. It'll make the crew feel more comfortable if they think I'm just another guy.*

Carl cheerfully said, "Mac tells me you're responsible for the chow. Did you fix something yummy for lunch?"

Not believing what he just heard, Charlie looked at Carl. "Yummy?" He smiled, "Bet your fat ass I did, our favorite."

"Marvelous. What's that?"

"Fried Mexican chicken. There's only three pieces for you, so don't get hoggy."

It was hard to conceal Carl's disappointment, but he tried; "Sounds good. . . . What's Mexican chicken?"

"It's a wild chicken sautéed in jalapeño pepper juice. Very chewy."

"Is there some place I can get some snacks, too?"

"Nope."

Headlights turned into the parking area and, once again, car doors shut, and Captain Mac led three men to the office. Each one, like the other men, was dressed in flight clothes and carried a duffel bag and a flight jacket.

"Morning, Miami."

"Good morning. Thought you said to be here at three o'clock sharp; it's almost four."

"Sorry, but breakfast took a little longer this morning. No one was too eager for Chuck's upchuck today. He uses a pepper that's just a little too hot for my taste. Are you all set to roar off into the wild black and blue kick-ass yonder? Ready to take Bunny's temperature?"

"Can hardly wait," he answered weakly, then faked a sneeze, then another. "But darned if I didn't catch a cold last night."

"That's too bad. Did you bring the clothes and money that I suggested?"

"I found some thick wool socks," Carl said, and pulled up his pant legs to show his new pride and joy jungle camouflage socks. Those coupled with his jungle jacket and boots, made a definite macho statement. "But guess my cold will take me out of the game this morning."

Mac smiled at the weatherman, while wondering where he found wool camouflage socks in the Virgins. He said, "Very sporty. Did you leave all the stuff that we told you to remove?"

"Why? I caught a cold, I can't fly. Besides, I thought you guys were just kidding."

"Do you see any of those things on us? Take them off . . . We're about to leave."

"Captain McCory, you said we can't fly if we have a cold." He fake-sneezed again and followed that with a dry cough.

"You're lucky that I can make exceptions. I know how you've looked forward to helping us out, so I'd never take that from you. Come on, Miami, we're going to shove that WC-130 over there right up Bunny's fuzzy little ass." He smiled at Carl. "Only, as you might expect, she doesn't like it that way so she's going to try to bunny-kick us the fuck out of there."

Carl did not like the way his morning was starting. A dead man had more confidence. "One more thing, Miami, don't be concerned with your safety. Sure, Bunny disintegrated two other aircraft, but I know how to fly these storms. Of course, I've had a few problems, some horrendous scares actually, but I'm still breathing. Watch out for the down drafts, they'll make you think you're dead for sure. One time I was caught in a heavy freefall at five thousand feet and finally recovered at seventy feet, but I survived and that's all that's important. We're going to get into trouble once in a while, but we can recover. So remember to stay strapped in and hang on damn tight. If we don't regain control, I'll guarantee you won't feel a thing. It's about the quickest and least painful way you can die. So relax."

Mac put his arm over Carl's shoulder and said, "Okay, let's go tickle the Bunny," and led the way to the aircraft. With Carl in tow under one wing, he could not run away, but he wanted to.

The ground crew was finishing up with their preparations and preflight checks. One of the men saluted the captain, telling him everything was ready. Mac returned the salute and introduced Carl to Sergeant Venerman. "Sarg, this is Miami. He's a honcho from Hurricane Center and, bless him, he volunteered to help out with Bunny and show us some new tricks."

Mac looked at Miami. "Sarg is our crew chief. Treat him nice because this is his airplane, and if something goes crazy on us, he's our only hope." Mac looked back at Sarg. "Why don't you show Miami around and explain everything. I'll help Meatball with the cockpit checkout." Before he walked away, he leaned over and whispered in Sarg's ear, "Keep him busy; he's scared shitless."

Carl was puzzled at the name Meatball. *The co-pilot was called Meatball? Why? Was he incompetent or stupid?*

After a few minutes of looking at various parts of the aircraft, Sarg led him to the vertical ladder that would take him into the belly of the metal beast that would transport him into a hellish nightmare. He was feeling strange sensations, as if his actions were ahead of his thoughts. He took one step, then another, as he slowly climbed the ladder.

Sarg led Carl down the crowded fuselage to his assigned position, and said, "This is the meteorologist's work station, and you be it." Then in the same tone a mother might use when speaking to her child, he said, "Be sure to strap in good and tight."

Seatbelts hung from the ceiling and dangled from all parts of a very sturdy-looking aluminum chair, but the sergeant did not tell him how to use the tangle of webbing. Carl gave Sarg a dirty look when he walked away; he could not understand Sarg not showing him how to use the complicated seatbelts. "What an ignoramus," he uttered.

"I'm not going to ask. I'll get slung out of this thing before I ask these people anything," he muttered. The first belt was for his lap, and once he figured out how to work the latching mechanism, he cinched it up tightly. Next, he snapped shut the left vertical strap, then the right vertical and pulled both as tight as possible. The lateral chest strap was snapped shut and pulled as tight as comfort permitted.

Sarg came back and glanced at Carl's seat belts, and said, "Oh no, Miami, that'll never do. When I said tight, I meant tight." He pulled the lap belt and jerked it until it stopped. The shoulder straps pulled tighter and the chest belt was so taut that Carl had trouble breathing. He was very uncomfortable.

"There you go, Miami. That'll get you to the Bunny, and then you'll have to tighten up some more."

Sitting uncomfortable and feeling alone in the dimly lit cabin, Carl heard the dreaded sound of an engine starting, then another. A minute later, all engines were running. He felt the vibrations, and heard the rattling of equipment around and above him. He hoped everything was firmly bolted into the built-in racks.

Suddenly something slapped him on his shoulder; it scared him and he jumped but went nowhere, as he was firmly fastened to the aluminum seat. "Hi-ya, Miami! Name's Jake and I'm the dropsonde operator. Hope you're tied in good enough; it's a real ball buster in there," he said with a thick southern drawl that was born and raised in Bay Minette, Alabama. He felt Carl's straps and added, "Well, it's okay for now, but just before we head in, you better tighten those straps up."

Carl was utterly confused; how could he possibly tighten the straps, when he could hardly breath. His fear mounted more with every moment.

"You know something, Miami, there's only one way to know for sure what a hurricane is doing and that's to fly through it. That means going through hundreds of miles of shitty winds to penetrate a howling eye wall of a very nasty storm. I really think that some of these storms are alive. I think that Bunny's actually pissed off at something," and he stopped briefly and looked strangely at Carl, and added, "Or at somebody. She tosses this mighty Hercules around like a toy when we're fighting our way in, trying to get into the calm of the eye. When you see her vicious eye wall clouds, you'll suddenly know she's alive, pissed, and evil. Man, that's a frightening experience.

"In all the hurricanes I've been in, I never seen such hate. . . This is one fierce motherfucker. Which one of you clowns named this thing Bunny anyway? The crew is convinced that her name is what pissed her off."

"Don't know," Carl lied. Bunny had been one of the names he had submitted. Then he asked, "Are you sure these straps have to be so tight? They are awfully uncomfortable."

"Am I sure? Shit man, I'm fucking positive, but don't worry, Miami; you'll get used to it. It's all in a day's work for a hurricane hunter."

"Why do they have to be so tight? It'll be a while before we get near the storm."

"My man!" Jake said in mock astonishment, "You're a weather scientist, a doctor of the clouds, you, above all of us, should know what to expect. The storm may be hundreds of miles away, but surely, you know about the weasels?"

He waited for a response from Carl. When nothing was said, Jake said in a condescending manner, "Weasels—you know—the pockets of dead air produced by hurricanes that float around unseen and unknown. What you probably don't know is that the Hercules doesn't react well to sudden air changes, and when we run into one of those, things suddenly go flying and slamming. It can be brutal."

Jake hesitated, then said, "Now you got to tell me, you're just trying to fool me that you didn't know about the weasels, right?"

Carl was unsure how he should react, but played it safe, "Yeah, I . . . just forgot."

"Thought so. Man, we caught a bad one on our last hop to Bunnyland. We were at ten thousand feet at night. We hit a weasel and WHAM! A second later, we're at five thousand feet and seconds later we were down to three thousand. Wow, it was bad at night. Mac couldn't see the water for reference and the rest of us knew, without a doubt, that we were shark food. Meatball had the throttles wide open while Mac strained at the yoke to get us out of the drop. If it happens today, don't be ashamed if you shit your drawers. Lots of folks do."

What in the hell am I doing here? Carl screamed at himself.

"Well, settle in, Miami. We'll be there when we get there; don't worry too much about the weasels, you can't see them coming. You need to work out the program you want to run as we approach Bunny. I need to know how many sondes you'll want before we really wade into the shit pool. After I strap myself in over the ejector, I can't move without fear of being hurt. If you want more drops, then you'll have to work yourself aft to give me a hand."

"It must be pretty rough inside. What's it like, Jake?"

"Can't describe it, don't have the education to be that articulate. Put simply, it's like you are in a huge deserted building and must run through pitch-black corridors, and you know open elevator shafts are everywhere and it's only a matter of seconds before you fall in one of them. It's fucking spooky. You can't see outside and it's dark inside when you're in the storm. Even when you're not in the heavy stuff and it lightens up, you still can't see the wing tips. If you're claustrophobic, Miami, you're in for a badddd time."

I can't do this! Carl's thoughts screamed.

"Remember, Miami, keep those headphones on. It's the only way you'll be able to hear the crew or me and they protect your hearing from the thunder exploding around us. Sometimes, it's like we are bouncing our way through a minefield."

"What do we do if we crash? Is there a survival plan?"

"Survive a crash in a hurricane?" He smiled and exploded in a fit of laughter, and then said, "You can't be serious," and he laughed more. There was not a doubt in Carl's mind that he was about to die. He promised himself that if he got out of this alive, he would never—never question Dr. Lewis again.

Jake continued. "It's my responsibility to be sure everything is strapped down and stays that way. If you see something breaking loose, call me on the intercom. Also, One-eye, our regular aerial reconnaissance weather officer that you replaced, helps me keep an eye out for the engines on this side of the aircraft. If you see hydraulic fluid or fuel leaking, let me know. Of course, if there's a fire, yell out loud and clear. The way we go in and out of these intense high- and low-pressure areas and the vibrations from the turbulence and explosions from lightning cause things to loosen up inside the engines in a hurry."

The plane jerked as the brakes were released. Jake left to get to his chair. Carl looked at the clock mounted twenty inches in front of his face. It was almost five o'clock as the big Hercules bounded down the uneven taxiway. He whined, "Dang! Still on the ground and it's rough."

At ten thousand feet, Mac came on the intercom. "Miami, you know what to do with all those dials and doohickeys on that equipment around you, don't you?"

"I know what everything does, but I've never used some of this stuff."

"Your job is to know how, when, and where, and the procedures to use everything that pertains to weather aboard this aircraft. It's up to you to coordinate the weather mission requirements with the navigator, the dropsonde system operator, and me. That includes the route, weather observation positions, dropsonde release points, special observation requirements, and altitudes you want to fly."

"I can figure it out, but do I have to be strapped in so tightly? I can't move."

Captain Mac motioned to Jake, who was sipping a cup of coffee at the navigator's station, to come forward. He removed his headphones to talk. "Jake, did you do the old corset routine on our weatherman?"

Jake grinned and said, "You should see him, Mac. He's got those straps on so tight, he's turning purple. He's not a very happy hurricane hunter."

"Damn it, Jake, I don't want him passing out on us. He has to do the meteorological work."

"Don't worry Mac," Jake said in a reassuring tone, "if he passes out, I'll revive 'im."

Meatball looked over at Mac and said, "Damn glad this isn't my maiden insertion with this crew. You guys take virgin-popping seriously," and laughed at the picture in his mind of the geeky little guy in his jungle suit all buckled in and anxiously waiting for all hell to break loose.

Mac put his headset back on and said, "Miami, don't forget to turn on the transmitter for your readouts when we get to your recording point. We don't want the fat-asses in Miami to miss anything . . . Right?"

Carl was angry and muttered, "Fat-asses in Miami! You...Captain Ignoramus, should know if it weren't for us in Miami, you wouldn't have a job. Nobody would know about the weather; thousands would be killed. You need to respect us mister big shot, poop-eating airplane driver. Think you'd know how to read and understand the correlation between these meteorological instruments, absolute altimeters, total temperature system, sea surface temperature instrumentation, dew point hygrometer system, meteorological altimeter system, and all the other facilities at my position? Shoot no...you Little Pilgrim, yourself."

After a moment, and in a humorous voice, Mac came on, "Miami, this is Captain Ignoramus, your poop-eating airplane driver. Your microphone is on." Carl wanted to die.

An hour later, his hands hurt and he realized he had a white-knuckle grip on the armrests. Then he noticed something else. Jake and Charlie were walking around; they were not concerned about the weasels, whatever they were. They went into the cockpit; Sarg was there already. Carl began to suspect that he was the object of a cruel joke. Suddenly Carl's attention was grabbed by fire-colored sunlight pouring into his window at the same instant that the plane banked in a turn. It was a beautiful sunrise and he found it hard to believe that a killer storm was less than an hour away.

Mac's voice came on the intercom. "Miami, we're getting into the area. Enjoy the scenery now, because it's going to change rather quickly. We just got a notice from a ship that reported waves at forty-seven feet high, which is about the height of a five-story building. I assume you want to start the first run at ten-thousand feet?"

"That's correct, pilot. I'm switching on the equipment now." Only minutes later, when Carl looked outside again, there was a different view, all dark and gloomy. Looking down, he saw that the earlier whitecaps were now large sections of white. The plane jostled around, and then suddenly it dropped as if gravity just went into overdrive. He heard Jake and Sarg sing out, "WEEEEEEEE," then, when the plane caught air and its descent stopped, they added, "SELLLLLL!" The plane then angled over against a strong broadside wind and Carl reminded himself that they were not even in the hurricane yet.

Mac said, "Okay, Miami, you've seen the weasel. You're now an official crewman of *Bouncing Betty*. Now loosen the belts a little so you can do your job."

The Hercules then began buffeting as the wind increased. Occasionally it jarred so hard, it felt like they were bouncing off the seas below. The noise was increasing; the excitement and his nervousness made him apprehensive about what was about to happen in the next instant. He neither loosened the straps nor thought about the dirty trick played on him. His thoughts were on finding the airsick bags; he looked in his storage compartment and, to his horror, there were no bags. He urgently needed one. Then he spotted two bags folded in the back of the locker and yanked them out. After fumbling in near panic to open them, he found that they were glued shut.

Charlie had played a trick on the new guy, not to be mean, but because they were always playing pranks on each other. It gave them something to laugh about, instead of worrying all the time. If Charlie bothered to look, he would have found that someone had glued his together, too. He and Jake watched as Carl desperately tried to find a bag of any sort to hold the up-and-coming mess; he could not ask anyone to help because to open his mouth was to spew. When his frustration was too much and he had given up all hope of finding a bag, he fumbled for his handkerchief. Only then did Charlie sail a bag across the aisle to him and say, "Sorry, must've forgotten to re-supply your barfies."

He managed to get one in place just in time, and did his best to fill it up. When he looked up and over the nasty rim of the brown bag, he saw Charlie grinning. Sarg said, "Shit, Miami, we're not even in the storm yet. Charlie, you better find more bags for him." Carl flipped them each a bird and then went back to his misery.

A short ringing alarm went off and Meatball came on the intercom. "All crewmen get to your stations. We're going into hurricane-strength winds in about 45 miles. Buckle up and stay put. No one moves in the aircraft until given the all-clear."

The chitchat and smiling faces ended; everyone was instantly professional. The hole, the vortex of the eye, was clearly visible on Carl's Doppler radar screen as was the brooding eye-wall packed tightly with severe thunderstorms. Carl knew when they had traveled the forty-five miles, not because of the radarscope, but because the plane moved as if it was out of control and the noise was deafening. He read the instruments as they did their jobs, but nothing registered in his mind. His thoughts were on what was happening around him and he was frightened. So were the other five guys on board.

"Holy shit! Aborting, aborting, aborting! Issuing mayday." Mac said in a very firm but calm voice. The Hercules banked steeply and turned. Carl heard the engines go quiet and he fought his bowel muscles to keep the hot brown lava from filling his pants. He had never imagined such fear was possible.

"What's wrong? We're crashing? Mac, what's wrong?" he yelled into the microphone.

"Damn it, Miami! Don't yell in the phones!" was the response, and then Mac said, "Hail broke our windscreen. Some water and wind is seeping through and it may blow in. We have to land ASAP."

Carl wanted to ask about the engines, why they were so quiet, but knew it did not matter; they were about to die.

Hurricane Bunny, advisory 7: Sept. 6, 0600 hours, AST. The center of Bunny is 16.4 degrees north latitude, 45.7 degrees west longitude. Movement is to the west-northwest and will continue in this direction for the next 24 hours at 20 miles per hour. Hurricane-force winds extend out to 180 miles from the center. Wind speeds are 140 miles per hour near the outer edge and building to 250 miles per hour near the eye wall.Tropical storm winds extend out to 240 miles from the center to the west and 450 miles on the southeast sector. The center of Bunny is 900 miles due east of the Windward Islands. If conditions do not change, the center of the eye will be over Guadeloupe in 45 hours. Bunny is a category 5 hurricane and is extremely dangerous. All marine and aviation activities should stay well clear of the area. A hurricane watch may be issued this afternoon for all Leeward and Windward Islands. Tropical storm warnings are in effect for these islands, and the outer islands should start feeling the effects of Bunny in 33 hours. Next advisory will be issued at noon, Sept. 6.

Pete came to the cockpit after plotting the latest coordinates and said, "Bad news old buddy. Bunny is coming to give our asses a thumping. With the size of that thing, hurricane-force winds will cover all the way down to the Grenadines. It looks as if we're back to our original schedule. I'm glad we ran the engine to maintain our speed."

"Can't believe it's so big. It has to be the biggest ever. Can you imagine the damage it's going to do? People are going to be dealing with Bunny for years after it evaporates back into the atmosphere."

"Don't know how recovery will be possible; the tourist industry will be wiped out overnight and that is the basis of the Caribbean's economy. We better find our treasure and get the hell out of the way while we can."

"We ought to be getting out of Dodge about the time the tropical storm starts."

"Not me, I'm staying on *Gypsy*. The only thing that'll save her is keeping chafing gear between the lines."

"You have to be shitting me. You'll have a ton of money and can buy lots of *Gypsies*."

Pete turned to look at Tom and muttered, "Maybe, but I owe *Gypsy*. I won't let her be ripped apart on some rocky shore."

Tom said, "Don't forget the drive-downs. Unless you're up wind, boats that break free will crush you." He thought for a moment then added, "But what the hell, I'll help you keep her in one piece. It'd sure make taking the treasure away a lot easier if *Gypsy* survived."

Pete said, "Well, if all fails, at least there'll be plenty of salvage work for us, right?"

Grady took a taxi to the airport and waited in his airplane while Bill filed the flight plan. By ten o'clock, they were on their way to rendezvous with Jerome and Abby in St. Lucia. All ships in St. Thomas were watching the hurricane closely and preparing to go to Venezuela to escape. The only other option was to run ahead of the storm and hope like hell that it turned north or ran out of gas before they ran out of ocean. He was sure Jerome's ship would pull out of St. Lucia and steam south to get as much distance as possible between it and the storm. He hoped Jerome would stay.

When Grady landed on the tiny airport in downtown Castries, he saw the stunning couple waiting.

After a quick but joyous reunion, Jerome said, "How things have changed. Going through Customs in the old days was not so easy with all of the cash we had to carry."

Grady smiled while nodding in agreement. "Today's so much better. No cash, no product, and we'll still leave the island with a ton of money we didn't have when we arrived. And there's no fear of being discovered.

"Unfortunately, this trip will be shortened. The ship's captain is concerned about the hurricane, so they are sailing in two hours to Tobago."

"Leave your stuff aboard, and stick around for some fun and possible profit. I'll fly you out of here."

"Good. What's the fun and profit thing?"

"Interested in a pirate's treasure in Martinique?"

Jerome looked at Abby. She was excited at the possibility of finding a real pirate's treasure, but then frowned. She asked, "What about the storm?"

Grady looked at Jerome and said, "Let's worry about that after we check in, have a great lunch, and get our business matters squared away." Normally, their meetings included all day and night reveling and tasting the best of the local offerings, but Bunny's proximity had put them on the clock.

They took a taxi to the Rendezvous Hotel and checked in as tourists. The hotel clerk reminded them of the impending hurricane and made them sign a statement that they would check out before noon the next day. Hotels throughout the Windward Islands were getting as many people as possible off the island before the storm hit. It was not because of concern for the tourists' safety, it was because it would be difficult to get off the island for weeks after the storm had passed, and there was only so much food and fresh water to go around.

Bill found the beach bar and ordered a cold beer while Grady and Jerome had their meeting. He was considered one of the family, but not in the financial way. Abby was also excluded from the meeting, but she was not interested, and never got involved in her husband's business. She spent the afternoon taking advantage of some terribly ridiculous sales, as merchants were selling everything at cost or less, before Bunny's wind could steal their goods.

Jerome gave Grady an attaché case containing a half-dozen tourist brochures and four slips of paper. One had the code for his new Swiss account and a notation "1.3." That indicated $1.3 million had been deposited. The next piece had the code name of Doc's Burger Joint, Antigua, and a number, "8," which meant the guy was an eight ball, a deadbeat, and no quarter was to be given.

Grady said, "This will make Bill happy; another Caribbean deposit." The next note had codes that told him what his territory produced in sales for the year-to-date; his people were up ten percent. The last was a full sheet of a cryptic message that he would have to sit down and decode in his own computer. It would be about the territory in general, any new people, any efforts by law agencies, any moves by the competition, and what areas to be careful in. The same old stuff, but it was nice to be aware of any efforts being made to slow their business.

They never discussed business vocally, unless they were far-removed from civilization. The governments had started randomly planting bugs everywhere, hoping for careless talk-a-lot criminals. Grady and Jerome were too seasoned to be careless; they were more prone to paranoia. After Grady read the notes, he transferred the new Swiss account number into his phone book to look like more phone numbers, then tore the note up and flushed it with the eight-ball's note.

Outside, they met Bill during his third beer. Grady slapped him on the back and whispered, "You just made yourself a hundred grand. Happy?"

"Damn right, boss, let me buy you a beer."

"Let me buy *you* a beer, but after this, you can't drink any more. You have to fly us to Martinique."

Abby joined them and they laughed and talked like tourists about Bunny's pending doom. Nobody would have ever thought that three of the four people sitting on the corner barstools were major drug dealers, calculating murderers, and conspirators with absolutely no compassion for their victims.

On the flight to Martinique, Grady said, "I have a plan that will expose us to the boys wherever they arrive. Keep an eye out for this boat," and he gave Jerome and Abby photographs of Pete's boat. He also gave them each a pair of binoculars and a cell phone.

Abby asked, "Who are these people? And what do they have to do with the treasure?"

"They have a map and are going to lead us to the gold."

Abby looked worried and asked, "You're going to take it away from them?"

"Hell yes, Abby," Grady quickly responded with a beaming smile. "That's what treasures are for. The strongest, most clever people capture the treasure; and then we must remain clever and strong, lest someone take it away from us. That's how the game is played; lost treasures do not belong to anyone other than the current custodian."

She added, "Well, I don't know about this. It doesn't sound right. Nobody's going to get hurt, right?"

Grady muttered to himself, *Fucking women*. Then said, "Abby, how else are you going to take a treasure away from someone without getting a little physical? Nobody will give up a buried treasure without a fight. Don't worry about it. I know these guys; they're friends of mine. If they end up with the gold, they'll just drink it up anyway. If we get it, I'll be sure they are properly compensated." He looked at Bill. Bill chuckled wickedly.

She had been excited at the idea of finding old treasure, but not at the cost of someone else, but she did not press it further. "Tell us about the treasure, Grady."

"All I know is one of them found the old map and the other guy is financing the deal. He wouldn't be in it if it didn't look good. Besides, they wouldn't tell me about it, so it has to be good. We're tracking them and we'll let them find it for us before we make our presence known. Then I'll offer to take them out of the storm area before it gets here. After they load the plane with our treasure, I'll deal with my pals."

Jerome knew how he planned to deal with his pals and had to be sure it did not happen in front of Abby. She did not understand the brutality of reality. The conversation ended as the plane touched down on the runway. After another session with the Customs' folks, they were standing at a car rental agency.

Gypsy Bitch pulled into Le Marin's peaceful little harbor at six o'clock. Everything was calm and relaxed; there were no webs of anchor lines surrounding the boats in the harbor. Tom said, "Maybe they know something we don't."

"Or they think it'll wait until tomorrow, Tom. I used to be the same way until Marilyn kicked my ass. At least it's good to see there're plenty of sheltered places to hide in."

The only other time Pete had been in the harbor did not count. He had been three-quarters blitzed and stayed that way all day, or worse, the entire week. He did remember a few people he had made met in the bars; some he preferred to forget. God had his own way of teaching moral decency to the puny humans on His planet. Pete's sordid and painful hangover lasted another week.

As they entered the harbor, they saw the little village. Small white buildings stood out against the deep greens of the surrounding hills. Tom's new chart showed a narrow but deep channel going into the village, and there was a good-sized hotel near the channel entrance. Pete's first priority was to find a secure place to rig the boat for Bunny's conditions.

Pete found an excellent place with nearby trees he could use for his extra lines and there was protection from the wind and seas on three sides. He was satisfied with his hurricane hidey-hole. As soon as an anchor had been set, he went below to listen to the last weather report they would get that day. He and Tom celebrated their good fortune by drinking several beers. After the weather report, they drank more beers, but were not very festive.

> Hurricane Bunny, advisory 9: Sept. 6, 1800 hours, AST. The center of Bunny is 16.2 degrees north latitude, 49.8 degrees west longitude. Hurricane Bunny is moving west-southwest and will continue in this direction for the next 24 hours. Movement is at 20 miles per hour. Hurricane-force winds extend out to 180 miles from the center. Wind speeds are 180 miles per hour near the outer edge and 250 miles per hour near the eye wall. Tropical storm winds extend out to 240 miles from the center on the west side of the storm and 450 miles on the southeast sector. The center of Bunny is 690 miles due east of the Windward Islands. If conditions do not change, tropical storm winds will make landfall in 24 hours. Hurricane-force winds in 27 hours. The center of the eye will be over Guadeloupe in 34 hours. The eye of the hurricane is 40 miles in diameter, and may reduce in size as the storm picks up more strength after it enters the warmer waters of the Caribbean. Bunny is a category 5 hurricane and is extremely dangerous. All marine and aviation activities should stay well clear of the area. A hurricane watch is issued for all islands, in the Leeward and Windward Islands, north of Grenada. Tropical storm warnings are in effect for all other islands. Next advisory will be issued at 0600, Sept. 7.

Tom sat at the edge of the door. "You know what? This stinking hurricane is going to kill a lot of us. Wind from 180 to 250 miles per hour and extending out 180 miles is just plumb hideous. That's just the front side, then add another 180 miles, and you have a hurricane 360 fucking miles wide. Moving at twenty miles an hour means we'll be in catastrophic wind for eighteen hours. There's no way to survive that. Forget about riding *Gypsy* through the storm; there's nothing you can do, buddy. We have to be on an airplane out of here by tomorrow at this time the latest."

"Yeah, I've been thinking the same thing. You sure picked the wrong place to find a treasure. Can you believe that thing is angling southward again? Somebody down here must've pissed Mama Nature off."

"Pete, *Gypsy* won't make it. You still have time to take her to Trinidad. I'll stay and try to locate the treasure and make sure it's in a high and dry place. Then I'll catch a flight out and join you in Trinidad."

"Thought about that, but if the treasure is as big as you think, you'd never be able to move it by yourself with the limited time we have. Besides, you know the last few flights out of here are going to be packed with the local elites; you'd never get a seat. No, Tom, I knew the risks when I signed on. Let's hope for the best."

That made Tom happier; he knew that without Pete, the treasure could not be moved in time. "If you change your mind, Pete, I'll understand."

Pete shrugged his shoulders and said, "The really sad thing is nobody down here seems to know what's coming their way. No one's boarding up windows or rigging boats."

"I noticed. Maybe the radio stations don't know?"

"That's the Caribbean for you." There was no more talk of the impending storm; they could do nothing but carry out their plan. With the boat secured, they took the dinghy to the commercial area to clear Customs. A handwritten sign said to come back at seven-thirty tomorrow.

Tom said, "We need to be out on the island at dawn."

"Screw it, Tom; they won't be here either. Let's find a truck rental."

After a few phone calls and an extra twenty dollars for the clerk, they arranged to have a covered truck sent over from Fort de France, but it would not be there for three hours. With time to kill, they went in search of a good restaurant and decent food for a change. They ended up at the yacht club; its second story was a restaurant. They gorged themselves on French cuisine and wonderful wine, and afterwards went downstairs to the yacht club to see what was going on with the storm. The place was empty, except for the club manager, and he claimed to speak only French, which they did not.

They walked around the village of St. Anne. It was a delightful little village, but large enough to have its own supermarket, a town square, and a dozen bars, in addition to several restaurants. The village was so clean it looked as though it was hand-scrubbed daily. Aromas of pastas and fresh coffee floated from the bars and cafes. A mixture of jazz, rock, and Caribbean reggae charmed their souls as they walked through the old narrow streets of the quaint village. It was small, but very much alive. Everyone seemed to have the attitude that the killer Bunny would not dare visit their village.

Then an unpleasant thought struck Pete. "Remember the volcano eruptions in 1902? It wiped out thirty thousand people, and only because the governor didn't warn the citizens of the impending disaster."

"I read about that, Pete. The politician was up for re-election and needed to keep everybody on the island to vote for him. He even hired a scientist to proclaim there was no danger."

"Didn't do him any good; he was turned into cinder like the rest of the population. Surely, this isn't the case today. These people have radios and televisions. They have to know what's going on." They went into a bar and tried to converse, but very little English was spoken. It took two more bars and several beers before they found someone who could, or would, speak to them.

Pete asked the man, "Don't you people know there's a very dangerous hurricane coming?"

He answered, "Sure. You Americans are not the only people to monitor the weather."

"Why isn't everyone getting houses and boats ready?"

"We have time for that tomorrow. Today was a time for work. Tonight is a time for festivities, to eat, drink, and enjoy life's offerings. Tonight is our last opportunity for fun, hot food, and cold beer. We know that tomorrow night we will be captive to our homes or shelters. The next day we will emerge to find much of what we had is gone. We will not have electricity to keep our foods fresh, our beer cool; everything that will spoil must be thrown into the sea. And, sadly, some of us will not be here when Bunny leaves. There will be the months of doing without, and that is why we appear to be unconcerned. This is the last night some of us will have; it's the last night of carefree living for the rest of us for months to come."

Pete said, "Well, that makes sense to me. I like the way your people think. Let's have more drinks," and he bought a round for everyone in the bar, all five of them.

Tom saw the rental truck go past the bar and ran down the street after it. Pete stayed to pay the bar tab, and then went after Tom. As he walked out on the street, he saw a face in the shadows for just an instant. It looked familiar, like his pal Grady, but with the beers in him, he forgot about it. Only the truck was on his mind.

That evening, Pete and Tom made sure *Gypsy* was as secure as possible. It took hours of hard work to get the sails off and move everything loose on deck into the cabin. Four anchors were set, and they tied the boat to three trees. Everything had double lines. Normally, Pete would have been happy with *Gypsy's* storm mooring, but eighteen hours of 200-mile-per-hour winds were too much. The mountains around would cut down some of the wind. With hope and prayers, it might be enough. Besides the wind, who could guess how high the deadly storm surge would be.

7

September Seventh

THE EMBARRASSMENT OF YESTERDAY did not matter. Nothing mattered except not having to fly through Bunny. His cold had not worked the day before, but Carl had a solution for that day. It was not one that would do his reputation any good, but he could not endure another experience like that. The constant level of fear was more than a man with his education and promise should be subjected to.

His fear had peaked before the windscreen cracked and every second of the flight afterwards was sheer terror. He constantly expected to hear the men in the cockpit scream as the windshield blew in on them. They would have died instantly, but it would have taken longer for him. He would have watched the pilot-less aircraft flounder its way down to splatter into the churning Atlantic Ocean.

He could not wait any longer; the crew was ready to board the Hercules. It was three A.M. when he dialed his boss's home in Miami. After several rings, a sleepy man answered.

"This is Carl Snow, Doctor Lewis. Good morning; I apologize for calling you so early, but it's important."

A few seconds later, the sleepy man said in a cheerful tone, "Is this Carl the flying weatherman? How does my weather aviator like his new job?" and he chuckled.

"Doctor Lewis, I erred in my judgment about the fly-through flights. You were correct; wind speed over 200 miles per hour doesn't matter. I think I should return to my post and work harder on the satellite data. The storm might be aiming for the Bahamas or the Carolinas."

Captain Mac had been standing behind Carl, listening to the anticipated conversation.

He came up, put an arm around Carl's shoulders, and smiled when he said, "Hold on, Little Pilgrim, we can't abandon this storm, especially now. I don't think Bunny is through with the islands. Looking at the tops of those big clouds yesterday, I think something is pushing them back to the southwest. We need to take another look this morning. If they are, then the islands have big problems."

"Yeah, okay, but I'll be able to see what is going on in Miami."

"Afraid not, little pilgrim, we need you here. You replaced our aerial reconnaissance weather officer, and that slot has to be filled with someone qualified."

"Call him back to work."

"No can do, partner. He went to the States on leave."

"Surely you have a backup?"

"Yep, and it's you. Besides that, Miami, you can't see the little changes on satellite images. You have to be there, to look at things with a three-dimensional view. I do believe those were your words, right?"

That kind of talk was not what Carl wanted to hear. He wanted to hear his boss tell him to catch the first flight home, and all was forgiven. However, his boss said, "I heard that. Tell Captain Mac to keep up the good work. Carl, you expected those men to be courageous enough to go out there and bring back data for your office, so you do the same. . . . Carl, don't call me again begging to come home. You're there for the duration, Little Pilgrim."

Carl had anticipated Lewis's response and was prepared to exercise his only option: quit the job he had dreamed of since he was twelve years old. However, since he had actually heard the refusal, he was not too sure. He would be giving up his professional life, and worse: everyone at the office would laugh at him for being a coward.

Mac knew what was going on in the young man's mind. He had seen people refuse to go into a rough storm the second time. In fact, so many people had quit their jobs that NOAA had to start using military crews. Military personnel cannot quit—they would go to jail. He knew Carl was not a bad guy, he was just full of himself and was probably brought up thinking that intelligence was all that mattered. If someone had a different opinion, it was because he or she was improperly informed. He had never lived and thought on any level other than that which made him feel comfortable. Life had been easy, with few disruptions and no danger. Carl had been forced out of his comfortable little world into something completely alien, a life-threatening situation where someone else's intelligence and luck were the only things separating him from life and death.

Carl's realization that his judgment about the penetration flights was bad, and being caught unaware that the storm was moving in a new direction, had rattled his self-esteem. Of course, he could not have seen the clouds, because the view of his world was limited to the edges of a brown barf bag. He had been so sick that he puked air for the last hour of the flight.

Mac thought it was time for compassion. "Carl, let's do our job. I promise it'll be better today. The first time is always the worst. Now you know what to expect, and more importantly, you know you're going to survive. I know it's tough, but after this is all over, you'll feel pride in yourself that you rode the worst hurricane in recorded history to its death and saved a lot of lives because of it."

That made Carl feel better, not much, but enough to get him to take the first step toward the waiting airplane. The short speech was not that motivating, but Mac had called him *Carl*; he had used his name, and to Carl, that meant he was accepted. That alone was inspirational.

Strapped in again, but more comfortably, Carl was very aware of the engines starting. "Please God, let them shut down, a mechanical problem, a flat tire, anything." He had been completely surprised when he arrived that morning to find a new windscreen had been flown in from Keesler Air Force Base and was installed overnight. The powerful engines revved up . . . The brakes released, the aircraft moved. Carl looked out his window; it was dark, as the plane was rocking on the rough taxiway. He prayed, "Come on tire. Blow out." In moments, they were airborne and climbing for altitude. "Come on engine, overheat. Catch on fire."

The storm was closer, so they did not have as far to travel. They would be in the soup soon and Carl kept busy fiddling with the Improved Weather Reconnaissance System (IWRS). He checked his intercom switch to be sure it was off, and then muttered, "Need to change my attitude. We'll be slicing through the atmosphere at altitudes I select for meteorologists around the world to analyze. That's exciting and important. Those . . . fat-asses," he smiled, "will be looking at data that I dig out of Bunny. They'll only see numbers and graphs; I'll be making the decisions and directing the pilot where to take me. It's my storm. This is my job."

He felt better knowing that he had purpose. He jotted down his plan, and decided he would start with a fly-through at 10,000 feet, go to sea surface at 500 feet, then up to 1,500 feet. The next pass would be at 2,500, then 5,000 feet, and then 10,000 again. Then he would take the crew to the altitudes and see what Bunny had to say about it. He said absently while writing, "And if I'm still alive after that, I'll make one more run through the oven at the surface. That ought to make Captain Mac and his band of dunces happy. They'll think they've driven me mad and that I'm one of them."

He set the on-board computers to display the data every second, and to show him a real-time graph-showing barometer and wind speed. "Mac, you may be flying this chunk of aluminum, but I've got control of its brains. I'm going to know this storm as well as God does before I pull out. This little bunny is being inserted by the best. Ha, ha, ha."

His machismo vanished when Charlie came by and said, "Guess what? Since you didn't eat yesterday, I saved, and will reheat, your Mexican chicken for lunch."

Pete and Tom, and most of the marine community, listened to the six o'clock broadcast. Unfortunately, many people living outside of towns and villages did not own a radio or TV and were not getting advance notice of the impending doom that was rumbling toward them at twenty miles per hour.

To the inexperienced, the weather looked beautiful that morning with clear blue skies, still winds, and a glassy sea floating on increasingly large swells. To the experienced, the stillness and the high-altitude clouds that began to approach were there because the raging fury was sucking all the moisture and wind into it.

> Hurricane Bunny, advisory number 10: Sept. 7, 0600 hours, AST. The center of Bunny is 16 degrees north latitude, 53.7 degrees west longitude. Movement to the west-southwest will continue in this direction for the next 24 hours at 20 miles per hour. Hurricane-force winds extend out to 180 miles from the center. Wind speeds are 140 miles per hour near the outer edge and 250 miles per hour near the eye wall. Tropical storm winds extend out to 240 miles from the center on the western sector of the storm and 450 on the southeast. The center of Bunny is 460 miles from the island of Dominica. If conditions do not change, tropical storm winds will make landfall in 11 hours. Hurricane force winds in 14 hours. The center of the eye will be over Dominica in 23 hours. The eye of the hurricane is 40 miles in diameter, and may reduce in size as the storm picks up more strength after it enters the warmer waters of the Caribbean. Bunny is a category 5 hurricane and is extremely dangerous. All marine and aviation activities should stay well clear of the area. Hurricane warnings are issued for all islands, in Leeward and Windward Islands, north of Grenada. Tropical storm warnings are in effect for all other islands. A hurricane reconnaissance aircraft is in the storm at this time and weather updates will be broadcast every 15 minutes. Next advisory will be issued at noon, Sept. 7.

Carl, ready for action, said over the intercom, "DSO, this is ARWC. Stand by to launch sonde; I want a reading to know what winds and atmosphere we have before we're in storm conditions. Set deployment of parachute ten seconds after ejection. I want a vertical velocity of one thousand feet per minute. Eject when ready and stand by with sonde two for my command when we hit the outer storm wall."

"Roger, ARWC," Jake responded. He was strapped down in the tail of the *Hercules*. His sixteen-by-four-inch sonde wind-finding system tubes were firmly lashed to a bulkhead and held in position to make his final settings. The handling of the one-pound tube of sensors, satellite receiver, and transmitter, plus a battery pack, was Jake's main responsibility to the mission. The irretrievable sonde would be dropped at the ARWC's command and tracked for a distance of 200 miles.

"DSO, this is ARWC. Set wind measurement to triangulate its position by GPS stations and not Omega radio. In addition, I want data transmitted to my receiver only, not satellite to Miami. I will forward everything to Miami."

"That's not the way we do it, ARWC. I edit the data and send it on."

"Not on my watch, DSO. Please do as you're told. This is my operation."

"Okay, Miami. Did you read that, Mac?"

"Yes, DSO. Miami's in charge; do as he says."

Carl could not contain his smile. He truly felt pride in himself. Or was it power? He said, "DSO, confirm sensor specifics for my record. Temperature by Rosemount thermistor corrected for frictional heating of the probe with accuracy mode set to plus zero-point five percent centigrade."

"Correct, ARWC."

"Edgetech Dewpoint Hygrometer at same accuracy mode."

"Check, ARWC."

"Combined Altitude Radar Altimeter is on and set to two percent if we get too close to the surface."

"Roger, ARWC."

"Air Research Pressure Altimeter set to reference datum of twenty-nine point nine two inches of mercury.... Navigator, this is ARWC. Are wind sensor probes computing true airspeed with side-slip according to the Self-Contained Navigation System?"

"Yes, ARWC. I'm getting accurate ground speed and heading information to complete the wind calculations. Position is confirmed by inertial and Doppler positions computed by the navigator's SCNS."

"Pilot, this is ARWC. All equipment and conditions are secure for insertion."

"Good show, Doctor Snow. We are ten minutes from the tropical wall. Advise me of your first-run plan."

"Continue present heading at ten thousand feet."

"Roger, ARWC, but I have set up this run so we can turn five degrees to starboard to take some of the punch out of her. Advise if that's not acceptable."

"Pilot, ARWC, take as much of the punch out of her as you want at this stage, but no changes at recording altitudes."

Mac turned to Meatball and said, "See, I told you he'd be okay when it was time to get to work."

"Yeah, but he sounds a little bossy for a first-timer."

"DSO, ARWC, drop sonde one." A metallic WHANG came from the rear of the aircraft and DSO said, "Sonde away."

The plane banked suddenly as a wind gust hit. Mac straightened it out and throttled down to lose altitude. The co-pilot announced over the intercom, "That was a shitty welcome to Bunny's hutch. Estimated wind speed at eighty plus."

"DSO this is ARWC. Drop two." The plane began to bounce from side to side and there was the first weasel, and this time Carl's voice was one of the six who sang out WEEEEE . . . SELLLL. Then it got worse, much worse.

Pete removed the dinghy's engine and gas tank, and took them to the truck. Both men carried the rubber boat. Pete said, "Call the airport to reserve two seats on the last plane out. Use this credit card to pay." He gave him a Master Charge card. Twenty minutes passed before Tom returned. He looked disappointed and said, "The only way you're going to get a seat out of here is to be there. They're not taking reservations. We stand a chance to get seats before the locals, as they are trying to get the tourists off the island. There's talk that some French military transports are coming in to take as many people as possible. The person I talked to told me not to count on it, though, because St. Martin is also going to be hit, and they'll get the military aircraft first. There's not that many French aircraft around to do much good."

"How about the Americans, Tom? Are they bringing in transports?"

"If they did, it'd be for the Virgin Islands. It's too big of a storm; they should've started hauling people out of here when they saw this thing building."

"Sounds like you're telling me we're stuck here, rich or poor."

"That's right, unless you want to go to the airport now. It's in Fort de France, maybe thirty miles away, and the crowd that's already there is getting unruly, the agent said. We might have to be there all day to get a seat, and we might not even get one. I vote that we go for the treasure and find a hole to crawl in on some mountain."

An hour later, they were moving out of town on the east shore road, going north. Tom plugged the island's coordinates into Pete's hand-held GPS. The GPS would tell them when they were near. They reached the area and could see the sea. Tom said, "Okay, we're about as close as we're going to get. Find a place to put the dinghy in."

"That's easy to say. Take your nose out of the GPS and look around. It's all jungle and cliffs to the water."

"Quit whining. We'll find a spot and look at the weather; it's incredibly good."

"And that's incredibly bad. This means when it turns bad it's going to be *real* bad."

"Look at the swells, Pete. Those are Big Eye Bertha's fart waves. She's a-coming." He pointed to a clearing to his right. "Right there; we can get down right there." With the truck parked on the washboard road, Pete grabbed the bow and Tom hefted the stern and carried the dinghy the twenty-five yards to the rocky shore. A moment was spent gazing at the little island a half-mile away.

Running the rubber boat out into the fringes of the surf was both exciting and terrifying. Pete yelled out, "You know what happens if the engine quits, don't you?"

"Sure. We won't have to worry about Big Eye anymore. Those rocks and breakers will turn us into fish food." Pete steered, following Tom's instructions; he had drawn a map, combining features shown on the old hand-drawn one and those shown on the new store-bought chart. He had the island in sight and was looking for the best way to get there without running up on the reef or being swamped by the breakers. Tom was standing to get a better view and pointed the way between the coral heads and rocks that were just below the surface. At one point, Pete lost confidence in Tom when he pointed to an obviously dangerous reef covered with breakers, but it turned out Tom had seen clear water behind it, and it was calm and deep all the way to the island.

"There it is, matey!" Tom yelled, "Our own Treasure Island."

Pete noticed a very strong surge flowing between the island and the reefs of the mainland. "This is going to be a treacherous place to be when the wind picks up." Tom acknowledged, but his attention was focused on his dream island. Pete found a place to wedge the dinghy between the rocks and they pulled it out of the water. He tied it to a rock, and they quickly began their search. Tom had his map and compass. Pete carried the shovel.

"Who would bury a treasure on this barren rock?"

"Someone who didn't want it found by accident, Pete."

In Miami's Hurricane Center, Miss Stein sat on her abundant backside typing the weather statement. She was weeping. The satellite image was horrifying; the huge mass of Bunny filled the Atlantic Ocean and was aimed for the—ant-sized by comparison—Caribbean islands. Speculation in the office was that the human population would be reduced by a third. Ninety percent of livestock and domestic animals would be killed; eighty percent of the homes would be destroyed, and communications, utilities, and potable water, non-existent for weeks or months to come. Most individual food reserves would probably be lost in the first hour of the hurricane. Warehouse storage losses would be at ninety percent, and one hundred percent, after hurricane survivors started looting. To expect better would have been folly; the wind was too strong and the duration too long. Category three storms actually break boulders with the pounding surf. This thing, the monster Bunny, went beyond the maximum category five. Categories were designations that measured the limit of man's mind to visualize destruction. Bunny's unique category was inconceivable.

The weather eggheads, with no lasting thoughts of those in its path, were locked on the storm's every move and were delighted to be able to experience such a phenomena. There were others, however, very much concerned with what was going to be left after Bunny had trampled the islands. The French had aircraft on the way from the homeland. They were fully loaded with food and water, medical supplies, and troops. They would wait in South America for the storm to pass. One troop carrier would land on each French island before the storm and would find secure shelter near the airfield. When the storm passed, those troops would clear the airfield of debris and set up portable airfield communications so the supply planes could land. The supplies would be swapped for survivors.

The islands belonging to the United States would be taken care of, but there was nothing in the works. In the American political structure, it was impossible to use common sense and make the moves beforehand that were going to be desperately needed after the storm hit. They would have to send experts in to survey the area after the storm and evaluate the extent of damage, make out a list of what was needed, and do mountainous paperwork justifying how much it would cost. Before they could even give you a sympathy fart, they had to kiss the budget god's ass.

The Dutch islands were in for a hard time, as were the British and independent governments. Thankfully, the Red Cross would clumsily arrive and try very hard to get food and water to the survivors.

Most of the populace was aware of the killer called Bunny. Police cars on every island traveled the back roads, broadcasting warnings to the public. Most islanders without the visual benefit of television pooh-poohed the notion that they were going to be swallowed by the strongest hurricane ever. They were being told not to stay in their homes, but to go to the nearest emergency shelter. All the islanders knew that to abandon their homes was to invite looters. When they returned, everything of value could be gone.

Most of the people who had television sets saw the massive size of Bunny as it marched toward the Caribbean. The experienced knew even the emergency shelters would not hold up under those kinds of conditions, so they went up to the mountains to find sheltered places behind the huge boulders and in caves. Unfortunately, many did not remember the mudslides that often occurred when torrential rains came.

Religious zealots were beating the drums of death and destruction to drive people into church to accept the various sons of God before the world ended.

Merchants were trading merchandise for any amount of cash, knowing everything would be ruined or looted. Businesses wrapped their office equipment and files in plastic garbage bags, and placed them as high off the floor as possible. Jewelers crammed their heavy safes with their merchandise, while keeping a few of the most expensive pieces to sell wherever they ended up. Business owners carried backup copies of sales and accounting histories. It might be a long while before those records would be used for anything but the tax collectors.

Boatyards were full of boats, with many more waiting to be hauled out and tied to hard ground with sand screws and chains. Every boat in every harbor had someone onboard, taking things off, setting more anchors or tying to shore the best way possible. By noon, there was not one foot of nylon line available for sale anywhere in the Caribbean.

Grocery stores were madhouses. By noon, most shelves were empty—bottled water gone, canned food gone, batteries gone, flashlights gone, oil lamps gone. Plywood, nails, screws, and tape were gone, also, as all homes not equipped with storm shutters were being boarded up and windows taped.

Children were outside picking up objects that would be blown away or turned into deadly wind-driven missiles. Family goats and chickens were herded in close to houses so they could be brought inside when the time came. Larger animals, like cattle, were left to fend for themselves, unless their owner had a storage barn, which practically none did, and it did not matter anyway; they knew the barns would be blown apart.

Airports were packed with panicky and pissed-off tourists. The smiling faces of pink skin and sun-blocked noses under green hats made of palm fronds were replaced with yelling, angry, nasty people who were truly scared. Most believed they were privileged; being rich tourists meant that their lives were more important than the locals' lives. Each demanded to be on the next flight—or else. Threats were hurled at ticket counter employees while children cried out of confusion and fear at the anger displayed by their parents.

Each island's version of the National Guard arrived to try to control the airport crowds that had turned into angry mobs. On Martinique, a sign made with butcher paper and a magic marker stated:

> *Attention all Persons*
> *1- Airport will close exactly at three o'clock P.M.*
> *2- All persons are to be secure in shelters by four o'clock P.M.*
> *3- Mandatory curfew begins at five o'clock P.M.*
> *4- Any person outside will be taken to jail.*

Carl Snow watched the instruments and the running graph on a computer screen. It was at 100 knots, the graph steadily rising. The barometer was steadily going the other way. "How low can you go?" Carl asked himself.

"ARWC, this is Mac. We are on track at ten thousand feet. The autopilot maintains altitude by barometer, so expect a steady or sudden decrease in altitude as we near the eye. It's not a pleasant sensation and no efforts will be made to correct unless we get too low."

"Okay, pilot. The pressure is dropping steadily."

THUMMMMP! The plane suddenly tilted over forty degrees as a very hard gust hit from the portside. Carl involuntarily yelled, but his eyes stayed on the instruments. A major gust had come out of nowhere; it had not shown up on the Doppler.

"That was 200 knots, Meatball," said Carl.

"Getting bad, ARWC; going to get worse."

Carl looked away from his instruments to see what it looked like outside. It was not there; he could only see about two feet of the wing before it disappeared into the dark gray fury. The plane bucked violently, nose down, then nose up, then side to side—like riding a wild bull.

Mac disengaged the autopilot to regain control. It only worsened. Carl noticed he was white-knuckled again. He pulled on his already tight seat harness to be sure it was secure. He tightly closed his eyelids, and thought: *The wind is trying to rip the wings off. That must be what happened to the other planes. Should've left the automatic data sender on, but I'd lose my chance. They made me do this, so I'm keeping the information. It's mine to share after I've analyzed it.*

When he opened his eyes again, he screamed into the microphone, "Another eye is forming!"

"Son of a bitch! Carl! I told you not to scream in the microphone. Now calm down and get back to business."

Carl was shaking, but forced himself to inhale deeply a few times and let the fresh flow of oxygen calm him, however slightly. He looked at his instruments and said meekly, "Another five degrees right, please. Keep right until I tell you to roll out." Silence for a few seconds, then, "Okay, roll out and bring me left a couple. Give me two more. Okay, hold her there . . . More right! Okay, mark it . . . Here! DSO, drop sonde!" Carl, suddenly terrified, screamed, "Oh shit! Rollout! Rollout! Now!"

Somewhere, in the midst of madness of that raging cyclone, there was a tiny band of very courageous airmen. No person on planet Earth could possibly know what those men were experiencing.

Hurricane Bunny, advisory number 11: Sept. 7, noon, AST. The center of Bunny is 15.8 degrees north latitude, 56.9 degrees west longitude. Direction west-southwest and will continue in this direction for the next 24 hours. Movement is 20 miles per hour. Hurricane-force winds extend out to 180 miles from the center. Wind speeds are over 140 miles per hour near the outer edge and over 250 miles per hour near the eye wall. Tropical storm winds extend out 240 miles from the center on the west side of the storm and 450 miles on the southeast sector. The center of Bunny is 330 miles from the island of Dominica. If conditions do not change, tropical storm winds will make landfall on all Windward Islands in 4 hours, 1600 hours. Hurricane-force winds in 6 hours, 1800 hours. The center of the eye will be over Dominica in 16 hours. The eye of the hurricane is 40 miles in diameter and may reduce in size as the storm picks up more strength after it enters the warmer waters of the Caribbean. Bunny is a category 5 hurricane and is extremely dangerous. All marine and aviation activities should stay well clear of the area. Hurricane warnings are issued for all islands, in the Leeward and Windward Islands, north of Grenada. Tropical storm warnings are in effect for all other islands. All persons should be well stocked for food, water, and shelter at this time. All islands affected by this warning will go into a curfew at 1700 hours and shall remain in effect until notified by local authorities. Hurricane conditions may last for approximately 24 hours. Next advisory will be issued at 1800, Sept. 7.

Tom and Pete stumbled around the rocky and brush-covered island looking for two rocks: one looked like an egg, and the other had a sail shape. Finding the tallest elevation was not hard; it was a solid rock cliff on the southernmost point of land between two rocky appendages of land going southeast and southwest. The average elevation was about ten feet and the highest was just barely over fifty.

As wind tugged on Pete's hair and clothes, he said, "This is the worst place to get caught in a hurricane."

"Fucking spooky, ain't it?"

"Killing a man and leaving his bones here to guard a treasure is spooky. With the increasing winds and rising water, this place is fucking scary."

The land tapered up from the north and west to the big boulder. Cliffs went from the sea to the boulder on the south and east sides. The primary growth on the island was the thorny bushes so prevalent in the Caribbean. They were so thick it was difficult to see through them. The trees stopped growing at ten feet high and the tops were trimmed flat by the constant tradewinds. Everything was pushed downwind, and while the windward sides of the trees were almost leafless due to the blowing salt air, the branches were still very much alive and full of inch-long, hard-as-nails thorns that were sharp as a needle. It was a foreboding sight and a painful experience moving though the offensive plants.

The only other plants were multi-limb cacti, countless ball-cacti with their razor-sharp needles and bright red centers, and the majestic century plants that grew in places where the soil was deeper. The spike of mature century plants stood ten feet above the tree line and constantly danced in the wind like mocko jumbies at carnival.

"The growth is too dense to be penetrated without a couple of sharp machetes. It'll be impossible to see anything until you get within a few feet of it, Tom. There's no way we're going to find those rocks. Maybe we need to let Big Eye prune this place and come back when she has finished."

"And let her sweep the egg and sail rocks off the island, too? No way, buckaroo! We're committed; let's get to it."

"Come on Tom, think about it. The rocks are either too small to be seen under the trees, or we're on the wrong island. The old mapmakers didn't have modern ways to measure land mass when this map was drawn, remember."

Ignoring Pete's logic, Tom said, "The map says, 'Line up the southernmost peak of the main island with Sailrock then walk fifty long paces in line. Eggrock guards the bones of my loyal crew. His bones, under a man's waist of sand, guard my treasure'."

Pete, normally not inclined to complain, but with his eyes still locked on the sea of thorns, grumbled, "Man, this is going to be too tough."

Tom, hoping to put a little more spark into Pete's attitude, smiled, and said, "Just keep saying to yourself, *chests* full of gold for El Morro."

Both men went quiet as they viewed their surroundings. It was as if they were in another world, a private world occupied by only the two of them. The sky was still blue but fading to gray near distant clouds. The clouds were fluffy white around the edges, and with their bellies full of water, the color darkened to deep blue. The various shades of the blue ocean, and the desolate island with its reefs being covered with long sweeping white breakers, was a sight they could have gazed at for hours. Unfortunately, only hours remained to locate and find a safe place to hide the treasure.

Finally, Pete responded to Tom's encouragement. "We don't even have a first aid kit to treat the punctures from those fucking thorns."

"Pete, if you want to head for town, go ahead, but I'm here and I'm staying until it's time to leave. I have to give this everything I've got. I'll use the shovel to beat my way into the interior. I might get lucky."

"You'll be lucky if you don't die from a thousand thorn punctures. Those damn things are tough, man. Shit, they'll stick you if you even look at 'em."

"I know, Pete. I've had my share of punctures. I'm going in there."

"Okay, but if I bleed to death, there'll be two dead men guarding the treasure, and one of 'em is going to be pissed."

They headed into the dense growth and carefully began whacking away. The thin limbs were resilient and bent more than they broke. They tried leaving the limbs and scraping the thorns off, but that did not work either.

"It's going to be a long afternoon," Pete whined.

"Stop bitching and push in there. It's not going to kill you. Just keep thinking about what we're looking for."

Almost three hours later, Pete needed a break. He went to the dinghy for a drink of water and to listen to the latest on Bunny. Walking down the rough trail he muttered, "It'd be great news if Big Eye stalled and stayed away for another…" He stopped and stood dead still in shock, not believing his eyes. "Fucking dinghy's gone?"

He ran around the island as fast as the rocks would allow—the rubber boat was gone. He went back to where the boat had been tied; the water level had risen above the rock he had tied it to. Pete looked around; the breakers covered the reefs, and the current had increased since landing, making it impossible to swim to the main island. After a moment to let realization seep in and strike home, he muttered, "We're stranded. Seaman Phuckewe's bones are doing a damn fine job."

He sat on a rock feeling exhausted. Fear gripped him as the seriousness of the situation hit home. Angry, he muttered, "It's a countdown to a brutal beating, and probably a very shitty way to die." His anger turned to sorrow when he thought of Emily. She would never know what had happened to him. He had been so afraid of commitments, thanks to a raving bitch, his ex-wife, Ann. He had never told Emily how much he loved her, and that angered him more. Emily would have been a wonderful wife, even though she was afraid to sail with him.

He stood and went back to the thorn patch to give Tom the shitty news. Besides screwing up with Emily, Pete accepted the blame for the dinghy's loss. He should not have used a loose double hitch to tie the dinghy, especially in crucial times, but it was a habit. He was sure that when the water came up and the dinghy floated, it jerked and pulled on the knot until it came free. It had happened to him before.

As he followed the beaten path through the mangled trees, he could hear Tom's relentless effort to find the rocks. He stopped about ten feet away, and still out of sight of Tom. He would need a running head start. "Tom! Take a break; we have lots of time now. Relax."

"The storm stopped. It's moving away?" Tom answered in a hopeful tone.

"Can't tell. . . . Can't find the radio."

"We lost the radio?"

"I couldn't find the radio . . . because I can't find the dinghy."

It took a few seconds for Tom to respond, and then he said, "You saying the dinghy is gone?"

"It's not where I tied it and I can't find it anywhere, is what I'm saying."

"You sure it didn't float to another part of the island?"

"I looked; it's gone. The water is piling up and it floated away."

"Used a half-hitch, didn't ya?"

"Yeah, afraid so. It probably pulled out when she started floating."

Tom suddenly sounded tired. "Ain't that some shit.Think we can swim it?"

"Not unless you're a porpoise in disguise. The current's running a good five knots."

"So, we might as well make ourselves at home."

"You're not pissed?"

"Why? It wasn't your fault. Stupid dinghies are always getting away. I've lost a few. I think there's a dinghy fairy that flitters around looking for unattended dinghies and turns them free."

Pete was relieved at Tom's attitude, but Tom had every right to be pissed, every right to get hostile, but he had instantly accepted his fate.

"Tom, I don't think it was the dinghy fairy this time. It was Seaman Phuckewe protecting the captain's treasure."

Tom answered with, "Those bones don't have anything to worry about. I planned to take them with us, and they'd still be protecting the treasure." Then he added, "Pete, I'd guess we have about three hours before we have to be in a damn good place to hide. You look for a place high up and I'll keep looking for the rocks."

"Grady! Don't you think we should go to the airport and get out of here?"

"We have time, Abby. It is only thirty minutes away and I've told the flight controller to be sure nobody ties the aircraft down. We'll be leaving around five."

"It better be sooner than that. Tropical storm winds will be here at four, according to the bulletin," said Jerome.

"Relax. Tropical storm winds are no problem for the Lear, and besides, we'll find the boys before then." Grady sounded confident, but the others were uneasy at waiting until the last minute. They had watched Pete and Tom take the dinghy down to the water and idle away. They could not see where they went, but Grady decided it did not matter; the treasure would be brought to the truck. If they returned without the treasure, they would surely have the map. Either way, they would get a ride off the island.

Grady had spotted his pals the evening before as Tom chased the rental truck. His crew arrived two hours later, and, not knowing when they would go to the treasure site, had been in the van ever since. They were all tired and irritable at being cooped up, especially Abby.

Glances to wristwatches became more frequent as time passed; everyone except Grady was getting more nervous with every tick. At two o'clock, clouds that had been on the horizon were moving over them in a darkening sky. Abby complained that she was hungry, was thirsty, had to use the bathroom, was too cramped in the van, needed to stretch, needed to sleep, Grady's cigarette smoke bothered her, and being a pirate wasn't fun anymore. The closest bathroom and food were four miles away, and Grady was not going to miss seeing if the boys brought something back.

Finally, she said, "Screw this stuff, Jerome. Who needs it anyway? I want to get out of here. We don't need the money, and I damn sure don't need to sit here hungry and uncomfortable. I have a real need to do a number two, and I'm not going to pull my pants down out in the woods with all of the bugs and mosquitoes and snakes, and God knows what else. I want you to take me back to that little place, and then you can pick me up on the way to the airport. Better yet, take me back to the hotel. Screw them and their pirate's treasure. I want to go."

Grady had hoped Abby's impatience would not rule, but feared it would. She was the only child in an old-money family and always got what she wanted. She was right though; she did not need the money, neither did Grady, but he thought she should be enjoying the adventure. The action was what it was all about; the old gold, silver, gems, and stuff to hold were just the winner's trophy.

Grady said, "Jerome, I'm not leaving. Everyone knew what the plan was before we started. The ten minutes it takes to get her to the store may be when they arrive with or without our treasure. We'll have lost our best, and maybe our only, opportunity."

Jerome had seen his wife get this way before and knew that the more someone argued, the more demanding she would get until she had her way. He looked at Abby and said, "Come with me." He stepped out of the van; she followed. He led her into the woods until they were out of sight and in a decent area. He said, "Squat and dump, darling. It's not going to do any good to cause trouble right now. Grady is right; we could miss them if we took you to a tinkle station. We did want in on this deal, so let's relax and do what we came here for, then we'll leave. By tonight, I promise you the luxury of the Old Grenada Inn, chilled martinis, and the finest steak south of the nineteenth parallel."

"Come on Jerome, I can't go to the bathroom out here."

He handed her his neatly folded, never-used linen handkerchief and said, "Wipe that beautiful little ass of yours with this. If it's not enough call me; I'll gather some nice cool leaves for you," and he turned his back to give her privacy.

Abby was not a happy lady, and when Abby was not happy…"Nice cool leaves? What do you think I am, a misplaced aborigine longing for the old days? Asshole!" Her thoughts were hostile, but in the end, the handkerchief was adequate.

Back in the van, Grady said, "Feeling better? Everything come out okay?" She silently fumed: *Smart-ass; I will get even. If you were anybody else, I would have Jerome beat you up.* She snorted with an ironic thought: *But they're the same breed. He would probably beat me up instead.*

At three P.M., not a tint of blue was in the sky; it was ominously getting darker. Swirling high clouds blew by much faster than the winds they were feeling. It was not bad weather, but showed definite promise.

Abby asked, "Grady, do your turkey-brain buddies even know there is a killer storm bearing down on them?"

"They prepared the boat for the storm last night. Relax, they'll show up pretty soon. There's no way they'd get caught on the windward side of the island."

"Okay. What's our absolute deadline?"

"Five o'clock," said Grady, but he got a questioning look from Jerome and a "you're dead meat" look from Abby.

"Alright, four-thirty."

She countered with, "That's not going to get the job done; curfew starts at five. We may not get clearance to take off after the wind starts. Let's make it four, to give us a margin of safety."

He looked at her as if she was a silly schoolgirl. "Clearance from the tower? Who gives a shit about clearance; we'll leave when we want to. Four-thirty gives us the time needed to get there, and we'll be airborne and headed to paradise ten minutes later."

Later, at three-thirty, Abby asked, "You don't suppose this is a decoy by your buddies, do you? They might've left the truck here and went by dinghy to another area where they had another car stashed."

"Don't be silly. Why would they go through all of that trouble?"

"Because they saw you. Did they see you?"

"Shit no."

"Was there a time when they might have seen you?" That caused Grady to think. He was almost sure Pete had not seen him the night before, but he had looked in his direction and hesitated. Nevertheless, he dared not admit it to the others. Abby would build on that possibility to bolster her decoy bullshit. Yet, he had lingering doubts—could it be a diversion? His pals would not hide from him, unless they had big treasure. And if that were the case, they would be hiding from everyone. Doubts, he hated being uncertain, so he decided to play it out.

"Well? Were you seen, Grady?" asked Abby once more.

"Come on, Abby," Jerome said, "give him a break. He said he wasn't."

At three-forty she asked, "Are you positive you weren't spotted?" Grady was not sure; time was running out as doubt increased.

Bill, who had remained silent on the matter, finally spoke. "Maybe it's time to pick up the marbles and run. They could have traffic problems at the airport and probably have cops blocking the airport entry because of the mass exodus."

As if Bunny had a schedule to keep, a massive black cloud that floated 100 feet above the ocean appeared on the horizon. They hypnotically watched it quickly become larger as it came closer. Grady resisted Abby's pleas to flee as it sped over them and a wall of wind slammed into, and rocked, the van. It was starting.

Grady said, "This is only the outer band of the storm and was low to the sea because it was the downpour of cold air from miles above." A few minutes later, another stronger gust rocked the van and that was enough for Abby.

"That's it, Grady. It's going to get a lot worse, real fast, and I know those guys set you up. They saw you and planted the truck. If we leave right this second we have time to go by the boat to see if they're there and we can look for them at the airport…Or we don't have to look for them at all. Either way, we're leaving; it's close enough to the time we agreed on."

Grady closed his weary eyes and thought about their situation. He knew she could be right, and it was a good idea to look for them at the boat and airport, in case he had been spotted. Pete and Tom had been gone for eight hours. If they had a good map, that would have been enough time.

He slowly drove down the mountain and did a slow drive-by inspection of the truck. Jerome had decided it was time to leave the Windwards for Venezuela, and Grady's unhurried driving was driving him and the other passengers nuts. Grady sped up to quell the looming mutiny and drove too fast to the village where Pete had left his boat. The boys were not there and no one had seen them.

Grady surprised everyone when he said, "Bill, drive the van back to the airport. Don't bother turning the damn thing in; the storm will cover all of that. Fly Jerome and Abby to wherever they want to go. Keep the plane safe; go to Venezuela. I'm staying here and I'll take your car. After the storm passes, come back and look for me. I'll be at the treasure site or around the airport."

Abby shrieked with disbelief, "You're not staying here?"

"Of course I am. I know those guys think they have something big, and I'm not going to walk away from it. I don't blame you for getting out, but running isn't for me. I'll survive the storm one way or another. I've been through enough of them."

"Yeah, you've been through hurricanes," Jerome said, "but never a Bunny. This thing is twice as strong as a normal hurricane. Do you know what you're getting yourself into? You do know that after it starts you'll have no options, don't you? If you make a bad choice now, you're going to pay the price when it's too late."

"Shit, Jerome, you think I'm a little kid? I know what I'm doing."

"Well Abby, kiss our friend goodbye, and make it a good one; it'll probably be the last time you see him." She did, but hurriedly, since time was running out and the wind was definitely blowing stronger. Bill tried to talk Grady out of staying too, but Grady was not interested.

By ten minutes after five, the truck had not moved, and Grady was damn sure on the edge of a tropical storm. The little Honda was not made for driving in forty miles per hour winds. The rain was heavy and blowing sideways. Tree limbs were swaying wildly; some were breaking. Thinking about what Abby had said about a decoy, he continued for several more miles, but did not see another vehicle or a sign of another human. He began to feel very much alone in a dangerous world. He liked the feeling and welcomed the challenge.

8

Heerrre's Bunny

"SECURITÉ, SECURITÉ, SECURITÉ, HELLO ALL STATIONS, hello all stations, hello all stations, this is United States Coast Guard Cutter *Point Pride* on channel sixteen. All persons still on board any vessel should secure the vessel as well as possible and then abandon the vessel. All persons are advised to seek safe shelter on high ground. Any area less than twenty-three feet above sea level could be submerged by the storm surge associated with Hurricane Bunny. Break—more to follow."

Every person with a VHF radio was glued to the set as the tropical storm developed. The warning was directed at foolish land dwellers who chose to stay in their oceanfront dwellings, and boaters who felt compelled by senseless reasoning to stay aboard and ride the storm out. Many of them stayed because everything they owned was aboard. Without their boat, they would have nothing and would join the ranks of the homeless. Others stayed aboard because of flagrant stupidity.

"Break, break—this is Coast Guard Cutter *Point Pride*. Any person requiring assistance to evacuate their boat should seek assistance on VHF channel 16 or on 2182 sideband frequency immediately after this broadcast. Due to the nature of Hurricane Bunny, we will not be able to assist mayday calls after the storm begins. Prepare now and leave your boat by 1730 hours. All vessels, regardless of size, should comply with this recommendation. Wind conditions are expected to make all vessels untenable in port. *Point Pride* will monitor channel sixteen during the storm and will be on station off Point de Sable, Fort de France. This is Coast Guard Cutter *Point Pride*, standing by."

Grady drove wildly in the rain and wind. He was not concentrating on the worsening weather, but on finding his fellow Lagoonies. Bill had called to let him know the boys were not at the airport. Back at the truck, there was no sign they had been there. He was sure the truck was not a decoy; Pete was too honest to be devious. However, time was running out; if they were on a barrier island, they had to get to the mainland very soon. Looking at a roadmap, he saw it was almost seven miles before another road led to another point to see the eastern shore.

He opted to take a look. If the truck was gone when he returned, he would know they went south and they would not have much of a lead.

The blowing wet world beyond his windows, and trees along the road that were swaying where only the limbs had been moving ten minutes ago, told Grady that things were rapidly turning to shit. He should be looking for a place to get out of the wind, but the game was on; he was not going to let those guys beat him. That was what it was about: competition. It would be a contest played in hell, his opponents being Pete, Tom, and Big Eye Bertha.

He had the road to himself, other than tree branches. It was getting darker and more dangerous. Through driving rain, he managed to see the side road and turned off. Ten miles an hour was the best speed he could do for the three miles to where he had a view of the shoreline. As expected, he was disappointed with the view, sunlight was disappearing, and rain restricted visibility to a half-mile.

The car rocked sideways from the wind as he looked over the harsh seascape. Nature's nasty side was awakening. As he drove back, Grady knew it was time to play smarter; if the truck was still there, he would go to the village of François. It was on the edge of a mountain where he could park the car in an elevated and sheltered place.

A sudden hard gust of wind hit Grady's car from the rear and it spun out on the wet road, and crashed into the forest. His head slammed into the windshield on impact, knocking him unconscious.

Finding the marker rocks under storm conditions was impossible, but Tom hoped to find at least one and get a bearing on it, in case the waves washed them away. The wind was too tough. Limbs covered with thorns whipping through the air were reminiscent of the ancient seafaring quartermaster's cat-o-nine-tails. He took great care to avoid the thrashing thorns, as they could easily penetrate an inch deep when propelled by stormy gusts. Finally, covered with blood, Tom gave up. He wearily and bitterly muttered, "Another golden horizon added to my failure list."

He did not need more teasing from the crows. He had had enough of that shit and had vowed not to return to the lagoon without success, no matter how long it took. That was one of the reasons he had wanted Pete as a partner; Pete never gave Tom much crap about his dreams. Grady had not either, and Tom suddenly wished he had invited him. It would have been good to have his help.

The wind was steady at sixty and gusting; it was past time to seek shelter. Pete had not returned, but Tom knew where to look; he would be on the backside of the high point. He hoped the place was not one of the steep, salt-rotten rock walls that were so common. Salt-rot rock was a dangerous condition that existed in the Caribbean. Salt was constantly blown into tiny cracks in the rocks by years of storms and daily tradewinds. As time passed, it expanded, causing rocks to break, and eventually crumble.

Yelling for Pete in the roaring wind was useless, so he made his way to the big boulder and began working up and around to the lee side. The hard rain, which had begun an hour ago, made the rocks slippery and greatly reduced his vision. After he was in the backside and out of the wind's direct blast and reduced rain, he was able to look around. There was no sign of Pete.

Tom continued slowly climbing over the fallen rocks and huge boulders of the salt-rot rock wall; it was not easy going. At the halfway point, he stopped to rest and tried calling again. No one answered.

A sudden thought flashed through his mind, his face twisted in anguish: *Had he been duped? Did Pete take the dinghy, and leave him to die. Then plan to return after the storm to have the whole treasure for himself? Was he once again a victim of another's greed?*

He started climbing again. He was sure Pete wouldn't leave him, but where the hell was he? He had to be on the lee side. Tom continued to work himself around to the east. While climbing over the steep, rough terrain, he was also looking for a place to get out of the weather. Not one spot looked good enough to call home for the next day or so. The only shelters were under ledges of rotten rock and they would not be there after the hurricane started shaking things around. With no success in finding shelter, Tom decided to go back to the windward side, hoping to find Pete.

Thirty minutes after leaving the windward side, it became noticeably worse. The rain was heavier and it was difficult to walk against the wind's force. Pebbles were moving; soon limbs, bigger rocks, and, shortly, the thorns would be airborne. It was starting; he had to find a windbreak. He searched the windy side and hastily made his way back to the lee side again.

Pete, like the dinghy, was gone. He had been betrayed. Huddled with his back to the elements, he muttered, "He must've found the rocks... I will survive ...I'll be waiting for the bastard."

Wind gusts chilled him in his soaking clothes; he knew the conditions that he was feeling were putting him on the edge of a very real danger: Hypothermia would drain his energy and strength; depression about the betrayal was corrosive to his will. Also creeping in, was the fear of being all alone in extremely furious winds, flooding seas, and a violent battering of ice-cold rains from frozen clouds miles above him. His next couple of days, if he lived, would seem like an eternity.

"So fucking what?" he screamed. "I'm going to make it." He grabbed a head-sized rock and placed it next to a beanbag-sized boulder. He took another rock and placed it beside the other; he was building a Caribbean igloo. He was breathing heavily with exertion as he stacked the rocks to make a two-foot thick wall around a foxhole-sized circle, just big enough to sit in. He would not have a roof, but the rain was blowing sideways anyway. He was completely absorbed with his plight when suddenly he jumped and yelped in fear as he felt a rough hand grab his shoulder.

"Where the hell have you been?" yelled Pete over the noisy wind.

Tom nearly fainted. He had never been happier; he wanted to hug his friend, but of course, he did not. Instead, he yelled with a big smile on his face, "Looking for you."

"You were supposed to wait for me, asshole. I've been around this fucking place three times. Follow me, I've found a place on the other side."

"That's the wind side."

"No shit! Come on!" Tom was so happy he would have followed Pete, even if he tried to swim for the main island. They worked their way back against the wind; it was much worse this time around. One hand was needed to hold on, the other to protect their eyes from flying debris. They peeked through a slight crack between their fingers to see in the hurricane-force winds, as small pieces of nature strafed them. They slowly made their way through swaying trees and slippery rocks. Pete led, and when he got behind one waist-high rock, he stooped to get out of the wind's blast and motioned Tom to do likewise.

"This is the place you found? Are you nuts? It's too low, the surge will cover this area, and we're totally exposed!"

Pete pointed to a rock, and said, "Look!"

Tom looked, but was confused; he had no idea what Pete was doing. "What is it?"

"Sailrock!"

All Tom saw were jumbled boulders and crumbled rocks. "You're nuts!"

Pete continued on, making his way to where he had been pointing. Tom followed as they climbed up to within five feet of the top before stopping. When Tom came alongside Pete, he saw it. Sailrock! It was not a sail as he had pictured; instead, it was the shape of the sails used at the time the map was drawn. It was a square-rigger, not a triangle, and it was not even a rock, but actually the absence of rock between four huge outcroppings on the mountain.

As they got closer, Tom saw that the sail was actually a small horizontal cave. Pete led the way into the cave with Tom literally on his heels. It felt great to be out of the wind and rain, and it was good to speak without yelling at full volume. "How'd you find this? I never would have seen the sail shape; I was looking for triangles."

"Dumb luck. Couldn't find anything on the lee side to hide behind, so I came back to this side hoping to find something. I stood in front of this place for a few minutes before it dawned on me, and then I came over to take a look and found the cave."

"It looks solid. If the cliff on the other side doesn't collapse and take this section with it, we could make it."

Pete said, "Guess you know we're going to have some company as the water rises. Rats, spiders, and bugs."

"Good, I'm hungry." Moving closer to opening, Tom could see what some of the flying debris was that had pelted them. "Damn, I've been porcupined!" Thorns blown off trees were imbedded in his arms.

A warm fire would have been nice but would not work in the cave, so they just sat and listened to the wind and watched the light in the entrance get darker as storm clouds increased and the wind and rain worsened. Soon they could hear the hurricane's cold roar grow to a chilling howl, and then to bloodcurdling screams, and then the indefinable voice of Satan that caused the cave to vibrate continually.

Tom and Pete repeatedly gave their own private thanks to God for the small cave that protected them from Big Eye Bertha's rage.

Hurricane Bunny advisory number 12: Sept. 7, 1800 hours, AST. The center of Bunny is 15.6 degrees north latitude, 58.2 degrees west longitude. Direction west-southwest and will continue in this direction for the next 24 hours. Movement is 20 miles per hour. Hurricane-force winds extend out to 180 miles from the center. Wind speeds are 180 miles per hour near the outer edge and 250 miles per hour near the eye wall. Tropical storm winds extend out to 240 miles from the center to the west and 450 on the southeast sector. The center of Bunny is 150 miles from the island of Martinique. All islands in the Windwards are experiencing hurricane conditions. The eye of the hurricane is 40 miles in diameter and may reduce in size as the storm picks up more strength after it enters the warmer waters of the Caribbean. Bunny is a category 5 hurricane and is extremely dangerous. All marine and aviation activities should stay well clear of the area. Hurricane warnings are issued for all Leeward Islands. A hurricane watch is in effect for the Virgins Islands and Puerto Rico. All persons should be well stocked with food and water and be in their shelter at this time. All islands affected by this warning will go into a curfew at 1700 hours; it shall remain in effect until cancelled by local authorities. Hurricane conditions will last for approximately 24 hours. Next advisory will be issued at 0600, Sept. 8.

No one heard the broadcast in any of the Windward Islands, as electrical power had been knocked out earlier. Radio antennas exposed to the wind had toppled. The broadcast was not important to the people anyway; they already knew they were in for a bad time.

Coast Guard Cutter *Point Pride* was riding out the storm okay. The captain, a man most sailors knew as Skip, had sent most of the men to shore. Only three sailors who had volunteered would ride out the storm with him. They would not be able to go after people in distress, until the winds were below sixty or so, but they could monitor radios, note distress calls, names of boats, and record the last words of mariners. When they could, they would know how many people were in trouble and where to look for whatever was left.

The first hour of a hurricane was the worst part of a killer storm for Skip. It was when unseasoned sailors, who had stayed on their boats, realized they had made a grave mistake. It was a time when men bawled while watching death approach. It was a time when men and women clasped the microphone of their radios to their chests, as it was their only contact with the living. Even the most experienced hurricane survivors had never gone through sustained

180-miles-per-hour wind, and that was just the beginning. With those winds came gusts that exceeded 250 miles per hour, tornadoes, and horizontal waterfalls, which pounded and sank anything uncovered. After a severe and lengthy beating, there would still be the matter of the constant 250-mile-per-hour eye wall. Then the storm's second half.

Skip had been in almost every Caribbean hurricane during the last fifteen years and could not believe what they were experiencing. He had known it was going to be a brutal storm, but could not fathom the severity. It was almost as if the storm was the physical presence of the devil herself. It was dangerous, deadly, and so sinister that it emitted a feeling of evil that permeated the air and all objects it touched.

He had expertly set out his eight storm anchors and chains that had held him fast in every other storm. Tonight, however, he doubted they would hold; there was going to be too much wind.

Earlier that day, he had stopped a freighter from entering port, and he was glad that he had. The windage of the high-sided freighters would have dragged any number of anchors as well as pulled the bollards off any dock. A ship sailing downwind in hurricane-driven winds would be devastating to anything in its path. For months to come, fuel would pollute and poison the pristine shores of all the islands. He had to do what was right, not what made frightened men happy, or allowed survival at a grave cost to others.

"Mayday, Mayday, Mayday, this is the sailing vessel *Polly Girl* with three persons on board! We're sinking! My pumps can't keep up! We need help!" said a very excited voice on the radio.

Skip responded, "*Polly Girl, Polly Girl, Polly Girl*, this is Coast Guard *Point Pride*, I acknowledge your mayday. What is your position?"

"Coast Guard, *Polly Girl*! I'm ninety degrees off Fort St. Louis. I'm sinking. All pumps are working and one man is using a bucket. My engine's water pickup has been routed to pull water out of the bilge and the engine is running hard. There's too much rain for the scuppers; water is pouring in. We might have loosened a plank in the pounding. Come get us, Coast Guard!"

Other people who heard the Coast Guard respond started calling in their pleas for help, too. Baby-chick mentality ruled the airwaves. Like the chick runs to and huddles against its mother when frightened, the mariners had their Coast Guard. It was impossible for Skip to communicate with any of them. He had to establish control or nobody would be able to talk, unless he imposed silence on all vessels within hearing range. "Seelonce, Mayday. This is United States Coast Guard Cutter *Point Pride*. Do not transmit on this channel until the conclusion of *Polly Girl's* mayday."

Skip clicked the microphone twice, and then said, "Coast Guard *Point Pride* to *Polly Girl*. No sir, captain. Our vessel cannot be moved under these conditions. The only help you can expect is from yourselves. Do what you can to save the vessel. I recommend that you do not leave your vessel now, unless she sinks. On the chart, there is a shoal shown to the west of you. You might let go your northeast anchor and hope it blows you onto the shoal. If you get in shallow water and can crawl, try to make the mountain before the main surge arrives. What are the names of everyone on board?"

The frightened man understood his position and spelled out the names.

With sadness in his voice, Skip said, "Good luck, *Polly Girl*."

Skip said to Charlie, a crewman standing next to him, "Why don't these people listen to our warnings?" Then he went back on the airwaves. "Mayday, hello all stations, hello all stations, hello all stations. This is Coast Guard Cutter *Point Pride . . . Polly Girl's* Prudonce. Seelonce feenee.

"Mayday, mayday, mayday, *Point Pride* this is *Just Write*."

"*Just Write*, this is *Point Pride*; what is the nature of your mayday?"

"I'm dragging my ground tackle. I was near *Polly Girl*, but I'm now in the main harbor and picking up speed. I think I'll go aground on the rocks at Anse Auane."

"*Just Write, Point Pride*. Give me the names of everyone on board."

"Only me, Jason McCurdy, and my dog, Skippy."

"Jason, you don't stand much of a chance going into those rocks. Leave your ground tackle dangling, maybe one of them will snag something before you hit, but with the wind force behind you, don't count on it to be lasting. You know the wind is going to be twice as bad pretty soon. If I were you, I'd do one of two things. Jason, I'm speaking to you as Skip now. This is not the official Coast Guard talking. Looking at the chart and wind direction, I'd either cut free from your anchors. Start your engine, run before the wind, and try to miss hitting Cape Salomon. You'll be in for some bad times, but at least the storm wind will be blowing you away from the center. You might make it. The other thing would be to cut free of your anchors and pray that you're driven up on the smaller rocks. If you do that, stay in the boat until it stops its movement up on shore. As soon as you're lying hard on your side, get out and crawl like hell. Find shelter behind a big rock at least twenty-three feet up from the surf. You might make that, too, but all your options are dangerous, Jason. Think it over and let me know what you are going to do."

"Will do, Skip...Thanks anyway," said Jason's dejected voice.

It was getting hard to hear the radio with the incredibly loud wind shrill. No matter how loud it got, he could hear even stronger winds blowing in the harbor. "Hey Skip! There goes another one," said Charlie. It was difficult to see, but with the high-speed rotary windshield wipers, he could see the ghostly image of a fifty-foot sailboat being pushed out to sea. Skip called, nobody responded.

Another call came on. "Mayday, Mayday, Mayday, Coast Guard. Something is dragging through the Trois Ilets anchorage. I can't see what, but I hear anchor rodes exploding upwind from me. It sounds like it's taking everything out. We need help!"

"Vessel calling mayday, what is your vessel's name?" After a delay, "Vessel calling mayday in the Trois Ilets anchorage, please give your vessel's name or call sign." There was no answer. Apparently, whatever was blowing down on them, did. The wind was getting stronger and that did not seem possible. It felt as if Skip had been in the hurricane for hours, but it had been sixty minutes. Seven boats in Martinique had issued maydays, and Skip had little or no hope for any of them.

Boats like *Gypsy Bitch* that were shoved up into the little nooks and crannies would take longer. More time was needed before the chafing of nylon ropes would cause the lines to separate and put more load on the surviving lines that, too, would let go. If the lines were oversized and well protected, then the strain on cleats would get to be too much and pull out, taking sections of the boat with them or whatever they were tied to. Tomorrow the landscape would look a lot different; goodbye to Martinique's magnificent beauty of quaint villages and lush tropical jungles. Anything in the harbor would be pushed up on the rocky beaches as high as the surge went; what was left of once noble yachts would be rubble.

Some calls brought tears to Skip's eyes, and made him want to risk *Point Pride* to help. While he was too seasoned to let his emotions dictate actions, he might have tried if the full crew was aboard, and he was damn glad they were not.

A woman called while crying hysterically. Her husband had crawled out on deck wearing a dive mask so he could let out more scope on his lines as the surge was silently swelling into the harbor. Something in the wind, a piece of house, or boat, maybe a child's toy from miles away, somebody's cat—who knows what, hit him in the facemask. He was knocked unconscious and the wind tumbled him back into the cockpit. When he revived, he was blind, leaving his frail wife alone to deal with the storm. She tried, but there was nothing she could do. She talked and cried to Skip for almost twenty minutes, and gave him their children's names and telephone numbers and begged him to call them when he could. "Please tell the children how much I love them," were her last words heard by Skip before a sudden loud report of the yacht's first contact with the horrifically steep rocks of Point de La Rose. A place of beauty just hours ago was collecting yachts; it would be haunted by the horrible deaths of the crews for eternity.

Pleas for help came from several boats. They offered everything they owned if someone could rescue them, but that was impossible. Skip, feeling bitter about life, stood helplessly at the helm of his ship. His emotions were raging between anger and a deep sadness. *Why didn't these people listen? Why, damn it? Why?* He was a witness to human slaughter, as the next to be exterminated were riding a fast-moving escalator to death.

The haunting calls came only from his small patch of the Caribbean. He did not have to contend with the same begging, open-mike prayers, sobbing, and screams from scared people on their dying boats in every other part of paradise. So many mariners throughout the tropics would never see another new day, enjoy the peaceful serenity of a Caribbean sunset, or know the warmth of love. For many, their loved ones in faraway places would never know what had happened to them, or if they were dead or alive. Bodies were rarely found. Skip knew it would get worse until no one was left to call.

A couple of hours after midnight tomorrow, they should get a temporary respite as the eye passed over. Then hell would quickly return to the same tortuous conditions until midmorning when the bulk of the super storm would have passed; but still, category-one hurricane conditions would prevail until a few hours after dark.

That's a mighty long time to spend in a nightmare. People could only take so much strain and fear. The never-ending roar of wind and screams of stronger gusts wore down the toughest nervous system. Muscles burned with fatigue, while straining to hang on to safety rails onboard, or to a mattress over their heads while hiding in a bathtub at home, or crouched down in a flooded cistern. The human spirit would fight desperately to sustain precious life, while an evil that lives deep within the heartless storm allowed no relief and was determined to take a person's soul before it snatched life away.

Always, at the pinnacle of desperation, the solitude of death would be stolen, leaving only increased fear and punishment. And, always, more was coming. Bunny's direct-hit survivors would need professional help dealing with such traumatic experiences. A segment of the population would come out okay; some people had attitudes about storms that enabled them to understand them for what they were. They respected and even, in an odd way, loved the storm, because it was as close as one can get to his maker while still living on earth. To these people, the storm ceased to be a problem and became a living entity, pure and natural, a tonic to tune-up Mother Earth, even if it was painfully destructive to the little animals that had recently started crawling over her surface. It was simply a tool designed by need.

These people would find the safest place possible, drink a few rums, and try not to think about the noise or the rain pouring on them or dwell on misery. They knew that, as it started, it would end. They just had to stay out of the way for a while. Then they would contend with the storm's massive tail full of rain that would take another few days, maybe a week to pass.

Skip was one of those people, but on duty, he could not stay out of the way. It was his job to man the radios and be ready the instant things were stable enough to get out and help. A minute or two could make a tremendous difference to someone hanging onto a lifejacket as they were swept out to sea, with no knowledge of what happened to their mates or boat. In so many cases, they would not even know how they ended up in the water. Tough times were ahead for those who survived.

At that moment, however, Skip's positive attitude was eroding. *Point Pride* was in extreme danger. She might ride out the first half of the hurricane, but after the eye passed and the blast from a 250-mile-per-hour wind hit from the opposite direction, he doubted the ground tackle would hold. Moreover, she would be exposed to a longer fetch—the mountain would not block any of the wind, and the seas could be unmanageable. The only factor in his favor was he had picked a spot that would give him a softer landing on shore. That was much preferred to being driven upon a vertical rock wall, as so many had already done.

9

Bunny Winks

A YOUNG FAMILY IN DOMINICA SAT IN THE DARK with only one candle burning to give them light. They were prosperous and owned a new concrete block home. Mom and Dad Le Antis had made the decision to stay in their home rather than go to a public shelter. They had good reason: once they entered the shelter, they would not be permitted to leave until the officials gave the all-clear. That could be days after the storm passed, as roads would have to be cleared of fallen houses and trees and bodies. By the time they returned to their house, nothing would be left; the looters would have taken everything Bunny did not take. The two little kittens their children loved so much would be lost, as pets were not permitted in the shelter. Besides, they had ridden out hurricanes before, in houses not nearly as good as their newly-built home.

As the wind increased, their candle danced wildly in the wind streams that, somehow, found a way through the block walls and tiny cracks in corners of windows and doors. The new home began to shake slightly; the noise was unrelenting, and Dad decided it was time to head for the safest place in the house—the place every resident of the Caribbean knew too well—the small bathroom in the center of the house. He carried a mattress in with him to act as a roof, or wall, in case the place started coming apart.

The kitties were brought in, too, and Dad's daughter, little four-year-old Maria, thoughtful of her pets, brought the kitty-litter box with her. Jammed into the tiny room, Dad could not hear the sounds of his new home being taken apart over the roaring wind. He had no idea that the plywood he had nailed over the windows was being pulled off one sheet at a time, at first, then suddenly, the pressure popped the remaining panels free at the same instant. The rear sliding glass doors disappeared so fast, it would have been impossible to see, even in daylight. It was as if a magic wand had passed over and everything vanished.

Every item in the house was moving, and then whisked out, as though sucked by a giant vacuum cleaner. Couches, chairs, tables, draperies, carpet, refrigerator, oven after the gas pipes broke, cupboards, pots, pans, dishes, clothes from the bedroom with beds, dressers, pictures on walls, nonreplicable photographs of the kids, of their parents, of happier times in their lives.

Their previous world had disappeared and they did not know it.

That was when the candle blew out and all the windows were sucked out, without a noticeable sound, other than a sudden and disturbing whistle from wind being sucked through the cracks around the bathroom door. The wet towel that had been jammed under the door to seal off the wind was gone, sucked out from under it. Seconds later, the front door was blown in and forced out of the rear of their home through a small window.

The family felt the sudden effect of wind increase and reduced air pressure: ears popped, Maria cried at the pain. The only door left in the house was the bathroom door; it was the only barrier separating the Antis family from death.

Dad, fearing what was happening on the other side of the cheap hollow-core plywood door, pushed the mattress against the pulsating door. The wind was battering it so strongly, he was sure it would not hold, and neither would he. With the mattress covering the battered door, Dad felt it buckling, as the demon did everything to get at those in hiding. To the struggling, crying family, the wild-thing on the other side was alive, a beast insane with desire to suck them into its mouth, mangle them, and spit them out to sea.

The roof lifted, just a little, but it held, thanks to Dad's purchase of hurricane clips that the lumber salesman talked him into buying. The unrelenting wind, however, eventually found a weak point on the right side of the house: roof, hurricane clips, and parts of the block walls instantly took off into the dark wet night. Dad did not hear that either. The family huddled in the bathtub, except for Dad, who tried to keep the beast on the other side of the door. They were not aware the roof over their heads was no longer there. In the absolute blackness and deafening roar, the only way to know the roof was gone was to shine a flashlight to the ceiling, where there would be only more blackness.

The children alternated between crying and screaming; they never knew such horror. They clutched their mother tightly, but could not see her. Mom and Dad were crying for the same reasons their children did, plus out of sadness in knowing their children were going to be violently killed, unless they could keep that damn door shut.

And it went on, and on, and on, and on, and on, and on, and on, and on, and on.

Grady thought he was flying the Lear through violent weather, it rocked wildly, and shook as if on a giant vibrator. The noise was unbelievable; it was the sound of a squadron of B52s with afterburners on. He sat up, his thoughts fuzzy, confused, he was in a black world. Then he remembered spinning out, and wondered how long he had been out. He looked at his watch, but it was too dark to see.

He turned on the interior lights and saw that not much inside the car had been damaged except the windshield on his side, which was a mass of spiderweb cracks. He attributed the cracked windshield to his aching head. Another glance at his watch revealed it was smashed. He turned on the headlights, illuminating the swaying and breaking forest in a horizontal rain. Tree limbs, leaves, dirt, rocks, and debris mixed with parts of trees zoomed by too fast to be recognizable. He felt insecure in his small and fragile universe.

Frequent jolts from stronger gusts hit, and Grady knew the car would have rolled and tumbled away if not for the tree stumps holding it. After a few minutes of bouncing around, he knew what he had to do. The integrity of the car interior was the only thing keeping him alive. It was only a matter of time before some object smashed a window and it would be all over; the inside would quickly fill with objects from the hostile exterior. He crawled into the backseat, got down on the floorboard, and pulled the backseat cushion over himself.

His timing could not have been better. Without warning or a noticeable sound, the roof collapsed, windows blew out, and the interior of the car was instantly alive with wind and flying particles. He had a good grip on the springs under the seat cushion but needed all of his strength to keep it in place.

Many mayday calls went unanswered by Skip that night because it was impossible to hear over the wind. The noise had been deafening. He compared it to standing behind big jet engines at full throttle. The low-profile cutter tossed about like a toy boat and Skip could not see anything outside in the rain-blurred night through the bulletproof windows. When using the spotlight mounted on the cabin's top, there was only the glow of a small, short tube of light; the atmosphere was too thick for the beam to penetrate.

Foremost on Skip's mind were the anchors, and he anxiously waited for the first indication that *Point Pride* had broken free of the bottom, or an anchor chain parted, or a cleat pulled out. Normally they could tell by the beeping of the anchor alarm, but it could not be heard. One man had been detailed to watch a handheld GPS to see if their position changed. When it happened, they had a plan—but not much hope it would actually work. The main engines had been on for hours and were running in gear to reduce strain on the upwind anchors, but it was doubtful they were doing any good.

Every sound, other than the constant roar, brought fear. There were many sounds that were felt, as chunks of civilization were hurled their way. Trees, parts of houses, and lots of corrugated tin from the roofs, which were lethal ten-foot razor blades spinning, tumbling, and invisible in the total darkness.

Going outside was to die. The apparent-wind instrument had blown away long ago, but they knew the wind speed was awesome without numbers. It was irrelevant whether they were in 150, 250, 350, or 1,000-mile-per-hour wind. They were already in the dimension where the demon lived. Each man was quickly learning his own limits. When the eye wall approached, the wind was no longer part of nature; it was pure evil energy. Only the spirit of death had the power to spawn such a fierce and terrifying force. That opinion was not shared verbally, but by personal thoughts, and was not exclusive to those aboard *Point Pride.*

Ears hurt and continually popped because of the extremely low and still-dropping air pressure. Uncertainty and fear ruled, and only each man's personal limits of courage protected him from catastrophic fear.

When wind reached the maximum force of the eye wall, a million steel claws outside tore at the hull. The noise shattered nerves, the entire steel ship vibrated so hard that anything not bolted down danced across the floor like players in a child's electric football game. It was too much to endure and each man's mental barrier ruptured, and horror sprung forth like flooding waters from a holed dyke, then flowed freely and without restriction. Without being told, each man ran from the pilothouse to the small bow section, where they huddled together for any semblance of protection.

The handheld GPS Skip carried with him was useless. The thick layer of rain, hail, and wind altered its readings. If they were dragging anchors, it would not matter because there was nothing they could do.

Strangely, Skip couldn't feel the rise and fall of riding over the waves any longer, then he realized there were no waves. The wind was too strong for waves to rise against it, but the boat wasn't still; it was constantly thrown around until one anchor chain or another stopped its movement.

With such violent action, the crew knew every second was borrowed time; the chains were the only things keeping the ship upright, and one of them would eventually pull loose and the boat would flip over as easily as a plastic toy boat in an unruly child's bathwater.

Then it happened. They heard nothing unusual, nor felt anything more than they had been experiencing, but suddenly the ship moved, seemingly in slow motion. It lifted and did not come to the halting jerk on the stretched-straight chain. It continued to roll, and they obeyed Nature's law of gravity and fell as the ship rolled. Everything else in the compartment did likewise. Skip's forearm was broken when a toolbox fell on him. Chuck was tangled in several coils of heavy one-inch nylon line. The other two men were okay, but were covered with all sorts of stuff that had been accumulating in the compartment for years.

The ship's interior lights were still on, so they could see their surroundings. That miracle would soon change, the batteries were now upside down and acid was rapidly pouring out.

Skip was in pain but his thoughts were only on his ship and crew. If they stayed upside down, they would soon take on water. The watertight doors and compartments were secured to keep it waterproof sitting upright, but air vents topsides could not be sealed. They were helpless.

Then it happened again, the ship was blown upright. The cheers from the trapped men lasted only a second, until it snapped over again and kept rolling. The anchors dangled like charms on a charm bracelet, as the chains wrapped around the hull with every roll. With momentum, *Point Pride* rolled over and over in the wind, like a tumbleweed, and was probably being rolled right into the big vertical rock wall graveyard with so many others. Not one man doubted that he was already dead.

Pete yelled, "Can't believe this noise!"

"Can't believe solid rock vibrates!" Tom yelled back. Rain blew in the cave's entrance, flooding the cavern floor, and it was already six inches deep and rising.

"One good thing about this water is we won't have any creepy company tonight."

"Don't worry about that. Everything outside is dead by now."

"Figure we'll have this for about eight more hours." Pete scooped up water in his palm, drank it and then spit it out. "Holy shit! It's saltwater. I thought the wind was keeping the water in here. It's the fucking surge."

After long hours of sitting on hard rock and soaking in the cold saltwater, they alternated sitting and half-standing positions one at a time in the low cave. Water rose almost to their knees in the cave. They knew the eye wall had to be close because of the incredibly high-pitched scream outside, and their ears popping like a string of Chinese firecrackers.

The last words that were audible over the incredible screech were Tom's. "Think we'll make it?"

Pete thought about what he'd do if the cave started to collapse or if the cave flooded with the surge. If he ventured outside, the wind would tear the flesh off his bones and scatter his remains to never be found. No, if he were to die, it'd be in the cave. Life or death was out of his hands.

Tom's thoughts were of gratitude. Had he stayed on the backside, he would have been sucked into the wind hours ago. He also wondered if the bones protecting the treasure played a part in the storm's severity. This could not be a natural event.

A lifetime of fear and confusion later, the wind seemed to be easing off. The noise changed from the incredible screech to an incredible roar that slowly turned into the sounds of gusting wind. Pete and Tom waded out of the cave and ventured into the pitch-black void. The rain had stopped, and suddenly the clouds opened to reveal moonlight and the most awesome sight ever seen by man. A beautiful moon bathed their world; everything looked peaceful, the sky was full of stars. The terrain was shockingly moon-like. It was barren.

"I've seen a lot of destruction, Tom.... This is beyond reason." Nothing that resembled a tree stood; only the surge and barren rock covered the island.

"The worst of it is, it's only half over, Pete."

The water separating them from the main island was alive with energy; it danced straight up into the air and then fell straight down again with no direction to the waves. The air was almost still with only ten knots of breeze. It was a sight, both pleasant and horrifying, and it was beyond comprehension how such destruction could be so closely bordered by the peace they were experiencing.

Tom muttered, "No sense in looking for the Eggrock now." For the first time, the treasure, his golden horizon was unimportant. He had a feeling of well-being, a sense of inner peace. He had witnessed one of God's ultimate natural forces and he was fortunate to have the presence of mind, to realize and be thankful that he had found the true treasure offered to mankind: life. Money was not going to make his problems disappear, and suddenly he strongly felt that he had been given his challenges for a reason. Someday he would understand why. Tom felt almost giddy with happiness, and for the first time since he was a child, found himself silently praying, giving appreciation to God rather than asking for help or bitching about something.

Time had actually stood still for Dad before the wind seemed to subside. Bunny's eye was over the island. His energy was expended, but he forced himself up, and woke his wife, who had fallen asleep with exhaustion. Their children were left in a deep sleep in the tub.

Dad carefully opened the bathroom door. The first view of their home brought an immediate gasp from his wife, then tears, then sobbing. He had expected to see what was before him, but had desperately hoped it would not be so. It looked as if a bomb had been set off inside, with nothing usable left to build on. She cried hysterically at what her home had been turned into. Her home, her life, had been destroyed. Anything still there was broken; walls were ripped apart with tattered pieces dangling in the gentle wind. The only thing left in her house was a demolished refrigerator from some other house. Everything she treasured from her past was gone: her grandmother's dishes; her jewelry, pictures—gone; and she knew she would never stop crying.

Her husband fought back tears at his wife's sorrow, but felt anger at God for destroying everything his family had worked so hard for. The house was wrecked beyond repair, and all of their money had been spent building it. There was no insurance; it was too expensive for island people to buy, and there was no way to replace any of their things. His job as the restaurant manager in a beachside hotel would be gone with the wind as all of his other belongings. At least his family was alive, so far.

Mom and Dad Le Antis, however, would soon learn something even more horrible: they were the only fortunate family in the neighborhood.

Grady had never experienced such misery. The hump in the floorboard caught him on the hip; he could move only enough to put it in under his waist, which was even more uncomfortable. His hands and arms were cramped from hanging onto the seat cushion, and he was exhausted from the beating he had taken in the wreckage of the car, as it had been shaking and battering itself to pieces against the remaining tree stumps. Those stumps were the only things between survival and being tumbled and torn to shreds like the cheap piece of tin that imprisoned him.

He became elated when he realized the wind was slowing and wanted nothing more than to get out of his cramped quarters. However, he was not sure if that was going to be possible. The doors would not open; the roof had been crushed down, reducing the windows to oddly shaped slits.

As the wind died, the area was bathed in moonlight. Grady could see the demolished landscape around him. The front of the car had been lodged into the three stumps. Behind him was a Bunny-cleared field with sparse stumps. When the wind returned, it would blow the battered car downwind until little was left. Grady had to get out and find a better place, pronto.

He pushed, pulled, and strained his guts trying to enlarge a window opening. With every move, thorns punctured his hide. Finally, he crawled out of the crumpled car, leaving only a few strips of flesh clinging to jagged edges.

Grady stood on the ground, stretched, and tried to get his aching muscles back in order. The easy wind and moonlight was as welcome as anything he had ever known. For a moment, he thought of using the light to look for Pete and Tom, as they would be easier to see without the trees. He could see the ocean and a small dark island offshore. He quickly realized how stupid that would be; his life now depended on finding shelter and the best place would be the small village down the road. It would be close, but, with a little luck, he could make it.

As he made his way through the fallen and shredded trees, looking for the road, he muttered, "If those guys are still alive, they deserve the treasure. Fuck it; all I want is to make it through the second half." He saluted the small island, and said, "Good luck."

He found the road; however, it was not easy telling where the forest stopped and the road began. Everything was cluttered with broken stuff. He needed to run to make it to the village, and that was impossible with the road covered as it was.

His world looked eerie in the moonlight; the jumbled wreckage of nature caused stark shadows, giving the illusion of being on another planet, or in another dimension. With no trees or branches to interfere with the breeze, there was no noise other than the pounding surf and the ringing in his ears caused by the low barometric pressure.

He hoped the last hurricane warning he heard was right about the eye being forty miles wide. He would need every second to get to the village. Traveling was difficult, and after an hour, he crawled over the crown of a small hill to see a horrifying sight: the entire area between him and the mountain village was underwater, completely submerged by the surge. He had no place to go.

"Fuck, fuck, fuck!" he yelled, and then turned to the east and started a frantic search for shelter. He worked his way to the shoreline, knowing the high water was already in, so there was no added danger from the surge, and the shoreline was covered with huge boulders and rock outcroppings. He would be uncomfortable, but could find something to hide behind.

After a quarter mile of rough going, he spotted an outcropping of solid boulders jutting above the horizon. He was encouraged; he could make it. The closer he came to the outcropping, the more confident he was that he would survive. While struggling, he uttered, "Not a minor feat surviving a super hurricane in the wilderness. Shouldn't have been so worried, shit; I'm a survivor."

He stopped for a moment to catch his breath and read the weather signs. The wall of clouds and lightning strikes were still miles away; it was still calm, but he knew when it started to change, it would happen fast. Stretching, and feeling confident, he thought: *Maybe I was wrong about the treasure. I've gone through all of this shit because they wouldn't let me in.* "Fuck 'em," he said aloud. "They're either dead or they tricked me."

Grady looked up at the weather-wall, which was noticeably closer; he pushed himself to make better time, but he was thinking about the moves to put on Pete to fox the treasure away. Suddenly he slipped on a wet, bark-less, and overturned tree trunk. He fell and landed awkwardly on one foot on another slippery stump, and then the foot slid into the tangles of broken limbs. His full body weight drove the foot deep into the twisted web of immovable limbs and broken tree parts. He cried out in pain as his leg snapped and shattered at the ankle.

After repeated and concentrated attempts to get free of the tangled trap, he knew the only way he would be released was to get help or cut his foot off. He did not have a knife, and felt he was surely the last man on earth. Grady leaned back to rest on the tree trunk that held his body upright, he was exhausted, in excruciating pain, and an odd feeling crept into his consciousness: it was fear.

He whined, "Shit, shit, this can't be happening." Grady surveyed his plight. When the wind returned, the tree that had him in its vice was going to move; he would be crushed, or at the very least, his leg would be ripped off. "Fucking future's not too bright."

He rested, thought, and cursed for thirty minutes before the black and streaked with lightning weather-wall approached. The moon and stars were rapidly lost in the approaching onslaught; thunder was steadily getting louder. In near blackness, a gust of wind, only twenty knots, hit. Behind the gust was a steady wind. Grady made another attempt to pull free, and then collapsed against his wooden prison wall.

He realized the horror of what was coming: He was trapped, facing the wind, and unprotected. Very soon, billions of needle-sharp thorns and tree limbs traveling a couple hundred miles per hour would find him. "Fuck this!" he yelled.

Those thoughts sparked fresh energy, adrenaline was pumping overtime; he ignored the pain; he had to get free. His mental state turned wild, survival instincts took charge, as a wolf would experience with its foot caught in a trap. He was ready to chew his foot off, if he could only reach it. He yanked at the limbs holding his foot, and finally yanked at his foot until the pain made him throw up. Then he leaned back to rest, his leg on fire with pain.

The breeze was stronger and a hard gust hit him. He thought: *This is it. All the shit I did...nearly killed a dozen times and now to end it like this, battered to death by Nature.* He snorted a laugh. *Maybe I'll get lucky and a fast moving tree limb will knock me out.*

Soon it was hard to breathe without holding a hand over his mouth. He kept his other hand over his eyes. He suddenly became aware of the thousands of pricks on his body and knew the thorns were airborne. The pain was not as bad as the thought of what was happening. It was useless to pull them out, there were too many, and were quickly replaced, anyway.

He wondered how long he would endure, wondered what that warm salty taste in his mouth was. He felt the inside of his cheeks with his tongue; the points of thorns were sticking through his cheeks. He tried not to think about what was happening to him, but his mental image of his body was nothing compared to what was really happening.

He started coughing as thorns worked into his throat and gums! Confused and panicky, he ventured one quick look. He moved the bottom of his hand away to glance down, and that was a huge mistake. The wind caught his hand and he was powerless against its force; the arm was snapped back and broke at his shoulder. Just as fast, the thorns found his eyes.

He groaned in agony, and then laughed, once, at his stupidity for moving his hand, which proved to be his final mistake; the wind filled his mouth and began tearing the flesh away.

Grady sat alone, alive and conscious, as his flesh was peeled back from his mouth to his ears. The power of 250-miles-per-hour wind was skinning him alive. The wind blew larger objects into his mouth that broke teeth, exposing nerves to the wind. The pain was unnoticed; it was nothing by comparison. His eyeballs were turned into mush and were blown out, leaving the eye sockets puffed in like mini downwind-sails full of wind.

His shredded clothes were stripped off. Hair was pulled out, and needle-like thorns covered every part of him facing the wind. The jaws of the wind, using thorns as teeth, chewed on his body. Chunks of flesh disappeared in the wind, leaving only pink craters. Blood was sucked away the instant it surfaced. Fortunately, Grady soon went into shock; he would not be a witness to the complete destruction of his body.

Half an hour later, Grady was a skeleton, and his bones were being tossed to the wind. The only piece of flesh left of Grady was still tangled in the broken and rolling branches. Big-time operator, Grady Fisher, free-spirited, generous at times, but always devious, had joined thousands of others never found after the passing of a Cape Verde hurricane.

10

Big Eye Passes

THE WIND WAS AS BAD, IF NOT WORSE, DURING THE second half of the hurricane, but it was easier on Pete and Tom. Their cave was in the lee of the wind and rain. Gradually, the wind dropped below hurricane force, and it felt almost like a spring breeze by comparison, but the rain continued its destructive downpour.

A scene of total destruction met them as they emerged from the safety of the shelter. The surge had receded and left the landscape looking as if a hydrogen-driven daisy cutter bomb had exploded. The island was bare, swept clean, as was the main island to the west. There was not even a loose rock left on the island, and not much soil for the eventual re-growth of the horrible thorn trees. The view of the island was surreal, as if a strange mind with an appreciation for the grim had created a living picture.

Fast moving clouds raced overhead; continual rain fell through the air in sheets to splatter on bare rock and splash on an ocean the exact same reddish-brown color. Gigantic brown waves crashed thunderously on the reefs and land. No sign of life was anywhere, no birds, insects, or other people. Wind gusts pulled at Pete's wet clothes, and he felt as if he were in a strange, cold, lifeless world.

Tom broke the eerie spell. "Think we're dead and this is hell?"

"I'd believe it."

Tom looked at Pete. "Earth or hell, it looks like we lost our treasure. Egg rock and the sand our treasure was under are gone. We needed one more day."

"Don't know about you, Tom, but I'm damn happy just to be breathing. The gold doesn't seem to matter much anymore."

"I agree. . . . How are we going to get off this rock?"

"I've given that some thought. We're eventually going to have to swim for it. After a normal hurricane, we could wait for the usual swarm of helicopters that come to take pictures and show dignitaries what storm damage looks like. That won't happen with this one. It's too big; too many islands have been affected. Anything that flies will be needed to get the injured taken out and to bring in supplies."

"You've got a point, but I'm not crazy about swimming it. That's some dangerous shit, Pete."

"We haven't eaten for two days already, and I don't know about you, but I'm hungry. We can drink the rainwater caught in the rocks for a day or two, but there's nothing to eat. Even the fish will be out in deep water. The longer we wait to do the swim, the weaker we're going to be."

Tom had a sarcastic smile when he said, "Tell you what, you swim to get help and if you make it, bring me a couple Egg McMuffins® and a big jug of steaming hot coffee, and you can have my share of the treasure."

Pete did not answer; in fact, he did not even hear Tom. His mind was trying to make sense of a strange feeling.

The ruthless hurricane had slowly passed, leaving only tropical storm conditions. *Point Pride* had come to rest at the high-water mark during the peak of Bunny's front side, but not until it had rolled all the way across the three-mile stretch of harbor. It ended up on the rocks with its stern at the bottom of a cliff; its bow angled steeply upwards following the terrain of the cliff. The bulletproof windows were gone and every square inch of the hull was dented or scraped. It was an incredible sight.

The wreck of *Point Pride* was not alone on the desolate shore; boats of all sizes were strewn about; pieces of boats cluttered everywhere. Not a single boat still floated in the harbor. Not a single soul moved about on the rocky shore. Stormy wind, rain, and the dark sky surrounding the massive destruction everywhere painted a grim picture of stark misery. It looked as if the entire population of the island had been blown out to sea. The once-lush green island was now the color of shit.

Jerome and Abby lounged on chaise lounges while enjoying the afternoon on their private veranda of the Old Grenada Inn. Abby complained that it was too overcast to get a tan. Jerome sat with a freshly-made margarita and looked at the massive blackness of the distant hurricane; its outer limits only 100 or so miles to the north.

"I'm glad I listened to you Abby. It's a good thing we left before the Bunny ate Martinique. Wonder how Grady made out?"

"How can we find out?"

"Bill is supposed to look for him today or tomorrow. We'll have to wait."

"There hasn't been very much about the hurricane on television. Apparently, Jerome, the islands have lost communications and the weather doesn't permit anyone to fly in, yet."

"If this happened to the States, it would be on 24/7."

Abby sighed and said, "Such horrible weather. Isn't it a shame about losing the hurricane-hunter plane? Wonder if any of the crew survived."

"Not in that kind of weather. Did you know that was the third hurricane reconnaissance plane lost in Bunny?"

"That's what I heard, but it's hard to believe. You'd think they'd have enough sense to know what kind of storms to fly through."

It was early the next morning before anyone felt like venturing out of whatever they had hidden in during the storm. Everyone was frightened and in various degrees of shock from the terrible punishment they had endured. The dangerous part of their ordeal had passed. Now they faced the next phase of survival: the slow plow through the dreary mess, hunger, depression, and hardships for months to come.

The team of French soldiers who had landed before the storm and had been secured away in the community's bomb shelter were the only people working. They were at work before dawn clearing the landing strip. All that remained of the airfield was part of the concrete runway. Asphalt taxiways, tarmac, roads, buildings, and the perimeter chain-link fences were gone. Some areas in the runway were unsafe; they were undermined by high water and heavy rains. The dangerous areas were marked with tree trunks spray-painted in bright orange. One hour past daybreak, the first military transport landed.

The airport was closed to all traffic, other than the French military. Aircrews were given landing instructions by a hastily made traffic-control center located in a tent. A portable generator provided electricity to run the field radio equipment.

More soldiers disembarked, along with tons of food, water, and tents for the military to use as housing and for a field hospital. More tents for emergency housing for survivors were on their way. As soon as each incoming aircraft was emptied, it was filled with the injured, and departed as another aircraft circled, waiting to land. That process would be repeated around the clock during the daylight hours. It would take weeks before the government was able to get a body count, and the number of dead was not indicative of the true death toll. Only the bodies found and identified would be counted.

A fast civilian aircraft came out of nowhere and made a low approach over Pete and Tom. They waved wildly, hoping to let someone know they were stranded. They had heard other aircraft larger than this one, but this was the first they had seen. The airplane did not acknowledge their signals, and they would never know that the pilot had seen them.

Bill continued his approach to the airfield. He could not fly over to inspect the runway, but other military aircraft had landed, so he knew he would make it. Bill quickly landed before he could be waved off, knowing he was going to catch hell from the authorities for landing on an obviously closed and damaged airfield. He had his orders. Ignoring military orders was easier to live with than breaking Grady's.

He dodged a couple of orange tree stumps, quickly taxied off the runway, shut down the engines, and was getting out of the aircraft, when a Jeep with armed men screeched to a stop only a few feet away. An officer in the Jeep announced through a bullhorn and in French, "Do not disembark the aircraft. This is a restricted area and you will be arrested immediately, if you fail to comply. You are to leave this area now. Do you understand?"

Bill did not understand a word, but knew that the contents of his message probably were, "Get out or go to jail." He replied, "No speaky French."

The officer repeated his message in English, again, through the bullhorn and with a thick French accent. The officer was ready for this kind of thing and knew the next few days would be a nightmare of invaders from the media looking for gore and glory.

Bill did not stop walking to the officer. "Sir, I'm here to find my brother, his wife, and two infant children. Just give me a day. I won't be a problem for anyone, and I know where to look. They are expecting me."

"You are not with the press?" asked the officer.

"I can assure you that I'm not. I do not have a camera, notepad, or even a tape recorder. I want to find my brother's family and get the hell out of your way."

"Didn't you realize landing here was a very dangerous and stupid thing to do?"

"No, I didn't. I'm a very experienced pilot with thousands of flying hours. I saw your markers, and since I'm here already and will have to fly out to leave anyway, why don't you give me one day?"

"Very well, monsieur, but if I find that you have lied to me, I will confiscate your airplane, sell it at auction, and put you in a French jail in Guyana for more years than you would like to think about."

"Fair enough, sir. If my brother comes looking for me, please tell him I'm looking on the other side of the island, where he expected me to be. His name is Grady." Transportation was Bill's big problem. "I don't suppose I could use one of your Jeeps, could I?"

"Monsieur, if you ask one more question of me, you go to jail. You are not supposed to be here. You're interfering with our mission of finding and rescuing many families."

Bill turned away and started walking. Fifty feet away, the officer laughed and said, "Besides monsieur, none of the roads are passable; they are full of trees and parts of buildings, wrecked cars, bodies, and boats. To get anywhere, you must walk."

"Then walk I will, thank you. But, think I better take some water with me." He returned to his aircraft, grabbed his water bottle, binoculars, and quickly shoved his nine-millimeter pistol into his waistband and concealed it with his raincoat. His smaller Walther .380 had already been strapped to his leg.

No security fences were left standing to separate the road from the runway, so he made a direct approach. All aircraft that were there when the storm hit would remain there forever or until their parts rusted away and faded back into the soil they had once been part of. Everything had been turned into twisted pieces. There was not one structure still standing. The trees, or what was left of them, consisted of twisted and shattered stumps. Some that did not break off were single, lonely figures of wooden poles, void of branches and bark. It was hard to imagine that a town surrounded by thick green jungles had once stood where he was. The wind's friction had burned every growing thing to death.

Bill was eager to find the two men waving on the island Grady had suspected was the treasure site. If it wasn't Grady, then it could be the treasure hunters. There was nowhere to hide on the tiny island; anyone who could go through the hurricane on that rock was very lucky. That was reason enough for him to believe it was Grady; he was lucky and always came out on top.

Pete had been quiet for a few minutes before he realized what that strange feeling was. He had been looking at something too obvious to be recognized. He said, "Tom, read the map's instructions to me again."

Without looking at the map, which was wet and wrinkled and in the cave, Tom recounted from memory: "Line up the southernmost peak on the main island with Sailrock. Walk fifty long paces in line. An egg rock guards the bones of my loyal seaman. His bones lie under a man's waist of sand guarding my treasure."

As Pete looked around, Tom said, "Forget it; I've already paced it off. There ain't anything but hard rock."

"Humor me." Pete walked to where the top of the Sailrock was in line with the peak of the southernmost mountain on Martinique. Then he turned and walked straight on that bearing for fifty long spaces. He was standing on top of solid rock just as Tom had said.

Tom, standing beside him said, "Told you."

"Yeah, you told me, but turn around and look directly back at Sailrock."

Tom turned and was surprised. At that distance from Sailrock, he could see a recess in the rock before the cave. It was a horizontally egg-shaped recess. Tom was stunned, "Holy shit, we've been camped out right on top of the treasure?"

"Not only that, if we had had a dinghy, we would've been gone and never would've seen it. And if it hadn't been for the storm, we could've looked forever through the trees and overgrown brush for an egg-shaped rock."

"There was sand just as we crawled into the cave. I'll bet that's our spot. Let's dig down there to see if Mr. Bones is on duty."

"Wait a minute, Tom. Do you think we might be smart to leave it there undisturbed, until we are rescued? I seriously doubt that *Gypsy* made it, so we'll need another boat to get off Martinique and that may take time. There's no way our truck is still there; high water took care of that."

"*Gypsy* might've made it. We could bring her up here, dig at night, and haul ass before anyone sees us."

"Tom, I seriously doubt that there's a useable boat on any of these islands. We need to get to the main island before we do anything else. Then we'll need to be taken someplace unaffected by the storm to find a boat. It's the only way to get it off the island, other than by helicopter."

"We're broke, Pete. How do you intend to get a boat?"

Pete, smirked, "How do you think? We'll borrow a charter boat. They'll be writing them off as lost anyway."

"We still need to see if a skeleton is buried here."

"You honestly think we'd stop digging if we found the bones? Shit, we'd have sand flying and scattered everywhere and that's not going to look natural if a rescue chopper flies over. Two guys stranded on a remote island with a freshly dug hole could make the wrong people start asking questions."

Tom's engineering background was working; "What's sand doing this high up anyway? I'll bet that was a natural hole in the rock and the captain brought sand from the beach to fill it up after he deposited his gold."

That sounded logical to Pete. The two agreed to be patient and do the smart thing: get off the island, find a vessel they could sail home, and then start digging. Starvation played a major roll in their decision to swim for the main island. Normally they could have trapped small fish in the tidal pools, but there were no fish. Nothing was left on the island to eat, no grass or seaweed, no birds, rats, or even bugs. It was time to get off the pot.

The weather was rotten, but the wind was down to twenty knots. They stood on the shoreline, delaying the inevitable. Tom said, "Last chance. Sure you don't want to wait to see if anyone on that jet saw us?"

"They didn't, or the pilot would've waved his wings. Law requires it when survival is in question. We might as well go ahead and get it over with."

It was a half-mile swim to the island if done in a straight line. Further, if you had to contend with a current running parallel to the island, and there was a swift opposing current to the big waves. It would be a treacherous swim, deadly if the current pushed them onto one of the numerous coral or rock reefs. They would be pounded and cut into pieces. Fortunately, both were good swimmers. Unfortunately, the water felt unnaturally cold and their bodies had steadily been losing internal heat since it started raining a lifetime ago.

Tom felt a shiver as he submerged in the water up to his chest. He was more susceptible to heat loss since he was all skin and bones. He said, "I'm going to give it an all-out try and swim directly to the island."

"Whatever blows your skirt up. I'm going to relax and slowly breast stroke it across. The current should help me with the waves. If we get separated, let's meet where we left the truck."

They looked at each other for a moment, and then Pete said, "If you start drowning, I hope your last thought is of me spending your share on cold greenies and hot women."

Tom chuckled, and then said, "And you can think of me, with my newly transplanted weenie, taking care of Emily for you."

They waved, and each pushed off, and became separated right at the beginning. Tom swam the Australian crawl strongly and directly perpendicular to the current and waves.

Pete let the current take him against the waves and he swam as needed to get around the hazardous reefs. Once clear, he swam as Tom had, letting the waves push him into shore, without the current. An hour later, landing and getting out of the water was not pleasant for Pete. Heavy sea swells carried him ashore and battered him against jagged rocks, broken coral, shells, and floating trees. He tried to get out of the surf by swimming hard onto the rocks, but suction of receding water from the spent giant waves only pulled him out again.

Bill had never seen so much destruction as he did when walking on the cross-island road. With all of the debris and mud, it was difficult to tell where the road was supposed to be. After an hour, he became aware of an odd noise that clearly was not one of the few military chainsaws trying to clear the road. It was a motorcycle, and that was exactly what he needed. It was a young man looking for something or someone. Bill waited for the motorcycle to reach him and motioned the driver to stop. The cyclist did not expect Bill's sudden blow to his chest, but he felt the pain as his breastplate shattered, sending bone slivers into his heart. He dropped to his knees and slowly fell over on his side to die painfully, but quietly. Bill, with a wicked smile, held the motorcycle and watched the young man during the dying process.

The way across the island was still slow, but at least he did not have to walk. In only an hour, he was on the other side and carefully looked for Grady and the other guys. He only saw a few people; they were locals who were milling about confused, in shock, and trying to find anything that remained of their past lives. Several tried to stop him, but they were ignored.

Two days ago, a quaint village stood where he was. All that remained was a mud field. Mudslides covered everything. He saw a few people making a lot of commotion around another pile of mud. It piqued his curiosity enough to stop and look. A man dug furiously with a shovel; other people scraped mud away from the hole with their hands. When the shovel hit a hard-concrete object, they all stopped. One woman cheered. The man dropped the shovel, fell to his knees, and began digging with his hands.

Bill got off his motorcycle and walked over to see what they had found. The mud-covered man, with the help of another, pulled at a concrete slab until it was free from a hole. Another man was the first to look inside. He instantly wailed a scream of sorrow. The others looked down and gave the same response. Bill looked down and saw that the concrete structure had been a cistern that several families had entered to escape the fury. Unfortunately, the mud had covered their only way out and rain had filled the cistern to the brim.

He mounted up and resumed his search, and wasn't surprised to see the truck was gone. Everything had flooded, and the only things standing were a few shattered tree stumps. He moved slowly, while looking for a way to get to the point nearest the island. Then he noticed a curious thing well off the roadway. He did not know what it was, but after walking closer, could tell that it used to be a car. It had been crushed and rolled; pieces were missing. The interior was as mangled as the exterior. Thorns were sticking out of everything. Thorns were something he had to contend with, a fact he had learned thirty minutes ago, when he had his first flat tire. The other tire went flat minutes later, but it did not matter, he rode on the rims.

He turned to walk away, and then looked back again. It was the same color as the car he had rented, the car Grady had taken. The license plate confirmed it was a rental. He looked more carefully in the surrounding rubble for a sign of the car's occupant.

Bill stood back and said, "No one could've survived in that, not even Grady." When Bill looked around, he saw a man slowly walking through the destruction about a quarter-mile away. He was too skinny to be Grady; it had to be one of his pals. When he was closer, he yelled out, "Hey buddy, want a lift?"

"Yes ma'am, he was a very brave boy," Lewis said, as he talked to Carl Snow's mother on the phone. "And so passionate about his work, he insisted on going into the most dangerous storm ever witnessed to fully understand what makes a storm like that tick. Finding a way to stop it from happening again was the most important thing in his life... next to his mother, of course."

Lewis impatiently listened, glanced at Miss Stein, smirked, and then said, "Your boy got thousands of people, caught in its path, out of harm's way. Thanks to his efforts, we were able to get the warning out earlier."

He was silent for a moment as Carl's mother wept, and then he spoke. "Yes ma'am. I heard Carl instruct the Air Force to be sure all family pets were aboard the evacuation aircraft."

He listened to her, then said, "Yes, ma'am; he'll be given a medal. In fact, I've started a new program of early warning that is called Snow's Advanced Storm Warning Procedure.

He was quiet again as Carl's mother wept into the telephone. Miss Stein, sitting across the desk whispered, "That isn't very nice. Are you really doing those things?" He shook his head, "no."

The only other crewman still alive woke Skip. "It's over, Skip. You're not going to believe what has happened to the island. Can you get up?"

"Whatever you do . . . Do not touch my arm."

"Shit, it looks bad. We have to get you to a doctor."

"Good luck trying to find one."

"Does it hurt?"

"Fuck you."

Tom said to the approaching stranger, "You know you have two flat tires, mister. I don't think that'll carry us."

"You might be right. I'll walk along if you don't mind the company. Where you headed?"

"I'm looking for a friend. We got separated a while ago."

"He wasn't driving that little blue car over there, was he?"

Tom looked where Bill pointed. "Wow! Look at that! No, he'd be on foot. Anybody survive in that?"

"Don't know. No one is inside."

"That was some blow, wasn't it?"

"I wouldn't know; I just got here. Came to find my brother, but just found out he had left before the storm hit. So thought I'd see if I could do somebody else some good, since I'm here. You don't look like one of the locals. You from around here?"

"No, my friend and I were sailing and we stopped to get out of the Bunny's way."

"What happened to your boat?"

"Don't know yet. We left it in Saint Ann and were out here at a friend's house."

"Where's your buddy? Did he stay back at the house?"

"No, the house didn't make it. We have been looking around for survivors."

"Not very many endured around these parts. I've only seen a few where there was a village a couple miles back."

"I hate to think of the number of people who were killed."

"It's going to be staggering. Listen, since my brother's family made it out, I'd be glad to give you and your buddy a lift if your boat didn't make it. And to be honest, when I flew my plane in, I came in over the harbor and there wasn't anything still floating."

"Hey, that must have been you we saw this morning. We waved, but guess you didn't see us."

"I didn't see you, sorry."

"That sounds great! I'm going down that ravine over there to see if Pete made it."

"Made it? Thought you guys rode it out together."

Tom looked confused for a second, then said, "We did, but we found a dingy floating and took it, thinking it would be easier to go along the coast. It sank and we had to swim for it."

"Oh, I see," said Bill, while thinking, *you lying schmuck. Now pick up Pete, and then find Grady, or his body.* "My name's Bill. What's yours?" He warmly said as he offered his handshake.

"Tom, Tom Roscoe. My pal's name is Pete Morgan."

It's not Pete Morgan, Tom old boy. His real name is Captain Morgan Blackburn, but I doubt that you'd know that. His ex-wife would pay big bucks to have that information. Grady, being a smuggler, had done a fingerprint check on Pete when they started hanging out together. Some undercover cops were damn good. "Well, Tom, I'll get you back to the States. Where're you from?"

"St. Thomas."

"That's good; we won't have to fool around trying to make military connections and mess with the paperwork to get you home. I have a place on St. Thomas, too. We'll have to get together and chase the ladies one of these days."

"Sounds great! I'll buy the rum."

Bill smiled. Salvage Tom had to have found something if he were buying. According to Grady, he was the poorest Lagoonie in that swamp. They walked down the side of a hill that used to be a road. It was slippery going, and messy too, but they made it to where the truck had been before it had washed away. Tom repeatedly yelled Pete's name as they walked.

While Tom looked for his buddy, Bill was scheming. Tom owned the map, so it would be on his person, or hidden. It looked like Pete did not survive the trip from the island. On the other hand, maybe Pete did survive and had the map or the goodies, and had split. If that were the case, he would have headed for his boat or the airport. He would not be stupid enough to take the goodies out of the country on a military transport. Pete was either dead or looking for a boat. Or maybe Grady had him.

Bill pressed Tom into looking for his buddy at the harbor and assured him the motorcycle would get them there. Tom reluctantly relented, as Pete should have been there before he arrived. Tom had run out of energy swimming against the elements and drifted almost a mile down the island before he could make landfall. Either Pete was buried in the surf where he landed or was pulled out to sea, or was caught in one of the reefs. Each of those possibilities meant the worst, but he refused to give up completely. After all, it was, and always had been, against his nature to admit defeat.

By four that afternoon, they were in the harbor. The picturesque little village Tom felt so much at home in before was not there; all that remained was rubble. Many of the foot-thick, seventeenth century coral walls remained, but everything else had been blown or washed away. At least the village's rubble had escaped the mudslides he saw everywhere else.

The harbor was void of anything floating; a few masts rose from the water. Many demolished boats had washed up on shore. All others either sank or were blown out to sea. *Gypsy Bitch* was gone, as were the trees she had been tied to.

A hundred or so bewildered people wandered around the wreckage. Women cried and children huddled against their parents' legs. Men were angry and all fought back tears every time they met another survivor. Sadness hung heavily in the air.

Bill said, "Guess that's that; your boat is gone and it appears your friend has been taken, too. Let's go over to my plane. I've some snacks and it looks like you must be starving."

"Maybe Pete's at the airport. He might've been here and headed for the next logical place to look for me."

"I agree, besides the military may have set up a feeding center by now. If he isn't there, though, I think you might as well give it up and leave with me. I want to help you guys, but I can't stay here past tomorrow morning. The military knows I'm looking for my brother and the top dog is going to be sure that I'm out of here in the morning. In fact, if we see him, I'm going to tell him you're my brother to make it easier to get out of here."

"Wonder how bad St. Thomas got hit? We may not be able to land."

"St. Thomas took a direct hit. By tomorrow morning, I'll land where I can find room, just like I did here this morning. If we don't get in early, we won't get in for at least a week. I was a Harrier pilot in the Marines, so I've got lots of experience in landing in places with no real runway."

Tom was impressed with his new friend and thankful he had been so lucky. He also had thoughts about giving Bill a share of the treasure if he did not find Pete. He still had the same problem: how to get it off the island and where to secure it. Bill and his aircraft certainly provided a good solution, and besides, he was a likable guy.

Rain poured over Tom, Bill, and the others standing in the chow line. The Army tent was packed to standing-room-only, as people came for food, and then did not want to go back out in the never-ending rain again. Threats and orders shouted from the military had no effect on the stunned mob. Each had been tortured beyond caring whether they pissed off some foreign soldier.

Finally, Tom and Bill got close enough to the tent for one of the cooks to pass out tin trays full of hot food that quickly became soaked with rainwater and turned cold. Bill ate a few bites, and then tossed the tray to the ground. He looked at Tom and said, "Go ahead and eat this slop; I'm not that hungry. When you finish, come over to the plane."

Tom, with a mouthful of food and half an ear of corn smeared over his scraggly beard, acknowledged he would. Ten minutes later, he banged on the plane's door, which was quickly lowered and closed again to keep the foul weather out. "Holy smoley! This is nice! This is your plane?"

Bill tossed him a towel. "Yep, I decorated it myself. The paneling is Burmese teak that I found in an old yacht in Calcutta. It belonged to the nawab of Bengal. That's the guy who killed all those Brits one night in the Black Hole of Calcutta. Ever hear of it?"

Greatly to Bill's surprise, when he finished bullshitting about the teak, Tom said, "They must have used a pretty interesting process to preserve the wood. The Black Hole incident took place in the mid 1700s, didn't it?"

Bill turned and pointed to a well-stocked bar in the rear of the Lear. "How about some of that? Think a couple of pulls will shake that chill out of your bones?" Tom's face erupted into a smile as he walked hurriedly to the bar. Bill pointed to a store-pack of Georgia Jimmy's Beef Jerky.

"And things just keep getting better," Tom muttered.

After Tom had a couple shots of straight rum, Bill asked, "Well, what are you going to do about your friend? You can leave a message with the army here; they'll surely set up a message center. I'll leave my satellite number for him to call, and if he does, we can come back, if the military allows it."

"That's nice of you to offer." After the soothing rum, he was feeling melancholy; his mind and body were reacting to the hardship, the cold, and demanding physical endurance of the last few days. He was weary, as he sat sprawled over two seats near the bar and looking outside into the darkening and rainy evening sky.

Rum was winning the day; he took another gulp and held it in his mouth, letting a squirt or two go down his throat every few seconds. He fought off sleep; he had to stay awake in case Pete showed up and made a trip to the chow-tent. Guilt and anger alternately flooded over him as he waited. The ugly side of paranoia also sneaked in: *Is Pete hiding, waiting for me to leave so he can take it all for himself?* Tom smiled at a thought: *I'll have the last laugh if he is. Glad I decided to trick his ass.*

Tom became aware that Bill, who was soaking wet, was talking to him, "Hey, you! You awake?"

"Sure," Tom slurred.

"I've been talking to the general about your pal. I gave him Pete's name and how to contact us if he shows up. Unfortunately, I have some bad news; the general thinks we might as well write him off. He said rain was washing everything into the sea and storm currents were pulling all the wreckage offshore. Already there's a thick debris line full of bodies, trees, houses, and everything else you can think of. He emphasized hundreds of bodies are visible."

"Don't mean nut'n."

"Not unless you want to face reality. Pete didn't show up where he was supposed to meet you. He wasn't at his boat. He hasn't been here, and this is the only place on the island where there is anything left. Survivors from all over the island have made their way here. Dead people, who tried just as hard to stay alive as your friend, are everywhere. God has reclaimed those he wanted and there isn't shit you can do about it other than to get on with your life."

"Don't mean nut'n."

"Have another drink, Tom."

11

Homeward Bound

MORNING'S LIGHT BROUGHT ANOTHER DREARY SKY; low gray clouds flew by, while soaking the island with rain. It was another soggy day. Bill woke Tom by roughly shaking his shoulder. He noticed an empty Mount Gay bottle and another was half-gone. Tom had been a thirsty boy last night.

"Time to trot or rot, Tom; let's get over to the mess tent for some strong coffee and greasy food."

Tom opened a bloodshot eye for a second, and then closed it as the headache registered.

"Come on Tom. Timing is right for us to pop off this place and get into St. Thomas before they can shut the runway down. Get up!"

"Can't leave without Pete."

"Pete is dead. Don't you remember what I told you last night?"

"Oh, yeah." Tom sat up and stretched. "Damn, I feel like shit. Must be your expensive rum. Not used to it. Give me rotgut any day."

"Maybe it's the quantity, not the quality. You drank almost two bottles last night."

"Naw, do it all the time. When I can afford it." Tom was awake and he knew it was time to make a decision; he was at the point of first tack, he had to jibe or keep sailing into the same old problems of poverty. Getting enough money to buy another boat or find another partner with a boat to return did not appeal to him. Bill had been a friend, so why shouldn't he trust him. He solved all Tom's current problems; and hell, Pete was dead anyway.

"Bill, I'd like to offer you a proposition. Pete and I were here for a reason other than what I told you. We were here to dig up a buried treasure."

"You're not going to tell me you bought a pirate's treasure map, are you?"

"No. I have an authentic map."

"How do you know?"

"We found the site. Pete and I wanted to bring his boat to the site before digging it up."

"You serious?"

"Very. I want to offer you a share in the treasure in exchange for your help. Interested?"

"Shit, yes. I'd love to go treasure hunting. Where's the map?"

Tom was silent for a second, then said, "It's hidden, in case one of us didn't make it back."

"How big is the treasure? What do we need to get it?"

"We need transportation to bring it here from the other side of the island, including some sort of boat to get to it. We'll need to cover it while loading your plane. And I'll need your help digging and toting."

Bill sat across from Tom, and while looking down at the floorboards, he muttered, "Dinghy won't be a problem, they're scattered everywhere. Getting it there will be. We could steal an army Jeep if we leave right now before it gets too active outside. I have a tarp in the storage locker. Do you have shovels?"

"Nope. The storm took it. But we can pick up some broken limbs and tin roof pieces that'll work okay."

Bill shifted in his seat and asked, "And just exactly what share do you have in mind for me?"

"Half. That's based on Pete being dead, of course. If he's still alive, then it'll be a three-way split."

"Sounds more than fair. Why don't you look in the aft storage compartment," Bill said and pointed the way. "Dig out the tarp while I scout up some transportation. I'll be back in a few minutes, so be ready." He opened the door and disappeared into the gloomy light.

Tom opened the refrigerator door, and then opened a cold beer. He took a long gulp, then uttered, "Damn that tastes shitty... but it's goooood fur ya!" He took another drink. "Well, Bill's a partner—too bad Grady's not here." He took another swallow. "Fucking Pete! What am I going to tell Emily?"

After pouring half the beer down his throat, he went over and opened the aft-locker. He looked through the small but crowded storage compartment. As he pulled the canvas out, he noticed a large pile of chain on the floor and was curious why chain would be needed on an airplane. Then he noticed a tag on the canvas: *Fisher's Rigging*.

Bill casually walked up to a soldier who was checking the oil of his Jeep. He asked, "I need transportation to go to the other side this morning. Can I use your vehicle?" The young man answered, but Bill did not understand French, and it did not matter. He maneuvered behind the young man, grabbed his head, and quickly sliced his jugular vein. Being careful not to get soiled in the process, he dragged the man into the bushes and watched as the soldier died quickly and in silence, as his blood pumped over the ground. Its color quickly dissipated into the muddy water.

Tom was on his second beer when Bill returned. The borrowed Jeep had a borrowed rowboat tied over the backseat. Bill, in a hurry, said, "Grab that canvas and let's split before they miss the Jeep." Tom guzzled the beer, tossed the can into the sink, picked up the canvas, and hustled to Bill without a word.

Bill drove the Jeep as if it belonged to him. No one in the early hours seemed to notice two civilians driving the military vehicle. It was a strange time for island people, and even stranger for the foreign solders. Nothing was as it should be, everything was displaced.

When they were well clear of the airfield, Tom relaxed a little and asked, "You know Grady Fisher?"

"Who?"

"Grady Fisher. The canvas has his name on it. Grady is a friend of mine."

"Oh, that Grady Fisher. I don't know him, but I bought that canvas from a rigger. I guess that must have been his name."

"What in the world are you carrying that chain around for?"

"Regulations, Tom. In high winds, it's necessary to chain her down. If the wind gets too strong, she'll try to fly away," he said, and he laughed. "When's the last time you saw Grady?"

"A few days ago, in much better times. He wanted to come with us. I should've let him; Pete might still be alive."

"Better hope Pete is dead, Tom. If he were alive, it would make me think that he's staying away for a reason. Maybe there was no sign of his boat because he's on the move. You ever think that maybe he's trying to take the treasure for himself?"

"No way," Tom lied. "Pete wouldn't do that. Besides, if that's the case, he's in for a surprise."

"What do you mean?"

"Pete only thinks he knows where the treasure is. I didn't tell him the last part because I planned to play a gag on him when we came up short."

Bill laughed unnaturally hard. He was pleased to hear of Tom's distrust. He was also cautioned that Tom might hold back on him, too. He would have to play it straight to the end, until Tom would be ready to fly like a chainbird. "So what didn't you tell him? Or do you distrust me, too?"

"I didn't distrust Pete. I was playing a trick on him for some laughs. I trust you, Bill, and appreciate your help. Other than Pete, or Grady, I couldn't have asked for a better partner."

"Glad you feel that way. So what's the gag on the treasure's location?"

"Pete can't read the map because it's written in an old form of French. I translated it for him except for a small note on a corner of the page that referenced a passage in a book written by Claude de Hours in the sixteenth century, *Gold of the Rainbow*. It stated, 'A treasure can only be safely hidden when its view is unseen when blinded by another.' I'm pretty sure we'll find only a small chest."

Tom turned to Bill and smiled, "But there was another notation below that with an arrow pointing down and an X. In the old days, an X represented a dimension of three feet. Three more feet down is the main chest and I'll bet anything the old captain figured that if someone found the map they'd stop digging at the small chest." Bill looked pleased.

The army had worked hard the day before; part of the road was cleared, so it was barely passable for four-wheel-drive vehicles. The going was slow; hard turns had to be made to swerve around the bigger trees. When they drove by the place the kid had been killed, Bill stopped the Jeep, and told Tom to give him a second. He went near the area to take a leak. He saw the toe of a muddy tennis shoe mostly concealed by broken tree parts. Bill really was not concerned about the boy being found; there were no wounds. His breastbone was shattered. It would appear that he either had an accident, or was killed by flying debris. Years later, if fingerprints on the bike posed a problem, it would be easy to say he found it in the wreckage.

Tom gave Bill the directions and soon they stopped at the place the truck had been left. They pulled off the dinghy and rowed out into the turbulent ocean. Tom's powerful strokes on the oars surprised Bill; the skinny man was stronger than he looked. He made a mental note to remember that when he broke out the chain.

Tom negotiated the crashing breakers and the tricky current until he planted the dinghy's bow on the island's rocks. "Let's be certain this thing is well up on the beach and tied. I don't want this one floating away."

As he walked up the rocky mountainside, he had mixed emotions. *What am I going to find? An empty hole? A treasure lost or a friend lost, and an enemy made?*

When he reached the boulder, he stopped, took a deep breath and prayed that his trust had not been betrayed. When he looked down, the ground was undisturbed. He uttered, "I knew he wouldn't take it. Got to learn how to trust other people. Sorry Pete."

"Is this the place?"

"This is it; let's dig," and he started chiseling the ground with a sharp stick to loosen the sand. Bill selected one of the small pieces of torn corrugated tin roof to shovel away the loose sand.

Before darkness had chased the ugly gray away the evening before, land was close to disappearing behind the horizon. Pete had spent the last twenty-four hours at sea trapped in a strong current that was sweeping him further away from land. He had lots of company; however, all of it was dead and bloated. He had found three large coconuts and knew he could survive for a while longer. The nuts would keep him afloat and he could drink the milk and eat the meat for nourishment.

He had sustenance, but he was terrified; the thought of sharks bothered him more than usual. If he had to die in the belly of a shark, it would have been more acceptable to him before he had become a rich man. Before, he didn't have much in the way of expectations about his life.

The deep-water eating machines would be lured to the surface to devour the rotting bodies. Cows, goats, dogs, rats, and people of all shapes and sizes were drifting in the weed line. All were stiff; most bloated, and had there been any birds left alive, they would have had a feast pecking at all the soft, tender and wide-open eyes.

Pete was not a religious man a couple of days ago, but he had found God during the storm, and during the pitch-black night at sea, when he heard the splashes of sharks in feeding frenzies. He and God had become friends. Finally, dawn and its meager light arrived; the skies brightened to a dull gray, and no land was in sight. He prayed aloud, "Please God, let the current wash me back to land. Just get me close enough to swim for it. I can make it, if you'll just let me drift into a current that runs between the islands. And please, God, protect me from your creatures under the surface. I understand they're here for a good reason, but there are plenty of other things that need to be recycled....Not me. Not yet, please."

Tom and Bill alternated with the pick and shovel, as there was room for only one man in the hole. It took three hours of hard work before the pick hit something other than packed sand. Bill was in the hole and looked up at Tom; both smiled.

"I think it's a bone," Bill said as he resumed digging. He carefully dug around the hard spot. Minutes later, he was digging with his hands. Then he stood up and handed an ancient tibia to Tom.

"Welcome to the twenty-first century Seaman Phuckewe. You've done a damn fine job," Tom grandiosely announced.

Bill stayed on his knees and continued to dig with his hands and a knife. More bones were freed from the sandy dungeon that had held them captive, and on duty, for so many centuries. The skull was the last major bone removed and the ancient seaman's expression shocked them. It looked like he was happy to be released. It was not natural. Bill held it up and said, "Look at him, he's smiling. Must've been a birth defect or disease that deformed his cheekbones like that. I've got the perfect place for the old buccaneer to reside, Tom."

"Actually, Bill, I had planned to keep the bones and make a real Jolly Roger and mount them on the bulkhead of my boat." He examined the skull more closely. "I hope that smile was caused by a deformity and not by some kind of ancient magic. I have to tell you, there were times while stuck in that little cave that both of us wondered if the hostility around us was being caused by this fellow."

Bill laughed and said, "Good thing you didn't see this skull then, or you might have run off. As far as keeping the skull; it's yours; I'll take the map then. You did say even partners, didn't you?" The disadvantage of having a partner began to surface for Tom, as he wanted the map. Then he thought: *There I go again; cool it. Be happy you got anything out of that hole. Be joyous you're alive.*

"Tell you what Bill; we'll split everything after we get back to St. Thomas. No sense in trading maps and bones when there may be some very nice pieces of jewelry in the chest, right?"

Bill smiled and resumed digging; *there was no need to be worried or stingy.* He chuckled and said, "I wasn't serious, Tom; this is your treasure and anything you do will be okay with me."

Tom took over the digging duty and was surprised when he hit something at just the right depth. Like Bill, he finished the dig with his hands and was tremendously surprised at the chest he unearthed. "Damn, Bill, did we miss the small chest?"

He dug around the sides until he could feel the bottom, but he still could not pull it up. Bill wedged himself into the hole to help. Both were laughing at the prospect of a gold-laden chest that was too heavy to lift. The chest moved, and then broke free from the earth, but it was still heavy, and there was not enough room in the hole for them to position themselves to get the best leverage. Nevertheless, they grunted the bulky box up, inch by inch, until it rested on the earth's surface.

They stood in silence looking at the three-by-two-foot chest. "Do you think this is the small chest, Tom?"

"That's hard to comprehend. Wouldn't that be something if it is? Let's find out. Hell, it's only three more feet."

Later, and much deeper than three feet, Tom was sure they had found the only treasure. He took one more stab with the pick before giving up. It scraped a hard object.

Both men were silent with knowledge that something beyond their wildest dreams lay only a few shovels of sand away. As they cleared the hole, it became apparent that the two of them were not going to lift it.

Bill said, "Tom, we need to cover the hole and pile some rocks on it to hide the dig. The smaller chest is all we can handle. We'd be smart to get it back to St. Thomas, buy a motor yacht and some tools, and then come back here to pull that big one out. What do you think?"

"Good luck finding enough rocks to cover the area, but I'm in agreement, except we should go somewhere other than St. Thomas. It's going to be shredded like this one. I doubt if we'd find a boat there. What do you think about going to Trinidad?"

"Caracas will have more to offer. I know the Customs people there, so they won't need to search the plane. I'd hate to have a shithead government official steal this from us."

"Caracas it is. But before we close the hole, let's open the small chest to be sure it isn't just rocks."

Bill's expression remained unchanged; he was happy. Tom found a piece of broken rock and pounded on a corner of the chest. The wood was iron-hard with age, but the repeated blows loosened a seam until it started splintering. He opened a small hole and peered inside. He sadly said, "Wish Pete could've seen this." He looked at Bill. "I'd say there's about two hundred pounds of... gold!" Bill's smile had a wicked curl.

They lugged the 200-pound chest to the dinghy. Once there, a horrible truth became apparent: the dinghy was not going to hold both men and the chest.

Distrust reared its ugly head again, but Tom was not going to let those thoughts control him again, and said, "Bill, why don't you row the treasure over and come back for me."

Bill smiled and said, "Nope. You're the better boatman. You take it and come back for me." Bill was not worried; Tom could not carry it to the Jeep by himself, or get off Martinique without him.

By three o'clock, most every island in the Caribbean had been beaten, was being beaten, or was getting ready for Bunny's beating. Not one soul in the Caribbean and Central America was unaware of the monstrous killer. News networks in the United States were going nuts trying to find out what had happened, or was about to happen. News' crews had been placed in sturdy buildings on some of the bigger islands. Each had its own power supply and satellite communication cameras. The airwaves were mostly silent.

Doctor Lewis sat in a quiet room full of people with their cold, half-empty coffee cups on the conference table. Also, on the table was a pile of satellite photographs of the Windward Islands. Lewis leaned forward and took a sip of coffee, unaware of its bitter, cold taste, and said, "We should've sent in the cavalry. The Air Force could have sent planes down there to help evacuate those poor people. It's not their fault; they had no idea what kind of storm this was going to be. It's our fault for not being stronger with our warnings and I can promise each of you, it'll never happen again.

"Based on the damage shown here and earlier reports, FEMA estimates that seventy percent of the population were killed or physically injured. All people will have psychological problems with the memory of the storm and coping with what's left. If the storm winds didn't kill them, the rivers of rain or the mud avalanches did."

He picked up another photograph and sailed it across the table like a flat Frisbee to Miss Stein. "See all those chunks floating in the ocean? A lot of those chunks used to be people."

Bill was not worried, but Tom certainly was; he was sure they would be stopped at the airfield, searched, and their treasure confiscated. "Just relax, Tom. We're not doing anything wrong. We're going to drive up to the plane like *we own* the place, load *our* stuff on *our* plane, and then you'll take the Jeep over to the parking area while I preflight the plane. No sweat, no strain; we're doing our thing. All we did was borrow a Jeep for a few hours, so just act natural."

Tom felt a little better until he noticed a truck with a covered bed coming their way. The closer it came, the more certain he was they were going to be arrested, but instead, it stopped at another aircraft.

Covered with the canvas, the heavy chest was hauled up the boarding steps and hidden behind the bar. Bill said, "Park the Jeep, and I'll have us ready to take off as soon as you get back. And then, partner, after I get some elevation, I'll put the plane on autopilot and we can count our gold, okay?"

Tom parked the Jeep and wanted to run to the plane, slam the door shut, and speed away before they could take the gold, but forced himself to walk.

He almost made it. As he reached the boarding ladder, he saw another Jeep racing toward Bill's plane. Three men were aboard, one carried a rifle, and this one did not stop at the loading transport.

Tom hurried up the steps, while resisting his overwhelming urge to slam the door. The Jeep started honking its horn, and the increased engine noise clearly indicated that it had sped up. *Shit! I knew it.*

A voice in French said, "Arrest monsieur! Je veux parlais avec vous!" The driver honked the horn twice more.

He did not know what the Frenchman said, but he damn sure knew what *arrest* meant. "Fuck 'em." He muttered, as he pulled the door shut and yelled at Bill. "They're here and want to arrest us. Get us out of here!"

Bill turned to look at Tom and said, "Too late; they parked right in front of us. Open the door and sit down. I'll do the talking." He unbuckled his safety harness and before getting up, he reached under the seat and pulled out his Beretta, and tucked it in the back of his waistband.

Tom sat at the bar, concealing the tarp-covered box. He grabbed a beer and tried to relax while Bill lowered the door.

"L'attente un moment, un monsieur," the armed guard said.

"Whoa ... hold on there, Pierre. I don't speak your language. No speaky Francais."

Tom was not happy. He looked at the beer bottle, knowing it would be the last he would have for a while. He was so close to his dream; he would have had big money, and instead, he would be doing time for stealing the jeep. They would surely confiscate the gold and find the map. With a disgusted snort, he took a big drink, and then muttered, "The crows are going to love this. Another golden horizon turned to a bucket of shit."

In broken English, the soldier said, "This man is a fellow American tourist; he must leave here. I'm glad you found your brother, so maybe you have room to take him with you, too? He has been hurt a little and needs rest. Please, you can take?"

"Tom," said Bill, "take a look at this character and see if you know him." Tom stuck his head out of the doorway, and the one wrapped in an army blanket suddenly became alive and yelled coarsely, "Tom! It's me!"

Bill was knocked out of the way, as Tom bounded down the ladder. "Pete! I don't believe it. I thought you were dead."

Pete looked like shit. He had aged twenty years, his skin was wrinkled from the water. With a hoarse voice, he said, "Made it to the beach, but got beat up trying to get a foothold and finally lost it to the current. I've been floating around out in the Atlantic ever since."

"You're a lucky son of a bitch."

"You don't know how lucky. It was a scene straight out of a Stephen King movie. I drifted offshore through bodies of people, cows, you name it, and I was the only thing alive. Luckily, a chopper saw me and plucked me out of the water." Bill chuckled and stepped in at that point. He told the military captain that they would be very happy to take care of the man. Everyone was happy as the trio boarded the Lear again. While closing the door, Bill had that wicked smile again.

With a friendly demeanor, Bill said, "Okay boys, let's celebrate and I'm buying. Unfortunately, I'm also flying, so I can't join you in the festivities, until we get to Caracas. I know what Tom wants, but how about you, Pete. What will it be, vodka, beer, rum, scotch, or brandy?"

Pete said, "Brandy sounds good; I'm really chilled. You wouldn't have a hot-water shower onboard would you?"

Bill smiled, then answered, "Of course. You think your pal would be traveling on anything less than first class?" and pointed to a cabin door in the rear. "Take the drink with you while you wash up. I'll dig out a pair of slacks and clean shirt that should fit good enough for the trip," He gave Pete a glass almost full of cognac, and three packs of Georgia Jimmy's Beef Jerky.

Pete looked hungrily at the first food he had had in days, as Bill said, "You guys get yourselves fixed up while I get this thing in the air and away from here. Tom will tell you the news and then we'll party."

"What are we celebrating?"

"Being alive, you stupid shit, and look at this!" Tom lifted the tarp to show him the old chest.

Pete looked over the bar and was completely dumbfounded to see the dirty old chest. He instinctively knew where it had come from and was surprised at its size. He looked at Tom. His confusion evident by his expression, he felt a touch of betrayal and was unsure what Bill had to do with it.

Tom understood what his pal must be thinking, and said, "We'll open it after Bill gets on autopilot." Then he told him what had happened since they separated. All thoughts of Tom's treachery vanished, and Pete did not mind the three-way split in the least.

Once Pete had showered and both men had had three very stout drinks, the booze began to take effect. Feelings of success only heightened their fun; life was great. Pete could not contain himself and wanted to remove the lid and see whether all the effort had been worth it, but Tom made him wait.

Bill finally had the plane flying straight and level; the autopilot was in charge, and he went back for the big moment each was so eagerly awaiting. He went into the storage compartment and returned with a crowbar. He handed the iron bar to Tom and said, "Do the honors."

Tom poured himself another glass of rum, and then toasted the old stained chest. "To the honor of the bones of Andre Phuckewe! You've done a great job keeping it safe. Thanks." He tried to be gentle with the old chest, but rum, anticipation, and a little greed soon won over patience. He popped a couple wooden slats off, gave the crowbar back to Bill, and then reached in and pulled out the first bar. Stamped on the surface was the head of a male lion with two crossed swords behind it.

Bill said, "It'll be interesting to see whose stamp that belonged to."

Pete grabbed another bar, handed it to Bill, and then he leaned over to get one for himself while saying, "How many bars are in—?"

Bill interrupted Pete's question by hitting him on the back of his head with the crowbar, knocking him unconscious. In the same motion, he twisted his body in a 360-degree swing and caught Tom on the side of his head, breaking the rum glass at his mouth. He fell straight down.

"Damn boys! That wasn't much of a challenge. I was hoping for a little rumble, but since there's so much treasure at stake, why take the risk, right? Too bad your pal Grady isn't here."

He checked his instruments; the plane was on course, the radar showed the skies were clear of other aircraft. The only things visible were thunderstorms ahead, but he would go over and around them.

Back at the storage compartment, he dragged an end of heavy chain out and selected Tom first. In Pete's condition, he would be too weak to do much damage if he came to before he was snugly bundled. Twenty minutes later, Bill was sitting in the comfort of the pilot's seat, sipping a glass of chilled club soda. He had two gold bars in the co-pilot seat. He picked up one and mumbled, "Well, Charming Billy, your life just got a hell of a lot better. Grady, wherever you are, dead or alive, I enjoyed working for you pal, but piss off. I'm rich now. No more doing the dirty work, no more risks. I'm free. I'll hire my own Dirty Bill…hell, I'll have three or four of 'em. Shit, with my money, maybe even little Abby will run off with me. YESSSIREEEEE!"

With a big area of clear air ahead, he dropped down to ten thousand feet and activated the autopilot. He went to the back. "Rise and shine me buckos! T'is time for your flight."

Pete's head moved; he was too dazed to realize what was happening. Bill poured a glass of water on his face to revive him. "It'd be a shame if you missed all the fun. Wake up, sleepyhead."

Bill poured water over Tom's face until he sputtered. Pete mumbled, "What's going on? Why am I wrapped in chain?"

Cheerfully, Bill answered, "Now, why don't you use that soggy brain of yours to figure it out. It shouldn't be too tough. Take a look at Tom. You guys are dressed like twins."

Tom was awake and pissed. Bill glanced at his watch and said, "Okay boys, I'm going to tell you like it is. I don't have much time before I have to make some maneuvers so I don't fly into that damned hurricane, so listen up if you're interested. Your old buddy, Grady, and I have been tailing you so we could steal your treasure. I don't know where Grady is right now, but it doesn't matter. Your treasure belongs to me."

"Grady? Grady Fisher?" asked Pete.

"Yep. Your old drinking buddy wasn't much of a friend, I'm afraid. It was his idea to throw your asses out of the plane. At least he was a good enough friend to keep your little secret, Captain Blackburn. Yeah, he knew about your adventure in the F-16 that got your ass in a jam. What the hell did you do with that thing—?"

Tom angrily interrupted, and yelled, "Throw us out of an airplane? What the hell are you talking about? There's plenty of gold for all of us!"

"No, there isn't! I'm a greedy son of a bitch. I'm going to land this thing at a friend's hacienda and trade it for a nice yacht and then I'm going back for the rest of my gold. By the way, thanks for the map." He held up Tom's map.

In anger, Tom spat out, "Fuck you! Turn us loose. You wouldn't have shit if I hadn't brought you in."

"I must've hit you a little too hard, boy. Didn't you hear me? Grady and I have been on your ass since you left St. Thomas. This gold was ours the day you found out about it. We just let you find it for us." Bill moved to the rear of the plane and said, "Hold your ears boys, I'm going to ease the pressure in here before I open the bums-a-way hatch. After the pressure is equalized, you know what's going to happen next, don't you? You guys have to leave, but don't worry, you'll be scared shitless all the way down, but it'll only take a couple of minutes until you splash. When you do, be macho, hit the water face first with your eyes wide open. Wow! What a rush that'll be! Don't worry about pain; you won't feel a thing....Or I don't think so."

He was enjoying himself while he opened the cabin's air pressure valve. He looked out of a window and said, "Wow, you should see the seas down there. Man, it's rough; but don't worry, those chains will make sure you don't bob around too long. Now I'm going to show you Grady's little bums-a-way door. Bet you never figured that your old boat-bum buddy owned a Learjet. You..."

"You're full of shit, " Pete coarsely yelled. "Grady had nothing to do with this."

"You wouldn't believe who Grady really is, how rich he is. I've worked for him for years, or used to, until I inherited a fortune from a couple of fucking idiots." He laughed again.

With the flip of a finger and a click of a switch, an electric motor started. The motor's sound was quickly replaced by blowing wind. The air in the cabin turned cold; it sounded as if they were back in the hurricane. Pete looked at the source of the noise and saw a sliding door opening vertically in the fuselage.

Tom yelled over the noise, "What are you doing?" Bill laughed again, and with a twinkle in his eyes, sang, "Off we go into the wild blue yonder."

The only thing Pete was sure about was that Bill was truly enjoying the moment. He also knew that he was about to slide out of a floor-level door two miles above the ocean. He looked at Tom, who seemed to be trying to find something within himself that would give him the superhuman strength needed to break the chain.

Bill looked at them and said in a mother's sweet voice, "Now which of my little chain cocoons wants to be first? No fighting, now, you both get a turn." He waited for a response for a moment, then said, "Neither of you wants the honor? Tell you what. Tom, to be fair, you get to pick; that's the least I can do for the guy that put all that gold in my pocket. How about it, Tom? Is it you or Pete?"

Bill was wearing a look of mock-disappointment, and said, "You're mad and not talking to me. Well, okay, I guess I can't blame you. But it's all your own fault, Tom. . . . You're just too damn trusting," and started laughing again, while he bent over and grabbed Tom by his chain and started dragging him to the bums-away door.

Out of frustration and anger, Pete raised his heavy-with-chain legs to block Bill's path. Bill stumbled; it was not much, but he lost his balance enough to fall backwards.

Then in a fraction of a second and before the mind could comprehend, Bill was not there. Moments in a strange howling-wind-silence passed, before Pete realized what had happened. Stunned, he chuckled and said, "The son of a bitch fell out."

Also stunned, Tom mimicked, "The son of a bitch fell out." Then both were quiet. Seemingly, minutes passed before Tom chuckled, and he started laughing. Pete joined him until they were laughing so hard, tears streamed from their eyes. And the laughter went on.

Finally, Tom got enough control and managed to say two words, "Chain cocoons!" before he erupted in another laughing fit.

Pete wanted to add something; it was painful trying to suppress his laughter. "You . . . know what this . . . means, don't you?"

Tom managed to blurt out between laughter, "You're an F-16 pilot? . . . Can you fly this thing?"

"Not in a chain cocoon." They resumed their laughter, as if the situation were horrendously funny. Later, in a moment of sanity, Tom rested his hurting sides and asked, "Captain Morgan? Thought you were a jungle grunt in the war. You were actually a pilot?"

"Both. Fighter pilot, until I was blown out of the sky over Cambodia. Was flying on the deck to take a little surprise package to the bad guys, who weren't supposed to be there either. No one knew where I ejected. A small band of Cambodian fighters found me, and it took almost a year to get out of there, so I was taught the art of jungle fighting."

Tom was impressed. Pete never indicated that he was anything more than just another enlisted man who had survived. "Is that the F-16 adventure Bill was talking about? You were sneaking over the no-fly zone and got caught?"

"No, but don't ask. I don't want to talk about it."

"Damn, Pete. Your secret is safe with me. Shit, look at us. Who am I going to be talking to?"

To change the direction of the conversation, Pete said, "Wonder when we'll run out of fuel." There was silence, and then Tom started laughing again. Pete joined him until he got his breath, and then talked very fast to get his next thought out. "May not have to worry about fuel. There're some mountains out there that are higher than we are." The laughter resumed.

Tom forced himself to talk through the laughter and managed to say, "Wonder if . . . we'll run into Big Eye . . . before the mountains? The laughter went on and on until they reached the turbulence of Hurricane Bunny.

The plane began to rock from side to side. With every movement, the chain cocoons rolled downhill; it was impossible to control their movements.

The open bomb-bay door beckoned. The laughter had ended and they only cursed with each roll. Tom still concentrated on finding that inner superhuman strength needed to get out of the chain.

Pete rolled down to the open door, he prayed that he would stop, but did not until his feet went out into the wind. He felt himself being pulled out by the wind's force.

Tom screamed, "Try harder! Don't let it get you!" It was useless; Pete had no control and was sliding out when the plane violently banked again and threw him inside, breaking his nose as he crashed into the other side of the cabin. Both men nervously laughed, briefly, at his near-death. The next jolt flung Tom at the open door and he stopped an inch from the sudden deadly drop off. He wanted to throw up, but was too scared. Pete was silent, knowing that the next jiggle would take his friend. He could not watch and closed his eyes as the next jolt struck. The moment became too traumatic and he threw up all over himself and choked on the chunky vomit mixture of brandy and Georgia Jimmy's Beef Jerky.

Book Two

The Lost Treasure of El Morro

1

Costa Rica

YOUNG CHICO COMANCHO SAT ON THE GRASSY HILLSIDE overlooking his father's tiny farm. It was only three hectares, but provided enough watermelon to pay for the cost of farming for the year and enough squash to pay the land rent. Rice provided enough for the family to eat, and some to sell for cash needed to buy other food and essential clothing for him, his three sisters, and their parents. A double line of mango trees ringed their land's perimeter; left untouched it would yield enough to replace worn-out equipment, but most of the crop would be eaten by anyone who was hungry, including the monkeys.

Chico's sisters worked in the house during the day, helping their mother. He and his father toiled all day in the hot fields, from before dawn to near dark. Spending six days a week in the field should not have troubled him; every boy he knew was doing the same thing. Nevertheless, it did; he had dreams, aspirations, and wanted more from life than his father had. He wanted to be someone important: the honcho who drove the truck on a big hacienda, the foreman of the hacienda, or the foreman of anything. He did not want to spend his life working the land until his father died and then making his sons work with him until he was finally given the everlasting rest. Nonetheless, that was all life offered; he was in a prison without bars, walls, or guards. His bars were poverty and, more importantly, a mentality developed over generations that fueled a lack of expectation that kept him, and everyone else, in their places.

This particular day, he was not daydreaming about leaving the farm; he was watching the sky, and he was impressed. His father told him a big storm was coming and he needed to bring the goats and chickens to the house so they would not be lost in torrential rains that might last for days. The danger of flash flooding from mountain runoff was great. He had chased the chickens back to the yard and herded them into the wire pen. The milk cow was tied to the front porch. His last job was to find their six goats that were grazing somewhere on the hill.

Chico knew he should take care of business, but could not keep his eyes off the swirling clouds racing across the sky. He was a veteran of many storms in his fourteen years, but this one was different. The clouds were moving faster, they were darker, and there was an odd feeling that something very powerful and sinister was coming. He was fascinated with the sensation.

Then he saw it. At first, he thought it was a bird, a moment later he knew it was an airplane, but no noise came from its engines, only the whistling sound of a large object moving through the air. The plane was unusual, not like the crop dusters the big haciendas used. It looked like the airplanes he once saw at the San Jose airport, but smaller. Its nose was down and headed straight for the big mountain behind him. As it went overhead, he ran to the top of the hill to see what it was doing. He ran as hard as possible but lost the race; the plane disappeared behind the hilltop. Nevertheless, he continued to run and when he reached the top, the plane was gone. He looked at the big mountain; its peak was three thousand meters high, and low flying clouds obscured the top third.

He was saddened that he had not been able to watch it fly around the mountain. His excitement passed and he turned away; time to catch the goats or catch hell from his father. Then he had an idea and turned back to face the mountain. Did the plane crash? He should have been able to see it before it flew into the clouds. There had been no explosion that he, for some reason, associated with a plane crash. There was no smoke, but the clouds would hide that. He had to know if it had crashed.

The goats were forgotten; he ran to his house with his news. His father, Fernando, was angry that he had not brought the goats in and that Chico had nothing else to do but fantasize about airplanes. Fernando was also angry at Chico's suggestion that they investigate. He was not going to go traipsing around the dreaded Mountain of Lost Souls.

His father grabbed Chico roughly by the shoulders and pulled him close. He looked in his son's eyes and in all sincerity said, "You are never to go to that place. I've told you this many times before. It is bad. People go there and die; they never come back. Big cats guard the spirits of the mountain. Poisonous snakes cover the forest floor; many of the vipers have never been seen by a living man. All the animals on that mountain are vicious. Even the plants that grow there are poisonous. Now, do not waste time with this foolish talk. There is much work to do."

His mother backed up every word of Fernando's advice; she was terrified of the mountain. Chico's little sisters cried at the thought that their big brother was going to the evil jungle mountain.

The short discussion of Chico going to the mountain ended with a hard slap to his face from his father. His father spoke very little because he did not like to waste time talking and used the slaps to end disagreements or potential arguments.

The boy held back his tears until he was out of the house and away from the family. Then he cried. The blow to his face did not make him cry; it was not that hard, and he had grown up being slapped. Chico cried because he wanted to do something different, do anything but be a farm boy. He wanted adventure and fun, but there was only work. He could not go to school most of the time, because there was too much work to do, and without his help, his father could not feed the family.

By the time Chico found the goats, the rain fell heavily. Before he could reach the shelter of home, the rain turned to hail. Being pelted by pea-sized ice balls made the goats go crazy, and for once, they were not stupid; they ran full speed ahead to the house with its protective front porch. Chico was the last to reach home and was glad the hail had not been bigger. Once he had seen ice balls the size of a bird's egg that had killed all of their chickens.

Hurricane Bunny had lost a lot of its punch; winds were only sixty miles per hour and the storm's most deadly feature now was its massive size and tremendous amount of rain. Central America braced for its arrival, knowing what was in store. Rivers would swell; bridges would be washed away, mountainside villages would be destroyed by monstrous mudslides. Hundreds of families would be killed, and all agricultural interest wrecked. Economies of nations would be ruined for years to come. Hunger and homelessness would become bywords for the developing nations in the storm's path.

The United States, already burdened with relief efforts to every Caribbean nation, knew it was expected to contribute heavily in getting food, medical help, and temporary housing to the millions of Latinos. Unfortunately, the government had never faced a disaster so massive and all relief organizations were stretched thin already. Military units were in the islands to help, and more were being called up to assist the Latinos, as soon as the massive storm moved off land and hopefully into the Pacific Ocean.

Doctor Lewis at the National Hurricane Center was not too sure that was going to happen, however. His computers were showing a strong possibility that it was going to turn north and meander its way up to the shores of the southern states on the Gulf of Mexico. Bunny the Beast had stopped killing with her wind, but still had a cauldron of other deadly forces.

Sometimes driving horizontally, sometimes pounding vertically, the rain seemed it would never stop. Hail had come, gone, and come again for days. Ice balls, some the size of grapefruits, had battered the countryside and badly dented the Comanchos' tin roof. It sounded like cannon fire with every impact, and made Chico's little sisters cry. The rice crop was destroyed, and the squash field smashed into small pieces of yellow mush. The hectare planted with the gringo's kenaf seed stock was demolished. Hail stripped every leaf and broke every stalk of the once lush, twelve-foot plants. The seed crop would have provided money that wasn't needed elsewhere.

The Comancho family was now destitute; they had no food other than what had been in the house, no money other than 300 colonies, about a dollar in U.S. currency; and they were luckier than most. They still had their house, goats, chickens, and milk cow. They would not starve, but would have to eat the family pets. Fernando, like most men in the valley, kept goats for emergency use at times like this. The children would not like it, but they would eat.

It had been five days of hard rain since Chico had seen the airplane, but during Bunny's water barrage, there had not been a waking moment that he did not think about the plane. He knew he was going to see if it had crashed, but he did not know how to do it. The only way was to run away for a few days and that meant he needed to take food. To steal food from his family under their present conditions was unthinkable; he would have to fend for himself. He had his knife; he could kill something to eat in the forest, he reasoned. All he needed was a few of his mother's matches, and those she would not miss.

He understood that he was about to embark on a dangerous undertaking, but was more afraid of coming home after disobeying his father than he was of the mountain's reputation. He had convinced himself that if he did find the plane, he would bring something of value back from the wreckage. Then all would be forgiven. Besides, his father could not do anything to the fields until they dried, and there were no seeds to plant, and no money to buy seeds for watermelons, which were to be planted after the squash harvest. Maybe his father could borrow money from the man at the big hacienda again. Still, it would be days before any fieldwork was possible.

He was about to take his first vacation and would return as a hero, the only boy who had gone to the mountain and returned. The mountain and the plane were exactly what the teenager needed. His hormones were screaming for excitement, for action. Nature was in control and making him respond to her insistence that he become a man.

Before dawn on the sixth day, Chico wrapped a handful of the big strike-anywhere matches in a well-used piece of tinfoil, put them in his pocket and slipped out of the house. Normally his mother and father would be up at that hour, but they, too, were taking a vacation. He worried that his mother would be sad at losing the foil, but Chico knew she would forgive him; she loved him best of the kids.

He walked in a straight line to the mountain; his path took him up and down several hills that sugar cane was usually planted on, but fortunately, for the farmer, it had been left bare with only grass growing to give the soil a rest. He also had to cross three miles of flooded rice fields and the going was soggy. By noon, he stood at the base of the mountain's forest. Land at this point was too steep for planting. He found a stout walking stick to help with the walk and to use against the snakes and cats.

The boy wanted to stop and think about what and where he was about to enter, but did not because he knew that if he did, fear of the unknown and the mountain's reputation would win. He forced himself to continue. It was not long before he began to think that he had erred in judgment. The trees and brush kept getting thicker as he climbed. It was no longer a forest; it was a jungle. Huge plants concealed the ground and the creatures that crawled or slithered on it. He thought about the snakes with each step. Howler monkeys in the trees continually hooted as he made his way from one pod of monkeys to the next. There were other sounds, too; most of them he had never heard before. It was more excitement than he wanted, but he refused to admit that he was afraid.

He walked the way his father had taught him when in dense crops, by stomping the ground every few steps to give the snakes plenty of warning that something was coming. Hopefully, they would get out of his way. His knife was out and at the ready should anything pop its ugly head out of the dense jungle. He sang a song he liked, to make sure the bigger wild animals would not be surprised, too. To wake a sleeping jaguar would mean a horrible death.

When the afternoon's light began to fade, he realized that he was hungry, and wondered where he would sleep. He knew the big cats prowled for food during the night, and had heard that they would not attack a grown man for food, but a fourteen-year-old boy might be just right.

By nightfall, he had proven to himself just how stupid he had been by not listening to his father. The jungle was indeed a scary place. He looked for some place to hide, but there was none other than the treetops. He selected a tree that had no flowers, which meant no monkeys. Chico had always been afraid of the big, white-testicular males that delighted in proving their masculinity by tossing other males out of treetops.

As long as Chico was the first monkey in the tree and there were no delicious flowers to eat, he should be safe from the aggressive males. He used vines and broken tree limbs to build a nest high up in a tree. When complete, he began to realize just how hungry he really was; he was starving, but a safe place to hide was more important than a happy belly. He was not as afraid after he settled into his nest and accepted hunger as a temporary discomfort.

The boy dozed off, but was suddenly awakened by the dreaded roar of a big cat. His brief feeling of security vanished when more big cats announced to the jungle's inhabits that they were awake and hungry. Several calls of the feared jaguar and his cousins came from all around him. He was very still, trying to be invisible to the cat's sensitive ears, nose, and night-eyes. So were the howler monkeys and birds. Only thousands of surround-sound frogs did not care, and continuously created a racket of high and low-pitched croaking throughout the night.

He had plenty of time to think in his world of darkness and knew his name would be added to the others who had been foolish enough to enter the jungle world of the Mountain of Lost Souls. He did not sleep, as every noise he heard from the jungle floor made his imagination soar. He was sure he could hear the claws of a cat climbing up to him, but it probably was not any more than a bird flittering. Every sound was a nightmare.

Chico also had regrets about running away; his parents would know that he went to the mountain and would be worried. His mother would be crying, his sisters, too; they cried at everything. His father would be mad enough to come after him, but he would not; he was too afraid of the mountain. As he sat alone in the tree, he would have been very happy to let his father beat him for causing them so much trouble. He prayed that everyone was wrong about the mountain, and promised that he would run home at first light.

As early morning light began to brighten, he closed his burning eyelids and fell into a deep sleep. When he awoke, the sun was a quarter of the way up and he was sore from sitting on the branches and vines. He felt rested, felt good, and almost invincible. He had spent a night in the mountain's jungle and survived. Last night's terror had vanished from his memory. His promises to return home if he made it through the night were buried under the bravado he enjoyed.

Hunger took control of his thoughts. He looked for frogs first, since there had been millions last night. Frog legs would have been good for breakfast. Strangely, none could be found. He was getting hungry enough to stick his knife into one of the white-balled howler males if given a chance. While slowly moving a large elephant-ear leaf, he found a sleeping iguana. He struck quickly as iguanas are incredibly quick when threatened. His knife caught it in the tail. The two-foot lizard turned and attacked the knife and the hand that held it. That was too bad for the lizard. Chico grabbed its neck and easily broke it. Iguana tail was one of his favorites but he did not eat them often, as they are difficult to catch in the open fields of the farmland.

Cooked over a small wood fire, the lizard was delicious. After eating, Chico felt great and thought about going back, but the challenge and his successes were more powerful. He had to go a little further; he had to bring something of value back to prove he had gone into the jungle. Ideally, he would bring back money since the dead people in the plane would surely have been rich. Being dead, it would be okay for him to take it. That would make his mother so happy, it made his venture and risk worth continuing.

Jerome Savage was nervously pacing the bedroom floor in his suite aboard the *Gypsy Princess*. "Where the hell are they?" he angrily asked.

Abby, concerned over her husband's attitude, said, "You have to settle down, Jerome. Maybe they were killed in the storm. It's been a week since the storm passed and Grady or Bill would've contacted you by now."

"Bullshit, his plane landed and it left with three people on board: The pilot, his brother, and one other American who had been rescued at sea. His brother, ha! He doesn't have a brother. It was that fucking Grady. He was seen driving a Jeep with his brother and later the military found a murdered soldier who was responsible for that vehicle."

Abby was shocked. "You're suggesting Bill or Grady murdered that soldier?"

"That's what the military thinks, and they have a worldwide warrant out for the plane and Bill."

"Maybe that's why you haven't heard from them. They may be in jail."

"If so, I would've been the first person they called. No, they've got that fucking treasure. I know it, and it has to be a whopper if it made Grady and

Bill take off. They don't want to give us our share and that means they're trying to fuck me, Abby—and nobody fucks Jerome Savage!"

"Oh, all you guys are alike," and she lowered her voice to mimic his, "Nobody fucks me. Nobody fucks me. Nobody fucks me." She returned to her normal voice, "You're just a bunch of chest thumpers. So he split with the treasure, big deal! He stayed there and faced the hurricane...we didn't. We left as fast as we could and have been thoroughly enjoying ourselves. We have more money than we can ever spend and can do anything we want. Jerome, your damn brooding is driving me nuts."

"It's driving me nuts, too. I'm going to show those pricks not to fuck with me. I've called my contacts and put the word out to find the bastard. Now I have to go to St. Thomas and find someone who knows where they went. I'll have those pricks and the treasure in a week, two at the most. Nobody fucks Jerome Savage."

"Do what you want; just leave me out of it; I'm staying on board. If you want to run off sniffing for your best friend, then go ahead. But you had better remember one thing. I'm rich, beautiful, and I'm definitely high maintenance. Don't be gone too long if you don't want to lose the best thing that ever came into your life."

"After I find the bastards, I'll make it up to you. We'll jump off this tub and go to our place in Buru for a couple of weeks. That place always zones me out, and that's what I need right now. That damn Grady has me all screwed up. I trusted the bastard. I'll bet they're sitting around that dumpy bar they hang out in, spending my money and bragging about how they fucked Jerome Savage."

"Jerome! Lighten up. ...I'm not kidding. It never was your money, never was your treasure, and those other guys don't even know you. Damn it! Get a hold of yourself!"

Villages in the north of Costa Rica took an awful hit from Bunny. Mudslides killed too many people; tornadoes killed many more. Most homes and businesses were destroyed or badly damaged in the stormy days of Bunny. Everyone was affected; people wandered about in a daze without eating, or caring for their wounds, and unaware of anything other than they had been visited by the devil herself. They picked through the remains of their homes, if there were any, trying to get their lives back. It was a sad sight for the Red Cross crews who were starting to make contact with each village by helicopter. Road travel was impossible.

Mary Carter had volunteered her services as a doctor aboard one of the Air Force helicopters. Looking out at the barren wasteland as they landed at the first village, her eyes watered with sadness and at the horror of the damage.

The helicopter sat down in the middle of what had been a small school's playground. A herd of zombies walked slowly to the helicopter, each hoping for help. Unfortunately, no help other than medical would be available that day. Emergency supplies were still a day or two away.

Two hours later, she and her team had patched up the most serious injuries, but more continued to straggle in as word got out to the outer areas of the small community. She asked one man wearing tattered clothes what his name was, but got no response. A man nearby said, "He's Tonto; don't bother with him."

She spoke Spanish well enough to do her job, but was not aware that tonto meant foolish. She laughed, thinking it was the Lone Ranger's friend.

She said, "Well, Señor Tonto, we'll get you fixed up in a jiffy. My, my, it looks like you've been through a rough time. You're covered with cuts and nasty bruises." Looking at a blue-back and purple mass on his chest, she asked, "What happened to you?"

"Don't know, just woke up hurting."

"Were you in your house? Is your family all right?"

"Don't know. I was in the woods."

"Do you have a family?"

"Don't know?"

"How old are you?"

"Don't know."

The man who identified Tonto came over and said. "He doesn't have anybody, Doctor. He is just a crazy man. The village to the north had a crazy man hanging around for a few months. This has to be him. I think he must have wandered into the woods between our villages."

"Can you take him back to the village?"

"Maybe you should take him to San Jose and put him in jail. He's just going to get in trouble since there's a food shortage. People won't be so willing to feed him anymore."

The doctor looked into Tonto's eyes and said, "He doesn't look crazy."

"Maybe not, but he acts crazy; and that's what being crazy is all about. He's stupid. He doesn't know anything. I tried to talk to him, but he knows nothing."

Doctor Carter asked the man to bring Tonto back the next day when she would return. He made no promises and reminded her of everyone's present concerns for drinking water and food. The following day, she returned to find that Señor Tonto was nowhere in sight. He was only one of the mass of people wandering about, trying to find themselves.

2

The Wreckage

THE JUNGLE WAS AN EXTREMELY MISERABLE PLACE during Chico's second night. The breeze that had blown the previous night and day had vanished at sundown; the rain fell straight down and hard at first, and then slowed to a drizzle that continued. Along with the dark and drizzle came the mosquitoes. He could not believe how bad the bugs were, even in his new treetop nest. He could only slap, swat and complain about the continual attacks.

Finally, he could stand it no longer and he lowered himself to the dark and violent jungle floor only to find that the bugs were worse. He quickly dug into the mud he stood on and smeared handfuls of it over his body. The cool cake felt good on his welted skin. The bugs would not be able to bite him through the mud; unfortunately, the drizzle kept washing it away. To climb back to his lofty safe-haven would be a waste of time; he would have to keep returning to his mud supply.

He sat down, put his back against a tree, smeared more mud over himself, and then sat very still. It was a gradual realization that something was very different, and he then realized that the jungle around him was completely quiet other than the rustling of leaves caused by light rain and the buzzing mosquitoes. What had happened to the noisy frogs?

Chico found out why everything went quiet when a loud roar came from behind his tree. It scared him so bad that he yelled, and his fourteen year-old lungs had plenty of power. His scream was so loud and foreign to the jungle creatures that it scared whatever had roared, and it ran off. Chico could hear it crashing through the brush; it sounded big.

The frogs came back and he felt secure with their noise that had only irritated him before. He had learned a couple of valuable lessons. His self-pity of only moments ago vanished and he was proud of himself, as an inner strength began to grow within. He was gaining confidence.

Later, Chico slowly opened his eyes and jumped from fright when he realized that he had slept on the jungle floor. Dim early morning light was finding its way through the dense, wet jungle. Like the previous morning, his promises to return home were pushed aside with thoughts that he would work his way up a little higher before turning back.

The going was getting rougher as the terrain slowly turned rockier. Rocks turned into boulders and rock walls, which meant fewer trees. Mostly he had to crawl up on the steep 45-degree angle. An hour into his morning climb he found himself in the clouds. The jungle was no longer lush green; it was light green, the air was gray. It was an eerie sensation, and another first for Chico. He had walked in the clouds.

Visibility was greatly reduced and he did not know how he would find the big rock outcropping near where the plane should be. His plan was to climb straight up the slope to the top, and, on his return, he would come down at an angle so he would not cover the same territory.

His sense of time vanished in near whiteout conditions. He just kept working his way up, praying the steep angle would level off and then start going down again. He was determined not to turn back, and the airplane was no longer his sole motivation. The sections of dense jungle were fewer, as were the big vertical rocks. The angle seemed to be less and he realized that without the tilt of the land in the reduced visibility, it would be easy to become hopelessly lost. Maybe that was what had happened to all of those other people. They never returned as they became lost in the cloud forest.

Chico was afraid, but refused to let his fear guide him. He constantly thought there might be a fearsome creature just out of sight and behind the white curtain of visibility. Fear and uncertainty about snakes, big cats, being alone, getting lost, and what would happen if he found the plane full of dead people constantly swept over him. He was terribly afraid of dead people, although he had never seen one.

The land kept getting flatter, which made it easier to make his way through trees that had been there for hundreds of years. If trees could sense things, they would know they were being visited by a different kind of monkey, one previously unknown by the jungle.

He began sensing something new, too. It was a good feeling; then he realized for the first time he was tasting freedom, and he liked it. The jungle was his private world. He belonged there. It was beautiful and he could do as he pleased. No one would scold him, laugh at his foolishness or slap him. He was in control of his life, but he was still cautious, except it was different; he felt secure knowing he was an important part of nature.

Suddenly he stepped on something that did not belong in his forest. It rocked under his feet and made him fall face first into the wet ferns covering the ground. It scared him at first, thinking he had stepped on a big snake, but quickly realized it was not a snake; it was too hard. He used his walking stick to part the ferns enough to see that it was a shiny piece of metal. Then he wondered what it was, how it got there. *Could it be part of the airplane?* He continued and a minute later found a bigger piece of the same metal but this one was almost a meter long and had lines of rivets in it. For some reason he labored to carry both pieces with him.

He came to a ravine in the land and through the fog's whiteness could make out a foreign-looking object on the other side. The ravine was deep; its walls muddy from days of rain and constant drizzle. He slid down to the running stream that only a day or two ago must have been a rushing torrent of rainwater run-off. Cautiously, he waded across in the waist-deep muddy water, his feet slipping several times on the unseen and slimy stones. His progress stopped when he ran into another metal object under water; it was too heavy to move and the water too muddy to see through, so he left it, as his hands were full anyway.

Going up the other side's muddy slope was not as easy. After an exhausting struggle to gain the top, he stood and could not believe what he saw. What had looked like a strange object in the fog turned out to be broken trees; some were knocked over. He followed the trail of broken trees wondering what was big enough to do that kind of damage, and then remembered the tornadoes. He stopped when he saw a shiny long object in a tree. It was part of a wing. Then there was another wing. He had found the airplane and it had broken the trees when it crashed. He was elated.

Pieces were scattered everywhere and his elation faded to dread; he was afraid of stumbling over a dead body, or part of one under the thick growth of ferns. With every step, he had his walking stick in front like a blind person, feeling for dead people and snakes. He found more pieces of twisted and torn metal, seat fabric, and headliner. At one place, he found a long chain and knew he was saved; he had found something of value to take back to his father. It would be hard to drag the heavy chain, but his father would be so pleased that there was no way he would go back without it. Unless he found something better.

When he found one of the jet engines, he stopped for the longest time and stared; he had never seen one before. He had to touch all of its bent and broken parts. He wished he could take that home too. Maybe his father could figure out how to work it. It would certainly be valuable to the big haciendas; his father could sell it. Maybe he would get some help and come back for it. Then he had a thought that pleased him: *I will not be able to find anyone brave enough to come to the top of the Mountain of Lost Souls. I'm the only one. This is my place.*

The next big piece he found was the tail section. It was intact but torn off the fuselage. Nothing was inside but torn headliner hanging down eerily from the rumpled ceiling. He was happy no dead bodies were inside and did not look under the fern mat. The rest of the fuselage was lying against a big tree at a near vertical angle. Its front end was flat, the windows broken out. The rear end had been torn off; jagged edges formed a threatening mouth-like hole that rested on the ground.

Chico hesitated before getting down on his knees to look inside. He knew that was where the dead people were. He called out, "Anyone in there? Hello! Is anyone in there?"

The mountain's silence seemed heavy in the fog; it was the sound of death, and the multitude of birds and frogs that were so noisy not long ago seemed to have vanished.

The wind was not blowing; nothing moved, as if time stood still. This was the place for lost souls. Fear was winning. Chico began backing away from the area; he did not take his eyes off the jagged mouth of the dead airplane. He wanted to run, but that would mean that he would have to turn his back to the place of the dead, and then the spirits would know that he was afraid and grab him from behind. Then he remembered the money that might be inside. He still did not want to go in that place, but times were going to be very hard for his family until they could work the land, plant more crops, and finally get a harvest.

He had no choice; he had to go inside, but he wasn't in a hurry. He walked all the way around the fuselage looking for a single good reason not to go in. After a while, it was time; he got down on the ground and crawled to the edge of the jagged opening. He felt something in the ferns but did not look at it. Inside it was dark; the only light came from the smashed cockpit and the portholes. He fought against turning back, as doing so would mean that he would not stop running until he fell, exhausted and far, far away from the place of lost souls.

"I don't give a shit if the fucking airport is closed. Find a way to get me to Martinique and St. Thomas today. I don't want any excuses, Jackson, you hear me?"

Jerome was on a roll. Abby had flown to New York to visit her mother, which freed him to get everything in motion. She was pissed at his attitude over Grady but he did not care. She had no idea what it took to be successful when working with the type of people who were in his business. Loyalty did not exist; trust was laughable, everybody waited for any opportunity to fuck the next guy.

He had already wired the photograph that Grady had given him of Pete's boat to his contacts along the coast of South and North America, including Panama. Central America and most of the Caribbean would have to wait for telephone service to resume. He had instructed a contact in Washington D.C., who worked for Immigration, to run checks on Pete Morgan, Tom Roscoe, William Rainer, and Grady Fisher. He wanted to know everything about them and especially their next of kin. He would have people watching the families, and soon would have the amateurs in his grasp. Grady would be another matter; he had no family, but it would be interesting to see if they could find anything he did not already know.

Ten minutes later, Jackson called back. He had made arrangements for a seaplane chartered in Trinidad, to take him to the east end of St. Thomas. Jackson would meet the seaplane with his high-speed Donzi that he'd have to drive from St. Croix, where he lived.

Jackson Julian, besides having a backward name, was a sharp operator. He was Jerome's administrative assistant. He knew the business in general, and many of Jerome's key men, but had no idea how the operation actually worked.

His main job was to control the complicated banking procedures, a job he did well.

He met the seaplane as it landed near St. Thomas's shit-brown and devastated countryside. As Jerome boarded the boat, he asked, "So, if St. Croix looks like St. Thomas and the rest of the islands I flew over, how did your boat make it? I didn't see a single boat afloat in the harbors."

"It was on a trailer at my house. I live in a small valley between the mountains. I didn't get the full effect of the hurricane. My house is still standing, too, but not many made it. The island is a mess."

Jackson knew Jerome had a major hard-on for Grady, but not why, and anyone who creates problems for Jerome is usually on the short-timers' list.

He asked, "With all due respect, may I ask what the problem is?"

"The cocksucker is trying to fuck me."

"What happened?"

"He's trying to fuck me. That conniving bastard is trying to go into business for himself. Grady was waiting for a storm like this. It's the perfect time to pull it off. With communications restricted to satellite phone use only, he can make his moves without me finding out, until it's too late. The treasure gives him the cash to make a big difference in his relationship with a supplier, which better not be Ortega."

"What treasure?"

"The lying bastard invited me to help him take a buried treasure away from some people he knew. He set it up so the timing would put us in danger of the storm. He knew Abby wouldn't stay, so I wouldn't either. And all of that just gave him an excellent excuse to break off our usual week-long meeting."

"So the treasure was bogus?"

"I'm not sure. It could've been a setup to kill me and blame the storm, but my instincts tell me it was real. That's one of the things we'll be checking on. Grady has money, but it's dispersed into real estate, stocks, anything of value other than the burden of heavy cash. But for him to buy trust with the growers and producers, you gotta have a big wad of cash, Jackson, and that's exactly what buried treasure offers. It is completely untraceable. It's perfect."

Jackson looked at Jerome before giving the twin 400 horsepower engines full throttle. He said, "I can't believe Grady would do that to you. Me, sure, he'd fuck me over in a heartbeat, but not you, you're his friend."

"Let me tell you something about how Grady treats his friends. We were in Leavenworth together for seven years; I know the man. I know he personally killed three guys because I watched him do it. He blamed the first one on the cellmate he had for a few years. He was a nice guy with only three years to go. Thanks to Grady, he moved up to lifer. The second one he rigged to look like the prison's head black guy, a Muslim doing time for running major drugs, did it. He picked up a life term, too. The black population knew it was a setup, but could never figure out who did it. I should have told them, damn it. We wouldn't be having this conversation right now. I'd be aboard the *Snow Eagle* with my wife.

"The third murder was a misguided homo-boy who had the hots for him. The kid worshiped Grady. It was funny watching Grady try to stay away from him; the kid just wouldn't quit. Finally, Grady grabbed him by the throat one day in front of the cellblock population. He held him off the ground and fucking strangled him with his bare hands, and then threw his body off the third floor tier. The guards never found out who did it. Everyone was too afraid of Grady to rat him out. Damn, I should have told them about that one, too. That's just the murders I witnessed. There's no telling how many lifers he gave an early out to."

"I didn't know Grady was gay. So he killed his lover."

"Most everyone is a little gay in long-term slammers. Grady was only on the receiving end—he wasn't queer. He wasn't a lover either. The kid didn't have to die; all Grady had to do was tell him what would happen if he didn't get out of his face."

"What was he in the slam for?"

"That's another good example of what he'll do to his friends. He was stealing munitions from the Army and then selling them to the terrorists who'd use them to blow the shit out of our troops."

"With him there?"

"Shit, no. He had blackmailed the base commander, a fucking general. The general kept him in headquarters as a quartermaster auditor. The bastard had a license to steal; and he did."

"No shit. Had no idea he was such a bad ass. Who are we looking for on St. Thomas besides Grady. I might know them."

"Pete Morgan and Tom Roscoe."

"Would that be Salvage Tom?"

"Don't know, but we'll find out pretty damn soon." Jerome was tired of all the conversation. He wanted action, wanted to kill somebody, which is a trait he managed to hide successfully from Abby. He had never accepted defeat in anything, or tolerated anyone putting pressure on him. When it happened, somebody got dead in a hurry. A prison shrink had diagnosed Jerome as having ZPS, Zero Patience Syndrome.

He motioned for Jackson to speed up; he was in a hurry.

Chico said aloud, "Remember your bravery for the last couple of days. You're not going to let a dark place scare you away from what brought you here." He scampered in and let his eyes adjust to the dim light. Soon he could see. There had been a fire; everything inside was charred. All the seats were empty, some had been torn out; a few were still attached to the near-vertical floor. He felt both relief and unhappiness; it would have been nice to take money home and he knew that he would have to look around the broken tree path to find the bodies. At least they would be outside in the light. He had to pull himself up from seat to seat to the front of the airplane to see if the pilots were still there. As with the rest of the plane, the compartment was empty. He was fascinated with all of the gauges, levers, and switches. He would have loved to sit in the seat and play, but he did not want to stay in there any longer than necessary. He lowered himself to the dirt and scurried out into the light, only to be stopped by shear horror.

Father Death was gazing at him from under a thick fold of ferns. He screamed as he had done when the cat had scared him, and raised his head with a jerk. He hit the opening's jagged edge, which made a three-inch cut in his scalp, and knocked him unconscious.

Not much had improved in the isolated Costa Rican villages. Just before dark, a helicopter hovered ten feet over one small community; a military crew threw boxes of food out of cargo doors like a high-tech farmer feeding cattle. Five-gallon water jugs were lowered with short lengths of rope. The pilot knew how desperate the people were and refused to land his machine; the people would swarm them and the strongest would take everything not bolted down, including their fuel and possibly their clothes. Many of the starving victims were nearly naked. They fought among themselves over the food and water, and then huddled in their own small groups to protect what they had taken. It was a survival situation, and each was doing what he or she felt must be done to preserve life. Those who had—had; those who didn't have—wouldn't have.

Tonto was one of those who didn't, and he was hungry. Thirst was not a problem; he did not know better than to drink the muddy water in puddles that were everywhere. He went to one group of six; three were little dirty-faced children. At their mother's command, they threw rocks at him to keep him away. The next group he came to did the same. Everyone called him names and acted as if they hated him. He wished he could find that nice woman in the white coat; she had cared. He finally quit bothering people and found a thick brush to crawl under for the night. It felt so good to sleep; his head did not hurt then, and his stomach did not hurt from being hungry. He wished he could sleep forever.

After a night lost to dreams of food, sunny skies, and friendly phantoms, Tonto crawled out from under the bush, and then relieved himself on it. Women and men from a group saw him and angrily yelled at him. He did not think he had done anything wrong; he just went to the bathroom. Everybody has to go sometime. A few minutes later, four men came over; one of them had a big chunk of hard bread in his hands. The other men held rocks, and none of them looked friendly.

The man with the bread said, "Hey, Tonto. I'm going to give you this bread, but you have to take it away from here before you can eat it. Do you understand?"

"You mean you want me to go away before I eat the bread?"

"That's right. You have to go very far away. You have to go so far away that you can never come back to this place. Do you understand?"

"You want me to stay away forever."

"Yes. And if you ever come back, then we will feed you these," and the men held out their rocks. "Do you understand?"

"He laughed at the man, and then said, "You can't eat rocks."

"You will, and you'll die. We will stone you to death. Do you understand?"

"You will kill Tonto if he ever comes back here?"

"Yes. Now take this bread and run as fast as you can." Tonto understood. He grabbed the bread and ran as hard as his bruised and aching legs would carry him.

Having worked in four villages that day, Doctor Mary Carter was exhausted. The image of the poor man, Tonto, haunted her. She had looked for him in each village but only saw more lost men and women who had their own problems. It was sad seeing people forced to live that way. At home in Minneapolis, that could never happen. Tonto needed to be institutionalized; someone needed to provide for his needs. It was not his fault that his brain was incapable of operating normally.

Chico awoke. Sunlight was fading and darkness was only minutes away. He did not know what had happened, or where he was, but his head hurt. He reached up to feel it. His hair was matted; he thought it was mud. When he pulled his hand down, he saw it was blood and was horrified. He felt the stickiness on his face; it was the same. Then he remembered the horrifying lost soul that attacked him. He jerked his head around to look. It was still there. He tensed, waiting for another attack. The skull was smiling at him. He thought the spirit was happy because it had killed him, and that made him angry.

He scrambled out of the fuselage and ran away from the airplane before stopping at the edge of the meadow. Chico felt his skin, he was warm; he heard his heart beating, his lungs were heaving for air and he knew he was still alive. The thing had hit him but it didn't kill him. He quickly turned around to see if the dead soul was following. Then he cautiously walked back, being sure to look all around him in case it was sneaking up on him.

After reaching the airplane, he carefully stretched out, as if he were going to pick up a rattlesnake, and probed the ferns. He gently grasped a fern and very slowly pulled on it. It opened enough so he could see the skull was still there. He nudged it with his foot; it did not attack. He nudged it again, but harder. It moved wherever his foot pushed it. He smiled with relief. "You're not a lost soul."

He had never seen a human skull before. He picked it up, and then he laughed at his foolishness of being afraid. He stopped laughing at a thought: *What happened to my head, the blood? Oh ... bumped my head when I saw the skull.* He laughed at himself again. Chico examined it with intense curiosity and wondered who it was, then realized it had to be the pilot, the only one aboard. The fire had burned his skin off. He looked around for the rest of his bones, but saw none. "The animals must have eaten him." He smiled and said, "I'm taking this back. It'll scare my sisters and friends for sure. And prove I found the plane." He laughed at another thought: *I'll tell Father this is one of the lost souls. He'll be scared. I'll say that he came back with me with to protect me from harm. There'll be no more slapping.*

He looked for more bones or bodies under the ferns, and for the first time, he was not afraid of what he might find. Before darkness arrived, he ended his search for bones to find something to eat. The closest thing he found to food was a bottle of whiskey. He couldn't read the label; it was in English, but recognized one word, Virgin. He thought it might be holy water and smelled it, then threw the smelly stuff away.

Unsuccessful at finding food, the boy crawled into the airplane's aft section. He tore off some the dangling fabric for a blanket, curled up and went to sleep. Morning came much sooner than the two previous mornings. He had slept all night. Even the mosquitoes were not bad. He preferred to reason it was because there must be a type of plant, maybe the ferns repelled them, instead of the idea that he was in the land of the dead.

He took another look around the area but only found torn up junk: seats, sections of metal, a smashed old wooden box, a magazine, a toothbrush, broken glass, a wheel, and small pieces of cloth. His stomach put an end to the treasure search and he started looking for something to kill; he was starving. He gathered up several small pieces of metal that he could throw at birds or bunnies, but he seemed to be the only living thing in the meadow.

Young Chico sat down to contemplate why there were no mosquitoes or animals. At that altitude, the storm must have been really bad. The wind would have blown everything out of the trees; the rain would have drowned everything on the ground and washed their bodies down the mountain through the ravine. That gave him an idea; he would use the ravine to go home and would not have to go through the jungle. It would be easier, and when he came back, he could follow the creek to the airplane. That was good because he did not have any idea how to find the place again. He also thought it might be easier to find food along the creek.

He looked around, and muttered, "Good thing my father wouldn't let me come up here when I wanted to." He grabbed the skull he had named Señor Smiley, and walked to the ravine. He followed it downstream, and it was not easy walking, but was a lot better than the jungle, and he felt much safer.

3

The Good Doctor

DOCTOR CARTER WAS WEARY, BUT FELT SHE WAS catching up with the injuries heaped upon the population. If they could get more food and water, everyone's health would improve; but that would take time. It was even difficult to get medical supplies, as the demand for everything was so great throughout the tropics. Soon it might be worse; Bunny, which had only been a tropical storm when it visited Central America, had moved north, was approaching the Gulf of Mexico, and was a giant hurricane again. She could not understand why God would let a killer storm like Bunny exist.

Only three people were left to treat, then she would be off to the next village. As her next patient sat down at the folding table next to the helicopter, she noticed a shy man in the shadow of a small tree. It was Tonto. She asked the boy she had just treated to go tell the man she wanted to talk to him. The boy brought him to her, much to the annoyance of the woman being treated.

The woman snapped, "Finish me first, so I can get out of here. I don't want to be around that crazy no-good. You should have the police take him to jail. He steals food."

"Well, has anyone been giving him something to eat?"

"Who wants to waste food on him? We have our own families to worry about and there isn't enough food to go around. Besides, he drinks dirty rainwater; the sickness will kill him soon anyway."

Doc Mary excused herself from the uncharitable woman and took Tonto's hand. She led him into the helicopter, told him to sit on a bench, and asked, "Are you hungry?"

"Yes ma'am. Real hungry."

"What have you eaten today?"

"Nothing, but I had a piece of bread yesterday."

She suddenly realized that she was speaking English, and Tonto was responding in Spanish. He understood. She opened the ice chest onboard and found a bag with a turkey sandwich and four olives. She gave the food and a quart bottle of water to him.

"These are for you. You must stop drinking the water from the puddles; it will make you sick. You come back here tomorrow and I'll give you more food and water."

He could only shake his head and mumble, his mouth was crammed full. He didn't eat the sandwich; he attacked it. She wanted to laugh, but felt she should cry at seeing such hunger. She said, "Señor Tonto, people are saying that you are stealing their food. You don't have to do that anymore. I will feed you every day if you will come see me. Okay?"

"I don't steal food. I've been real hungry, but I never stole anything to eat. People will not let me get close to the food; they always chase me away by hitting me with rocks. No ma'am, I never steal anything."

I believe you, Señor Tonto. You just leave those people alone and come see me. Can you speak English?"

"Don't think so."

"I'm talking to you in English and you understand me. I bet you can; try it."

He looked very confused. He asked, in Spanish, "What do you want me to say?" She handed him a sheet of paper, which were instructions on how to operate the portable blood analyst machine. He read it aloud.

"You do know how to speak English and very well, I might add. Those were some hard words you spoke. You sound like you're an American. Did you live in America?"

"No. Don't think so," he said in English.

"You don't think so? You can't remember?"

"No ma'am. I don't know what happened before the storm."

"I'll be dammed. I knew something was wrong. You're not stupid; you just don't have a memory. Are you sure you don't have a family?"

"Don't know."

Doctor Carter dwelled on the man's problem until the woman she had left waiting at the table yelled, "Listen, Doctor, I was here first. I have kids to take care of, and there were other decent people here before that bum came. Finish taking care of us decent folks before you start messing with the lowlifes."

Mary gave the woman a dirty look and said, "You good and decent people have been starving this man to death, and you call *him* a lowlife? You had better pray to God to forgive your sin against one of His children. This man isn't a lowlife. He isn't a thief, as you lied to me. He is just a man who has lost his memory from an injury in the storm. You should be ashamed of yourself. Now you pick up those bandages and get out of here. You can take care of yourself. I'll not help someone who can't help others." She yelled at the scowling woman, "Get out!" The stress she had been under while treating so many injured and dying people finally had found a release.

The angry woman scurried away. She was going to get her husband to chase the troublemaker out of the village. The next man who sat at the table had felt the same way, but realized he should have been more charitable.

Doctor Carter had an idea; she told Tonto to wait and went out to take care of the last two patients. Fifteen minutes later, she returned with a magic marker and rubbed the ink on one of Tonto's thumbs, then the other, and pressed them on a sheet of paper. Tonto looked at her as if she were the crazy one. She realized he did not understand. "Don't worry, the ink will wear off, it will not hurt you. I'm doing this so I can send your fingerprints to someone. They may be able to tell me if you have a family." She jokingly asked, "You're not a criminal are you?"

"Don't know."

The walk home was torturous, but quicker. It had been extremely difficult where other tributaries fed into the stream, which appeared to be the main watercourse off the mountain. When he came to a waterfall, he thought it would be impossible to continue, but after a half hour of serious mountain climbing, he was able to stay with the river.

By nightfall, he was at the mountain's base and no longer had to contend with the over forty-degree terrain. He was very tired but needed to get home, sleep in his own bed, and eat his mother's cooking. He wondered which of the goats his father had slaughtered, and that thought made him sad; they had been his playmates since he was a child.

His homecoming was better than expected. Only his mother was awake; his father had gone to bed early as he had had a hard day in the fields. However, his mother was so overjoyed to see him that she screamed with delight, which woke the rest of the household, including the chickens outside, that started cackling. With so much commotion, he was glad he had decided to leave Señor Smiley on the porch.

His father came out of the only other room in the house, the bedroom. Chico wanted to run, but stood his ground, ready to take his punishment. He was surprised when his father, with tears of happiness in his eyes, hugged him for the first time in his life. His little sisters ran out of the bedroom and hugged him at the same time.

Finally his father spoke. "Please tell me you did not go to the Mountain of Lost Souls."

"Yes I did, Father…" His mother gasped in horror, then his sisters followed mom's lead. "…but I wasn't harmed. I didn't see any ghost and I went all the way to the top and found the airplane that I saw. It crashed."

"What happened to the people?" asked his horrified mother.

Chico smiled and said, "I'll show you," and he stepped out on the porch. He came back in holding the skull behind his back. Then said, "Here he is!" and quickly held the skull in front. Every one of them screamed in fright and scattered like the chickens at butcher time. His father included.

Jackson Julian steered his way through the masts of sunken sailboats in the lagoon. A marina's docks were smashed and splintered; boats that had been tied to it were sunk, leaving only the parts sticking above the surface. Only an old weathered sailboat, and a trawler tied to broken pilings behind Dirty's Beer Joint were floating. Yachts that were out of the water before the storm all lay on their sides and were strewn about like matchsticks. Mangrove trees around the lagoon were stripped of limbs; some hung broken and held together by a piece of their fibrous bark. Like the rest of the Caribbean, it looked as if the place had been bombed.

Jackson pointed out Dirty's place. Jerome was not impressed. Grady had talked a lot about it, but it was too unrefined for Jerome's taste. A boat bum's paradise maybe, but he was no boat bum.

He was not aware that the patrons had only found the bar half-floating in the lagoon yesterday. Thirty now-homeless boat bums picked up the old hull and physically dragged it back into place, an inch at a time. Yesterday also marked a big day in the Lagoonies' lives; Dirty had managed to get his generator running on his trawler and he had the only cold beer on the island; maybe they'd even have ice next week.

Jerome examined the rickety handmade barstool to be sure it wouldn't collapse with his weight. As soon as he sat down, a three-foot iguana walked over to within inches of his foot and stared at him. He had seen iguanas before, but not that close. He was unsure if it was aggressive and intended to bite him or was just unafraid of humans.

The bartender, a dirty man in a stained T-shirt said, "Don't worry, he's just begging for a handout. Ignore him, he'll go away unless one of you sweeties aren't wearing shoes and have painted your toenails red. Red toes look like cherries to him. Now, what do you want?"

Jackson said, "Miller Lite, please."

Jerome was irritated with the ugly beast at his feet and the dirty asshole with a shitty attitude behind the bar. If he didn't need information and if the idea of having a drink wasn't so appealing, he would have left. Instead, he dismissed the bartender's attitude and ordered his favorite drink: "Old fashioned with Jack Daniel's, easy on the bitters, lots of ice, and a twist or orange slice...and three drops of Curacao on top."

The bartender bellowed with laughter. Then he looked at Jerome and said, "An old fashioned with lots of ice, a twist, and three drops of Curacao on top? What does this fucking place look like? You don't think we're a bunch of sweeties, do you? You want to drink old fashions, then get the hell out of here. You want beer or room temperature booze then you can stay, but forget the fucking ice, shithead, there ain't any. Which is it going to be, pokey?"

The crows were snickering; pokey was the islanders' word for pussy, and was not associated with cats. Jackson was noticeably uneasy; he knew about Jerome's temper in the best of times, and Jerome certainly wasn't in good times. He was dangerous. To break the tension he said, "We're not here to cause any trouble. We're just looking for Salvage Tom. You guys know where he is?"

Jerome had never been a patient man. He stood up and said, "I don't like your attitude. I'd like to take you out back for a minute and—."

Dirty interrupted him. "Why? You want to give me a fucking blow job?"

Jerome swung at him but Dirty had anticipated it and stepped back; the blow missed. Dirty smiled and said, "Hey, you bunch of crows, look at this; the pokey wants to punch me. Ain't that great!" He looked at Jerome, the smile faded. "I'm ready for a little punching, but you don't need to leave the bar to fight in my joint."

Dirty picked up his shillelagh, an old dinged-up baseball bat, and scampered around the bar. In his earlier career as a wrestler and fighter, he fought dirty, and as the bouncer for his bar, he was just as bad. He charged Jerome with the bat raised high. There was no doubt in Jerome's mind that the bartender was going to work him over with the bat, and he was not armed. Reluctantly, he retreated, but Jackson was ahead of him and moving outside. The crows watched another tourist being chased away; the attack ended as Jerome exited.

Jerome was quiet as he listened to laughter coming from the bar. He was not mad anymore, he was enraged and had decided to kill the belligerent bartender. "I need a gun. Give me yours, Jackson."

"Come on, Jerome, that asshole's not worth it. You go in there shooting, it's just going to cause trouble."

"I'm not interested in your opinions. Give me your gun."

"I don't carry one, Jerome, and for the same reason you don't. I'd be breaking parole."

That was all Jerome said about killing the man, but there was no way it was not going to happen, gun or no gun. Then he heard someone behind them say, "Hey mister, can I talk to you?"

A short redheaded man came up to them. He offered his handshake and said, "They call me Roosterman around here. I heard you say you're looking for Salvage Tom. Strangers can't come into Dirty's, ask about one of us, and expect to get an answer. Everybody around here likes privacy for one reason or another. I know Tom. Why are you guys looking for him?"

Jackson replied, "A mutual friend suggested we speak to him about his project off Martinique. We may want to purchase his find."

"Who is your friend?"

"Grady Fisher. Know him?"

"Sure. He hasn't been around since the hurricane. We thought he might've been killed in the storm. His boat bought it, big time. Is he okay?"

"We haven't seen him since the storm either. Have any idea where he could be?"

"Nope."

"How about Tom? Is he around?"

"Haven't seen him since he took off with Painter Pete. They went out on a salvage job before the storm hit. Maybe Grady went with those guys. He and Pete are pretty good buddies."

"Is there someplace those guys might have gone after the hurricane?"

"Anywhere, I guess; but I'd think Grady would have hauled ass to get back here for his boat, unless he knew it had sunk. Then they're probably down in Trinidad or Venezuela, some place not fucked up by the storm . . . . Oh, they could be in Costa Rica. Grady goes down there once in while. I think he has a cabin in the mountains."

Jerome smiled with a thought: Forgot about that. *It isn't a cabin, it's a home isolated in the mountain jungle. It'd be the perfect place to set up his new business.*

Jackson knew what Jerome was smiling about, he was going to insist on going to Costa Rica. And he would put the shit on him to make it happen. After they paid off Rooster for his information, Jackson was surprised that Jerome didn't want to bust balls to get to Costa Rica, but wanted to stay in the lagoon that night.

After Roosterman and Jerome had parted company, Rooster hurried over to Red Hook's Tent City where he checked in and stood in line to use the only telephone on that end of the island. It was a satellite phone provided by the U.S. Army, so survivors could keep in touch with families. People were allowed to call anywhere in the world, but five minutes was the cutoff time. Hanging up was not an option, the system disconnected automatically to prevent long-winded conversations.

An hour later, it was Rooster's turn. He looked up the number carried in his billfold and dialed Paris, France. A digitized voice answered; Rooster said, "This is Rooster in St. Thomas. Two men are here looking for your salvage diver, Tom. They were interested in Tom's find off Martinique. They may want to buy it."

The man standing behind Rooster said, "Come on, man. Get off de phone." Rooster ignored him, and continued. "One of the guys with Tom has a place in Costa Rica. These guys are going down there to look for him. With two of the watch words used that I'm supposed to be listening for, Martinique and treasure, I thought it related to your idea that Tom might be coming into a lot of money. The fancy dressers from off-island might be buyers for your property."

A woman standing further down the line, yelled. "Damn it! Get off the phone you long-winded little bastard! I got to call my kids!"

Rooster continued. "This is still the only telephone I can use. I'll call back in the morning, Monsieur Beloit, to see if you have any further instructions. Your investment in paying me to keep an eye on Tom may be paying off."

Jerome had other plans that could not happen until the dumpy little bar closed. They went back to Jackson's boat. It's bow had been pulled on shore so they didn't have to wade.

Jerome turned on his satellite phone and got through to Smith at Immigration in Washington. The name of Pete Morgan did not match anyone with his description in the FBI's files. Fingerprints were needed. He learned that Tom was a wounded war hero, a graduate of MIT, and divorced. His ex-wife was hostile and had filed papers to make him stay away, so there was little chance he would go there. Both parents were dead and there were no other names in the files.

Grady's trail had ended when he was released from Leavenworth. No family was listed.

Jerome had to smile at the news that Pete Morgan was not whom he said he was. That meant he was probably on the run, another positive element that he was in cahoots with Grady. Tom Roscoe, however, was a puzzle. Why would a man with his education be a sleazy boat bum in some Caribbean saltwater swamp? Was it all a cover? Had the three of them been working their own deal all along? It made a perfect team: Grady's larcenous mind, Pete's criminal talents, whatever they were, and a very educated man camouflaged as a bum.

As night flooded the remains of St. Thomas, the island was very dark. Only houses with enough left standing to house their owners, and those with generators and fuel to run them, had lights. The six o'clock curfew was in effect and was taken very seriously by everyone. Only those with intentions to steal were on the streets.

Small communities formed their own security teams that stood guard at night against the few roving bands of human scum who stole food, fuel, and money from Bunny's survivors. There were no security teams guarding the boatyard, however.

Most of the Lagoonies had no place to go, but refused to move to the military tents set up on each side of the island. Instead, they found corrugated tin sections that had once been someone's roof, or canvas that had once been someone's sail, and built their own shelters. They were scattered around the boatyard. Some guys used turned-over and wrecked boats as their shelter; they were survivors who were fiercely independent and self-sufficient. Their only luxury was their common living room: Dirty's bar.

After closing time at Dirty's, and when the one light that hung in the bar shut off, Jerome said, "Stay here, Jackson. I'll be right back."

Jackson had noticed that Jerome's attention had constantly been drawn to Dirty's, and knew Jerome was not going to give it up until he had satisfaction. Jerome had Jackson's eight-inch diver's knife in hand.

Jerome lowered himself to shore from the bow and walked into the night. Jackson did not like what was happening and went below so he could proclaim his innocence when there was an investigation into Dirty's murder. He tuned in the VHF radio; the airwaves were silent. A bottle of Virgin Island Rum was opened and he took a big gulp; the cheap booze burned all the way down. Its harsh taste lingered. He was getting fond of the stuff.

Dirty might look like a scumbag, and for good reason—he was a scumbag. He was also very aware of the personality the groomed black man had under the thin veneer of expensive clothes, elocution, and respectability. Dirty was from the same breed, and was sure the criminal underworld had paid for the fancy duds. He knew they were aboard the sleek powerboat that had pulled its bow on shore that afternoon.

Dirty was almost positive they would be sneaking up for retaliation after all witnesses left after closing, and he was ready. He only heard a slight sound of gravel moving under someone's step, but it was enough, and he positioned himself in a place that would give him the first shot. He had left one candle lit and positioned it to put out enough light to identify the approaching intruder; he would hate to wallop one of the crows.

The silhouette of the man he expected slowly emerged. A big knife was in his hand and that was all Dirty needed. He swung the bat in a manner that would have made a steroid-packed professional homerun hitter envious. The blow caught Jerome at both shoulder blades; the force of its impact knocked him six feet away. He fell to his knees, and then his face, totally unprotected by his hands, planted hard on the dirt, breaking his nose. The sudden shock of the blow rendered him useless. He could not move or breathe, but was fully conscious and felt the pain. He did not know what was broken, but his body felt like it was on fire.

A strong hand grabbed his shoulder and easily flipped him on his back. He wanted to scream in pain, but without air in his lungs, he couldn't. The dark shape of a man loomed over him and said, "Well pokey, you still wanted to play, and that's the second mistake you made today. Now I'm going to give you something to remember me by, in case you ever think about coming to my bar again. Remember one thing; if I ever see you, I don't care if it's downtown Cleveland or the heart of Joliet Prison, you will get five times the pain as you're going to experience tonight. I know you've done hard time so you've figured out that I've been there, too. You know what this is all about, and you know that I'm telling you the way it is and the way it will be. Stay away from me, and if you send some shit-bag to do your dirty work, I'll know who sent them. I'll find you."

Dirty punched Jerome in his solar plexus further delaying any hope Jerome had for getting a breath of air. Then he said, "I'm going to leave your feet alone this time because I want you to walk out of here. But you won't be sticking a knife in anyone's back for a while," and slammed the bat down on his left shoulder. Jerome moaned in pain but still no air could be expelled to make a sound.

Dirty grabbed the other forearm and put it on the ground. He stepped on it with one foot, and slammed the bat down again and then again, breaking every finger, every bone, on his right hand. "Now you have one good hand and one good arm. When you get that shoulder in a cast, you'll be able to reach your zipper and hold your dick to piss. But I'm afraid you'll have to get your buddy out there in the dark to wipe your ass.

"Here's another little present from me to you," and he slammed his fist into Jerome's cheek, placing the knuckles just right to break the teeth on the right side of his mouth, which cut the inside of his cheeks. Dirty said, "See what a softy I am. I'm leaving teeth on the other side so you can eat .... my people would laugh at how softhearted I'm getting in my old age. Now you tell me, have I done enough to make you realize you don't want to ever fuck with me again?"

Jerome, on the verge of passing out from a lack of oxygen, still could not answer.

“Come on pokey, you have to say the words. I won’t believe you if you just nod your head.”

It was impossible to speak, but Jerome managed to mutter a guttural sound that resembled a painful “Yes.”

“Good. Now you’ve got ten seconds to get off my property. If you’re still here I’m going to think you haven’t had enough. In case you don’t know how to count that high ... be gone before that candle on the other end of the bar goes black.”

Moving was incredibly painful, but Jerome knew it was his only chance to stay alive. There was no doubt that the bartender would kill him. Only two men had ever beaten him; now there were three, and all had come from the same part of hell, a maximum-security prison. Some men are really-bad, and there were a few who scare the shit out of the really-bad. He had just met one.

Jackson heard a scuffle on the bow. He listened for a second until he heard a faint and pitiful, “Help me.” He bolted out to see Jerome huddled up and kneeling on the ground. Something had gone wrong. “What happened?”

A very shaky and weak voice answered, “Never mind. Get me to a doctor and be careful ... got broken bones.”

Jackson wanted to laugh. Apparently, the greasy barkeep was too much for big bad Jerome Savage to handle. He dearly wanted to say, “Well, it looks like somebody does fuck with Jerome Savage,” but of course, he wasn’t that foolish.

4

Chico's Guerdon

CHICO WAS BACK IN THE FIELDS, HIS GREAT ADVENTURE over. Señor Smiley was condemned to stay outdoors and well away from the house, outhouse, and water well. It was placed in a tree so that the surviving goats and chickens could not be exposed to, or even see, it. Chico, after carrying it down from the mountain, was not allowed to touch it. It was evil and belonged to the mountain.

He longed to show it to the other boys and men of the village. He needed to let everyone know that he, alone, had gone to the top of the wicked mountain and had brought back death's head. *What good is it to be brave if nobody knows?* Instead of enjoying his triumph, he sat in a muddy field doing a job he hated above all others. He had gathered all the kenaf seedpods he could find and had to open each pod and check its seeds to see if they had germinated with all of the rain. Those that looked good were put in the sun to dry. Every pod was made entirely of fibrous slivers that got under his skin, itched terribly, and got into his nostrils, which made him sneeze and cough. His father hoped to get enough to plant; there was still time to get a small harvest, and any harvest might prove to be the only way to keep his family fed.

At the end of the day, he knew what he was going to do tomorrow. Going to work in the kenaf field wasn't on his list. He had enough for his father to start planting and he would finish with his seed chores the following day. Señor Smiley was going to town. That night after dinner, he decided to be a man in his own way again, but did not want to cause his family to worry and be sad like the last time. He announced, "Father, I have cleaned and dried twenty-five kilos of seed. That's all you can plant in two days. I'm going into town tomorrow to see my friends. I'll finish the seeds when I get back." Then the boy sat quietly, waiting for the slap.

His father looked at him and said, "Okay." As always, he was a man of few words. As far as he was concerned, his son had proven his worth; he was a man. Then he added, "It's time for you start looking at the girls in the village. You'll be fifteen and you should be married soon. Perhaps you'll be lucky enough to have sons. We sure need the help."

His sisters squealed with delight that their brother was getting married. His mother just got up and took the very few scraps out to the chickens. Chico was not interested in girls, although he had heard about doing it from some of the older boys and was naturally curious. He had seen his parents discreetly engaged in the act since there was only one bedroom. It was a normal function of mothers and fathers, certainly nothing to get excited about. It was how humans made babies, same as the animals.

The next morning Chico walked into town. His mother warned him, "If you have to take that nasty thing with you, cover it up in a burlap bag so you won't scare every decent citizen into an early grave. They've all had a tough enough time. It wouldn't take much for those people to blame you for the storm and all their misery."

"But I didn't go up there until the storm was over."

"That has nothing to do with it. They'll say the mountain knew you were going to offend it and brought in the storm to stop you. When you become an older man, you'll know how mature people think."

Like all teenagers, he thought his own mother was full of shit. Smiley made the trip in the bag, but Chico took it out as he entered the village. He carried Señor Smiley under his arm like a watermelon. A group of men sitting under a tree called him over. The youngest of the group said, "Chico, what is that under your arm?"

"I watched an airplane crash into the Mountain of Lost Souls so I went up there to see if anybody was alive. It took me three days in the jungle to get to the top, but I found the plane. This was the pilot. The fire burned him up."

They laughed at such a foolish notion. Nobody goes up there and comes back. After the laughter died, the man said, "Okay Chico, good joke. Now where did you get the skull?"

He did his best to convince them. He went into detail about sleeping in the trees, the jungle cats, and described the wreckage and his search, but they refused to believe him. They just laughed until they tired of the boy and shooed him away. They knew that graves were destroyed during the heavy rain and bones were washed up everywhere. The head had to be from an old Indian because it certainly was odd looking.

Next, the boy came up to three women; all were his mother's friends. Like the men, they did not believe a word. While young Chico was not prone to lying, they knew he was a man and that meant he would love to play jokes on them. Besides, his mother would not allow him to go to that dreadful place; his father would have skinned him alive. Chico insisted; they shooed. One of them said, "What's the matter with your mother? Why would she let you carry a dead man's skull around? Don't you know that's wrong?"

As he walked away, feeling dejected, he heard another woman say, "It's his fault! Chico brought the mountain's curse upon us." The other women babbled in agreement. Moms may be full of shit, but they're always right about the damnedest things.

Several boys saw him, heard his incredible story, and did not believe him either, but they followed him around because he had a neat skeleton head. Chico soon lost all hope of being a hero and put the head down and started playing cana demonio, a rough game of tag that normally was played in sugarcane fields. With the cane destroyed, however, they played in the village, annoying the adults with their running around the houses and yelling the required jeer, ¡Feo diablo—tú heder! (Ugly devil—you stink!) to the demon, who had to follow the sounds in order to catch someone to become the next devil. Usually, it was a difficult game, as it was impossible to see in the tall cane fields.

Tonto was early. The helicopter with the nice doctor and food would be coming soon. He waited close to the landing zone, but well away from the others who also waited to see the doctor. Several noisy boys were playing, and every time one ran past him, they would make an ugly face, stick out their tongue, and call him names. They thought crazy people were scary, but fun to tease. Soon the game changed from tag to keep-away. They tossed the skull from one to the other, while Chico tried to get it before it was dropped and broken. They played all over the village and Tonto once again found himself in the pack of wild boys. He enjoyed watching them play, but felt sorry for the one, who never could catch the object they played with. At first, he thought it was a ball, and then decided it wasn't.

Suddenly one of the boys was tackled just as he threw the object and it went off course and flew right over Tonto's head. He reached up and caught it. It was fun; he hoped they would let him play. When he looked at the object a strange electric-like jolt hit him, making him confused and dizzy. The object in his hands was a human skull and he knew its odd smile.

Chico cautiously approached Tonto and reached for the skull, but Tonto pulled it closer and wrapped it under both arms as a fullback would a football when running through the line.

"Give it to me. It is mine and I want it now."

Tonto wrapped his arms tighter around the skull. For some reason it was important to keep it.

The other kids loved it and laughed. Chico said, "If you don't give it to me, I'll get the men to take it from you, then they'll chase you out of the village for causing trouble."

Tonto said, "I know this head. Where did you find it?"

That bothered Chico. He desperately wanted someone to believe him, but not the village idiot. He said, "I found it on the Mountain of Lost Souls. Are you a lost soul?" and he laughed.

"I don't know, but there's something important about it. If I give it to you, will you show me where you found it?"

"No. It is mine. I can't show you because it's too hard to get there and it's so scary that you'd only run away." Finally, he was able to say the words he had hoped the others would have said.

Then he thought he should take advantage of the unexpected opportunity. "It's way up on top of the mountain where ghosts live and no one has ever gone there and returned alive—except me. This head came from the dead pilot of a big airplane."

"Please show me. I don't know what it is, but something in my head tells me I must go there."

Chico continued, "Everyone else was burned up and then washed away by the rain." Some of Chico's friends stopped laughing when they began to realize that Chico was serious. He would not hesitate to play a trick on them, but he would never seriously lie, and he had never been a braggart.

One boy wanted to call Chico's bluff; he said, "Okay Chico. Prove it. If you take the crazy man, we'll go with you to see if you're lying."

That made Chico happy—for an instant, until he remembered his promise to his father to finish the seeds tomorrow. If he declined for any reason, his friends and the whole village would think he was lying. He could not let that happen.

"I don't think the crazy man should go, but I'll show you where it is."

"No!" Tonto insisted, "I'm going. I have to. I don't have to go with you; I'll just follow your trail." He then begged like a child, "Please."

Chico was happy that his friends were willing to go, but knew when he did not turn back after getting on the mountain, they probably would. Maybe they wouldn't, if the crazy man continued. Curiosity about the crazy man might get some of them to risk the adventure.

Joseph Carter received the fax from his daughter, Mary, who was helping the storm victims in Costa Rica. As director for the Federal Bureau of Investigations, he complied with her request. Two hours after he got to work, his people identified the man's prints and he had Morgan Blackburn's file on his desk. Included in the file were the telephone numbers of the man's wife. Ten minutes later, it was faxed to his daughter's satellite receiver.

Every hour on the hour, Mary Carter switched on her satellite receiver to check for messages and return any important calls. She was delighted to know there was hope for the lost man. She wasted no time calling his wife. "Mrs. Blackburn, this is Doctor Mary Carter. I'm calling from Costa Rica. There is a man here who has lost his memory. I believe he's your husband. Is that a possibility?"

"Yes!" she answered excitedly. "Morgan has lost his memory? That's wonderful. Where is he?"

Mary thought it odd that a wife would think her husband's memory loss would be wonderful. "He's in a little village in the northern part of the country. I can get him to San Jose for a flight out to Houston. Can you make the ticketing arrangements?"

"Yes of course. How do you know he has lost his memory? He's been missing for a long time."

"He doesn't even know what his name is. Everyone thought he was just a crazy man, but I knew he wasn't. I questioned him; he speaks excellent English and Spanish, but couldn't tell me a thing that happened before that terrible storm hit the country. He was hurt, but not badly; that's how I came to know him. I wish he were here right now to talk to you. I'll see him later today. I can call you then, okay?"

"No, no. I need to be there. Maybe it'll trigger something to regain his memory. I'm so happy you found him. I just can't believe it. Thank you so much. If there's a flight, I'll be in San Jose today. How do I get to the village?"

"I can only carry military personnel or storm victims. It's the rules. Several private helicopters in San Jose that carry food and the media are there. I'm sure you can charter one, but they are expensive."

"I don't care about the money; I just want Morgan. Where do I tell the pilot to take me?"

Mary gave her the information, and she felt good all over that she was able to help the man. Just before Mrs. Blackburn hung up she had asked Mary not to mention anything to Morgan—she wanted to surprise him. The good doctor planned to be there to see the reunion, no matter what her schedule was. She was delighted. A moment like that made all the misery that had surrounded her worth it.

5

The Bitch

JEROME SAVAGE'S ATTITUDE HAD CHANGED; he had become a gentle person—at least for the time being. Broken teeth, a broken left shoulder, and a crushed right hand have a tendency to take the fight out of anyone. Aside from the obvious injuries, Jerome was certain his shoulder blades were broken, too. Without a car and following the complete demise of island taxis after the storm, Jackson had to take him by boat to the Army's hospital on the other end of the island. Every movement, every wave, sent excruciating surges of pain gushing through his body.

He was well aware that the bartender's concern about him sending others to do his dirty work was foolish. He occasionally forgot his pain when delightful thoughts of vengeance controlled his mind. He would never share that experience with anyone. His pain was nothing compared to what the bartender would feel.

The army doctor was rather skeptical about Jerome's story on how he was injured. How a man could have fallen in a boat and sustained so many broken bones was not realistic, but he had seen many odd injuries during the last two weeks. Jerome's earlier compulsion to get to Costa Rica would have to wait a day or two. The doctor insisted that he stay in the hospital overnight and Jerome did not resist; the thought of traveling that night had vanished. The doctor's suggestion that Jerome be airlifted to Miami by military aircraft the next day was even better news. But not for Jackson, as Jerome had insisted he would accompany him.

The only thing pleasant that happened to Jackson on this venture, so far, was spending the night in his boat—alone. He frequently stayed there on weekends, and loved the solitude. He knew the next morning, he would have to find a safe place for the boat, set his anchors, and hope his $300 thousand plaything would be there when he returned. He was to be a wet nurse to his boss and that was repulsive enough to make him look for a new job; however, one does not quit in their business. Retirement meant being murdered, or retiring after all the bones are paid for with old age and favors—but nobody ever quits.

The next day, Jackson was pleased to see the bulky cast on Jerome's upper torso. Both shoulder blades had been broken in addition to his shoulder. The cast on his hand had wires sticking out of the end of his fingers; that would slow down his maniac boss. The thought of brushing one of the wires against something made Jackson's skin crawl and he hoped Jerome would do it frequently. The shoulder cast extended down his forearm and added another foot to his width requirement.

Jackson wondered what he was going to do the first time Jerome wanted him to wipe his ass. As far as Jackson was concerned, it was not going to happen. Jerome could call Abby or walk around smelling like shit and feel like a baby with a diaper full.

Doctor Carter hoped she could keep a straight face and her surprise a secret as the helicopter settled to the ground. She was disappointed that Tonto, Morgan Blackburn, was not there. Then she worried that maybe the nasty woman of yesterday had instigated the others to chase the poor man away. If he didn't show up, then Mary would put the fear of God in the self-righteous woman. Morgan had to be in the village the next morning, when his wife arrived.

Morgan was a no-show. The nasty woman admitted she had tried to get her husband to chase the man away, but he had refused and told her to start minding her own business or he was going to chase *her* away. A few people had reported seeing him in the morning talking to some boys, but nobody had seen him since. Mary stayed for an hour longer than scheduled; she had hot food for Tonto in a container that she had scrounged from the military. She also had found new clothes so he would look good for his wife. She prayed that he was all right, and convinced herself that he had simply forgotten. Maybe he had found food somewhere else, but he damn sure better show up tomorrow.

Beautiful Ann Blackburn sat in first class; her two traveling companions, lovers, and employees, traveled in coach. While they munched on free pretzels and drank Pepsi, courtesy of American Airlines, Ann enjoyed a glass of chardonnay and tray of fresh hors d'oeuvres, and a steak would soon follow. After the meal, she looked forward to a glass or two of brandy, then a nap.

Kevin and Kevin did not like each other. Kevin One was forty, with white skin, and short. Kevin Two was in his mid-thirties, black, and well built; his hair was in dreadlocks six inches long. They put up with each other for two reasons: their well-paid jobs and it was the only way to be near the woman they both loved. They had wanted to sit apart on the trip to Costa Rica, but Ann insisted they travel together to study the map, and come up with solutions to her problem. That was their job: solve their mistress's problems, whatever they might be. Moreover, they did an excellent job, no matter if it was balling the horniness out of her in a ten-hour sexual marathon, or killing a jerk that made a snide remark to her while standing in line at the bank.

Ann was beyond beautiful, her face and body were perfect. She would be the perfect model for an angel. Her black hair framed a perfect, innocent-looking face. In her teenage years, she never even had a blemish. Unfortunately, all of Ann's beauty was limited to her appearance; she had been a raving bitch since birth, and perfected the art of making others miserable during her forty years on earth. Ann also had enormous wealth; she was born with that, too—but it had never been enough; as with sex, she always needed more.

The Kevins, as Ann called them, were in the process of solving her biggest and lingering problem. She did not care how it was handled; she just wanted it done. Her chicken-shit husband needed to be dead, and she wanted him to see it coming. She often fantasized about painfully slicing him up with a sharp knife until he bled to death. Her hate for Morgan was pure.

Ann planned to grab her husband and be long gone before the do-gooder doctor could interfere. Her pleasure could not be totally achieved until Morgan's memory returned. Killing him would be useless if he did not know that his treachery had cost him his life and, surely, the best pussy he ever had.

Kevin One had arranged for a charter pilot to meet and take them directly to the village. The Kevins planned to scoop up Morgan and fly him to a house that Kevin Two had already rented through a Costa Rican realtor found on the Internet. From there, pilot Wally's job was over.

Wally Rasp met them at the only door exiting Costa Rican Customs and Immigration. An hour later, he set the chopper down at the village. Lots of folks came running, thinking he was bringing food.

Nobody in the village knew where Morgan was and Ann was told that the doctor could not find him either. Everyone thought he had gone to another village to find food, as there was not enough in the village to feed their own families, much less give it to a crazy man. Ann's true self was apparent in her fury at not being able to find the man known as Tonto.

As darkness was slowly arriving, they looked in the next village, but had the same results. Ann told Wally to take them to their rented house but he refused, stating that he was expected home that night and he would not be able to find the house after dark. Ann insisted.

Aggravated, but richly bribed, Wally flew to the Pacific Ocean, then up the coast to the village of Playa del Coco. Storm damage was minimal along the west coast. Their biggest problem, like most areas, was isolation. Everything that came into the village had to come by boat or helicopter. Wally had the little village's undivided attention as they circled and then landed on the beach. Most of the villagers ran to see what, or who, had arrived.

Kevin One found a taxi driver in a little waterfront bar who knew where the house was located. Ann insisted that Wally stay with them in order to get an early start the next morning. He explained that he needed to go to Liberia to refuel and would stay there with his in-laws. Again, she insisted, saying they could stop for fuel on their way back to the village. He explained that the airport was only used to fly in relief supplies from North America. Their refueling service was only open in the afternoons. She told Kevin Two to make the arrangements, which proved to be difficult, as he didn't speak Spanish. Nevertheless, as always, Ann had her way, a man would be there at eight the next morning for $100, American currency.

Ann had plans for Wally that night; the Kevins had suspected she had and were not happy. Wally was happily married and devoutly faithful to his wife, but that did not deter her desires to sexually humiliate and then dominate him. He gallantly resisted—she cruelly prevailed. After it was over, she rudely kicked him out her bedroom.

The next day started with hope and ended in frustration for Ann. Morgan had disappeared. Her temperament didn't improve when Wally told her that her charter was over; he had another scheduled for the next day. She did not intend to lose her only means of transportation. She faced him eye-to-eye, and said, "If you're saying that because you're afraid that I'm going seduce you, don't worry. You're a lousy fuck. I promise to leave you alone."

The Kevins were delighted to hear that. With Wally's ego destroyed, he was more determined to return home. He said, "Sorry lady, but I'm going to San Jose. I'm expected to be home and besides, I can lose my license for canceling a booking. I'll drop you off in Coco, or you can go to San Jose."

Ann smiled at him, as if he had just said something ridiculous, and said, "That's bullshit, Wally, and there'll be no further discussion of the matter. You are going to stay with me until I'm through with you."

Wally was about to tell her what she could do with her demands but Ann looked at Kevin One and said, "Be sure Wally understands me." After a light beating and severe scaring, Wally saw the error of his ways and cancelled the next three bookings.

Walking up the ravine had been much easier than going up through the dense jungle, but still, three of the four boys turned back. They claimed it was too hard, but Chico knew that when they saw the steep walls and wild jungle, they were afraid. He had finally won their respect. Juan, the remaining boy, was scared, too, but refused to show it. If Chico and the crazy man could do it, so could he. Tonto had trouble keeping up with Chico, not because he was older, but due to a lack of food, his energy level was low and he tired easily. He did not complain; he was compelled, for some obscure reason, to see where the skull had come from.

Chico did not want to leave the man behind, either; he was sure Juan would go back if Tonto turned back. He needed to show Juan the wreck to prove his story. Besides, the crazy man did not seem to be too bad, and it was good to have the company, so Chico slowed his pace.

The creek water was cleaner than before and he found a wide spot to make camp for the night. He was not worried about sleeping on the ground, as the cats would surely stay away from three humans. Juan and Chico had often hunted together and made a good team. They went into the woods to find the night's fare. Their task was made easy by a slow moving tortoise and they had lots of experience cleaning turtles, since it was a mainstay of most farmers' diets during bad times. Normally it was tasty, but neither boy had eaten one raw. No one had matches for a fire.

Tonto surprised them. He did not know that he had learned how to start fires when he was fighting in a Cambodian jungle. He easily had smoke, then a flame, by rapidly rotating the right piece of wood against another piece that he had carefully selected. He ignited the dry moss and fed the fire small twigs and then larger sticks. Looking at the bloody mangled remains of the turtle; both boys were glad that the crazy man had come.

The crazy man muttered strange words never heard by the boys. He was angry with himself after seeing the boys bring in the turtle. He had been without food for days, except yesterday, and had forgotten that he could have found food in the mountain jungle only a few miles from the village. He knew how to hunt.

Sitting around the fire that night, they talked about many things and the boys realized that Tonto was not crazy, and he was not stupid, either; he simply could not remember anything before the storm. They felt more secure knowing the man was not going to do anything spooky or dangerous. They all slept soundly that night, especially Tonto.

Roosterman wished he could tell the crows that a French millionaire was flying in to take him to Costa Rica, but could not let them know he had been spying on Salvage Tom. The Frenchman was concerned that Tom had found something of value on his sunken yacht. He did not think the diver would be stupid enough to turn up with money right away, but eventually he would and it was Rooster's job to tell him when it happened.

Instead, Rooster told them the Frenchman had heard about his fishing abilities from some French people he had on charter. The man was picking him up to go fishing in Central America. The crows were drunks, not stupid, and no one believed him. Rooster's personality stretched the limits of anyone's tolerance for arrogance, and he was a lousy fisherman, to boot. Besides, no private planes were allowed to land on St. Thomas.

They were wrong. The Lear did land; money buys influence and influence buys everything else. Rooster also discovered that Monsieur Pierre Beloit was not aboard. Maurice Perdue handed him a note as he entered the aircraft.

My dear Roosterman,
I'm terribly sorry but I cannot make the trip with you. A once-in-a-lifetime opportunity to collect a very extensive set of works by the artist Le Barri demands my attention. My associates, also collectors, will be with you instead. If you locate my salvage diver and his friends, my associates will know if he has taken my property.

Good hunting,
Pierre

His three associates were on board; however, they did not look like collectors of anything other than maybe the balls of Beloit's enemies. To make matters worse, they did not speak much more than a few words of English. All spoke French and Spanish fluently, but Rooster did not know more than *cerveza por favor* and *donde los baño*. Three hours after leaving St. Thomas, they landed. Roosterman was surprised when they would not let him off the plane. They had landed in Panama where they took on fuel and another passenger. The Frenchmen greeted the stranger as an old friend, but did not bother to introduce him to Rooster, who was almost afraid to look at the new man; he had never seen someone who looked so mean. He thought, how bad have I fucked up by getting in with this bunch?

Roosterman had another surprise that day; they landed in San Juan's downtown airport, and not the required international airport. Customs and Immigration had been easily bypassed. A limousine met them; the four men knew its driver. Their arrival was like an everyday occurrence. Rooster did not understand a word, but knew they had Grady's place located, as they passed a map around so all could see the red ink circling a spot in the middle of nowhere.

Chico led his companions as if he were an expert at climbing over rocks, boulders and through jungle. If it was not so much hard work at times, it would have been enjoyable for Tonto. The scenery was spectacular and food was easy to catch; turtles were apparently unaffected by the rains and mountain trout had weathered the flooding. Tonto had made a bow from a strong young tree and arrows from straight limbs of another. He used thorns for the pointed ends and barbs to prevent the arrows from pulling out. His skill was amazingly effective with the weapon and he killed a sleepy but, unfortunately, gravely endangered owl for lunch. He had no idea why the boys were in awe at his woodsman skills: he assumed it was only natural.

A noise slowly became more noticeable to Tonto as they followed the creek higher into the sky. Looking back, he could see the valley and the tiny farms well below. The village looked small from their height and he could see a helicopter circling the village but could not hear its rotors. It sparked his memory that he was supposed to meet the pretty lady doctor yesterday, but with the excitement of the skull and the trip, he had completely forgotten. However, that was not the doctor's military helicopter; it was painted red.

When the gorge made a sharp turn to the right, he could see where the noise was coming from. A magnificent waterfall was cascading down from a ledge 100 feet above. Instantly, he had the same feeling as when he saw the skull. He had been there before. The feeling was frightening; he could not understand it.

They climbed the steep rock face and had to make a small side-trip through the jungle where the wall turned to an overhanging angle upwards. When they reached the top, Tonto knew it had been worth the effort. The view below was stunning. The flowing water ended abruptly and fell the distance into an indigo blue pool, deep from the ages, as water carved the bottom away. The valley below looked like a miniature land; the same tiny red helicopter flying unheard was in another part of the valley.

A flat place near the edge of the falls looked like a good place to rest for the night. Chico knew it was only another two-hour climb, but it was not an easy one. It would be better in the morning when they were fresh. Most of the conversation around the fire that night was what was going to happen to Chico and Juan when they returned. Juan knew he had a real shit-kicking coming but did not care; this was real adventure. Chico was sure his shit-kicking days had ended. His concern for his family was not so great, as the other boys would tell everyone where they were. Also, he alone, had already conquered the mountain; his parents shouldn't be too worried this time, knowing that he was traveling with other people. He just hoped they didn't know that one of them was crazy.

The boys told jokes; they were full of them. Tonto did not know any, but enjoyed listening, even if they were corny.

Jerome was under the influence. He was comfortable and should be. He was not in a hospital room, but at the Biscayne Hilton's penthouse suite in Miami. A fresh Crystal martini sat on his bedside table; two others sloshed in his belly. The butts of two Jamaican Dragon Puffs layed crushed out in the ashtray. The third was still lit and being inhaled.

Jackson was busy on the telephone, and sober. He had made progress; Edmundo, in Costa Rica, was checking the government's records to find Grady's place. Jerome had been there once, but couldn't remember how to find it. He also had talked to Jerome's man in Washington D.C. to find out who the real person was behind the guise of Dirty Dick Farrar. He had given him the best description possible, including the tattoo under his chin of a multi-headed snake that Jerome had the misfortune of being in a position to see. The snake was small, but he could see it had a head on each end; there was no tail. Behind the heads were lion's manes.

He had placed twelve calls to Jerome's mother-in-law, but no one answered, not even the house staff. That told Jerome that the old bitch had persuaded her dutiful daughter to go somewhere for fun. Whenever her mother went anywhere for a stay longer than overnight, she took the whole damn bunch with her. Abby had not left a message at the hotel or the cruise ship, which meant she wanted him to know how pissed she was at his obsession. He was irritated, not at that, but because he needed her to take care of him. Jackson refused to wipe his ass and doing it with a rigid arm or broken hand with protruding wires proved not only awkward, but also messy. If Abby did not check in soon, he was going to hire a hooker.

Jackson had also made flight arrangements to Costa Rica; Edmundo would meet them and have everything ready, including a longhair Spanish dictionary—and ass wiper. Edmundo could not believe how a normally hard man like Jerome could be such a baby over some broken bones. After Jerome had passed into the happy-zone, somewhere between Miami and Mars, Jackson got his first response to his earlier calls. The man in Washington couldn't do anything with the description, but passed him on to another man in New York, because of the tattoo.

The New Yorker, Sam Pano, explained, "The tattoo sounds like the mark of the Hydra. They are an exclusive group of Italian men who, for the most part, come from the Bronx and Brooklyn. It's a very secretive, membership-by-invitation-only group. Some people think it's the Mafia's elite, others think it's nothing to do with organized crime; it's a cultural thing. Personally, I think it's both, but you'll never find an outsider who knows for sure. Anyone outside the group who learns anything gets dead quick, and so does the guy who told him. The type of weenie that would talk about it would never get in; they are very selective."

Sam Pano was quiet for a moment, and then added, "Also, I doubt very much that it's a phony. Another of their rules is that every snake is different in small details. One man in the organization, usually the oldest, is present at each tattooing; he designs and photographs it for his records. There is only one name, one set of fingerprints, for each design. If there's ever a question of identity, it's very easy to check. Anyone wearing the Hydra, who isn't one, is unceremoniously murdered, no matter who they are or how young they may be. With that, there isn't any way that snake can be identified, even if I had a picture."

"No way on the tattoo. How about a picture of the man?"

"I might recognize him, but you have to understand, I won't ask one of the Hydra. Shit, if he's one of them, or I'd get a one-way trip out of Brooklyn on the evening tide."

"I guess fingerprints are the only way, but that'll take time. My boss expects information as soon as he wakes up."

The man from New York was silent again, and then said, "It's not much to bank on, but I've known some of those guys. Of the Hydras, I know there are only three…no, four, that I can't account for. Judging by the man's size, he fits the description of three of them. Can you tell me anything else?"

Jackson thought for only a second, and said, "Yeah. He's a mean son of a bitch."

"Were losing ground, pal; that description fits them all."

Jackson said, "He's a hell of a fighter; he beat the shit out of a tough hombre with no problem and left him as a pathetic cripple."

There was a silence, and then the caller said. "I think I know who it could be," said the New Yorker. "But I doubt that it's him. I can't believe he'd still be alive. Where is this guy?"

"I'm not sure I want to tell you. Sounds to me like somebody would like to know where to find him. I'd better give my boss first crack at him. Who is the guy?"

"I'll tell you, but part of the deal is you tell me, and nobody else, where I can find him after your boss is finished, okay?"

Jackson chuckled, "I doubt he'll be good for anything when my boss is through with him."

"All I want is the Hydra tattoo." Jackson agreed.

"Roberto Caponio was raised in the Bronx. He was a tough baby and got meaner. His pop worked for the mob boss, Gamboilli, but had no ambition; he was useless, chased the whores, and gambled away everything he could steal. He was shot dead when Roberto was only about eight. I know this because I lived across the street. I wasn't included in the same group as Roberto, as I'm not a pure blood. My mother is a black, only Pop is Italian. Young Roberto had the right stuff even then, and Gamboilli took him under his wing. Roberto was a made-man at the age of twelve."

Astonished, Jackson said, "You have to be joking."

"No, I'm not. To get that status, Gamboilli told him to whack a bad debt. As a boy, he walked up and put a pistol under the guy's chin, looked him dead in the eyes, and said, 'You know you shouldn't have done that to Don Gamboilli,' and pulled the trigger three times, blowing the guy's head off. Blood and brains splattered all over Roberto, but it didn't faze him. He looked across at the guy's horrified wife and said; 'You know what's going to happen to you, too, if you feel like getting talky about this.' From that time on, he was one of Gamboilli's favorites, and that's about the time he got his Hydra, if I remember correctly. The guy had it made until he suddenly disappeared when he was in his thirties. At first, I thought he had been whacked, but some of the guys said he had fucked up with Gamboilli and hauled ass. I don't know what he did, but he sure pissed off the wrong guy. Gamboilli has been dead for fifteen years and there are still big bucks on Roberto's head. That means his hit was paid for before Gamboilli died and the money is sitting there waiting for the guy who finds him."

Jackson said, "Sounds like my boss might want to pick on someone else, doesn't it?"

"If he wants to stay healthy, I'd definitely say so. The only way I'd fuck with him would be from a block away and with a high-powered scope on the biggest fucking gun I could find. In a hand-to-hand match, you can't beat him. He used to box and wrestle and he never lost, even when he was supposed to. I think that caused his problem with Gamboilli. He killed a guy in the ring that was supposed to win big."

Jerome did not move the rest of the evening and Jackson made sure he wouldn't. He had injected him with a healthy dose of Valium. Tomorrow was going to come too soon as it was, and he did not want any potty trips to wake him up.

If Jerome shit the sheets, let the maid clean it up; they had to be at the airport by nine anyway.

Ann spent her days making life miserable for the Kevins. She had Wally by the balls, and threatened to tell his bride about his romp in the sack, if he did not stop trying to get out of his obligation to her.

People on the ground were all looking for the crazy gringo to collect a thousand dollar reward offered by his wife. Ann chased a dozen false reports each day, and she was getting pissed. Calling the doctor and threatening lawsuits against her, her hospital, the Red Cross, and the countries of the United States and Costa Rica did not help, either. Ann, if she had been aggressive before the hunt for Morgan, was approaching a manic state. She had not been this close to catching the bastard in years, and he damn sure was not going to slip away again.

6

Resurrection

TONTO AWOKE TO A MISTY MORNING; THE CLOUDS had come in again. Yesterday, the sky was completely clear and they could see the peak only a mile in the distance. The mist was pleasing to him; everything was gray and still, and it was cooler. The embers of last night's fire were flamed, and the warmth on one side and the coolness on the other side of his body accentuated the freshness of a new day. All of their food had been devoured the night before, but they were not hungry; all were too eager to get to the wreckage site.

Chico was last to sit up. He brushed his bed of dirt and leaves off his clothes, stood and stretched, and then led the way. As they worked their way up and around one obstacle or another, Tonto wished he could understand the strange feeling he had since seeing the waterfall. It was a nagging feeling that wouldn't leave him.

Slowly, the angle of land began decreasing. Walking became easier and the creek wasn't moving so fast. The mist was thicker, reducing visibility.

Chico pointed, and said, "Over there, that's one of the trees." A tree was broken in half, its bark shattered and twisted as if a tornado had danced on it. The broken half lay at an angle; its branches sprawled on the ground, still connected at the break by strands of shattered wood fiber. As they walked on, they saw more trees and soon they were in a large meadow, with sparse trees and ground thick with green ferns. The mosquitoes had returned since Chico's last visit. He wished that he had brought Señor Smiley instead of hiding him at the mountain's base, maybe his presence was what had chased the hungry bugs away before. In the gray mist, a white object slowly appeared as they continued. It turned out to be the rear section of an airplane.

Its appearance affected Tonto. He had the same feeling as he had when he first saw the skull and the waterfall. He touched its outer skin with his hands as if he were trying to bond with the strange object to learn its secret. He slowly went inside, touching everything.

His actions were unnoticed by the boys; Juan was excited and proud of Chico for finding this treasure in a forbidden land and proud of himself for coming to see it. Chico was proud, too; now the village people would believe him. Tonto came out of the fuselage, looked at the surrounding area, and asked, "Did you look around carefully? There should have been bodies."

Chico described how he had searched and continued following the trail of broken trees. Chico was excitedly describing what they would see next, and next. The boys' excitement was lost on Tonto; the strange feeling was getting stronger. When he saw the main fuselage he wanted to cry, but didn't know why. Surging emotions made him feel that maybe he was going insane.

Chico stooped at the edge of the fuselage to show them where he found the skull, and told them about being so scared that he bumped his head on the jagged edge of metal. Tonto crawled under the opening and stopped in the charred black interior to let his eyes adjust. The other two boys wiggled in and Chico was first to show them how to crawl up the forty-degree incline to the pilot's seat.

Tonto was last; he did not want to see it, but the excitement and the egging-on of the boys to stop being a *pollo*, piqued his curiosity.

After pulling himself into the cockpit, there wasn't room for all of them. Chico sat in the burned remains of one seat; Juan was in the other. Tonto wedged into a space between the seats at the center console and used the co-pilot seat's mounting bracket to hold on. While Chico and Juan thoroughly enjoyed themselves, Tonto squirmed around trying to get comfortable. He kept brushing his hand against something so smooth to the touch that it almost felt soft. Finally, he pulled the object out from under the seat. It was heavy, and in the misty light shining through the busted windscreen, he saw its yellow color, imprinted seal, and suddenly understood what it was.

Realization came so hard that he turned loose of everything keeping him in the cockpit and tumbled down the aisle while yelling in a panic. The boys laughed at first, and then became quiet after they realized that Tonto had suddenly stopped yelling. They became concerned that he was hurt and scampered out of the seats and crawled down and outside. Tonto stood several feet away from the fuselage, looking in all directions as if the lost souls were calling him.

Chico whispered to Juan, "Something happened; he's crazy again." Juan was frightened as he walked over and tapped Tonto on the back. "Tonto, are you okay?"

He slowly turned around; the smile on his face scared the boys; both recoiled. He said, "Tonto's not my name. Pete's my name. I was in this airplane when it crashed. ...Seeing the gold made me remember."

Chico asked, "Gold? Real gold?"

"Come look." He crawled back into the wreckage. When his memory had returned, he was on fire and had panicked; he had to get out of a burning airplane. In his tumble down the aisle, the heavy bar had fallen to the dirt. After he escaped the burning memory, he remembered being hurt and his only way out had been through the shattered windscreen.

Pete handed the gold bar to Chico and said, "This is your reward for bringing me here. It made me remember. I knew something important was connected to your Señor Smiley. He wasn't the pilot, Chico; he's a pirate that lived over 300 years ago."

Chico was stunned and speechless for a moment, then looked up at Pete, and with a puzzled expression, said, "You're giving this to me?"

"Yes, Chico. You deserve it."

Chico started shaking with excitement, and muttered, "Gold . . . you're giving me gold." Tough little Chico, the fearsome boy who conquered the Mountain of Lost Souls began to cry.

Pete had a sudden and sickening thought: Tom! He grabbed Chico by the shoulder to calm him down and asked, "There was another man with me, Chico. You didn't find a body?"

With his red and teary eyes still on the gold, he answered, "No, but I didn't look real good."

"How about more gold? Did you find more bars like this one?"

"No."

"How about an old wooden chest?"

Chico thought and said, "I didn't see one, but some pieces of old wood might be a smashed-up box." He pointed the way, and then led them back down the crash path. He let Juan carry the heavy gold bar and had decided to let him have part of it; there was enough for both families. His father was going to be so happy; his mother would probably cry for a week. Best of all, he would not have to work in the kenaf seed field, and that made him happier than the riches the gold would buy.

On the search, Pete was in deep thought: *Tom has to be here. He couldn't have survived the crash, he had been standing up in back just before we hit. How did I survive? . . . Plain luck. No, it wasn't luck. Thank you, God.*

He delayed looking for the wood so they could search in and around the tail section. The only place he couldn't see was under the wreckage and it was too heavy to move. Chico was sure the heavy rains had flooded the meadow and had washed most everything down the ravine. The smashed treasure chest confirmed his theory as a likely possibility. A heavy cast strap that held four slats together had snagged on a tough meadow fern and was all that remained.

Pete reasoned that If Tom had survived, he would not have been able to carry the gold, and if he lived, he would have found him. Pete couldn't remember anything after bailing out of the windscreen, and falling thirty feet to the ground. The impact must have caused the amnesia. He did remember that he had followed the creek down and had been alone.

They spent the night in the tail section and smeared mud over their bodies to keep some of the mosquitoes away while they ate another turtle. The next morning the trio searched the other side of the creek before the first impact area. Tom was not anywhere. Juan's theory was that a jungle cat had dragged Tom to its den, which is what they do if they have babies to feed. Juan and Chico's ideas were realistic.

Pete was disappointed that Tom died after all they had been through. It bothered him that he had survived, and he hadn't even strapped in before the impact. There hadn't been time. Aside from some bruises and being knocked stupid for a couple of weeks, he was fine. He suddenly had hope: maybe Tom was wandering around stupid, too.

At the creek, Pete showed the boys how to sit in the water and to use their feet and legs as shock absorbers on upcoming rocks as they drifted down the creek. The first time Pete went down the creek he was not aware that the noise was a waterfall and had drifted up to the edge before he realized what was happening. It had been a struggle to get out of the water. It was possible that happened to Tom, and if he had had a couple of gold bars in his pockets, he would be on the bottom. If not, he could have washed up on the bank.

From the top of the waterfall, Pete marveled at the clear water, but it was too deep to see the bottom. The thought of almost being dragged over the side to plunge 100 feet into the deep blue pool sent shivers through his body. He hoped that hadn't happened to Tom.

That evening they camped at the foot of the falls and Pete repeatedly dove into the water, but with all the air and foam from the churning water, he could not see, or go deep enough to find the bottom. While he dove, the boys were hunting for food along the creek bank and looking for Tom's body. They did not return empty-handed.

The gray limousine stopped; the thick forest hid it from Grady's hideaway. The mean-looking Panamanian, Jorge, got out and worked his way through the jungle to the house. Ten minutes later, he walked back on the road, waving his arms, motioning them to come in. The limousine was parked in back and out of view.

Rooster had expected a shack, and knew someone had erred. *After all, Grady was just another Lagoonie, a boat bum, wasn't he?* The place was in the middle of a jungle all right, but it was a large, modern concrete-block house. The swimming pool in back was huge and beautiful, with black tile.

Jorge, in French, said. "They're not home, but it looks like they will return. Water is still warm in a teapot and three plates are in the sink, one still has egg yolk clinging to it. Men's clothing is in three of the five bedrooms."

Maurice, in badly broken English, told Rooster they would surprise the gringos when they returned. They thoroughly searched the house while Jorge and the chauffeur positioned themselves on the top floor to watch for Grady's return.

Rooster was curious about what they were looking for, but they would not elaborate. So, with nothing to do, Roosterman went to the bar where he found a generous supply of Virgin Island Rum. He was content, until he started thinking about what the Frenchmen were going to do to Grady, Pete, and Tom. He felt like a rat for a few minutes, but the feeling passed.

The Frenchmen overlooked nothing; every book was searched, every carpet removed, and floors inspected for trap doors or safes. Every drawer was removed to see if something was taped to the underside. No safes were found and that bothered the Frenchmen. Anyone living in a remote area and having the money to build that place, had to have a place to stash cash. They were determined to find it.

As darkness arrived, they formed into two groups, leaving Rooster to himself. Two men assumed guard positions, the others cooked food. It was not fancy French cuisine, but the cans of stew, chili, and peas were filling. Rooster was barely able to eat, as he had been drinking all day, and passed out right after the chili course.

As morning's light began to announce a new day, Rooster awoke. He felt like shit because of the cheap booze, but also because he had slept all night sitting in a dining room chair; he was still at the table when he awoke. He assumed the others were upstairs. Rooster wished he were home on his beloved *Coop*, his 28-foot Endeavor, with his wife Biddy, or at Dirty's for a plate full of Dirty eggs and a cold greenie. The thought of cold beer struck a cord. There was no beer in the house and he had not seen any empty cans when he watched the Frenchmen search the garbage.

That was odd. Grady, Pete, and Tom would not go anywhere without beer. He would have thought they had the wrong house, but several of the books had Grady's name on them, and besides, these people, the Frenchmen, were too thorough to make mistakes.

Jerome was not a good traveler, even when occupying two seats in first-class. His broken bones hurt and the casts were uncomfortable. Besides, his body was swollen from all the drugs he had the night before, and the chest cast was too damn tight.

They had stayed outside of San Jose so they could get an early start the next morning. He wanted to surprise his old pal for breakfast. Edmundo provided a seasoned whore dressed like a nurse who tended to Jerome.

The next morning, Jerome sat alone in the back seat of the rental car; the whore had the day off. Edmundo drove, and Jackson was in front and was uncomfortable with the weight of a shoulder holster holding a big 357 magnum under his windbreaker. Edmundo would be carrying a short-barrel twelve-gauge riot gun. Jerome dearly wanted to shoot somebody, especially Grady, but it was impossible, thanks to Roberto Caponio.

After Jackson told him what he had learned about the bartender, he was not as bent on personal revenge. If Jerome popped him, then another of his kind would not rest until they popped him. It was a no win; therefore, he had Jackson call Sam Pano, the man in New York, to tell him where to find Roberto Caponio, alias, Dirty, alias, Great Walking Eagle, and soon to be "Chum" Caponio, for some Italian mobster's next fishing trip. He would have paid big money to see how obnoxious Roberto would be when he learned who had fingered him.

The Costa Rican government tried to keep the country's roads in good condition, but the country was still developing, and needed money for all sorts of other essential projects. Potholes were alive and growing every day. Jerome let Edmundo know every time he hit one with a curse and sometimes a sincere threat. When they left the main road and took a dirt road, Jerome was horrified. The road resembled a small canyon filled with gullies, holes, and boulders, big and small, littered everywhere. It was not slow going; it was a creep going the six miles to Grady's place. The road was worse than it had been on his last visit.

Jackson was openly delighted at Jerome's pain and jeered at every jolt. It was not a good career move, but he had nothing to fear from the helpless man, and he was tired of taking Jerome's abuse. He had decided that if Jerome got nasty, he would pull the big pistol out and end Jerome's bullying forever.

When Edmundo saw the house, he abruptly slammed on the brakes, creating more ill-will toward him and his family, forever, from the back seat. He did not need Jerome's whining and threats and certainly didn't need Jerome's help in reeling in a wayward associate. But he kept quiet, as he wasn't stupid.

Jerome said, "Well, are you going to sit here all day?"

Edmundo asked, "You want me to back up out of view and then go in by foot to see if they are there?"

"Fuck no, you idiot. If they're here, I want to see them. Why pussyfoot around? Drive up to the house and get me out of this fucking car. Jackson, and don't let them see your gun. Edmundo, you stay off to my side. Keep that splatter gun ready, but it stays under your coat unless I tell you, and when I do, your move had better be spontaneous. If you pull it out, use it on every one of the bastards."

Jackson said, "The place looks empty. No cars, dogs, or people; maybe this has been a waste of time...or it's a setup."

Jerome said, "You mean that guy, Roosterman was working for Grady, and he sent us here to get me out of their way?"

"That... or maybe he sent us here to die. Maybe this is Grady's way to get rid of Jerome Savage. Maybe this is a way to take Abby from you, too. He has the hots for her, you know." Jerome had never felt such anger and frustration at not being able to punch Jackson's teeth out. Jackson was turning out to be an insolent bastard.

Edmundo asked, "Yeah, where's Abby this trip? I thought she always traveled with you."

Jackson, with a smile that irritated Jerome even more, responded. "She's off traveling somewhere... with her mother. Jerome doesn't know where she is, and Abby hasn't bothered to return his calls. Maybe Mom, Abby, and Grady are going over Jerome's accounts on some luxury liner in the Mediterranean at this very minute. Or, I wouldn't be surprised if she answered the door we're about to knock on." His smile plainly said that he enjoyed tormenting the crippled man. It was only harassment a coworker might provide for a few sadistic chuckles, but he should have known it was not the sort of thing to do to a pissed-off and case-hardened killer.

It was a good thing Jerome couldn't hold a gun right then, because the windshield would have been covered with Jackson Julian's brains and teeth from his big mouth. Jerome had just put Jackson's name on the list of people he would kill, but not right then; there was work to do. All he could do was threaten: "If you open that fucking mouth one more time about this shit, or mention Abby's name, other than being complimentary, you're a dead man."

Ann led her troop of willing and unwilling crew away from the helicopter shortly after landing. She had hired four more men to travel to the villages with them. It was their job to get out to the far reaches of each community to show photographs and find Morgan. She had reached the limits of her patience and was determined, more than ever, to get her hands on her chicken-shit ex-husband. She would have her revenge for the betrayal. He had embarrassed her in front of her most prominent business contacts, and he had left her. No man left Ann; she discarded them when spent.

From behind the curtains, Roosterman said, "That's not them, but they're connected. They were looking for Tom in St. Thomas. They're the guys I told Beloit about. I wonder what happened to the guy with the casts. He's the boss and thinks he's some kind of bad-ass. It looks like he talked himself into a good ass-kicking."

All of a sudden Maurice could speak excellent English, "Tell me everything you know about them all." Rooster was pissed at the deception, but told him what he wanted to know; it was not enough to be helpful. He wondered if the others could speak his language, too. He somehow knew they could, and just had nothing they wanted to say to him. He was just another lowlife Lagoonie, not a lowlife hood.

Maurice said, "Rooster, we don't want them to feel threatened. Go answer the door and invite them in. Be friendly; there's nothing wrong here. We just want to have a little chat about their friends."

As the trio approached, Grady's front door opened and Rooster stepped out and said in his best gringo-Spanish, "Hola Señors. Welcome to casa de Grady Fisher."

Jackson recognized Roosterman and turned to show Jerome his delightfully wicked smile, and said, "Ha!" He pointed to Rooster, and said, "See! I told you so! Grady lured us here." Jackson then looked at Roosterman, "I bet Abby's here too, right?"

Jerome was too pissed to be rational; he had warned Jackson. He yelled to Edmundo, "Shoot that bastard!" and tried to point with his lopsided arm. He had meant shoot Jackson, but Edmundo slid the short-barrel shotgun out and put a bunch of new holes in Roosterman's head.

It wasn't much of a fight; in fact, it wasn't a fight at all. The Frenchmen witnessed the murder and knew what was in the hearts and minds of Grady's men. Jerome felt four impacts on his body, but did not understand what had happened. Seconds later, he realized the truth as he lay in his own blood, struggling to get a breath of air. Four bullets had entered both lungs and blood was pumping out everywhere. He heard a raspy noise that sounded like a porpoise blowing an air-water mixture through its blowhole and that was exactly what he was doing. His last thought: *Nobody fucks with—.*

7

Flared Nostrils, The Kill Imminent

Either carnivores had eaten Tom, or he washed out to sea, or he was on the bottom of a very deep pool. Pete had given up all hope of finding him. He had to be dead. The boys, using Pete's bow and arrow, brought back a three-toed sloth for dinner. The poor animal, at its best, could only move in slow motion so it was an easy target, but their aim wasn't as good as Pete's. It took three hits before the soft, big-eyed and cuddly creature lost its grip on the tree and tumbled to the hard ground. The boys finished it off with their knives. It was delicious, and tasted a lot like a manatee.

Pete's restful sleep was interrupted by a bad dream. He had been dreaming about his ex-wife and her activities over the years to bring him back under her control. Also in the dream, was the young and beautiful doctor who had sent his fingerprints to be identified. "No!" He screamed aloud in his sleepy haze. "Don't do that!" He was fully awake with a jolt, rolled over, and looked out into the dark. He thought about his predicament: *She sent my prints to the States to learn if I have a family. I won't be hard to identify and she'll have called Ann. She'd love to catch me when I don't have a memory. ... She's probably here already, and with her money, she could have a mob looking for me. . . . Damn! What now?*

In the early morning darkness, Pete had an idea, rolled up to a sitting position and then laid back down again, when he realized it wouldn't work. He sat up with another plan, rejected it, and lay back down. Finally, he was satisfied that he had come up with the best possible action, and got up and restarted the fire. Breaking sticks for firewood made enough noise to wake Chico, who moved closer to the fire.

"Something has happened Chico, and I need your help."

Chico smiled, "Sure, I'll be happy to help you. What do you want me to do?"

"There's a chance that red helicopter we saw flying around the valley could be my ex-wife. She hates me and has learned that I'm here. If she finds me, she'll have someone kill me."

Chico was confused. "Your wife wants to kill you?"

"Yes. She's a criminal. I turned her in to the police and she wants revenge."

"Why would you marry a woman like that, Pete?"

"You'll know when you see her. She's beautiful, and she hides her mean side completely, except when she is angry."

"What can I do?"

"You and Juan go down the mountain and show your gold to everyone. It won't take the greedy woman very long to zero in on you. You tell her the crazy man with no memory is still on top, looking for more gold. That's all I'll need to get her out of the village."

"Why? If you're here, she'll find you? I could just tell her you died."

"She'd insist on seeing my body. This is the best way. The mountaintop is covered with clouds so a chopper cannot land. She'll surely have her roughnecks with her and they'll climb up to find me and the gold. She always maximizes her benefits. And I'm not going to be here; I'll be on my way to the ocean to look for a boat ride out of here."

"But I wanted you to meet my family. They are going to love you for your gift, Pete."

"Wish I could, Chico, but staying alive is more important. Somehow, I'll get out of the country without her following me. If Ann thinks I'm wandering around lost in the jungle, it will buy me enough time."

"We just say you're up here looking for the gold, that's all?"

"You have to be very careful, Chico. She will try to take your gold from you. Maybe you should have your father with you when you talk to her." Pete frowned. "Bad idea; that would put her in charge. When men meet her the first time, she can make them do anything. She's very conniving . . . You're too young to be vamped, but your father, anybody's father, wouldn't stand a chance against her. She's an expert at sexual persuasion."

"What does that mean?"

Pete put his hand on Chico's shoulder. "She'll use it on you, too, but surely, you're too young to turn loose your treasure for sex. Only older men do that sort of thing; you'd have to be at least sixteen before you get that stupid."

Chico smiled, but did not really know what Pete was saying.

Ann had fire in her eyes, as finally, she had information. The chase had provided hope that she was getting closer to Morgan. One of her men had found two boys who said the crazy man and two other boys had gone up the Mountain of Lost Souls a few days ago. The boys told him about Chico's claim to have gone to the top, where he found a crashed airplane and the pilot's skull. They had not returned, and that surprised no one. Nobody had ever returned who went there. Finding the mountain was easy; it was the big one with clouds obscuring its top.

She laughed heartily at the villagers' foolish superstition, and said, "Grown men afraid of a mountain . . . scared of a big clump of dirt and rocks. Now I hope my big bad brave men are not going to have those childish fears, because that's exactly where we're going, if we don't intercept them coming down. We'll go to the base and wait for Morgan to come by. If they aren't here by tomorrow morning we're going up." The four men from the coastal village refused. They knew of the mountain, too, and besides, their families expected them home that night.

Her only real problem with the mountain was that Wally refused to fly into the cloud-covered top. He said, "It's certain suicide. There is no place to land in the jungle and if there were, I wouldn't be able to see it. The best I can do is drop you off at the mountain's base and wait for you."

Ann's reaction was a sarcastic laugh and she snapped, "I don't trust you to wait, so don't talk like an idiot. If you're too afraid to fly us up there, then you're going to walk with us. And don't think for a second that I'll won't tell your wife about your infidelity if you don't."

Wally had almost reached the point where it would be worth the hurt to his wife to get away from the domineering woman. Unfortunately, Ann sensed his attitude and changed her tactics. She entered Wally's domain, the helicopter, and closed the door behind her. Wally was leery but male-curious, and that was his downfall. Ann emerged thirty minutes later, freshly screwed by the aviator and fully in control again. The Kevins had known the pilot did not stand a chance, when they were chased away from the chopper and told to go mingle in the village. They also knew that the pilot would be treated like royalty until she had no further need for the helicopter, but until then, he was in for some great sex, and that really hurt her devoted Kevins.

Ann was not going to break off the chase now, and she refused to take the four village men home that evening, but promised to pay them each twenty-five dollars for every day they were away from home. They could not refuse such an attractive offer. It was three times what they normally made, but each had made it clear that he would not go up the dreaded jungle-mountain.

She had Wally fly to the mountain, while staying low enough to be able to identify anyone walking. He landed in a clearing near the creek the boys had said they followed. She chased all of the men, except Wally, out of the helicopter again and told them to spread out and bring her anyone they saw coming down the slope. With everyone gone, she closed the chopper's door and went forward. This time she was horny; anticipation of Morgan's capture made her entire body tingle. She gave Wally the best he had ever had.

About an hour before dark, Kevin Two came to the helicopter with two teenagers in tow. One of them, a lad named Chico, told the story Pete had instructed him to; he was very believable. The gold bar was proof and the idea that more was up there and was being sought by Morgan struck Ann's greed-button. The boys gave her directions to the wreck and assured her that it was easy to find. She discarded the little scary stories about wild jungle cats and spooks as childish gibber. She would head up at dawn. Fortunately, for Chico, she was so excited about nailing Pete that she did not try for the gold.

That evening there was a commotion in the village. Chico was back with Señor Smiley and a shiny gold bar. Juan, who had to pass by his father's farm before reaching the village, had gone home to a tearful reunion. Three fat men walking through the village stopped to see what was causing the excitement. They could not believe a boy would go to the mountain and live to return; and that he would find such a treasure. Surely, he was blessed. Best to give this boy all of their respect, and while they were envious, it wasn't enough to go to that mountain.

They were still talking about the boy as they walked into their new home at midnight. They were shocked when pounced upon by strangers, and frightened when they could not answer the questions asked about men named Grady, Tom, and Pete. They had found the house months ago, and since it was not used and had not been used for over a year, they had claimed squatter's rights. They moved in and the house now belonged to them. It was a Costa Rican law that has been infuriating foreigners forever.

At first, they thought the previous owner had sent the thugs to drive them out or kill them, but that was not the case. The men were looking for the previous owner. The foreigners' attention suddenly changed from Grady to the crazy gringo, when they learned about the boy and his gold bar stamped with a seal.

The Frenchmen were told the story about the airplane, the mountain, and the gringo who was still up there looking for more gold. Maurice and his friends had been well schooled by their employer. The marking on the bar was identical to the markings used on every gold bar in the treasure of El Morro. That treasure belonged to their employer and it was their job to return it, and the thief, to the rightful owner.

Maurice wanted to talk to the boy and retrieve Beloit's gold, but the village was asleep; there was no way to find him. The squatters were not happy to learn that they were going with the strangers to lead them to the mountain. At first light, the Frenchmen left the car and followed the Costa Ricans through the brush that would quickly turn into jungle. They all were greatly surprised to find a red helicopter parked in a small clearing. The four Costa Ricans who were being paid to watch the machine were also greatly surprised and ran into the brush. The three squatters were told to return to the car and tell the driver to wait for them in San Jose.

Maurice, who had been a helicopter pilot in the French Foreign Legion, was delighted. After years of flying through massive dust storms, landing in a cloud did not bother him in the least. After ten minutes of becoming familiar with the controls, he tried to start the machine, but it failed. Several more attempts later, the engine roared to life and minutes later, they lifted off. His love for flying came second only to his love of women.

The sound of his helicopter spooked Wally as he stood knee deep in the cold creek. Everyone looked around in disbelief as the red chopper flew above the tree line. It was going toward the mountaintop. As it gained altitude, it disappeared into thick clouds. Its engine could be heard, but the sound grew faint, then that, too, disappeared.

Wally was incensed and that was nothing compared to Ann's anger. Someone was beating her to the gold and to Morgan. She should have made Wally fly them to the top and that infuriated her more.

She turned around and punched Wally in his stomach as hard as she could, and yelled, "You chicken-shit!"

Not expecting the punch, Wally had the wind knocked out of him and fell backwards into the water. His foot did not move, however, as it was lodged against a large rock and his ankle snapped as his body weight shifted.

Much to Wally's protest, Ann left him to fend for himself. As she walked away her parting words were, "Stop acting like a baby. Be a man for once in your miserable little life. Crawl back to your ugly slut wife." She laughed in contempt, and added, "This is what you get for not doing as you were told."

Pete had parted company with Chico and Juan, while watching the red helicopter land in the distance. Chico had been sad that the gringo would not be going back to the village. He wanted to show everyone that the gringo was not crazy and he had fully regained his memory. He was a good man and a pilot who had survived the crash. Pete, however, had made him promise that he would not tell anybody. It was important for everyone, especially Ann, to think he was still crazy.

He had gone through the jungle to get around the mountain to be sure Ann did not spot him. He left the brush behind and walked across open fields that had once produced great quantities of sugar cane, but now grew only weeds. Tractors were working in distant sections trying to get the land ready again for planting. Dust from plows rose into the air—a sure indication that the extremely wet conditions had passed.

There were no fences as far as he could see, which meant he was on a single hacienda. The person owning it had to be very wealthy. As darkness approached, he saw another dust cloud moving on the horizon. This one was moving too fast to be a tractor, and the dust was coming his way. Pete hoped whoever it was might be generous enough to give him food and water. Hunting food in open, barren fields would be difficult, unless he stumbled over a snake.

A fast-moving pickup stopped on the dirt road a quarter-mile away; the dust cloud enveloped it briefly. Pete walked to the truck. The man in a new, air-conditioned pickup lowered his electric window and asked in a loud, deep voice, "Who are you and what are you doing on my land?"

Pete answered respectfully, "My name is Pete. I was lost in the jungle when I went hunting. I'm on my way to the ocean, but I'm looking for work along the way, and I'll work only for food and a place to sleep."

In his deep, commanding voice, the man said in English, "You're a gringo aren't you?"

Pete responded in English, "That's right. I came here just before the storm hit and haven't been able to get out yet. Lost my money, clothes, everything."

"Seems to be a lot of you gringos around lately."

"What do you mean?" Pete asked defensively, thinking that the man was another who despised North Americans.

"Nothing. Get in; I'm Juan Carlos. I'll take you to the chow hall and get my cook to feed you. As far as working, what can you do? You have any agricultural experience?"

"I can drive a tractor."

"Sure you can. And you'll put one of my men, who worked hard in the fields to get that job, out of work. No thanks; go ahead and eat. You can stay in the transit peons' quarters tonight, eat breakfast in the morning, and then be on your way. And don't cause any trouble."

"I'm too tired to be of any trouble, and thank you very much for your hospitality. I really appreciate it."

The cook had fed everyone and had gone home early. Her daughter was due to have a baby and that was more important than feeding the few straggling workers who came out of the fields too late for the regular feeding. Pete and his stomach were disappointed; he asked where the sleeping quarters were.

Juan Carlos said, "Come on, you can eat with me tonight. I don't get many strangers on my land. Maybe you can fill me in on what's going on in the States."

Pete was delighted. He said, "Your English is perfect. You sound like a gringo yourself."

"My grandfather was a North American. He made me go to school in the States until I graduated from Texas A&M."

"You're an Aggie?"

"That's right and damn proud of it, so don't be telling any Aggie jokes or you'll find yourself eating what's left over in my dog's food bowl."

"Wouldn't dream of it. My best friend went there."

"Yeah, it's a big school. What's his name?"

"George Smith, he was—"

"You don't mean Clumsy George, the quarterback, do you?"

"Yes, that was his burden in life. I never knew a man so adept at most anything, who was also so clumsy. We flew F-16s, and while he was probably our best pilot, he damn near crashed several times on landings when he'd get his feet tangled up in the foot pads, or a sleeve caught on this or that."

"You're using *was* a lot. I take it that George was clumsy one time too many?"

Pete was silent for a moment, feeling the sadness of his past. "No, he was shot down by guerrillas using a hand-held rocket launcher. Clumsy was flying low, trying to keep them away from me. I tried to make him leave, but he turned to strafe them once again, and his plane blew to pieces. He died trying to save my ass."

"Sorry to hear that. I never knew what happened to him."

Pete was impressed with Juan's home. It was old, big, and perfectly maintained. Everything was made of rich-looking Costa Rican hardwoods. He noticed an extensive collection of ancient pottery, stone axes, and other relics from the past. Juan Carlos was pleased to point out that some pieces were dated to 300 BC from the Mayan Indians. Most of it had been found on his property. It turned out that Juan Carlos's main purpose in life was to collect things from the past, especially anything rich in Spanish history. Each room in the big house contained everything from weapons and armor from the conquistadors to paintings by early Indians. It was impressive, and probably worth a fortune.

Juan Carlos had noticed the gringo's tattered and dirty clothes. They weren't what a man capable of flying a F16 should be wearing. He thought Pete must have had a pretty rough time. That made him even more curious about finding him wandering in the fields. Juan Carlos intended to find out if there was some kind of connection to another mystery in his life. He told Pete, "There's a guest bathroom down the hallway. Why don't you clean up; my wife will find you some clean clothes. Looks like it's been a while since you've had either. You can sleep in the guest room next to the bathroom."

The evening was enjoyable for both Pete and Juan's family. Educated in the States, they spoke English as well as Pete. He felt at home with them. It was the first time in weeks that he hadn't been on the prowl for food, his every motion and thought on survival.

Pete slept in a real bed, rather than on dirt, and overslept until noon the next day. The household cook met him as he sluggishly walked into the sitting room, looking for his host. She said, "Señor Juan Carlos left instructions for me to feed you. He wants you to stay until he returns. He has taken the family back to their house in San Jose, and will return this afternoon. Tomorrow he will take you to the coast." Pete ate until he was overly full, and then went back to bed.

Juan's son, Juan Carlos Junior, called JC to avoid confusion, disturbed Pete's sleep when he knocked on the bedroom door. "It's JC. How would you like to meet a fellow gringo?"

A couple of gringos were leasing land and the hacienda's agriculture expertise to develop a new crop in the country, but thanks to the weather, they lost the crop and were also stranded. When JC and Pete pulled up to the mill, which was a sophisticated assortment of equipment on a forty-six-foot trailer, he could see they were not happy. Both were dirty and covered with sweat.

JC explained, "These guys have been breaking their balls trying to get this thing going. They lost 300 acres of prime kenaf to the weather, and their seed requirement for next year was lost too."

The dirtier of the two waved an invitation to join them. He was a man with a snow-white beard, balding head, big smile, and a body that would make Santa Claus envious. His belly was as big, but it did not shake like a bowl of jelly. JC said, "I brought another gringo to meet you guys. Pete Morgan, this is Jake Mongomery, call him Mongo. The other man," he pointed to the man standing on the mill, "is Robert Cline."

Robert climbed down from the trailer and said, "What is your country coming to, JC? You're being overrun by Yankees."

JC smiled and said, "Gringos are okay—as long as they don't want to marry my sister." They all chuckled at the overused racial slur used by all cultures.

As they all shook hands, Pete looked at Jake, and asked, "Mongo?"

Robert responded with a chuckle, "Remember that old movie *Blazing Saddles*? The guy who knocked out horses was Mongo. Jake uses the same stroke playing tennis or when golfing. He loves killing round things." Pete chuckled.

JC asked, "So, Jake, what are you guys going to do now?"

Mongo answered, "We've had it for this year. As soon as the roads open, we're going back to the States and try to scare up more finances. But before we do anything else, how about a cold beer?"

Pete jumped at the chance. It had been a long time since he tasted his favorite beverage. Normally, Pete was not an opportunist, but these were difficult times, and he found himself hoping he could hit the Americans up for a loan to get back to St. Thomas.

JC didn't stick around for beer, as he did not drink. One beer led to another, and by the time the Igloo cooler was empty, Mongo knew Pete as well as Pete wanted him to. They got along fine, and Mongo invited Pete to stay at their hotel as their guest since he had lost his money. Mongo told him they would take him to San Jose with them as soon as they could get over the bridges, which should be soon. The United States Army was erecting floating bridges everywhere. Mongo's generosity almost choked Pete up when he said they would get him a ticket home, too.

Pete left word with Juan Carlos's housekeeper that the gringos were going to get him home, and left a note thanking Juan Carlos for his hospitality. Pete had his own room at the Flor de Italia Hotel in Playa del Coco. It was ironic that the woman, who hated him so, had rented a house only a mile away.

His first evening in a public restaurant and bar in weeks turned into a drinkathon. There were no winners. The next day, Pete lay in bed, and for the first time since the hurricane, he thought of how his pals might have made out. *Who survived? Who didn't?* He was sure Dirty's bar didn't make it. He knew that Tom's death, the loss of Dirty's bar, and the truth about Grady, would kill the little community's Lagoonie spirit.

He was not sure what he was going to do about Grady, if he were still alive. The first thing he was going to do was beat the shit out of him. If everything Bill said was true, he would entertain the idea of killing the son of a bitch. He damn sure couldn't turn Grady over to the law. Grady would buy his freedom by telling of the buried gold.

Life was a hell of a lot easier with telephones. If they had had service, he would have called Emily to let her know he was okay, and the guys in St. Thomas to warn them about Grady.

8

Pursuit

MAURICE, FLYING 100 FEET OVER THE TREETOPS, carefully edged his way into the clouds. As long as he was rising, there would be little chance of running into the mountain. His teammates did not share that confidence, however, and were expecting a jarring crash at any moment. The ground proximity alarm continually chirped, as large rock formations would suddenly be located at less than the instrument's setting. From the chart on board, he knew the mountain was three thousand meters high and when he reached that altitude, he pushed forward, waiting for the alarm to tell him to pull back. His nervous copilot was reading the GPS and counting off the changes. Maurice mentally calibrated the changes into meters and after he reckoned that he was over the top, he slowly descended.

Maurice yelled, "Open the side doors and look below. Tell me what you see."

Jorge was the first to sing out, "Visibility about ten meters." Everyone was nervous. "Tree top directly under me!"

Maurice immediately asked, "How big?"

The other watchman said, "I see ground. Looks flat—covered with ferns or small trees."

Jorge: "Estimate about four or five meters."

Maurice snapped back, "High or wide?" At that point, they heard a screeching noise coming from the bottom, and then felt a lurch as the tree's topmost branches were broken away.

"That's the tree, Maurice. You broke it," yelled Jorge.

"No shit. Keep looking; I'm going to break it some more. Look out the sides to see if the rotors might hit other trees." He began lifting the chopper's weight off the tree then letting it settle down again, slowly breaking limbs and the main trunk to find ground.

The other man said, "I can see better . . . no trees this side. Then there was a zinging sound as the rotor caught a sapling on the other side. Jorge sang out, "There's one, but it's gone now. You're clear this side. The ground looks to be a field, overgrown with ferns or something."

The helicopter then jarred as its skids hit ground. They were down. Everyone, including Maurice, was happy the tension was over. After a quick check of the instruments for signs of damage to the electrical and hydraulic systems, Maurice shut down the engine and they dispersed to look for the wreckage. Maurice discovered several broken trees and knew it had to be close. Ten minutes after landing, they found the tail section and had the main fuselage in sight.

A thorough search followed. Maurice's instructions were to look at everything. If something could be moved, they were to move it and look under it. Look for a map as well as the gold. Two men worked each section.

Minutes later, one of them found a gold bar under the copilot's seat. Now they knew the treasure was there, or had been. Its trail would not be difficult to follow if the salvage diver tried to sell it.

Jorge said, "There're no bodies here; but if the diver survived, why did he leave a bar behind?"

"Don't know. It was under the seat; he probably forgot it. I wish I had been able to talk to the boy to see where he found the other bar. I'll certainly find out when we find the man who is supposed to be up here."

Jorge, with a quizzical expression on his ugly face, said, "I'm surprised we haven't seen him; he surely heard us coming."

"Since he hasn't approached us for a ride down, he must have something to hide, or the chopper scared him into hiding. Or, he is on his way down."

One of the men searching the tail section yelled out, "Hey! I found a body!"

If a rattlesnake had long and shapely legs, its name would have been Ann Blackburn. Anger was driving her to race up the mountain. Screaming demands at the Kevins to move faster were making them take chances that could result in a nasty fall that could mean the difference between life and death. If either were hurt, it would be too bad; she was not going to stop or turn back. Both hoped the other would make that mistake.

While going over difficult terrain, she had one Kevin in front, pulling her and the other behind, pushing, and both hanging on tightly to be sure she did not fall. When they reached the waterfall, she didn't see a thing of wonderment, only another time-wasting obstacle.

Fortunately, she was tired at that point and let them rest; besides, it was starting to get dark and she was unsure about traveling at night. She was also hungry, so they ate the sandwiches they had brought from home that morning. None of them was experienced in the wilderness and all wished they had brought sleeping bags and more food, but their minds had been on expediency, not endurance, when they left.

That night they slept under the stars with Ann in the middle to keep warm. The magnificent beauty of the star-filled night was lost to the trio; and even though they covered her body with theirs, neither Kevin felt desire for their mistress. They were exhausted, and she was snoring.

Juan Carlos's return was delayed, due to a tire blowout on landing on San Jose's damaged runway. He decided to put all new rubber on his twin engine Piper since all of the country's landing fields were in bad shape, and, as he had learned, a blowout on a touchdown was not fun. When he did return, he was happy to learn that Pete's fellow countrymen were going to get him home. He liked the two Americans, who had been working as slave laborers, which was unheard of in Costa Rica. Usually gringos would rather spend money than work. He had considered financing the money they needed to finish their project, but farming, with its constant possibility of crop or market failure, was all the risk his health would permit.

His housekeeper came to his private study and said, "Fernando Comancho and his son Chico are here. They are asking if they might speak to you."

Juan Carlos said, "I've been expecting Fernando. He, like everyone else, has lost everything." Juan Carlos knew Fernando needed to borrow money or seeds and fertilizer to get his next crop in the ground. He worked very hard to support his small farm and family. Fernando was an honest and honorable man. Juan Carlos would not add to his burden; besides that, he wished he had someone to turn to when times were tough. "Send him in."

Fernando and son shyly entered his office. "Patrón, thank you for seeing us. I have brought my son." He looked at Chico, "I consider him to be a man now and he has something to ask you."

Juan understood the importance of this seemingly small occurrence. He, too, had been introduced at one time as a man to another important man. It was a moment that went to the grave with every boy so blessed. He stood to shake the young man's hand; it was trembling. The boy had never spoken to a rich, powerful man before and everyone, especially the boys in the valley, were afraid of Juan Carlos. He was the patrón of the valley and a friend of the President. That, along with his rough demeanor and strong voice, intimidated all but the strongest of heart.

The boy stood tall, though, and tried to lower his voice to sound more like a man, but it cracked in mid sentence. "Patrón, I have asked my father for guidance on a matter of which I have no experience. Father said you are the only man I can ask. I have something of value that I want to sell. Our farm has been destroyed by the storm and if I can sell this to you, we might be able to replant." He looked down into the burlap bag he carried; he lowered it to the floor and reached in with both hands. Chico pulled out the heavy gold bar.

Juan Carlos was astonished. "Where in the world did you get that?" He took it from the boy and hefted its weight; it was heavy. He smiled and said, "If this is real gold, and not gold-plated lead, it will be worth a lot of money, Chico. Where did you get it?"

"I climbed the Mountain of Lost Souls right after the storm. I thought an airplane had crashed on it the day the storm started. I found the wreck and the gold was inside."

"You . . . went up the Mountain of Lost Souls?" Chico nodded his head; Juan Carlos was impressed. "That must be why your father considers you a man at such a young age. That is indeed a brave act for a young boy. Was everyone killed at the wreck?"

He pulled Señor Smiley out of the bag and said, "Only this one." Juan was too educated to be superstitious, but he didn't like skulls that had come from a dreaded place to be in his house. After all, one can't be too careful about some things.

Chico said, "I thought this was the pilot, but I met the pilot. Everyone thought he was crazy, but it was only because the crash had caused him to lose his memory. When he saw the skull in the village, he begged me to show him where I found it. His memory came back on the mountain when he found this bar. He gave it to me to thank me for taking him up there. He's a very nice man. There was one more man with him, but we think that his body was eaten by the cats or was washed away in the rains."

Juan smiled at the possibility of a cat eating, or rain washing his body away, there was a more-likely possibility. He asked, "So, Chico, who is, or was, this skull?"

"The pilot said it used to be a pirate named Phuckewe or something like that. It's very old."

Juan Carlos smiled at the boy's pronunciation of the pirate's name and thought it was a good thing his father did not understand English. He noticed the markings on the bar; they looked familiar. He went to his bookshelf where he selected an old, leather-bound book. He leafed through several pages until he found what he was looking for: a drawing of a gold bar with the same mark; it was from the incredible lost treasure of El Morro. Men had been searching for the treasure ever since it was taken from the Spanish in the eighteenth century.

He was quiet for a moment, dwelling on the importance of the discovery. As a successful businessman, he naturally thought of what he could do to preserve this secret until he could find the rest of the legendary treasure. But, as usual, decency overwhelmed his greed and he decided not to be devious with the boy. This was the boy's first experience as a man and it was important to teach him to be honorable.

The picture was shown to Chico. "This is a very important treasure you have found. Are there more of these?"

"No patrón, we looked everywhere, but this was the only one. The pilot said there were more, but I think the rains must have washed them away."

"I don't think these would wash away, they're too heavy, but they might have been buried."

He forced himself to deal directly with the boy, as it was only instinct that made him want to address his father. "Chico, I will buy your gold bar and give you the fair market price. As you can see by all the old things I have in my house, I am a collector of such things. I will buy this gold from you only if you agree to two things. One, you are to tell nobody about it, and two, that you and I become equal partners if we find more of the bars. Is that a fair deal for you?"

The grin Chico had been unable to control faded. "I'm afraid that I have already shown the gold to people in the village. There is a woman, the pilot's used-to-be wife. She saw it, too, and went to the plane to look for more gold and the pilot. The pilot said she is a very evil woman."

"When you get older, boy, and have pockets full of money from all the gold in the Lost Treasure of El Morro, you may learn about ex-wives." Then he thought: *However, I've never had that misfortune.* "Does the pilot know that woman is looking for him?"

"Yes. The gringo doctor that came by helicopter every day after the storm found him. She sent his fingerprints to America. They told her who he was and she told the woman. His wife hates him and has been looking for him for a very long time."

"Sounds interesting; what is this pilot's name?"

"His name is Pete." Juan Carlos was not the least bit surprised.

It took the whole crew to move the tail section enough to get a better look at the body. Still, all that was visible was a foot and an old well-worn boat shoe covered in dried blood. Jorge complained at the work, saying, "What's the point in doing this. He's dead, already."

Maurice responded, "We have to see if it was the diver or the other man." Rope and tackle were found in the helicopter and Maurice tied it to a nearby tree. With the added leverage and three stout poles, they moved the section. When the tail section started moving, it was unstoppable; it slammed over on its side. What was under it was a big surprise. Only a foot and part of a leg was under the fuselage; their attention was captured by the glitter of gold in the crushed and matted ferns scattered around the leg.

They all cheered in victory. Monsieur Beloit had given them a difficult job and they had succeeded. The Lost Treasure of El Morro was theirs and soon would be in France. Big bonuses would be their rewards.

Maurice decided not to push his luck with the early evening mountain fog. It would be dark soon and he would not know where to go in the dark. He could not go back to the car, since those who owned the helicopter would be angry and could be waiting with the local police for them to return. Of course, they would insist on taking the gold, too. It would be better to stay on the mountain overnight and leave at first light for San Jose.

There was no way in hell that Ann was going to let her husband and the helicopter thieves steal the gold. She had the Kevins up and moving at first light. Soon the slope began leveling off, and she could see the red helicopter though the trees. They crouched down and approached the helicopter slowly.

Kevin Two whispered, "Should we try to take them now?"

"Not now. I want to see Morgan before he knows I'm here. This reunion has to be perfect," she whispered, while watching three men milling about and another who seemed to be working on the engine. Then she added, "I don't see Morgan; he must be inside the helicopter counting the gold."

Her mental picture of Morgan with gold bars was too much for her temperament to handle. She couldn't wait another second and abruptly stood up and marched directly toward the men. The Kevins followed a few paces behind. She yelled, "Okay assholes! Get away from my helicopter!" She wanted to laugh at their surprised faces. Without hesitation, she boldly strode to the open door, stuck her head inside, and said "And you, Morgan . . ."

She was stunned when she saw the gold bars stacked against the aft bulkhead. She wheeled around to face the four men who had said nothing but grouped together near the door. She yelled again, "You bastards stole my chopper and now you think you're going to steal *my* gold? It's not going to happen!"

The Kevins instinctively moved in and pulled their switchblades, their only weapons, but they were proficient with knives. The four men still had not said anything, other than chuckling at the situation.

Ann yelled, "You think this is funny? I'll stop by your prison cells in a few years to see if you're still chuckling. I've called the cops and they're on the way. They know that you're trying to steal my husband's gold. I'm going to make sure they put you people away for a very long time."

The men were still chuckling, which only made her madder. She pushed the Kevins into the helicopter's cabin, crawled in after them, and quickly slammed the sliding door shut. Kevin looked at Kevin, confused about what she was doing. None of them knew how to fly the helicopter. No police were on the way; how could she hope to get away with such a bluff?

Maurice moved closer, as he was eager to hear how the treasure happened to belong to her husband, who must be the salvage diver, the thief. He put his face near the glass, and asked with a heavy French accent, "Who is your husband, mademoiselle. Are you the owner of the crashed airplane, and this helicopter?"

"Of course," she seethed with hated. "Who gave you the right to steal my helicopter and try to steal *my* gold?"

"We heard there was a plane crash up here, and wanted to try to save any survivors. We were going to bring your helicopter back, but it wouldn't start after we found no survivors. Our intentions were pure, mademoiselle."

"Bullshit! Where's my husband. If you have hurt him, I'll cut your balls off and shove them down your fucking throat!"

The men behind Maurice snickered. It was a funny situation: an aggressive woman and her two lackeys armed with little knives were threatening four of the most dangerous men in Europe. The Frenchmen were not concerned about the knives; they had Uzis in a cargo compartment only a few feet away. Maurice played it straight; he wanted to learn more about the husband. He was also captured by the woman's beauty; he had to have her. In rapid French, he told one of his men to bring the foot, but keep it hidden.

"I do not know your husband. Is he supposed to be here?"

"Yes."

"Mademoiselle, no one is here."

"Liar!" she screamed.

When Jorge gave him the leg, he held it up in front of the window and asked, "Is this your husband?"

She screamed in horror. Maurice apologized for scaring her, and explained how they had found it and the gold. She began crying. No man could ever detect her pretended tears; she was an old pro at faked emotions.

It appeared that the Frenchman was affected by her sorrow, but Maurice was an old pro, too. With compassion, he pleaded, "Please mademoiselle, come out. You are safe with me," and he slowly opened the door.

Kevin One reacted immediately and lunged at the open doorway with his blade. Maurice easily sidestepped the thrust, grabbed Kevin's arm, and pulled him out. Kevin landed roughly on the ground in front of the other three men. One of them stepped on his knife hand and casually bent over and took it from him.

Maurice paid the captured Kevin no attention. He said to Ann, "Mademoiselle, please, I mean you no harm. Tell your man to put his knife back into his pocket. He does not need it. Then why don't you come out so we can get everything straightened out."

Ann was disturbed at how easily they had neutralized Kevin One; he was the tougher of the two. She made a quick mental note to replace the Kevins with a better pair. The ruggedly handsome Frenchman standing in the doorway would be perfect. She snapped at the other Kevin. "Look at all the trouble you've caused me! Get out!"

Much to the Kevins' horror, she had changed tactics. She looked as helpless as a lost kitten. She sat on the floor, and her shoulders slowly slumped. Then she looked up at the Frenchman with her big, beautiful, blue, innocent eyes and whimpered, "I don't know what to do. Please sit with me. I need someone I can talk to, someone I can feel comfortable with."

Maurice looked sympathetic as he moved to her side; he also slid the door closed with his foot. She did not protest.

Juan Carlos looked into one of his recent financial folders to find the current price on gold. He showed it to Chico and his father. "This is 320 dollars. Do you know how much money that is?" Both shook their head. "It is 96,000 colonies per ounce."

Young Chico said "Wow!" His father, suddenly weak-kneed, smiled and looked for a place to sit down. Then Chico excitedly asked, "You mean I can have ninety-six thousand colonies for this gold?"

Juan had weighed the twelve and a half kilo bar on a bathroom scale brought in for the occasion. As he keyed the numbers into his calculator, he said, "No, Chico. You get 2,688,000 colonies for that bar. What do you think of that?"

Young Chico did not understand such a large number and his father was dumbfounded. Their troubles were over.

"To be honest with you, young man, this bar would be worth more if I sold it to another collector. It could be worth five-hundred times as much, but it will not be sold, so I don't think I should have to pay more, do you?"

"No, patrón; that is too much already."

"Good, and don't forget, we're partners on any other bars we find. For every one of those, you will get half of the gold value, which is . . ."

Chico could not contain himself any longer. He had tried to act like a man, but he broke down in tears and ran to his father. Between sobs, he kept saying, "We're rich, father, we're rich." His father had tears, too. Never in his life, or his father's, had they ever had more money than was needed to just exist.

It was a touching scene for Juan Carlos; he was glad he had been fair. He understood how it felt for the hard-working peons, men too proud to complain when things were bad, to suddenly have more money than they could ever have expected. It was theirs because a curious boy risked death for nothing more than an adventure.

After the boy calmed down, Juan said, "Chico and Fernando, how do you want this money. If I give it to you in cash you could lose it, or someone could steal it if they thought you had this much. If you want, I can give you 100 thousand right now and you can leave the rest in my safe. Whenever you want more, just come here and ask me, or my wife, or my son to give you what you want. I'll keep a record and you'll have one, too, to show how much you have taken and how much is left."

Fernando asked, "You have that much here?"

"Of course, Fernando. It takes a lot of money to keep this place running. Don't forget that I must pay hundreds of people every week. Maybe someday, people will think differently and accept checks for their pay. Maybe someday there will be a bank in the valley to cash them."

Fernando said, "I think you have given us a good deal. Taking 100 thousand colonies now is good, but if you do not mind, can I bring my wife and daughters over to show them how much money Chico has provided?"

"Of course, bring your family over tomorrow night and have dinner with me. I'll send my son over to pick you up."

Fernando was getting worried, frightened. Things were getting out of hand. To sit at an evening table with the patrón was unthinkable, wrong. It was against the way every generation had lived by and respected.

Juan quickly realized the position he had put Fernando in, and said, "Señor Comancho, you are a man of means now. You no longer are a peon; you can hire your neighbors to help in your fields. Please accept my invitation; but I will understand if you feel uncomfortable and decline."

The idea that he was no longer on the bottom rung of society pleased Fernando and he, with humility and embarrassment, accepted. After they left, Juan Carlos got into his pickup and went to see the gringos. He had a dinner invitation for them tomorrow evening.

As he pulled up to the mill, the Americans were just wrapping up work; the cooler was empty. Without leaving his truck, Juan Carlos said, "You guys come over here. I want to show you something." When they were standing next to the window, he said, "Take a look at this," and handed the gold bar to Pete.

Pete could not hide his reaction, but tried. Juan Carlos smiled while thinking: *This poor degenerate that I fed, housed, befriended, and felt sorry for is the man who has possession of the legendary treasure. Well, Pete the pilot, I have someone who may want to meet you.*

Jerome had not returned Abby's calls and she had left messages at all the usual places. She had spent a wonderful time with her mother until she started missing Jerome. Mom had never liked Jerome; there was something wrong with him, a hidden defect, and an unacceptable character flaw that only a mother-in-law could sense. She never tired of pointing out his faults. Ann loved her mother, but had to obey her heart, even though she knew her mother was correct.

Jerome's business upset her, and she had seen the beast that dwelled deep within his soul. She had wanted to run from him when she first found out about his business and flawed nature, but could not; she was already in love. Since then she always had mixed feelings; she loved Jerome, hated his business, but also thought it was exciting. Unlike the liberal politically-correct people of her nation, she did not feel bad or sorry for the users of Jerome's products. The users were just plain stupid; they knew exactly what they were doing when they threw their lives away just to feel exhilarated. Even the kids, they knew better, too. Knowing how much money Jerome made off the users, however, did make her feel uncomfortable, even though, if it were not him, there were thousands of other men standing in line to take his place.

She knew, but could not understand, that sometimes violence was a tool he used as a last resort to stay in business. She had pleaded many times for him to retire; she had all the money they could ever spend. He refused to consider it. That was his thing and always would be, with or without her. To ease her conscience, she privately funded several drug rehab centers.

Jerome's lack of response to her repeated calls scared her. The message his man Jackson had left did not sound good. It sounded like he really needed her, but he was not at any of the places he should have been. Something was wrong. Grady had better have some answers.

It took a couple of days on the phone to get a seat on the few passenger flights to the islands, but she finally succeeded in getting booked on a flight to St. Thomas. That nasty beast that usually hid so well had emerged and taken control of her husband, and the best place to start looking was at the den of the other beast, Grady. She was not overly concerned that her husband might have been killed; he was too tough. Besides, she knew that when he faced Grady, everything would be all right. He would realize that he had another berserko-reaction, and would recognize it for what it was. He always had in the past. They probably were partying somewhere or maybe they were trying to turn the treasure into cash. Either way, she would find them, and then she'd give her husband hell for not calling.

When Abby arrived in St. Thomas, her mother's old friend met her with a loaner Jeep. He also had a room for her in his hotel. Abby drove through the massive destruction to Grady's boat. It wasn't there. When she inquired at what was left of the dockmaster's office, she learned that the hurricane destroyed it and no one had seen Grady. That bothered her. She got directions to find the next likely place to find Grady. It was his favorite watering hole, Dirty's Beer Joint.

She managed to park her Jeep between two wrecked boats in the gravel parking lot. The little bar Grady had talked about so often turned out to be exactly as described. She thought it was cute, rustic perhaps, salty and beat up for sure, but still cute. It had the look that so many restaurant chains tried to achieve by buying phony old stuff and hanging it on their walls.

Every man froze in motion as Abby walked into the bar; all conversation stopped. She felt conspicuously overdressed and quickly found one of the dented beer barrels used as barstools. She sat gracefully at the scarred old bar. The dirty-looking bartender moved over and said, "For shit's sake lady, did you make a wrong fucking turn?"

She promptly responded to his gruff attitude. "Why? Is this a gay bar? If so, I promise not to bother any of you sweeties." Her sweet smile faded. "I don't make wrong turns, bozo. Now give me a beer; make it a greenie." She stared right into Dirty's eyes, not showing the nervousness that she felt. With her attitude, she belonged there. Abby had always belonged everywhere she went, but in this case, she remembered Grady's stories about the treatment tourists received, and she was not going to be chased out before she found Grady.

The crows snickered in delight. Dirty smiled and opened a Heineken, then asked, "I suppose you'd like to have a clean glass, too?"

"I doubt that you have such a thing. No, I'll manage," she said, and put the bottle to her beautifully painted lips and chugged half the bottle. She put it down daintily, then wiped her mouth with a fresh, frilly lace handkerchief retrieved from her Gasöppî purse, and said, "That was delightful; I was terribly parched."

Dirty was spellbound. He had never seen such a mixture of moxie and beauty. She looked at Dirty, who was giving her his undivided attention and said, "Don't you have anything else to do? I'll call you when I'm ready for another, but I do appreciate your attention and service. I'll certainly show my gratitude when I leave your tip. Now, be a good boy and move along, you're in my way; I can't read your menu."

The crows howled. Dirty shrugged his shoulders and moved away. She was happy. That meant that the hardened bunch of Grady's friends had accepted her. She had thought it was going to be much rougher. According to Grady, the bunch of men who hung out here were odd, some were crazy, and they were all unique individuals. Nevertheless, they were still men and had trouble keeping their eyes and thoughts off her. She was accustomed to the attention she naturally attracted everywhere she went. It was the curse of being beautiful and she had learned how to deal with it at an early age. By the time she finished her second beer, she only received the usual attention from the men.

When she ordered her third beer she asked, "Where's Grady today?"

Dirty could not conceal his delight that the woman had cheated. She had known how to react. Grady must have sent her. He smiled again for the second time that month and said, "So you know Grady. Where is that asshole?"

"Grady and I are old friends. He told me about you, Dirty. I hope you don't think badly of me, but I knew you were going to try to scare me away." For the first time in months, Dirty laughed heartily.

She took another swig and wipe, and then said, "I don't know where he is. I just got here and they said his boat was destroyed in the storm. I though he'd be here."

Dirty hated all *where-are-they* questions; there were too many warrants, too many pissed off ex-wives, too many ex-partners, and too many dangerous men seeking revenge and offering head money to give information to anyone. Dirty's philosophy was that if you do not know where someone is, it is because they do not want you to. He felt that way about Grady, too. He didn't know where he was and if he were alive, and that's the way Grady wanted it. However, he was pretty sure Rigger Grady wasn't among the living, and neither were Painter Pete or Salvage Tom. He thought the three had probably bought it on whatever golden horizon Tom had chased.

Dirty answered with, "When was the last time you saw him? You must be his ex-wife? Girlfriend?"

She politely smiled. Dirty's heart fluttered. She said, "Grady said you don't like questions, but you sure are full of them. I'm not an ex-anything. I'm a long-time friend, and to answer your next question, no, he's not boning me. We're not that kind of friends."

Dirty said, "Wish you hadn't told me that. I'd prefer to think that he was. He was always such a lucky son of a bitch."

"Sorry to have ruined your day. I saw him in Martinique just before Bunny came along. The people at the marina said they haven't seen him since then. How about you?"

"It's the same around here. So Grady was in Martinique; was he with two other crummy assholes?"

She knew it had to be the treasure hunters he was talking about, so she answered, "No. He was there with one of his sleazy girlfriends. We had planned to have dinner that night but I was on a cruise ship and they made us leave. You don't suppose that he would stay there during the storm, do you?"

"Lady . . . What is your name anyway?"

"Abby Savage."

"Well, Abby Savage, you can never tell what any of these crazy bastards will do. Two more of these shitheads haven't been seen since either. We know those two went somewhere to chase some kind of fucking—pardon—stinking, phantasmal fortune. Grady had expressed an interest in the project, so they probably met up down there and are together, either on earth or in hell." He laughed silently at himself: *Now I'm correcting my language in front of a woman, no, a lady. That's a fucking first.*

"That's not a very nice thing to say about your friends."

"Fuck nice. Err, pardon, screw nice; those guys are nuts and know what a hurricane can do and wouldn't hesitate a New York second to stick their balls, err, pardon, heinies, dead in the middle of it if it gave them a kick, or a few bucks. If they didn't survive the storm, it's because they deliberately put themselves in a position to get killed. You can't feel sorry or worry about speaking nicely about people who'll do that. They wouldn't like it."

She shook her head negatively and said, "Grady wouldn't have done anything like that." Then she realized that was exactly what he was doing the last time she had seen him.

"If you believe that, Abby, then you don't know the same Grady I do. That guy will climb up to the top of these fucking, err, stinking sailboat masts any day of the week for a few bucks. He couldn't care fucking less; err, less if it's raining in a twenty-knot wind. I'm telling you, these guys," he sweeps a hand around to encompass the crows, "every fu . . . stinking one of 'em is nuts."

Abby enjoyed Dirty's attempt to clean up his language. She did not use the "F" word herself, but certainly did not mind if others did. Maybe she would stick around for a while; she liked the place and maybe she could clean up Dirty's image and the crows' reputation a little. Besides, she needed to know when Grady, Pete, and Tom showed up, if they ever did.

She watched as a tattered rubber dinghy idled in to Dirty's bar. The man in it slid the bow into the tangled ruins of what had been lush mangrove trees before Bunny. He loosely tied it to a stump and stepped into the bar. Since he arrived in Lagoonie style and dressed in Lagoonie fashion—rags—he was accepted by Dirty and the crows as one of their own. By his dress and actions, he was obviously a cruising sailor, but he looked very familiar to her.

9

Tricks

WHILE CLASSY ABBY WAS SITTING IN DIRTY DICK'S getting blitzed, nasty Ann was getting hammered. Her mental mastery and sexy charms had bought her a victory once again. Maurice, in a fit of passion on the floor of the helicopter, agreed that she was entitled to her dead husband's gold. As passion turned to bliss, they smoked cigarettes and discussed Ann's offer for Maurice to work for her. He was readily agreeable, but wanted her to hire his other men, too. That would be the best and most secure way to protect her interest in the gold. She was delighted, and secretly could hardly wait to have the Panamanian brute, Jorge inside her.

The Kevins sat on the grass outside of the chopper with the other Frenchmen. There was no communication between the two groups, not even an exchange of glances. Tension was high.

Finally, the door slid open, and Ann came out, wearing only a wicked smile. The Frenchmen gawked in appreciation. The Kevins were horrified, something was wrong. To Ann, the Kevins were loose ends, and when fired, they would surely tell Maurice the truth about the gold, or worse yet, tell the authorities, who would confiscate her treasure.

Without fanfare she said, "You two are fired! I've decided to upgrade my staff."

Then she turned to Maurice and said, "Maurice, these idiots will send the Costa Ricans after us, and we'll never get out of the country. Even if we do, they could come after us. I don't want to be looking behind my back for my ex-bodyguards or a foreign government trying to steal my gold. Shoot them!"

That surprised the Frenchmen. It sent panic through the Kevins, but neither knew if she was joking and neither knew what to say.

Maurice expected trouble, but not this kind. Thinking she was only trying to frighten her bodyguards into remaining quiet, he went to the storage compartment, retrieved an Uzi, popped the clip out, and tossed the gun to Ann.

Without hesitation, she smiled wickedly and turned to the Kevins. Kevin Two shuddered in fear. His eyes were squeezed shut until he hear the click of the firing pin. He opened his eyes to see Ann look into the magazine.

Angry, Ann commanded, "Never again hand me a weapon that isn't fully loaded."

"Oui, mademoiselle," Maurice said and tossed her the clip. She deftly loaded the weapon, and as she raised the muzzle up and towards the Kevins, Kevin Two's mind kicked in. He turned and sprinted away. He was fast, but he couldn't outrun the two speeding bullets that entered his back and knocked him to the ground. Kevin lay on the ground rolling over in pain; blood covered his back.

Kevin One was a Texas jackrabbit in headlights. He was frozen with fear, but not for long. Ann blew his head into pieces by emptying the clip on him. She tossed the smoking and empty gun to Maurice and said, "Give me another."

Maurice motioned to Jorge to get a gun; Jorge doubled checked to be sure it had a full clip and took it to Ann.

"Good boy, Jorge." she said. Then she went to the badly wounded Kevin Two, and emptied the clip into his face. "Now there are no faces to tie them to me." She motioned Maurice to follow her to the helicopter. Fifteen minutes later, Ann, dressed, led Maurice out of the chopper.

At the engine compartment, she stopped and turned to face him, then said in a loving tone, "I have a couple of surprises for you, lover. First, is the foot; it isn't big enough to belong to Morgan. He wears a size twelve and that couldn't have been much bigger than a ten. Maurice, he's a tricky son of a bitch. He wouldn't have left that treasure behind if that's all there had been. I know how he thinks; he's not here because he has taken the treasure with him, and planted ten lousy bars and the severed leg to throw anyone who's looking off his track."

Maurice was definitely interested in what she was saying.

"We have to find him before he leaves this country or he'll disappear again. I have no idea where he has been hiding, but he has been impossible to find."

Maurice was appreciative of Ann the beautiful. He had thought that ten gold bars was a puny cache for the fabled Lost Treasure of El Morro. Hiding a token amount and taking the bulk was a great idea that would have worked if Ann had not shown up. Beloit would not have been fooled, however; and he would have hung Maurice by the balls.

Maurice smiled, and said, "Have no fear my dearest, I know where he and his partners have been living. As soon as we get this damn thing to start, we'll get in motion to search Costa Rica and then we can go to St. Thomas in the Caribbean and make love while waiting for him to show."

"So that's where the bastard's been. I'll be damned." Feeling great relief, and at Maurice mentioning making love, she began to get that old feeling and she rubbed herself on him until he was hard. Then she quit, feeling pleased with her power. She murmured in his ear, "Before I let you take me again I must tell you the other thing. I know you'll be pleased. I know the trick to starting this thing."

"The trick?"

"Yes, the pilot has been having problems with a doohickey in there and hasn't fixed it because it only happens once in awhile. He showed me." She leaned into the compartment and said, "You have to jump the electricity from this fitting to this one. I don't know what it does, but the engine will start."

"Shit, we were about ready to start walking down. We tried everything to get that damn thing started and you knew it all the time." He smiled, then lovingly muttered, "I wonder what other secrets you possess in that beautiful head. You are a woman that will surely drive me insane, my love . . . and I will love every second of the process."

Maurice began caressing her; he looked into her eyes and said, "My little kitten, it will be best if you do not say anything about the treasure." He smiled, "You and I may want to keep the rest just for us."

She responded in her passionate way, which created an enormous boner for Maurice. It was a reminder she wanted him to live with a little longer to make the passion more urgent and his animalism wilder when *she* was ready. Ann pulled away and unbuttoned her clothes and let them fall to the ground, and then said, "I am going to give you such pleasure when I return, my stallion."

"Return?... Surely, you jest. This thing is going to explode if I don't have you now. Where are you going?"

"While you get the chopper ready, I'm going to wash in the creek. I want to be fresh when I give myself to you on the trip back. It'll be glorious, lasting love."

He protested, "But I'm the pilot!"

"I know. You'll fly us both at the same time." Her saucy smile widened as she turned and teasingly walked to the creek.

Maurice looked down at his raging hard-on and said, "Too bad, my friend, but you might as well go back to sleep."

Ann found a nice place to bathe. The tranquility of the cloud forest, the cool mountain water that made tinkling sounds as it sloshed around rocks and branches, the still air with its cloudy mist dulling the wild green jungle all around her, was an intoxicating combination. She wished Maurice were with her now to make love in the wilderness Eden, just as the other wild animals do as lusty beasts.

She heard the engine starting and knew it would be useless to yell for her lover. The engine noise increased, and sounded as if it were taking off. She bolted out of the water to see what was happening, but could not see through the fog as she raced to where the helicopter had been. The fading engine noise had not lied; the helicopter was gone. The only things left were dead Kevins. They had even taken her clothes.

The female in her wanted to sit down and cry, but the monster that lived under her beauty was enraged. She yelled threats and shook both angry fists into the gray sky until she was nearly exhausted. Then the female in her thought: *They're going to come back. Maurice would never leave me.*

An hour passed and she had tired of cursing herself for being so stupid. *Why did she show them how to start the damn thing, and then walk away?* She could not understand Maurice, he had wanted her so badly. She, for the first time in her memory was completely alone. Being alone and naked in the middle of a wild jungle and on top of a mountain as darkness neared, was terrifying. She became aware of the jungle's sounds, the birds, bugs, and all the other things that were calling or screaming. Animals were eating things and animals were being eaten.

She had never noticed the noise before, and began to think she had not noticed the noise because it had not been there. It was there now because the carnivorous animals were coming to get her. They were going to rip her beautiful body to shreds and eat her.

With slumped shoulders and hanging head, she muttered, "Ann Blackburn, rich and beautiful, now just another lost soul who dared venture to the Mountain of Lost Souls. . . . If the next person up here finds my skull, one thing for sure, it definitely won't be smiling."

That thought hit her hard, she straightened up, took a deep breath, and angrily yelled, "What's wrong with me? I've never given up. I've never lost, except once to that bastard, Morgan. I won't be beaten this time, either."

She ran over and started tearing the Kevins bloodied clothes off, as she said with an evil vengeance, "Now I know where to find Morgan, and Maurice, you stupid bastard—you should have killed me. I will enjoy your torment for many hours or days before I cut out your heart and feed it to the dogs." She started laughing.

Pete and Jake left the hotel that evening for their dinner with Juan Carlos. Robert did not go; he was passed out in his room. As North Americans, they were right on real time, not Latin time. Juan Carlos had anticipated as much and had made sure that his other guests were early.

The housekeeper met them at the door and showed the gringos to the sitting parlor next to the dining room. Pete entered wearing his friendliest smile that instantly disappeared when he heard the voice and saw the boy moving toward him, "Pete!"

The boy ran to him and hugged him. His father followed; he was beaming the biggest smile Pete had ever seen. He grabbed Pete's hand and began shaking it while telling him thank you in every way he knew. Chico's mother followed with tears streaming down her cheeks and hugged the rest of his upper body. Chico's little sisters were crying because their mother was, and they ran over and hugged his legs.

Mongo was perplexed and skirted the emotional circus to stand next to Juan Carlos. He had to ask, "Who is this guy? These people act as if he saved the world."

Juan, enjoying the show, took his eyes off the commotion to briefly look at Mongo and answered him. "He saved their world."

Then Juan moved to settle everyone down. He gently pried the sisters away, then the mother. Chico got the idea and disengaged, and his father, still beaming, stopped pumping Pete's hand.

Juan said, "Pete, I thought that was a very gallant thing you did by giving the boy that gold. It was a gift, right?"

Pete was dumbfounded. *How could that happen? Chico was supposed to say he found it.* He answered, "Sure."

Juan said, "Not many men would have done that. I don't think you can understand what that bar will do for the Comancho family. Not only will it let them survive the wreckage of our country, but it also elevates their position in the community. Fernando can buy more land; and hire help so he can produce more crops. It probably will permanently improve his family's way for future generations. He no longer is a peón or a dirt farmer; he owns his finca."

Pete looked surprised, "Really? How much was it worth?"

"That, my friend, may depend on you. Let's talk about it over dinner. I'll bet you guys are hungry."

As they moved to the dining room, Mongo grabbed Pete and asked, "That gold bar was yours? You're dead broke, and you gave it to a kid?" He was astonished that he could be so stupid. "Do you know what that bar is worth?"

"Apparently it was enough to make a real difference in somebody's life. I figured it was around four grand."

"I knew I liked you for some reason; you're fucking nuts. You're wandering around wearing rags, starving, penniless, and you give gold that you think is worth four grand away to a kid that'd be happy with a hundred bucks."

"I didn't have a hundred bucks. All I had was the bar, and it was worth it, Mongo. The kid did me a huge favor. I'll tell you about it sometime."

"I'd like to hear it. By the way, Pete, that bar would be worth eight or nine thousand dollars. I hope that doesn't ruin your appetite."

Pete shrugged his shoulders, and said, "Such is life." That attitude caused Mongo to have another thought: *or you've got more gold stashed.*

After a generous helping of rice, beans, chicken, and a two-inch thick sirloin, freshly butchered from one of Juan Carlos's steers, they adjourned to the parlor again. Juan Carlos told the women to go into the kitchen and talk to the cook. The men had business to discuss. The remark was not insulting, it was just the way they did things in Costa Rica.

Juan started the conversation that Pete had dreaded since he walked in. "Pete, Chico tells me you looked for more bars at the crash site. He said you didn't find any. Mind if I ask you where you got the gold, and how many bars there were?"

"I don't know if there were any more. I just looked in case there were."

That's bullshit, thought Jake.

That's bullshit, thought Juan Carlos. He translated for Chico.

That's bullshit, thought Chico; *he said there were more.*

Wonder if they'll believe that bullshit, thought Pete. Then he said, "As far as where it came from, I have absolutely no idea. I was just as surprised as Chico to find it."

"Yes, I'm sure you were, but you were Tonto until you found the gold, weren't you. That bar is what jolted your memory back, isn't it?"

"No. I slipped and fell down the aisle and hit my head. That's when my memory returned."

Mongo asked, "What the hell are you guys talking about? You were Tonto? Crash site? What's going on?"

Juan Carlos looked at Pete, waiting for an answer. Everyone else at the table awaited Juan Carlos's translation.

Shit, shit, shit! Can't tell them, Pete thought, but then said, "Tonto as in stupid. I was a passenger on a private plane that crashed into a mountain. I was damaged in the crash, lost my memory. I was the only survivor, so I came down and was spending my time trying to find food. I had no memory of the past; didn't even know I was a North American or that I spoke English. Chico had seen the plane disappear into the mountain clouds and figured there was a crash. He disobeyed his father and went to the top looking. He found the plane but no survivors, only a skull. He carried the skull down to a village where I was waiting for a doctor. When I saw the skull, something in my mind sensed there was something very special about it. I begged Chico to take me to the place he found the skull; he led me there."

They had to speak in English as Mongo had only completed one day of his Spanish class. Juan translated.

At the end of the translation Fernando immediately said, "It's an evil place; only those with a truly brave and innocent heart may go and hope to return." He proudly patted his son on his knee. Juan translated for Mongo.

Pete continued, "He showed me the wreck site and I felt I had been there before. It was an eerie feeling. I had the same feeling inside the aircraft. When I fell down, I hit my head and my memory returned. That's all there is to it."

Mongo asked, "What were you doing, or where were you going in the plane?"

"I heard this guy in St. Thomas had a plane and was going to Costa Rica. I always wanted to come here, so I asked him for a ride."

Juan Carlos said, "Chico said you told him you were the pilot."

"Not me. It was another guy, but his body was gone. I don't remember telling Chico I was the pilot."

That drove another shard into Juan Carlos's respect for Pete, and made Pete's whole story totally unbelievable. He had talked to Doctor Carter earlier that day and learned that Pete's real name was Morgan Blackburn and Pete had already acknowledged that he had flown F16s with Clumsy in the Air Force. Then there was Pete's wife, Ann Blackburn, who had flown down the same day she learned of Pete. Pete told Chico to find the wife and feed her a phony story so he could escape. *Why?* He hoped to learn soon.

The story sounded fishy to Mongo, as well. He was an honest man and expected the same from anybody he called a friend. He asked, "Where did you learn to speak such good Spanish if you've never been down here?"

"What's with the interrogation, guys? I've lived in most every country along the Atlantic coast of South America. They speak Spanish, in case you didn't know."

Juan said, "Sorry about the questions, but a man crashing into a mountain and living, and then giving a young boy a gold bar that equals the total wealth his father could make in many years, makes one curious. Mind you, I didn't say suspicious. If you didn't know anything about the gold bar, then why did you tell Chico that the skull was a pirate's and was hundreds of years old?"

Pete sighed, tired of the questioning, and looked at Chico. He thought: *Chico, you little jabber-mouth.* He said, "I thought it would make a good story. The gold looked old so I thought it would be good for his imagination. That's all. It was a harmless lie."

"So where did the skull come from?" asked Mongo.

"It was in the airplane or it belonged to one of the lost souls that mountain is supposed to have."

Juan Carlos then said, "And you told Chico to find the evil woman looking for you and tell her that you are on top of the mountain looking for more gold in order to make good an escape. I guess you must owe her back alimony or child support."

"That's right . . . err, that's alimony. I don't have kids."

Juan smiled, but thought: *Right. The woman is going to spend money to come down here and then charter a helicopter for days to find a husband who owes her alimony. I don't think so. What's your secret, Morgan? It can only be one thing, the lost treasure of El Morro. You have the treasure and you are trying to hide it. You know what will happen if the government can connect you with digging up treasure, they'll confiscate it. If I only knew for certain, Morgan, I could make your life a lot easier.*

Juan decided to see what would happen with a little deception, "By the way, Pete, I sent word to your ex-wife that we would be here tonight. I'm sure she'll be here as soon as she gets the message. I heard she's very eager to rest her eyes on her rebellious husband." He wanted to laugh at Pete's expression. It was a sudden change from being rankled to being frightened.

Pete said, "No problem. I just don't like her, and I owe her a couple thousand bucks that I have no intention of paying. My real reason for not wanting to see her is she's a nasty person who wants my life to be miserable."

Juan said, "Well, if she doesn't get here tonight, maybe you'll see her in San Jose tomorrow. By the way, I can fly you guys there in the morning. The car rental company said that, under the circumstances, you could leave it here. They'll pick it up at no charge after the bridges are fixed."

Pete felt like shouting with relief.

Mongo, still not too sure about his new friend said, "Yeah, my wife will be happy. Thanks, Juan Carlos."

Pete, in an obvious hurry to be any place other than where Ann could find him, said, "Well, it's late and it's been a long day. Thanks for everything, Juan Carlos." He stood and on his way out, he said goodbye to the Comancho family.

Pete's urgent need to leave piqued Mongo's curiosity even more. A couple of thousand dollars and a nasty relationship was not reason enough to make a man like Pete run away from an ex-wife. Moreover, his rude departure from their host was not what he considered acceptable behavior. Mongo deliberately lingered longer in Juan's house while looking at some of his relics. He wanted to see what Pete would do.

Outside in the cool night air, Pete felt better. He walked around the yard, his eyes scanning the blackness for approaching headlights or helicopters. As he walked near the house, he heard Juan Carlos translating the rest of the English conversation to the Comanchos. Then he heard something interesting; Juan Carlos said that JC had been sent to get equipment they would need to look for more gold at the crash site.

Juan Carlos had not planned to look for the gold until he found out if it belonged to Pete. Since Pete claimed not to know anything about it, he had forfeited all rights to it. He also asked Chico to go with his son and three other men to show them the way and to protect his interest in their partnership. Young Chico was proud that Juan Carlos would even ask.

On the way back to the hotel, the car was quiet. Mongo broke the uncomfortable silence by saying, in a cold tone, "Your story sounded phony. I tried to see an angle to it that was believable, but it's too screwy. I keep thinking that the most logical explanation would be that you were involved in a gold-for-dope deal. That would be a good motive for trying to conceal your reasons and the lack of other bodies. I think I'd better rethink my offer to get you home. If you are a smuggler, then I could lose my trader's license and I do have a family to support. Your wife is here; she can get you home now."

Maurice and his chums wished it had not been so foggy on the mountaintop. They had wanted to see her face, watch her reaction as they lifted off. With a grin on his face, Maurice said, "Let that treacherous woman fuck the monkeys and boss the jaguars around. Stupid woman, did she think we were so inexperienced as to align ourselves with a person who'd kill her faithful employees? The fact that she thought she could walk up, fuck me, and buy me, pissed me off."

Jorge, also with a grin, said, "But you did a masterful job of masking your anger. I was beginning to think that you were in love with her." All the Frenchmen laughed at the ridiculous notion.

Maurice said, "She made a good point that ten bars wasn't much of a treasure. Beloit wouldn't go through this trouble for such a small treasure. By the way, she's convinced that the leg did not belong to her husband, and said he's a crafty bastard. Ann thinks he has the treasure and will go back to his hideout. That makes sense to me, too. I think it'll be worthwhile to stop off at St. Thomas to see if he or the others show up."

Jorge said, "One of them will be easy to spot; he'll have a hell of a limp."

"I don't remember if I told her the name of the island, hope not; if that nasty bitch manages to get down the mountain, my name is going to be on that same list as her husband's. You guys will have to protect me." They all laughed, but Maurice was in a hurry to put distance between him and the Mountain of

Lost Souls. He could envision the venomous woman running down the mountain at full speed, snarling and sharpening her claws in anticipation of a bloody massacre.

As light faded into dark, Maurice landed the red helicopter in an open field not far from the airport. He had Jorge walk to the airport where their car would be waiting. By ten o'clock that evening, they were sitting around a hotel bar getting drunk and gorging themselves with zesty Latin food.

It still was unknown what the thieves were doing in Costa Rica, but Maurice reasoned they either had a buyer for the gold there, or had planned to hide out in Grady's house until they could land their plane in St. Thomas. Pierre Beloit agreed when Maurice called. The Frenchmen's orders had not changed, Beloit wanted revenge; he wanted to personally put the thieves to death.

The brief conversation about Pete getting his ex to take him home was the last they had on the drive back to the hotel. Mongo was not his usual jovial self and that bothered Pete. The man had been a friend and he had clumsily lied to him. Pete understood that the friendship was badly fractured.

As they pulled into the dimly lighted parking area Pete said, "Mongo, I'd like to explain what I did tonight. It isn't as you think; I'm not a smuggler... well maybe I am, but not drugs, or in the usual way. It's a story not easily believed, but it'll be the truth. I lied to Juan Carlos for a good reason tonight. There was a pirate's treasure on board the aircraft. If I told anyone and the Costa Rican government got involved, it would get the other government involved, too. Between the two, neither would believe that there was only one gold bar or that the storm's rains washed the others away. Of course, the other bars may still be up there, but if they are, they're under the airplane, and it'd take some heavy equipment to move it."

He looked at Mongo, "For ten gold bars, it wasn't worth the risk to have to answer questions that would surely end up with me in legal battles, or in jail."

"Why would you go to jail?"

"Entering a country illegally is one reason. I'd have to explain how I happened to be on a private jet that belongs to a man who disappeared. Digging up a treasure that another government figures they have a right to is another reason. And most importantly, they'll try to make me show them where I found it, and that, I will not do."

"Ten bars like the one we saw is worth almost ninety thousand dollars." Mongo said. "Plus, if it is from an old treasure, it has added value if you can prove it. Are you telling me that you're so flush, you can't use ninety grand?"

"I'm broke. My sole possession was my sailboat that was lost in the hurricane. My checking account in St. Thomas has about 300 bucks in it."

"What's the deal about the guy with the jet?"

"That's the unbelievable part. He and one of my best friends were following my partner and me as we looked for the treasure. It turned out that my friend was a longtime thief, a smuggler, and very rich. He owned the Lear. His buddy tricked us into getting the treasure. Then he knocked us out, wrapped us up in heavy chains and was about to shove us out of the plane at ten thousand feet. He tripped over my feet and fell out himself."

Mongo snorted in disbelief, "So neither of you could fly, and the plane crashed?"

"I do know how to fly, but couldn't, because he had us both wrapped up in chains. How we got through Bunny without being dumped out of the open doorway, I'll never know."

"So the chain protected you when you crashed?"

"No. My partner, Tom, saw me throw up all over myself. He was a smart son of a bitch, rocket scientist smart, actually. He figured out that if we got our clothes wet, reducing the friction of dry fabric hanging on the chain, we could possibly wiggle out of the coils. He rolled to the back of the cabin where the rain sprayed in and got thoroughly soaked; he got free about the time the airplane ran out of fuel."

"You're bullshitting me."

"No, I'm not. He freed me as fast as possible, but it wasn't soon enough. I reached the controls just in time to pull the nose up, which took some of the punch out of the crash. How I survived is a miracle; somebody up there wants to keep me on earth a little longer. Maybe it was my ex-wife's prayers to let her find me before HE takes me."

"What's she so hot about? Did she catch you fucking her best friend? Owe her some serious money? Kidnap your kids?"

"It's nothing as mundane as that. I made her look bad to some people she wanted to impress. I refused to steal and deliver an F-16 to a base in Panama for a drug lord she was screwing at the time. Instead, I took it to McDill in Tampa, and spilled the beans on her and the drug runner. I had hoped they would drag her off to the slammer, but her money bought the lawyers that put her above the law. Ever since then, she has had detectives around the world looking for me. I've managed to escape because I completely changed my lifestyle."

"So you weren't too happy to hear that Juan Carlos told her you were at his place."

"Weren't too happy? I was scared shitless. You'd know why if you knew her. She's the most beautiful woman I've ever seen, but her insanity equals that degree, too. She's a natural born con artist, a treacherous criminal with not a shred of conscience, and to make her more dangerous, she's a genius. I doubt that a minute goes by without her scheming about something to make herself richer. She knows how to get everything she wants; always has and always will, except for me. I split, leaving her high and dry."

"That sounds kind of nutty. Hell, she's only a woman, Pete; you're a big guy. It looks like you could take care of yourself."

"Yeah, but she doesn't fight fair; she has a thing about losing. Besides, she has her bodyguards to do the muscle work."

"Are you serious, Pete, or is this just another case of the ex-wife miseries?"

"Well, you'll never know because I'm not going to be snared by that blood-thirsty maniac. I'll step in front of a semi-truck first."

"All right, I believe you. I'll get you back home. I guess with only $300, I won't hold my breath to be repaid. So don't worry about it."

"Bullshit, I pay my own way. I'll send you the money in a couple of weeks."

"Oh yeah? Going to take up bank robbing?"

Pete smiled, and there was enough light from the dashboard for Mongo to see that smile. Then he said, "No, there's no need for that. There's enough treasure left for me to pay you back, buy my new boat, and finance your kenaf company. That is, if you and Robert stay on and run it. How does that sound?"

"Sounds like a plan to me. Damn, Pete, how many more bars do you have?"

"Don't know; it's still buried because it was too much to carry out."

"So that's why you gave the ten bars away. It's easier than explaining its existence until you have the rest of the treasure secured. And that's why you'd never show the authorities where it was found."

"Eggg-zakely, Doctor Mongo."

10

Truth

ABBY WOKE WITH A HANGOVER BORN IN HELL. She needed to vomit, and as she put her foot on the floor to race to the bathroom and slipped on the slimy mess at her bedside, it was obvious that she had been sick the night before. After barfing, she crawled back into bed and lay there in her morning misery. She hated herself for drinking so much; she normally would only have two or three drinks.

A lot of brain-fog surrounded her evening at Dirty's bar. Then she remembered that Dirty had picked the two soberest men to drive her home. He sent them off with a stern warning about not treating her in any way they would not treat their own mothers. She remembered liking that; she felt secure being under his care. Dirty was not such a bad guy and he had been very nice to her; it was only the crows that he was gruff with.

Then she remembered talking to a brusque old woman, Alice, who, despite having the biggest rear-end she had ever seen, did provide more information than she wanted on Grady's pal, Painter Pete, and the island's bottommost Lagoonie, Salvage Tom.

Then the memory returned of a man she had watched come to the bar in a dinghy, as did the feeling that something was not quite right. She had seen him somewhere before, and suddenly she knew where. Something had to be wrong. He had been on the flight from New York to Miami with her, sitting in first class and across the aisle from her, and he was with another man. Both were well dressed in expensive black suits. One of her talents was being able to read a person by the way they dressed and acted. She had labeled them as native New Yorkers because of their obvious fuck-you personalities.

On the plane, he definitely looked and acted like a powerful businessman. His traveling companion could have been a gangster because of his rough and ugly face, but she sloughed off that possibility because he was dressed too well and his mannerisms were too refined for a hooligan. The contrast bothered her: *Why had a polished businessman turned up in a remote Caribbean dive dressed like a bum?* No one seemed to know him. Every time she glanced his way, he was watching Dirty, but he never spoke to him.

Grady had said Dirty was concerned about outsiders coming into his place, and he thought Dirty was probably hiding from someone. She looked at her watch; it was noon, her usual hour to get up and get going. She would be brave and have breakfast at Dirty's place. An hour and a half later, after showering and pampering her skin and getting her beautiful face just right, and her hair carefully combed to look as if it had been tossed in a carefree manner, she was ready. While looking for her car keys, she found a note from Dirty.

Good morning, pretty lady.
I wouldn't let the boys drive your Jeep so they brought you home in mine. I have your keys. Come by for breakfast tomorrow; it's on the house. And in case you're wondering if you did anything wrong last night the answer is no. You were a perfect lady and if you did anything wrong it was to make every crow around here fall in love.
Yours truly included. (Don't tell Fat-ass Alice, she'll be jealous.)
Dirty

Abby laughed and called the front desk for a taxi. The taxi driver almost refused to take her to Dirty's bar. He warned her that it was infested with riff-raff and it was not safe for an unescorted lady to go in there. She wanted to correct the driver, the men were not riffraff; they were just tired of society's bullshit and were no longer interested in the politically correct. Besides, with Dirty there, nobody would dare get out of line. She had found a friend.

Dirty smiled when Abby walked in, and he made a couple of crows move to give her room at the bar. She felt at ease. Against her better judgment, she ate Dirty Eggs, the name itself was not appetizing and the mess piled up on her plate was not visibly acceptable for breakfast. However, it was hot food and tasted good; she had started the process of turning into a crow, but did refuse a beer that early in the day. Cultivating that aspect of crowism would take a little longer.

After breakfast, she asked Dirty if they could talk in private. He showed her to the storeroom, which was also his office and sometimes home for one or two of the crows if they were too drunk to find their way home.

"Dirty, it may be nothing, but I thought I should tell you something. Grady told me that you didn't like Statesiders coming in and asking questions, or snooping around. He said you might not want to be found by someone. He also said many of the other crows, as you call them, felt the same way. And that is one of the reasons Grady likes your place. He's in the same boat."

Dirty did not know how to react. He had liked Abby in a fatherly way, but not if she was going to be the nosy kind. He started to tell her so, but she continued, "Also, I'm sure my husband would feel comfortable here. And that's why I want to tell you about a man I saw here yesterday." Dirty felt better about her.

She told him about the New Yorker, and the only bit of news that bothered Dirty was that his eyes followed Dirty's every move.

"I'm glad you said something, but don't be too concerned. You'd never know it, but some of the crows have big money. Some still have a business; they use my phone to call occasionally to check in. Some rely on the stock market for support. There are three millionaires that I know of who are crows and even they charge their fucking, err, stinking beers. But did you notice anything more about the other man on the flight?"

"I though he was a gangster at first, as he was somewhat scary to look at, had a strong Bronx accent, but also had an expansive vocabulary. I know that's no reason to rule him out as being a gangster, but he could be a cop or an attorney. Or he may be nothing at all."

"So tell me, Abby, what makes you so suspicious? What kind of business is your husband in?"

She looked uncomfortable at the question when she answered, "Just intuition, I guess. My husband's business is his own affair, but you can say that he fits in the plays-the-stock-market-income bracket, like some of your millionaire crows."

"Fair enough. Thanks for alerting me about the new guy. I'll check him out. Now I hear the crows getting unruly out there. Must be thirsty, and how about you? Ready for a beer yet? It's on the house."

Abby smiled and hugged him and said, "Dirty, that's not necessary. I'm not one of your crows; I can pay for my own, but thank you."

"Oh, you're such a classy broad. If I were only ten years younger, I'd take you away from that husband of yours."

"I don't know about that. He loves me and he's pretty big. Besides, what would Alice say?" They laughed.

Dirty said, "Sorry, little lady, but you can't spend your money in my place. You're too good for business. All the crows stayed, not one of them left while you were here last night. A lot of them, not wanting to look poor in front of the only dignified lady to grace this joint, paid cash for their drinks, Besides, I like you for some reason; hate to admit it, but in a fatherly way. And since I'm feeling fatherly, I have to ask about your husband. Where's he and what would he say about you being here looking for Grady?"

She was embarrassed about her husband's business, but felt she did not have to worry about fatherly Dirty. She hesitated briefly, and then said, "He and Grady are pals. He was coming here to see him and I haven't been able find either of them since. That's a couple of weeks ago. I thought if I found Grady, I'd find him. Was a man here looking for Grady?"

Dirty had a sinking feeling; *he was about to make one of the people he liked feel bad.* He asked, "Was he a black guy with a light chocolate complexion?"

"Yes. Was he here?"

"A big guy with lots of muscles?"

"Yes. Where is he?"

"Does he speak well and dress in fancy clothes?"

"Yes, yes, that's him! Is he still here?"

"I haven't seen him." He smiled at the old joke routine, but behind the smile was sadness.

"Where is he?"

"Why are you married to a no-good son of a bitch like that? Good thing you aren't my daughter; I'd have to turn you bottom side up and give you a good spanking. He came in here with another jerk-off, err pardon, guy, and I ran 'em off. I didn't like them. And I'm afraid that I pissed him off, Abby."

She quickly asked, "Was Grady with him?"

"No, little lady. Like I said last night, Grady hasn't been around since before the storm."

She hesitantly asked, "What do you mean you pissed my husband off?"

"Abby, he's a fucking loser, err, pardon; he's a loser. That man has done hard time before. Did you know that?"

"I know he was in jail once for something that he didn't do."

"That's bullshit, err, pardon, baloney. That man wasn't in a jail; he's done time in a maximum-security prison. I know, so have I. It leaves a mark on a man that all hard-timers can recognize." He stopped talking, looked at her, and then asked, "Do you mind if I curse? Being careful with my language is kind of hard."

She smiled and wanted to say, fuck no, but shyly said, "Shucks, no." He would have preferred to hear the fuck no, but was happy that she didn't swear. He continued, "Well, I knew he was trouble, and if I have a fault, it's that I don't like phonies. He came in here like a big shot so I treated him like the phony he was and he threw a punch at me. I humiliated him in front of the crows and that really pissed him off. He's no good, Abby. Do yourself a big favor and dump the fucker, err, jerk."

"And what happened then? I know you can't mess with him and get away with it. He has a crazy temper."

"Yeah, and that's a good reason to stay away from a . . . creep like that." His cursing habit was improving. "The guy waited for the place to close, and then he sneaked in here as I was leaving. He planned to shove a knife in my back." Abby was horrified.

"But I was too good for him. I beat the shit out of him, Abby, because I know guys like him very well. I knew he'd be back the next night or the next unless I killed him or slowed him down so he could reflect on the errors of his ways. I broke both his arms so he wouldn't be a threat. . . . Sorry."

Tears began pouring from her eyes. "You beat him up and broke his arms?" He genuinely felt sorrow and nodded his head.

"You must be talking about another man, Dirty. Jerome is in top shape. He's tough, and please excuse me, but he's about twenty years younger than you."

"Nope. He's the only chocolate man fitting that description that's been here looking for Grady. I'm telling you, as someone who cares about you, dump the guy. You may love him, but he's bad news."

"You sound just like my mother."

"Really! She beat the shit out of him, too?"

Juan Carlos was waiting at the hangar when the gringos arrived three minutes early. He was eager to get Pete into a position to make him talk about the gold. He had to know. If it were still on the mountain, his son and Chico would know soon enough. If it were not, then it would be traveling with Pete, if he had it, or the cash from its sale. If Pete had neither, then Juan was ready to play hardball. He was going to have the lost Spanish treasure, and while he did not mind paying a fair price, he would get it one way or another.

If his suspicions were confirmed, it should open the door to negotiation. If not, he was not sure of what he was going to do. The only legal thing he could think of was to get his friend, the chief of police, to arrest him on smuggling charges. It would cost him a share of the gold, but that would be better than losing it all. His other option was to forget about it, cherish the one bar and let the treasure slip through his fingers.

The flight to San Jose was bumpy as another rain system was moving over the country. More rain that was not needed would fall for a day or two. But bumpy or not, Juan Carlos loved flying over the countryside. Tiny villages were scattered over the mountains with dirt trails leading to roads that led to larger villages in the valleys, with more roads that led to the main artery of his nation, the Pan American Highway. And that led to the central city of San Jose and southward to Panama. It was a beautiful sight with mixtures of farm browns and mountain jungle greens. White clouds settled down on mountain-tops, as if resting. Their lower sections turned from snow white to various shades of gray, some to near black where there was rain. He loved his country and was proud to be a Costa Rican.

His landing in San Jose was delayed at the last minute when the controller instructed him to turn off. A private jet had taxied without clearance and had taken off. Both the controller and Juan Carlos were angry and knew it had to be foreigners who had no respect for his country and its rules. It was always the super rich Americans or Europeans. Had he known that nine of his gold bars were on board, he would have shot the plane down—had he been in a fighter plane—as he often fantasized when flying.

Juan Carlos's plane, after landing, taxied up to a big black Lincoln left by Juan's chauffeur on the tarmac. As they drove away, Juan Carlos asked, "We have three hours to get you boys to the International airport; it's only twenty minutes away. Would you mind giving me a hand on the way? I've got to drop off some things." The gringos were busy clowning around; they would have agreed to anything.

As he passed the hospital, he said, "This is the place. It won't take long. Pete would you mind helping me carry some books?"

All the gringos offered, but Juan kept it to only Pete, saying, "Three happy gringos are almost more than a civilized man can handle. Besides it's hospital rules to restrict visitors to only two." Juan led Pete, who carried four novels, past the front desk without checking in and through a maze of corridors crowded with over-used equipment and sick people. The elevator, used to go up three flights, looked like it might have been the very first one installed in

Costa Rica. It made Pete nervous and he was glad he was not going any higher. He followed Juan like an obedient puppy into a small and crowded hospital room with four patients in beds. It was obvious that it was an orthopedic ward, as legs or arms were hung in traction devices. The one patient not in traction was in the last bed. Pete was happy that Juan had not led him into a ward where everyone was moaning in pain and sickness, or coughing and sneezing, or puking; he hated that stuff in hospitals. Broken bones were okay; they were not catchy.

They went to see the last man, but he was asleep and facing the wall. Pete noticed that there were no stacks of books to carry, only a couple of newspapers and a very over-read and tattered *Playboy* magazine. Juan shook the patient's shoulder; the man stirred and then groaned.

The man rolled around, still in the edge of sleep, and squinted to keep the light out of his eyes. His beard was scruffy, long hair disheveled, and he looked confused, as if trying to get his brain to recognize the two shapes at his bedside.

Pete was stunned. His brain refused to process the information his eyes were sending. Juan was quiet but watched closely; it was the moment of truth. Pete turned to Juan as if he needed help to comprehend. Finally, it seemed like minutes, but in only seconds, he asked, "Tom?"

The sleepy man wiped his eyes, looked again at the pair, and then focused on one of them. His emotions went berserk. "Pete! Pete! You're alive!" Excited, he jumped out of bed, only to fall flat on the floor. He had forgotten that he had lost a leg in the crash.

Pete was stunned at the sight of his one-legged friend; he was supposed to be dead and eaten by animals or drowned in the deep pool. Both men were emotional and confused; the only one who had his wits was Juan Carlos. His hunch had been right, they both came from the crash; both knew of the treasure, and at least one of them knew where it was. While Pete was helping his friend to his foot, Juan went for a wheelchair.

Pete and Tom's conversation quickly turned boring. They kept saying, "I couldn't find you. I thought you were dead."

"I thought you were dead and burned in the wreckage."

"I thought you were dead, I couldn't find you. I thought . . . ." Both were intellectually stunned.

Juan wheeled Tom out. Pete followed and was so happy that if he had a tail, it would have been wagging crazily in the air. Juan found the waiting room and politely asked the three people who were there to leave. The three recognized the manner of a superior macho and left without ill feelings. An important man needed privacy or he would not have asked them to leave.

Juan said, "So you both survived the crash. That's beyond belief, isn't it? Normally, people who fly into mountaintops do not. I only hope you two don't die of a sudden heart attack at finding each other. Why don't you guys settle down and tell each other your stories, one at a time. You probably want to be alone, but because you both owe me something, I'll settle for the truth. I'll clear up a couple of things first."

He looked at Tom and said, “One of my men found you crawling in my fields. You looked like you were dead, but didn’t know it. You were covered with your own blood. He knew you were a gringo and brought you to me on his tractor. I’ve never seen such a sad case; your leg had been torn off, but you refused to tell us what had happened. You were nearly naked; the only clothing you had was not much more than the waistband of your pants. You had a tattered rag that I guessed had been a shirt, tied around your stump as a tourniquet. Your old injuries were exposed. You’ve really had a tough time of it, haven’t you?”

Tom was too embarrassed to acknowledge the statement; he was ashamed that someone had seen his scarred torso and had the audacity to talk about it. But that was by Juan’s design; he had checked on him after he was in the hospital. He wanted Tom to open up, but Tom had refused to tell anyone how he had lost the leg or where he came from. The Immigration Department was very interested in where he had come from, too, but Juan used his influence to have them wait for his release before pursuing the truth.

Juan said, “I understand that you don’t like talking about it, but I found out that your injuries were caused by the war. I also learned that you sustained them while trying to save two of your men, who were pinned down by machinegun fire. You were awarded a Bronze Star for the act.” He looked at Pete and said, “Did you know your buddy is a bona fide war hero?”

Pete looked at his friend strangely and said, “No, I didn’t. Why didn’t you tell me that part? You said that you wanted respect from the guys in your outfit and wanted to make a difference. Sounds like you did, if you saved those guys. Shit man, they don’t give Bronze Stars for nothing.”

Tom was even more embarrassed. He said, “It doesn’t count when you get torn to shreds in the process. I’ve always hated myself for going after them.”

“You said you were hit with mortar fire, not a machinegun. Why would you hate yourself? That was a gallant act.”

Tom was irritated. “It was a stupid act. Had I known what life has to offer a blown-up guy, I’d have stayed in hiding and dug in deeper. I took hits from both weapons actually. Didn’t mind the holes so much, just the missing parts. Now I have more parts missing. With my luck I’ll eventually lose everything, and when I die, I’ll just be a head.” He looked blankly at them and laughed.

“Well, relax, partner,” Pete said with a smile, “I’ll hang your head up in Dirty’s so you don’t miss anything.” The boys were getting back to normal.

Juan continued his story, “But your luck sure as hell was working for you the day my man found you. Ten minutes after you were brought to me, a Red Cross helicopter with a doctor on board flew overhead to see if any help was needed.

Pete asked, “A woman doctor?”

“Yes, Doctor Mary. Everyone in our valley thinks she was sent by God.”

“She sure helped me,” said Pete, remembering her pretty face and unselfish actions.

Juan said, “Then, Tom, you were brought here. By the way, I’m paying your hospital bill. I'll need your help when you're ready to leave to recover my cost from the Veteran's Hospital program your country has. In addition, our government insists that you clear up a couple of things. You will not be able to refuse telling them how you were injured. Run over by a tractor, as you tried to tell us, won't work. They also want to know why you were found in the middle of nowhere, and why you had never legally entered our country. In fact, they want that information from you both. I know these people; I've asked them to hold off questioning until you recovered. You look recovered enough to me, now, so it's time to bring in the law and get this all behind us. You know you won't be able to leave here without clearing Immigration, don't you?"

Pete was angry. "You knew this all the time, didn't you? You tricked me into thinking that we were going to fly out today."

"Sorry, Pete, but you deserved it for lying to me. I'm not any more of a rat than you were. I found out through Doctor Mary about you. I know who you are, but I need to learn more from you. Things like why your ex-wife is so intent on finding you. From what I've heard, it isn't love. She seems to be a very liberated woman."

"She's a bit more than liberated; she's a crazy woman with a nasty disposition and blind ambition. She's pissed at something I did to cause her a great deal of embarrassment." He went on to tell the story. He finished with, "Now are you happy?"

"Not hardly, but I feel better about you. Now, what about the gold?" He was watching Tom for a reaction, and he got one: a look of guilty surprise. He continued, I know where that gold bar came from, boys. It's known as the lost Treasure of El Morro in many books on Spanish history. There have been all kinds of speculation as to what happened to it. Not a bar has ever surfaced in the hundreds of years that passed since Captain Newl disappeared. If you boys found it, I want to buy it from you. I'm a collector of Spanish artifacts and the treasure would be my centerpiece. If you have it and plan to melt it down and sell it off in small quantities I beg you not to. That missing gold represents a major change in Spanish history. Spain's forts depended on it to support them for a five-year period. Without it, they were not able to trade for much-needed supplies, including gunpowder. Spain had no more to give them. It shifted the balance of power, allowing the English to capture more territory. Even the pirates of the day were not afraid of the forts, or the soldiers. They had lost their fighting spirit."

Tom looked at Pete and said, "You have the gold?"

"I found one bar. Do you have it?"

"No. I didn't even look for it. I just wanted to get down that mountain. I figured if nobody knew about the wreck, I'd go back when I got fixed up. It was so cloudy up there, no one could have seen the crash."

Pete said, "Someone did see it, a young boy, and he's responsible for me being here." He told Tom his story, and ended up with, "I thought you might have tried to carry some of the gold with you and drowned at the base of a waterfall."

Tom interrupted, "I did! I didn't have the gold but I was floating down that river and I went right over. How I lived through that one, I'll never know."

Juan said, "It appears you two are pretty damn hard to kill. I'll have to tell my government to be sure to use silver bullets when they line you up for the firing squad," he joked. Only he laughed.

Tom looked at Juan and said, "How did you find out about the gold?"

"Your partner gave it to the boy; I'm not sure why, but I think it was going to be a burden to explain, and he wanted to reward the kid, too. The boy brought it to me to buy. Of course, I checked the seal and found out what it was. I paid the boy the current value and made him an equal partner if we found more. That was before I connected Pete with it. After I began to suspect that he had something to do with the gold I respected the idea that he had found it and it would rightfully belong to him. I was willing to pay his price, but he refused, as you have, to talk about it.

"I must tell you boys that I have sent Chico, my son, and several other men up there to look for the gold. If they find it, it still belongs to you, but I hope that you'll let me buy it. How much is up there?"

Pete thought Juan Carlos could not have been any fairer. He was the moneyman they had to find somewhere and they had landed right in his lap. He asked, "Before we talk, tell me how much trouble we're going to have leaving here."

"The authorities don't know about you, Pete. I didn't tell them or your ex-wife about you. I'm afraid that I lied to you. Tom, they do know about you, but obviously, not your plane crash. That will remain our secret, as I didn't want the police traipsing all over my land trying to solve the mystery of the one-legged gringo. I made up a story that you were on the way to San Jose from Nicaragua and crashed your Piper on my property. The plane burned and I cleared the wreckage so I could plant. All they were concerned about is that you were not running drugs. I assured them you were not. They accept my word here. I *normally* never lie."

Pete said, "I'm glad you lied about my wife, but you scared the shit out of me last night." Then he looked at Tom and said, "What do we have to lose?"

Tom shrugged his shoulders, and said, "Okay, Juan Carlos. Your dream comes true, but we expect fair payment. We have spent years researching it, invested everything we had, and have gone through the worst hurricane possible to find this treasure. We've lost our only possessions, which were the boats we lived on. There are nine more bars. I expect the market value plus 150 percent for our finder's fee and to establish the collector's value."

Juan Carlos looked at him in disbelief. Pete expected Juan Carlos's disgust was caused by the finder's fee that even surprised him. That was not what angered him. "Nine bars? Why do you lie to me? I told you the significance of this gold and you tell me you only have nine bars! I treat you kindly; I could take the gold away from you if I wished, but I offer you fairness and you offer me a lie!"

Juan Carlos looked at Tom who looked like he wanted to laugh.

Finally, Tom said, "Juan Carlos, you asked about the gold on the aircraft. Only ten bars were aboard and you have one of them. That is all of the gold we have seen so far. There is more, but we don't have a clue how much. We left it where it was buried because we couldn't carry any more than the ten bars. It weighed close to 300 pounds with the wooden chest. The other chest was much larger."

Juan Carlos looked relieved and said, "I knew it! Oh, thank God! Please tell me all about it, where it was, who took it, how you found it…Everything."

"There's only one way you'll get that information; you'll have to come with us. And bring your calling card to transfer the money to our international account after we get one set up."

Pete said, "I know just the guy," and he told Tom about the gringo kenaffers who were sitting in the car.

Juan said, "Don't be concerned about your buddies. I had someone drive them to the airport; their flight actually was leaving at nine."

He laughed; Pete did too, but while appreciating and fearing Juan's deviousness. He said, "You'd be a good match for my ex-wife."

Abby had been able to get a room at the hotel because the manager was her mother's personal friend. Someone else with more pull than Abby's mom had placed a call and demanded at least one room. With a full house, the manager moved Abby to his own guesthouse, which was okay with her.

Beloit's four henchmen moved in as Abby's things were being removed by bellmen. One room was fine, as the men split up to work twelve-hour shifts. Maurice and Jorge worked from noon to midnight, the other pair from midnight to noon. It was a twenty-four-hour surveillance at the place called Dirty's Beer Joint, where the salvage diver called home.

Each team split up, one would sit in the bar for an hour or so nursing a beer or eating, the other was free to roam. The bartender, who was an asshole, did not make their job comfortable. They constantly scanned the marina for the diver, or men matching the description of the other two, and listened to pick up key words associated with Pete, Grady, and Tom. They soon learned that this was the right place, but the trio had vanished.

Maurice was startled on his first trip to the dirty little bar. Boat-bums lingered about, as expected, but there was one beautiful woman dressed as if she were going to a garden party. Her beauty fascinated him. He briefly wondered how Ann was making out on the mountaintop. Too bad, she had been such a bitch. He really should have left her clothes, but it had seemed like the thing to do at the time. *C'est la vie.* Maurice considered making a move on the lady but could tell the bartender had declared her off limits; he was overly protective, and since he was already difficult to deal with, Maurice did not need another problem.

Dirty was on full alert. Something was going on; he had a bad feeling that his past was catching up with him. He started carrying his Beretta Minx again, a habit he had managed to break years ago. Its weight in his pocket was uncomfortable, but reassuring. The permanently stained apron hid it well.

The man Abby had told him about came in and avoided looking into his eyes. Abby was right; he was up to no good, and after a brief conversation that Dirty initiated, he knew the man was a problem. When the man introduced himself and they shook hands, Dirty knew at once that those were not the hands of a sailor; the nails were clean, manicured, polished, and weren't calloused; the man was clearly a city-born-and-raised boy of Italian ancestry. Alarms were sounding. If the Hydra had sent him, he would be a professional killer. He would not make mistakes. Dirty knew he wouldn't have anything to worry about in the bar, but closing time, or at home on his boat, he'd have to expect the man to make his play.

There was another possibility, too. Abby's husband might have hired the man to hit him. Abby had seen the stranger with another New Yorker; neither were her husband's friend or associate. Besides, Jerome was not the type to let someone else settle the score for him. He was a mean son of a bitch and would want that pleasure himself.

Dirty was curious about the connection between the New Yorker and the Frenchmen, who had suddenly started coming to his place. He did not think they were there for him, but they were looking for someone. It had to be Roosterman; he had something going with a Frenchman. If not, it could be related to the disappearance of the three crows. What had Tom gotten into? It was time for a heart-to-heart with Abby; he felt that she knew more than she had said.

Abby was talking to Fat-Ass Alice; they seemed to be getting along very well for being on opposite ends of the social scale. Dirty roughly grabbed one of the crows by the shoulder, led him behind the bar, and said, "You're the bartender for awhile. Your drinks are free but don't you give any away to your crummy friends."

Then he motioned Abby to meet him in the office. Abby looked puzzled as she went in, and he sat her down on the rumpled mattress. He then sat beside her.

"Abby, I love having you here, but I'm curious how long you're going to wait for Jerome or Grady to show up."

Her expression changed to worried. "I don't know what to do. I think something has happened, and I don't know how to find out." Her expression turned sad, and tears began filling her eyes. It gave Dirty an excuse to hold her and he briefly wished she were crying for him.

"Abby, I'm going to help you sort this out, but you have to be honest with me. Will you do that?" She nodded her head while sniffling. "What frame of mind was Jerome in when he came to see Grady?"

She hesitated. If she started talking, it would lead to other things that she did not want him to know. He might not like her after he found out what kind of person she had been, but there was no one else she trusted. She said, "He was mad at Grady. He thought Grady had taken something from him on one of their business deals. Jerome is funny that way. He's scared to death that someone is going to take advantage of him and he got obsessed about Grady."

"Be honest with me. I know what kind of man Jerome is. He wouldn't hesitate to kill someone if he justified it to himself. Do you think he'd kill Grady?"

"I don't think so. Those guys were like brothers, and they have been for many years. I was sure he'd face Grady and they'd yell and scream a bit, maybe punch each other a few times until Jerome came to his senses. Then they'd go off and get drunk for a few days. They loved to go on drinking binges once in a while."

"They ever run off for this long?"

"No. Jerome truly loves me. Even on their binges, he'd call me every day. I just know something's wrong."

"Where did they meet, college, work?"

She looked down, hesitated, and then answered the difficult question, "I guess you could call it work; they were in jail together."

Dirty's expression suddenly showed his satisfaction. "I knew Grady had done time. I can always tell, but the son of a bitch always denied it."

He thought for a minute, and then asked, "I won't ask what they were doing, but are they working together on something illegal? It's important for me to know, Abby."

"Yes."

"And that's what Grady was doing in Martinique when you saw him last?"

"Yes. It started as one of their regular meetings, but they got sidetracked on some kind of deal."

"And what was that?" She looked at him; her eyes were red, her expression pained, and her sorrow apparent. She remained quiet, blew her nose, and finally said, "I don't want to tell you, Dirty. You'll hate me," and she started weeping. There was nothing she could say or do to make Dirty hate her at that moment.

"Abby, I've done a lot of stupid things and I've broken most of the laws in my lifetime. I'm no angel; I understand these things. There's nothing you can say that will ever stop me from being your friend." That made her cry even harder, she sobbed.

Finally, her tears ebbed; she wiped her eyes with her dainty little hanky that was soaked with salty tears and slimy mucus. "If you hate me, I'll understand. It wasn't my plan, but I went along because it sounded exciting. I didn't know them; they were Grady's friends and it was all his idea."

Dirty had a bad feeling and was sure Grady had something to do with Pete and Tom's disappearance. He stayed quiet waiting for Abby to resume her confession, but staying calm was hard.

"Grady and Bill, the man who works for him, found out that either Pete or Tom had found a buried pirate's treasure. They followed them in Grady's airplane to Martinique. Grady offered Jerome a split on the treasure if he'd help. I went, too, but I got afraid when I learned they planned to take it away from the other guys. When the hurricane started getting close, I made Jerome take me away. Bill flew us to Grenada."

Dirty did not want to interrupt her but had to slow her down a bit. This was hard to believe. "Grady has a man working for him named Bill? Grady has an airplane? Grady was going to waylay Pete, his buddy?"

She shook her head and said, "Bill's been with him for a long time. He does Grady's dirty work. Yes, Grady has a Learjet. You wouldn't know it, but he has a lot of money."

"How do I find Bill?"

"I have no idea. I don't know where he lives or even his last name. I just assumed he lived on St. Thomas."

"In a way, I'm not surprised," he muttered. Then he looked at her and said, "But I can't believe he'd waylay Pete; they were friends."

"Grady really wanted that treasure for some reason. He was prepared to do anything to get it. He even stayed out there by himself watching the truck they used as the storm was approaching. Moreover, I don't think Pete and Tom were his friends; Grady doesn't have friends; he has buddies. Jerome is the closet thing to a friend that Grady ever had, and that's because they are exactly alike."

"Where was the truck parked? Was it on the east side of the island? And did Grady have a shelter to get into?"

"There was a small village a few miles away, but there was nothing but trees where the truck was parked."

"Well, that probably answers the question about Grady's whereabouts. He's fucking, err . . . dead."

"Dirty, after what I just told you, please stop worrying about cussing. I'm no angel, either. You should cuss me out for not telling you all of this before."

"Don't be silly." He was silent while thinking. Then he said, "Jerome was here with another man who had a high-speed boat. There was no way Jerome could have landed here from Grenada. He must have come by boat. No. A seaplane. He checked out Martinique first. That means Grady wasn't there."

Then he remembered something and said, "Abby, come with me. I have a hunch about something. One of the crows, Rooster, followed Jerome outside after I threw him out of here. They had a long chat about something. Then a few days later, Rooster told everyone that a rich Frenchman was flying him to Costa Rica for some fishing. That was fucking odd, err . . . odd. . . . I prefer not to swear in front of you, sorry. Now Rooster's gone and I've got Frenchmen hanging around. Umm, something is happening. Let's go talk to Biddy, Rooster's wife."

He led her out to his boat; its generator was running to supply electricity for the bar's beer cooler with a very long extension cord. He used the VHF to call the Rooster's boat. "*Chicken Coop, Chicken Coop* . . . this is Dirty." There was no response from *Chicken Coop* but someone else said, "She's on the boat, Dirty. The dinghy is there. She's probably laying an egg right now."

Dirty led Abby to his dinghy and they motored the half-mile to *Chicken Coop*. The boat was jammed into the mangroves with many other boats, but it was still afloat. Most were not. The mast was broken off and the hull was covered with gouges from beating against the mangroves during the storm. The sunken and tossed-about boats, the naked trees in the lagoon, made Abby want to cry. All the boats were pushed up, in, or on top of trees that were all brown, completely leafless with most every limb broken and shattered. It was a scene of destruction straight out of the *Twilight Zone*.

Dirty held on to the boat's stern and called out "Hey, Biddy! You in there?"

"What you want, Dirtyman?"

"Where's Rooster?"

"Why? He owes you money?"

"That's not why I'm here. Come outside, Biddy, I want to talk to you."

"I can talk just fine where I am. What you want?"

"Where's Rooster?"

"He's fishing."

"Where?"

"In the water, stupid."

"Damn it, Biddy quit fucking around and come out here. I want you to meet someone."

"It's that fancy woman that's been hanging out in your place ain't it? What she want with me?"

"She's looking for her husband. Rooster was the last one to talk to him. It happened a day or two before he went fishing with the Frenchman. I need to know where he went, Biddy."

She came out and her appearance shocked Abby. Biddy had short red hair combed straight up like a long flat top. The sides were shaved short. Her nose was long, thin, and hooked. Her body was thin but with big tits, and she was no taller than five feet. Her skin was snow white as if she never exposed herself to the warming rays of the sun. With feathers, she would have looked like a big chicken with tits. As she took the four steps to the stern, her head rocked forward then back with each hen-like step. She walked like a chicken, too. Abby could not contain herself and giggled; thinking Biddy was doing it for a joke, her giggle turned to laughter.

Biddy looked at her and said, "Ain't you got enough troubles without trying to piss me off. I'll drag that fancy ass of yours up here and beat the shit out of you if you laugh at me again. Where'd you get that fancy bitch, Dirty?"

Any need for giggles vanished and Abby was frightened. Dirty explained, "Biddy thinks she's a chicken. She loves chickens and thinks they are man's spirit while waiting to pass into their next lives. Normally she has a flock of them on the boat, but they were killed during the storm. Biddy's been distraught ever since."

Biddy interrupted him, "That's right. I'm in fucking mourning. Now what brings you all the way out to the turd pile? Who is her fucking husband anyway?"

"His name is Jerome, and he was here looking for Rigger Grady. Rooster talked to him, and I thought he might have mentioned where he was going."

"He did."

"Come on, Biddy. Where?"

"Why should I tell you anything? You don't let me bring my chickens in the bar no more. You cut us off if we get a penny over your limit. Why should I tell you shit? You're an asshole."

"You need to tell us so we can find her husband. He may be in trouble or be hurt. Besides, I told you that you can bring your fucking chickens in, but only one at a time and it has to be on a leash. You can't let them get on the bar and peck at the crows. It's not right. And you're always over your tab and I don't say shit to you. I've never cut you off, unless you get too drunk and start squawking your chicken songs. You know that."

"You think the rigger done fucked her husband up, eh? That why Grady ain't been around?"

"Don't know. That's what we're trying to find out. Can you give us anything to go on?"

"I might." She smiled. "But it'll cost ya."

Abby said, "I'll happily pay. How much?"

Dirty muttered, "Oh shit."

"It'll cost you both. Dirty, you got to do the rooster call and fancy pants you got to cluck-cluck sing *Yankee Doodle Dandy* for me. And give me ten dollars, too. And Dirty, you got to keep crowing until she clucks the whole damn song."

Dirty gave Abby a solemn look and said, "She's serious. Start clucking to the tune of *Yankee Doodle Dandy* and give her the ten bucks." He started crowing and flapping his arms at his sides.

Abby's embarrassment turned to acceptance after the first few bars were clucked. Heads popped out of nearby boats and cheered her and Dirty on. They knew what was going on; it happened a lot in their saltwater swamp. When she finished, everyone applauded, including Biddy. Abby's life had changed. She suddenly understood and loved the Lagoonies.

With the ten dollars shoved into her tattered shorts, Biddy said, "Rooster told the stranger about Grady's shack in Costa Rica. Her husband said he was going there. Rooster called the Frenchman and told him, too. That's when they came and got him."

"Why would Rooster tell a man in France that Grady has shack in Costa Rica? Why would a Frenchman be interested in Grady?"

"It weren't Grady, bozo. The Frenchman paid Rooster to keep an eye on Salvage Tom. He wanted to know if Tom suddenly became rich. So Rooster, being the fucking genius he is, put two and two together and figures that Grady, Pete, and Tom, since they're thicker than fucking fleas anyway, were together and were gone because Tom was hiding the money he stole from the Frenchy."

Dirty asked, "Who said Tom stole something?"

"Use your head for something other than a place to hang that big mouth of yours. Why would that Frenchman pay Rooster for over a year to see if Tom gets rich or starts acting strange? Tom did a salvage job for the Frenchman and Rooster figures that he found whatever it is that's so valuable. And he couldn't bring it here because of the hurricane so they went to Grady's place in the mountains."

"Rooster was spying on Salvage Tom?"

"Why not? The Frenchman was going to pay somebody to see if Tom stole something. Might as well be us. We need the money as much as anybody."

Abby said, "I wonder if the men—"

Dirty cut her off thinking the same thing. *If the Frenchmen who had come to the bar were the same as those who took Rooster, then where was Rooster?* "When is Rooster coming back?" he asked.

"I thought he'd be right back. He was just going along to identify the three assholes. He figured a day there, a day back, and two days there. I guess he was wrong. He's been gone a lot longer than that. You think he's all right?"

Dirty said, "Oh yeah. Don't worry about Rooster. He probably got a handful of money from the Frenchmen and he's not going to come back until he spends it in every whorehouse in Costa Rica." Biddy looked around for something to throw at Dirty as he cast off. The conversation was over.

Halfway back to the bar, Dirty stopped the dinghy, and looked at Abby. "Time to sort things out," he said. "We better find out what those Frenchmen want. One, are they all together? Two, did they hire Rooster? Three, where is Rooster? And four, did they find the crows? It makes sense, since I've learned that Grady has a jet. He and Bill could've hooked up with the boys. That would also mean that there was a treasure."

Abby jumped into Dirty's thinking and said, "And that could mean that Pete and Tom wouldn't have let the treasure be taken away. That would surely mean a fight, wouldn't it?"

"A hell of a fight, but there's something else. If the Frenchmen are the people who had Rooster, they're here now; that means whatever they were looking for wasn't found. They're expecting to find it here. They're taking turns hanging out; there's never more than one at a time in the bar, so they are expecting somebody to show up."

Then he pointed to the only sailboat still floating in the lagoon and said, "That's Salvage Tom's boat. He is as poor as a grown man can be. I can guarantee that he's not a thief. The only thing he has is stuff others have lost or thrown away." He stopped speaking as realization flooded over his rum-soaked brain. "That's it. About a year ago, he did a salvage job for a rich Frenchman who had lost his yacht. Tom found it and salvaged it for the insurance company. That was about the time Rooster was hired to watch Tom. Tom must have found the treasure, and I'll bet anything, it wasn't included in his contract. That would mean that it became salvageable. That's what the Frenchman wants."

"You're almost right. Grady said Tom had found an old treasure map."

"That's it. They must have found it. I fucking hope so, err . . . hope so. Maybe his luck has changed. Do you know that his boat, *Lulu*, was the only boat that didn't sink during the storm besides mine and one more?"

"I know, Dirty. Alice told me. She said you had it hauled and fixed for Tom before you knew Bunny was coming in. You're not such a hard-case, are you?"

"I'll show you hard case if you blab to anyone. I just felt sorry for the guy. He's a decent person; doesn't hurt anyone and would give you the shirt off his back, but he's had nothing but trouble. I wouldn't say anything, but it doesn't matter anymore because I'm pretty sure he's dead, but he and I have a mutual friend. Her name is Whorehouse Lou; she's the local madam."

Abby smiled, "What would Alice say about that?"

Dirty waved away the answer, "Lou and I have been the best of friends for years. Tom used to do some work for her. He didn't go there for sex; he went there just to talk to Lulu. He had some problems that all men fear more than death: a conniving ex-wife, war wounds that left him with very ugly scars, and no manhood." Abby was horrified.

"According to Lulu, it's really a horrible thing for Tom to endure. He never complained about it to anyone other than Lou. Poor guy, it's a good thing the crows never learned his secret; they'd never let him forget it."

"Speaking of being cruel, Dirty; why did you hurt Biddy's feelings by saying her husband was in a whorehouse?"

"I'd ruin her whole day if I didn't take a shot at her. She expects it, and if I tried to be nice all of a sudden, she'd know that I'm worried about Rooster."

"You really think there's a problem?"

"The answer is yes. The question is, for whom?" He gently touched her arm and said, "I think you better prepare yourself, Abby. If the Frenchmen and Jerome were all going to the same place, I'm afraid that Jerome might have come up the loser."

"I know." She teared up. "He would've called by now. Maybe it's for the best, anyway. The way he lived, it was only a matter of time, anyway. . . . Wish I had never gotten involved with him, but it was exciting and I did love him, but I've never liked his dark side. Does that sound screwy to you?"

"Yes, of course it does. Feminine logic always sounds screwy to me," he quickly answered, but with a warm smile. Then he said, "I'm going to have a chat with the Frenchmen."

Still tearful, Abby asked, "What makes you think they'll tell you anything?"

"I don't know Abby, maybe because of my affable nature. Or maybe because I'm such a persuasive motherfucker."

11

Closing In

TOM WAS STANDING UNASSISTED WHEN PETE AND JUAN CARLOS came in. He spread his hands out wide to both sides, took a slight bow and circus-chanted, "Da Daaa!" An ornately carved peg leg supported him. "Made it myself," he boasted.

Tom sat on the bed and held his leg high for all to see. The top, near the stump base was carved with jumping porpoises circling it. The next row had mermaids with oversized breasts. Below that, the *Lulu* circled the shaft. She looked better than she did in real life. At the bottom was a pirate's skull and crossed bones to complete Tom's masterpiece. Pete was envious, he almost wished he had one, too; all the real old salts of bygone years had peg legs; it was a seaman's badge of derring-do.

Juan Carlos had been busy making arrangements. He was excited about going hunting for the lost fortune of El Morro. It had captivated many men's fantasy for centuries, and soon it would be his.

Juan Carlos reported to Tom, who was the expedition leader. "I used my plane's radio to patch a call to my friend in Venezuela. I didn't tell him what we're doing and he didn't ask, but he's going to meet us in Port of Spain. He'll take us to his brother who operates a charter yacht company. Then he'll fly my plane back to his hacienda."

"Very good. How soon can we leave?"

"My aircraft is being serviced as we speak and will be ready shortly after four today. We're all set."

Tom said, "And the bank account?"

Pete answered, "It's still impossible to make long-distance calls, so I haven't been able to get through to Mongo to set up the IBC account. I'll try again after we get out of the storm-damaged area."

Juan Carlos said, "My bank is expecting my call to make the transfer to your account, and I'm carrying enough cash to charter the boat and keep us alive for a couple of weeks. This treasure, as wonderful as it is, is costing me a fortune. I hope it's all there. I'd hate to spend this much and not have the complete treasure."

"It'll be there," Pete said. "All you have to do is find the other nine bars on the mountain. If you can't, it's because they are buried up there."

By dark that evening, they had checked into a small parador near Punto Fijo and were sipping rum at Sonya's Pequeñito Café. Tom's diet had been restricted to bland hospital food, so he was looking forward to dinner. Pete was going to do the one thing he had wanted most since his memory recovered: call Emily. He found a commercial communications center a few blocks from the hotel. St. Thomas still did not have telephone service, but he got her parent's number from the stateside operator.

Emily answered after the second ring, "Hello."

"Hi, Emie, it's—" Emily bust out crying at the sound of Pete's voice. After the storm passed, she expected Pete would have trouble calling, but knew he would find a way. There would be SSB radios around and she knew the military had emergency satellite stations set up. He should have called sooner. The first few days she had been mad, then she worried and began to have serious doubts that he had survived. She knew he had stayed on that damn boat during the storm and it had taken him with it to the bottom. Still, she seldom strayed too far from the telephone, hoping for the best.

When the call happened, it was too much for her emotionally stretched state of mind. Her mother had to take the telephone, and that concerned Pete. There was not much time; the call was expensive and Juan Carlos had only given him twenty dollars. He would be cut off in four minutes.

After her mother explained her daughter's condition, Pete said, "I understand and wish I was there for her. Mrs. Hill, I'm in Venezuela right now calling from a pay station. They are going to cut me off in about three minutes. Please tell her that I love her and hope she can meet me in St. Thomas. I'll be there in five to seven days. I lost my boat in the storm and ended up in Costa Rica. I haven't been able to call until now. This was my very first opportunity. It's a hell of a story, though; she's going to love it."

In the background he could hear Emily's sobbing winding down; she was composed enough to talk. Mrs. Hill, being the motherly person she was, said, "Pete, you have scared my daughter out of her wits. She's been moping around here like a whipped puppy. You should be ashamed of yourself. But I'm so happy you're all right. I thought you were dead, so did Dad, but Emily was convinced you were tougher than that old hurricane. I guess she was right. Sorry to hear about your boat, but maybe it's for the best. Now maybe you two can find a nice, stable house and make it a home. Raise children instead of hell for a change."

The whole time her mother was jabbering Pete could hear Emily pleading with her to give her the telephone. Finally, Mother said, "Well, here is little miss smiley face. I better let her talk to you or she'll rip this thing out of my hand. Here you go. . . Oh, goodbye Pete, come see us. In fact, you can live here while you look for a house."

He heard the telephone being forcefully pried from her mother's fingers. Then Emily's silky voice came on, "Hello Pete, I've—." Time was up; the telephone went dead.

Jorge complained about staying on St. Thomas; he wanted to either visit his wife in Panama or his wife in Paris. Sitting around in a car or bar for twelve hours and then sleeping for twelve was getting to him. Maurice told him they had no choice; they were not to leave St. Thomas until they found the elusive thieves and Beloit's treasure. It could have been worse duty, but it was boring.

A little excitement was headed his way, but it would not make him any happier. He ordered a beer from the same old grungy bartender, looked at the same old wreck of a bar, and heard the same old voices that spoke of the same old stuff. He was so bored he was falling asleep at the bar, and didn't know it.

Dirty had a couple of the crows carry Jorge into the storeroom. Abby was there and had parked at the rear door. Dirty's sworn-to-secrecy crows carried the sleeping man through the room and out to the back seat of Abby's car. They drove to her apartment where they tied and gagged him. Dirty dismissed the crows and waited patiently until the effects of the Mickey wore off.

When Jorge awoke, he was thoroughly confused, blindfolded, hog-tied, and lying on what felt like a tiled floor. His head ached from the chemical that had sent him into dreamland and he had a strong need to throw up—but could not; his mouth was tapped shut. As the need to vomit became greater, confusion quickly passed to fear, then to terror, and then panic. Then he could not stop the involuntary action; his stomach convulsed and sent its contents up his throat only to be stopped by the sealed opening. The churning mass jammed into his air tubes leading to his nostrils and two streams of chunky vile painfully jetted into the air.

A hand grabbed the tape and roughly ripped it away, taking hairs from his neatly trimmed mustache with it. He spewed. He sucked in fresh air, spewed again, and was silent as his panic subsided. He knew that he had been drugged, but did not know why or who had taken him. His first fear was that the ruthless black-haired beauty on the mountaintop had found them. *How could she have gotten down the mountain so quickly? How could she have known where we were? Did she use her sexuality to persuade Maurice into betraying Beloit? Who else would grab me, Interpol? Wasn't their style. The thieves?*

Many years ago, about the time Dirty went on the run, he stopped talking like a New Yorker. He even had a touch of Texas as an accent now. However, the New York was still there when he wanted it. Using his Bronx voice he asked, "If you don't want your mouth covered with that tape again, you're gonna have to use it. What's your name?"

"Ben Dover," he quickly responded.

"Cute, but that name's a bit overused, but if you like it, I'll call you Ben. Now Ben, give me the names of your buddies."

"Which buddies? I have many."

"I only want to know about the other three who go to the wreck bar."

"I don't know what you're talking . . ." His speech was interrupted with a hard blow to his stomach, which expelled every bit of air from his lungs. He struggled for a breath. After he could breathe, the voice asked, "Sorry. I didn't hear their names. Would you mind repeating them?"

Jorge, a product of a lifetime in the underworld, was a realist. *Our surveillance was blown . . . or is this a ruse to throw any suspicion off Maurice and Ann? No, not Maurice, he knows everything I know. Think I'll play the game and not take the punishment. Have to stay alive.* He said, "Maurice Letmar, Jaquie Salvador, and Paul Pash."

"And your name?"

"Jorge Valdez."

"That's too bad, Jorge. I liked Ben Dover better. If you get out of here, you might consider changing it. Now tell me everything I want to know, and you'll be turned loose. I got no problem with you. Where can we find the little rat-fink who went to Costa Rica with you to put the finger on the salvage diver and Morgan?"

Shit, it must be the thieves. After a brief hesitation, Jorge answered. "He's dead."

"Glad to hear it. Tell me more."

"We didn't have anything to do with it. Roosterman was shot in cold blood by three guys in Costa Rica. He didn't see it coming."

"Too bad. Then what happened?"

"The killers thought we were somebody else, and tried to kill us, too. There was a fight. We won, but believe me, it was completely in self-defense. They came in blasting."

"Who were they?"

"We checked the identification they had on them, but I can't remember their names. Really I can't."

"Describe them."

"One guy, the leader, was a big black guy. He had one broken arm and a broken hand. I guessed he was there to get a little payback for his injuries."

"Was his name Jerome Savage?"

"Yes! That's it."

Abby sitting in a chair, watching, was shocked at the sudden truth, and infuriated at Jerome's destructive forcefulness, she screamed. "That stupid son of a bitch!"

Shit!. . . It's her! Must've been her crew. . . . Blowing the Kevins away had been a deadly deception to make us lower our defenses. . . . She was going to have those guys ambush us. No wonder her offer was so generous.

"And the other two?"

"One guy was a white guy. Had a funny name . . . It was Julian. Jackson Julian! The other guy was Costa Rican. . . . His name was Ernesto something." He heard the woman stomp across the floor and a door slam. *Yeah, those guys were on her payroll.*

"Did Grady survive?"

"He wasn't there. We don't know anything about him other than Roosterman said he was a friend of the diver.

"Okay, tell me everything you know about Morgan and the salvager, including the value of the prize the diver took.

"The gold belongs to my boss. He devoted years searching for it and paid the salvage guy to find it. The salvager kept it for himself. My boss has been cheated and he wants it back. I have no idea of the value. We only found a few bars and the diver's leg in the plane's wreckage. He's dead, but the other one, Morgan, survived."

"And you're waiting for him to show up here, right?"

"Right."

Dirty knew Tom too well to believe that he'd steal, but apparently he had, or at least had in the mind of Jorge's employer. He said, "You ever find the rest of the diver's body?"

"No. It was probably eaten by animals. The leg was under the fuselage, but human bones were scattered around the area."

"Why do you assume it was Morgan who survived?"

"He was seen in a village and fingerprints identified him. His ex-wife flew down from Huston when she learned he was there. She said the foot we found was too small to belong to Morgan."

Dirty was surprised that the information flowed so freely. It was as if Jorge thought the answers were already known. Tough guys don't give it up so easily unless it's a lie, or they know the game is over. Then words are his bullets, his only tool that will keep him alive.

Dirty stayed quiet for a moment to consider what he had learned: *Pete is, or was, alive, but how and why would an ex-wife be so interested in him?* He hoped to learn more with indirect questions. Maybe his ex-wife had taken him home.

"That's a very thoughtful ex-wife, isn't it, Jorge?"

Without much hesitation, Jorge said, "She's a piece of work, a real beauty, but apparently Morgan really hurt her." He wasn't about to expound on the neurotic bitch. "I'm sure he deserves whatever she has in mind. I wouldn't want to be in our man, Maurice's, shoes, either. I tried to talk him out of it, but he did her dirty, too."

"Well, Jorge, if you guys didn't find him, why wouldn't you think the ex took him home to Houston for her moment of glory? And why would he come here, if he knew she was hot on his tail for some payback?"

Jorge became nervous at those questions. His inquisitor knew she had been left to die in a Costa Rican mountain jungle. To answer with the truth or a lie would only release the cord and let fall the blade of Madame la Guillotine in the next room. He would be the first sip in her thirst for revenge. With a dry throat, he muttered, "She doesn't know Morgan lived here."

"Why do you think that she doesn't know where he lived?"

"He was still alive."

Dirty had to smile at that statement; Pete's ex must be a real handful. Maybe that's why he never mentioned that he had been married. "Okay, we've made progress, Jorge. Don't run off, I'll be right back."

He heard a door open and then close. Jorge stayed quiet, waiting for the door to open again and the ax to fall. *How did she know to come to St. Thomas?*

There was only one way, Maurice must have said something while in a mind-weakening fit of passion.

In the next room, Abby's eyes were red from crying, but they were dry. Her first hurdle into widowhood had passed. She and Dirty had a hushed conversation. He was going to keep Jorge out of circulation for a while. To release him would alert his companions.

Pete would return, if for no other reason than to tell them about Tom and to see Emily, if she ever came back. He needed to be warned about his ex-wife and the Frenchmen, but that was impossible until he made contact. Dirty knew the Frenchmen were professional thugs, and probably knew how to play the game. It would not do any good to kill them; they were only following orders. If they did not return with the goods, then the rich guy would just send more men with instructions to use more force.

Sanchez, Juan Carlos's friend couldn't wait. To beat an approaching weather system, he had to get the plane to his place, pronto. Juan Carlos, introduced as Señor Gomez, greeted the yacht broker at the airport.

The broker was surprised to see they were not carrying much luggage. Juan Carlos had an average-sized travel bag, and the other two men had only one small bag each. It certainly was not enough for a month's charter unless they were nudists. He had three boats lined up that would fit the requirements as given by the one named Mr. Smiley, Pete. Names were changed to protect the soon-to-be-guilty.

They had decided it would be better if the treasure could not be traced back to the treasure site. Juan Carlos did not intend to keep the find a secret; this was a godsend to share with the world, but it had to be discovered somewhere that would not invite greedy governments to take shares and do battle for years in this or that courtroom. Juan Carlos was positive that some people were not going to believe his story. Too many people had invested time and money to find the fabled treasure. He would make sure that when some zealot collector tried to track down the treasure site, there would be no tracks.

The men chose the only catamaran in the offering, which was much faster, and, with its shallow draft, could be beached with its bows on the island to load the gold. Sanchez had furnished the information for all the paperwork. Juan Carlos paid for the charter with cash.

By cocktail hour, they were sitting comfortably aboard a thirty-six foot catamaran. Cocktail hour was not spent sipping martinis that night; they were traveling by taxi to get their supplies. Pete wanted to be gone by midnight; this was going to be a quick incursion under cover of darkness.

Pete plotted their course to arrive with enough fading light to allow him to navigate the shoals without using a spotlight, which could be easily noticed from shore. He figured they would average ten miles per hour by using the engine if the wind slacked, or by slacking the sails if the wind was too strong. The voyage went as planned; Tom and Pete drank beer and sailed while Juan

Carlos worried. He was concerned that the only people who knew how to sail were drinking too much; worried that the treasure had been found by others; scared about pulling the yacht into the shallow waters; worried about being seen, and terrified at the possibility of getting caught. The only worry Pete had was losing the wind; sailing the fast cat was exhilarating.

Pegleg, as his friends would forever call Tom, enjoyed the sail. He loved the sea and the freedom it granted. His only problem was the discomfort his artistic leg gave him. He only took it off when the pain became too great, knowing he needed to get used to it, and he only had a few days to get ready. Tom wanted to dance a jig on the deck of his shiny new and sink-proof yacht when he returned to Dirty's bar. He had mixed feelings about his next boat; *Lulu* was still his love. He had planned to re-float and fix her up with his share of the treasure, but Pete's jabbering about the new boat he was going to buy was contagious. The idea of everything being new was appealing. Whenever he tried to make a firm decision on the boat, he had another beer instead. Deep inside, he knew which way he had to go; *Lulu* would win if anything was left of her.

The sailors were amazingly sober as the island neared and darkness approached. Pegleg read the chart as Pete began his approach. Juan had to drink a beer to calm down. Atlantic swells were ending their journey from Africa with thunderous crashes on the shoals. He prayed Pete was not going to take the boat into that area. His nervousness increased when the bow pointed directly at the rolling and boiling white water. He went below and put on a life jacket. When he came out, he offered jackets to the sailors; they looked at him as if he were crazy. Juan Carlos drank another beer, his second of the day.

Under sail alone, the fast moving cat crested on the first massive breaker and Juan was uncomfortable. He wanted to go below so he would not have to watch, but was mesmerized by the danger. Pete changed direction slightly and skillfully sailed down the length of the big wave's back, which put an extra five feet of water over the shoal. Then the charging white boiling water chased them through the rocks and into the deeper water around the small island. Juan thought Pete's skill at handling the wide boat under sail, and racing between the narrow jagged rocks, was supernatural. Repeatedly, disaster faced him, but he maneuvered out of harm's way and onto the next challenge.

At exactly the right instant, Pete said, "Now!" Pegleg released the jib sheet, slacked the main, and then quickly cranked in the jib; the main sail luffed while Pete ran to the bow. He picked up the previously prepared anchor and jumped to shore just as the hull gently nudged a rock. Juan had never known such sailing mastery was possible. He was truly amazed.

He did not understand, however, why Pete was so intent on wrapping the anchor rope around three different rocks before placing it under a rock ledge. Surely, he was a better seaman than that. When he asked, Pete only said, "fucking fairies," and walked away.

Juan could not believe the barren landscape; everything was dead. He wondered how Tom and Pete could have survived being there during the storm. To his mind, there was only one answer. Surviving the storm, surviving the man's attempt to roll them out of the plane, the crash onto the Mountain of Lost Souls, one makes an extremely difficult descent with a lost leg, the other finds his way down with a lost mind, both survive independently of the other. All of those things coupled with Pete's unnatural skills in handling the boat, dodging certain death with each wave, pointed to the obvious: his partners were protected by God.

He thought that was why they were the people chosen to find the Lost Treasure of El Morro. That was why the criminals were brought in with their airplane. God was taking them to Costa Rica to meet Juan Carlos, knowing that he alone would share the treasure's beauty and history and never allow it to be destroyed. Juan Carlos suddenly had a big grin; he was no longer worried.

He watched the powerful waves slam into the island and noticed the blowholes where waves drove into timeworn crevasses in the rocky shore. The openings constrained the passage of water so much that he could hear the sound of air being compressed, and then a sudden swooshing out of the holes proceeded the gushing water as it was forced out and up into the air for fifteen feet. The wasteland and its sounds made him feel that he was in a very primitive, powerful, and mystifying place.

Pegleg could not walk to the top, but he tried so many times that Pete lost his patience and carried him piggyback. Juan took the first digging shift. He wanted so much to photograph the island, the site, and the treasure, as it was found, but could not. If there were pictures, then someday someone would see them, and the treasure would be divided between lawyers and governments.

Tom was useless in the hole, so Pete did most of the digging. It was easy; the ground had been broken before. He began to worry when he did not hit anything and was below the point where Tom said he should hit the other chest. He dug harder, faster, and still, no chest. Juan Carlos was panicking, thinking that someone had found it.

Dirty and everyone else watched Biddy chicken-walk into the bar. Nobody laughed; everyone was always pleasant to her. They feared her wrath. She was an undersized and redheaded girl from a dirt-poor family in the Texas plains. She grew up scrapping for everything she could get. Now, at the age of forty, she had only the old boat and her stupid husband to show for herself. That made her an unhappy woman.

A long time ago, Dirty had made the mistake of telling her that chickens don't drink rum. She had responded by snapping, "Now, how in the hell would you know? Since when did you become a fucking chicken expert? I'll bet $100 that they do!" Dirty poured her a strong rum and coke, which she put on the floor; her chickens scurried over to the plastic cup, circled around the rim, and began drinking. Only then did Dirty realize that they also drink and eat anything on the floor, including small pebbles. A drunk chicken was not any prettier a sight than a drunk who thinks she is a chicken.

She asked Dirty, "You hear any more about Rooster?"

As he slid a rum and coke to her, he said, "Nope, but there are four Frenchmen hanging around here. Maybe they are the guys who took him fishing. One of them is usually here in an hour or so. You'll know him by his accent."

When the Frenchman arrived, he looked around, and then walked to the head, then around the boatyard, looking for his teammate. He had not spoken yet and Dirty couldn't wait to see how he handled Biddy. Finally, Maurice said to Dirty, "I was supposed to meet a man here. He speaks with a French accent. Have you seen him?"

Before Dirty could answer, Biddy verbally pounced on him. "Hey, you're a Frenchy, ain't ya?" The man nodded his head, obviously amused at the woman's appearance.

Biddy got off her barstool and chicken-walked directly to the stool next to him. His amusement turned to anxiety about the weird woman sitting next to him; she was clearly nuts.

Dirty was quick to answer his question before Biddy could chase him away. "Yeah, there was a Frenchy here for a while. He was talking to another guy, a stranger around here. I think they left together in the guy's dinghy."

Maurice was confused; Jorge would not leave unless he had a lead on Pete or Grady. He did not have time to dwell on it; the crazy woman was in his face.

"Hey Frenchy, you know my husband?"

"What is his name?" he answered politely

"Roosterman."

"Afraid I don't," he said, and he tried to turn away to his freshly served drink. She pulled on his shoulder to get his attention and said, "I bet you know Pierre Beloit though, don't ya? He's a Frenchman, too."

"No madam. I'm afraid France is a big country. I don't know the man, and in fact, I don't know most of the people there."

"Are you getting smart with me?"

"No. I just want to drink my beverage in peace, that's all."

"Well, if you want peace, why don't you drink at home? All you foreigners are alike, unfriendly. But you Frenchies aren't so fucked up when you want something, are you? No, then you're as sweet as a baby chick's ass. You people can't do shit for yourselves; we had to go to your country and beat up the Germans to make them stop kicking your asses. It cost us lots of good American men, but do you appreciate it? Shit, fucking no! You just get smart with a poor woman who is trying to find her husband who was doing a big favor for you people."

The Frenchman tried to say something in his defense and he was terribly tired at the Americans saved-your-ass shit. Biddy would not permit it; she kept right on talking over his words. "So Frenchy, now it's your turn to do something to pay us back in a very, very small way. If you don't know Beloit, well, a lot of your countrymen do. He's a very rich man. I want you to call your friends at home and find out what his phone number is. I want to talk to that turkey fucker about my Rooster. I'll be here tomorrow at this time; you better have that number for me."

Then she did a trick her girlfriend Bertha had taught her; she tightly closed one eye, opened the other as wide as possible and stared at him with a very mean expression on her face. The Frenchman decided not to argue or stay there a minute more. He gulped his drink down, left three dollars too much on the bar, and escaped.

Biddy chicken-ran after him and yelled, "Did you hear me, Frenchy? You get that phone number for me, or I'll put a bone-snapping whopping on your foreigner ass! Don't forget that you're dealing with an American now, not one of your turkey-shit Europeans!"

When she returned, Dirty told her the drinks were on him the rest of the day, but didn't say why. His plan had worked perfectly, and he would be sure she knew of the other two Frenchmen, as well. His plan to blame Jorge's disappearance on the New Yorker had been set in motion, but more work was required. Framing the man would be easy, but he had to find out whom, and how they had found him. For that, he would need Abby and Quick-draw Sidney.

When Abby showed up, Dirty selected another of his trusted crows to bartend. They took his dinghy out to Quick-draw's boat, *Traftnelis*. He was aboard, as always. He never left his boat except to buy food, parts, or to get drunk at Dirty's bar. The boat was not in the water; it was resting on top of crushed mangrove trees at an angle to starboard. A makeshift rope ladder hung down to the water's edge.

Abby asked, "He's living up there? Why doesn't he get it back into the water?"

"Can't, there's a big hole in the bottom that needs to be fixed first. Besides, it isn't easy to get a boat out of the trees. Salvage crews want ten grand to put him back in. He doesn't have the money."

Abby was incensed. "That's a shame to charge like that. His boat has an unusual name. It's a pretty name. Is it a foreign word for something nautical?"

"No it's an English word spelled backward. Quick-draw has an odd sense of humor." She looked at the word for a moment, then chuckled.

"Why Quick-draw? Is it like in Quick-draw McGraw, the cartoon?"

"Nope. It's because he's an artist and can draw a picture of anything in a couple of seconds. He worked for LAPD for years as a criminal sketch artist. I'd like you to give him the best description you can of the other man you saw in the airplane. Maybe I'll recognize him, and if I don't, then I'll send it to a friend of mine who can find out who it is."

Abby did not have much hope of giving him a good description; it was not her nature to study people's features. It had only been a couple of weeks since she had seen Jerome and she couldn't even describe him, other than that he was big, good looking, muscular, and a light-colored Afro-American.

It took a few minutes to convince Abby to climb up the shaky ladder. An hour later, he had an excellent rendering of Three Toes Sammy. A birth defect had caused him to be born with three toes on both feet. They had lived only a block apart and had been friends as kids. As an adult, no one would dare call him Three Toes Sammy; he was Sam Pano, and was a made-man in the family. He would have been much higher ranked, even allowed into the Hydra, had his father married an Italian.

While looking at the rendering, Dirty sarcastically muttered, "Obviously, our childhood friendship means nothing if he sent a hitter after me. How in the hell did he find me? Guess I'll have to put Mickey to work again, but this time, Sammy Three Toes, there'll be no witnesses." The stranger had told one of the crows yesterday that he was sailing off in a couple of days. That, to Dirty, meant the killer was ready. He would know Dirty's pattern, schedule, and where and when was best to have private access to him.

The hitter had been coming in later and later every day. Last night he showed up at nine and stayed until closing. Dirty knew he would do it again that night. Three Toes was careful not to show his face on the island and had sent an unknown whacker. Without Abby's tip, he would not have had a chance.

The hit man showed up late in the evening again and Dirty did not hesitate. Mickey was put into the first drink, and at the same time, Dirty bought a round of tequila for the bar to toast the passing of Big Eye Bertha. It had waddled onto the Texas and Louisiana coasts as a category three storm, blew down everything it could, and then pissed on everyone until the entire area was flooded. It had finally turned into a gigantic rainstorm as it drifted up the Mississippi River Basin. The tequila was a mask to cover an aftertaste of the Mickey that an experienced player could recognize. Everyone downed the shots and he poured them another. The passing of Big Eye merited a couple of drinks. Ten minutes later, the hit man was asleep in his chair.

Dirty said, "I'm getting tired of you guys drinking somewhere else and coming in here to pass out." He had a crow help him carry the sleeping man into the storeroom.

After the bar closed, Dirty carried the hitter to his dinghy, and idled out into the dark night. When in position, he shut the engine off and let the wind blow him to the stranger's boat by making silent adjustments with the oars. He would leave the same way and only start his engine when he was well clear of other boats. He did not want any reports of visitors that night.

When the hit man became conscious, he was in his boat's cabin and tied to the mast. He tried to clear his mind by shaking his head, but couldn't remember anything, or how he got there. Then he realized that he was tied up, and suddenly he knew the pounding headache was caused from a substance that had been put in his drink. How the fuck did Roberto know?

He heard footsteps and looked behind him. He moaned, but was not surprised to see Dirty. He asked, "Where'd I fuck up?"

"The only mistake you made was to be seen by a very lovely lady. Too bad; bad luck happens to the best, and I'll say you were damn good. That's why Three Toes Sammy hired you. Who, besides the two of you, knows I'm here?"

The hitter knew it was over, and acting foolish or trying to beg out was not going to work. He knew of Roberto's old ruthless reputation.

He said, "What do I get out of it if I tell you?"

"An easy out, no pain; that's the best you can expect."

"I thought so. What if I just take your tattoo back? You'll have a scar, but you'll be free of the bounty forever."

"You're shitting me. I told you the best you're going to get. Do you want to hear the worst?"

"No thank you, Roberto. No harm in trying, was there?" Dirty shrugged. It was good to hear his real name for the first time in over a decade.

"Only the two of us know. Sam did not want the word out in case you still had ears in town. He did not want another hitter down here trying to scoop the reward. You know he'll be sending more troops, don't you?"

"No, he won't. He'll be joining you before the sun sets today. I have more than ears up there. How in the hell did he find me?"

"A guy who ran afoul of your talents was making calls to find out about you. He has plans to pop you, too, but not for the reward. He wasn't going to tell Sam where you were, but changed his mind for some reason. Guess he figured out you weren't the killing kind."

"That makes sense. That was a guy named Jerome. He was looking for revenge, but he wasn't having a good week. He picked on another wrong guy."

"After all these years, Roberto, it looks like your luck is still holding. Would you mind telling me what got you into so much trouble?"

"I was supposed to let a guy win a match, but the guy pissed me off. I never liked the son of a bitch so I beat the shit out of him, and then I killed him in the ring in front of television cameras while the world watched. I could have beaten the rap legally, but Gamboilli had placed a heavy wad on the match. It pissed him off; I mean really pissed him off. He was so mad that he shot his best friend because he cheered me for knocking the fuck out of the jerk. Fortunately, his friend didn't die, but he's in a wheelchair today." As he finished the sentence, he pointed to the wall, and asked, "What's that?"

The guy looked, and Dirty pulled the trigger from the unseen gun held in his palm. The Beretta Minx sent two 22-caliber rounds into the back of the stranger's skull. He had done as promised; he had given him an easy out. He reloaded the gun and put the spent cartridges in a pocket.

While the hit man had been under Mickey's spell, Dirty had been busy. He had gone to his boat where he had previously transferred Jorge's sleeping hulk the night before. Jorge had been kept on heroin since their last conversation. He was too high to be fully conscious and there was no way he would remember a thing, other than maybe a dream-like memory of someone in a dark room asking questions. He had been lowered into the dinghy.

Dirty lifted Jorge out of the dinghy and guided him into the sailboat and down into the saloon. Jorge was completely unaware of his surroundings; the dead man slumped and hanging on the mast didn't register. Dirty moved Jorge's hands to touch the man, the mast, rope, counter tops, empty beer bottles, the dope kit, and its needles, dope, and everything else. He then put the untraceable Minx in Jorge's hand and fired off two shots into a pile of pillows. Only two shots would have been heard that night and Jorge's hand and body would be marked with gunpowder, his fingerprints on the weapon.

Dirty said, "That's enough credible evidence to ensure a first year law student could convict you, Jorge. Lucky for you, though, not in these islands, all it takes is a friend in a high place or money. You have both. You'll be sick for a couple of weeks from the overdose, probably go to jail for a few hours before your buddies can spring you. Then you'll be whisked off to France. Case closed. Our cops aren't very good in the best of times, but in the midst of a devastating hurricane recovery, they aren't even interested. It's only a white man killing another white man; they couldn't care less."

Dirty gave Jorge another injection that would keep him on his back until midday and opened up the boat. He left, taking the cushion with its captured bullets with him. It was four A.M. before he silently slid back into his slip. He was tired and wanted sleep, but five o'clock was coming up. If he were not at the bar with fresh coffee, the early, early flock of crows would just wake him up with their whining. Besides, he had a phone call to make.

After locking the office door, he opened his hidey-hole by removing several Phillips head screws from the bare wooden plank floor. With the planks removed, he had access to the three-foot waterproof safe buried in concrete beneath the building. He dialed the combination, opened the heavy door, and pulled out a black attaché case. He took it to a makeshift desk, opened the case, took out a portable antenna and placed it just so.

His safe and satellite phone were known only to Dirty. From memory, he dialed a number. Finally, a sleepy woman with a nasty attitude answered. Dirty said, "Don't say a word more. Wake up Tony."

A sleepy man with another nasty attitude came on the line, "Who the fuck is calling me at this hour?"

"It's Roberto, Tony. I need a favor this morning."

"Roberto?"

"Yeah. Need you to do a hit. It has to happen at his home, and then take a hard look around to see if there is anything about me in files, safes, and the usual places. Any problem?"

"Any problem? Shit man! You fucking disappear; everyone thinks you're dead except the young hopefuls who want to stretch your tattoo across their foreheads and collect the bucks and brag about what a tough motherfucker they are. You call me once every couple of years and now you wake me up and want me to whack some fucker. Who is this guy anyway? And where the fuck are you?"

"You know I'm not going to tell you where I am. You might run short of cigarette money and decide to turn that patch of skin in yourself. The guy is Three Toes Sammy. Can you do it?"

"Of course, but I want to know why?"

"He found out where I am and sent a hitter after me. It didn't work. He's the only guy living who knows where to find me, so he has to go."

"Yeah, I never liked the guy that much anyway. What's in it for me?"

Dirty fingered a file folder he had removed from the safe. "I have one file I was saving for that rainy day," which was a lie; he had a dozen such files. "I'll send it up by registered mail to you. It's about Senator Kent, you know, the asshole, who swears he doesn't have a past. I set him up a few years ago; he likes young boys. I got negatives and glossies showing the senator's ass, so to speak. I figure he'd pay anywhere from a half million to a couple million, depending when you spring it."

"Sounds good. When you gonna come back and square yourself, Roberto. It's been long enough, and if you told them why you killed the son of a bitch, they'd cancel the bounty."

"Nope. I have a good deal where I am. As long as I can keep those guys away, I'm happy. Besides, you know it was snake business and Hydra rules forbid divulging that information to anybody."

"Why not tell me where you are? You know you can trust me."

"I know. I just don't want you to see my luxurious way of life and all of the redheads around here. Shit, then I'd have competition."

"Okay asshole, take care. But call me more than every couple of years. For shit sakes, we're brothers. Family is supposed to be closer."

"Yeah, I know. Visit dad's grave for me, and piss on it while you're there. Listen; don't forget to be there when Three Toes crawls out of the sack. That means you have to leave now."

"What a fucking asshole you are. You haven't changed. I know what I'm doing," his brother said and abruptly hung up.

As Dirty put everything away, he was hoping that life would return to normal, though he knew he would never be safe. Eventually, someone would hand over that patch of skin to the current Don.

To complete the current phase of his plan, the only thing left undone was telling Biddy where the Frenchmen were staying. The Frenchies, between putting up with Biddy and the heat from the murder rap, should pop off the island soon, but he was sure someone else would take their place unless the Frenchman's anger was quelled.

"If I could just get Pete clear, or at least get word to him that they're here. . . .Maybe he knows and that's why he's staying away."

12

Surprise

JUAN CARLOS HAD NEVER FELT SUCH DISAPPOINTMENT. He had lost millions of dollars to bad crops before, and as recently as Bunny, but losing the treasure that had been within his grasp was painfully distressing. He had counted on going down in Spanish history as the man who had saved the treasure of El Morro; but that was not to be. In his disappointment, distrust crept into his consciousness. *Was it all a setup from the Virgin Islanders? A con?*

Then a dull THUNK came from the deep hole. Then another, and Pete yelled excitedly, "It's here!" Juan, overwhelmed with emotion, hurried to look into the hole.

Tom laughed, and then yelled, "Gotcha!" The nasty look Juan flashed at Tom for letting him believe it had been taken made the trick even funnier to Tom.

While chuckling, Tom explained that he had had the same feeling before, when he was the one doing the digging. The only logical reason why the pirate had buried it deeper than shown on the map was to give him an edge that the main treasure wouldn't be discovered by accident.

Pete could not believe how big the chest was, and while he appreciated Tom's humor, he desperately hoped there was not another trick in store for them inside the box. Tom and Juan rigged the double pulley block and tackle to a nearly overhanging rock. After Pete dug around the big black wooden box, he passed the line under it to see if they could get it out in one piece.

All of them put their weight on the line; the tackle creaked under the strain and it began moving. It was slow going but it was coming up. Near the top, Pete manhandled it away from the hole and positioned it on earth's surface for the first time in over 300 years. Everyone was out of breath from the laborious task.

Juan Carlos was first to speak. "May I open the chest?"

Tom had already had that honor and deferred the answer to his partner. Pete said, "Be my guest. I'm beat, and besides, it is soon to belong to you anyway."

Juan took the big knife, which he gently inserted in the seam between lid and box. It had been made the same way as the small chest. It was a rugged shipping container designed to be difficult to open. Finally, he lost patience; there were only two hours of darkness left and it was impossible to carry it down in one piece. He roughly pried a plank loose, and then cupped his mini-flashlight in his hand to shield unwanted light. The light beam pointed down to what he had hoped to see—gold.

After he reverently inspected a bar, he pulled more bars out and passed them to Pete and Tom. They filled duffel bags with as many as a man could carry over the rough terrain. Tom could not carry anything, so he removed the leg and placed it on the bow, and positioned himself on the boat to put the bars below through the front hatch. A faint light in the east became apparent as earth was spinning rapidly to the sunlight. Juan and Pete raced up and down the rock in a marathon to beat the morning's arrival.

As the sun sliced up through the watery horizon, the three men laid in the cockpit exhausted. Pete said, "Well, we managed to beat the sun, and my sore back is going to remind me of this victory for days. Everywhere hurts."

Juan Carlos, still sweating from the workout, said, "You think you hurt now, wait until tomorrow."

"Hey, did anybody see my leg?"

"I put it on the rocks;" Pete said. "It was in our way. I'll get it for you as soon as I rest and finish my beer."

Tom looked at him with a funny look, and then asked, "Left it on the beach? We have tides, you know. I'll get it, myself." He hopped his way to the bow, and then lowered himself onto the rocky surface. There was silence for a minute then Tom shouted, "Pete! You son of a bitch, you did it again! The fucking tide took my leg!"

It was unusual for Tom to display temper, but he had been through too much, and a good deal of those problems had started when Pete improperly tied the dinghy. Pete, too tired to get up, yelled back, "Shit, man, I'm sorry! We can buy you new lightweight aluminum one. You can carve another one, but if you ask me, that thing was too heavy."

"Fuck you. I'm not wearing one of those aluminum poles. I'll crawl first. You shithead! I spent a lot of time carving that leg. That was the best damn image of *Lulu* I ever did."

After Tom made his way back to the cockpit, he gave Pete an angry look. Pete nonchalantly opened another beer, took a sip, and shrugged his shoulders while raising his eyebrows. He said, "So what do you want me to say? I'd let you kick the shit out of me," He smiled, "but a one-legged fellow can't kick, can he?"

Juan Carlos had been thinking about something else; the missing leg debacle barely even registered. He moved to the navigation station and entered numbers in the calculator. He came back to the cockpit to interrupt the irritated sailors.

"There's something wrong here. El Morro's treasure was supposed to be twice this size. According to the records I've studied, this amount would only support the forts for two years at most. The ship's manifest specified gold for a five year supply."

Tom, still pissed, snapped, "Well, I guess Captain Newl had plans for the rest of it. He damn sure didn't bury it here, and there's nothing else shown on the map."

"You guys work it out;" Pete said, "I'm going to us get away from here before someone spots us."

"Tom, do you think he might have buried another chest below this one?" Juan asked.

Tom's face brightened. He thought for a moment, and then said quietly, as if thinking aloud, "The map had said chests of treasure. I assumed they included the first one, but that was a sacrificial box to hide this one....We better take a look."

Pete snapped, "Easy for you to say when all you have to do is sit on your ass. Bet you wouldn't think so if you had to do the digging." Juan Carlos was getting concerned; it was not like these two to be argumentative. Then he remembered the old Bogart movie when the three prospectors had found gold, and what happened to their personalities as greed came into play.

Tom shouted back, "Well, I offered to dig. And I'd damn sure dig now if you hadn't lost my fucking leg!"

Pete said, "Ha," reached in the starboard locker, tossed Tom's peg leg to him, and said, "Here. I just paid you back for fucking with me with about the treasure." Pete broke out in laughter. It took a moment to cool off and feel foolish for a flash, but Tom started laughing, too. Juan joined in. All was well with the salvagers of the Lost Treasure of El Morro.

Pete thought they were wasting time, but Juan Carlos was correct, they had to look. Juan insisted on doing the digging, and Tom stayed on the boat. Pete stood watch on top of Eggrock for approaching aircraft or boats. A large canvas tarp had been positioned by the hole and would be spread out to cover the dirt and hole if their privacy should become threatened.

Juan was in the pit for ten minutes when Pete heard the THUNK. He quickly scanned the area for anything approaching and then climbed down into the hole. Juan Carlos was wide-eyed and delirious. "It's here! Pete! It's here! It at least as big as the other one! It's here!"

Pete was as happy, but a problem deluded his joy. He said, "We should move the boat away, but stay in view until darkness returns. Then we'll set up the tackle again and repeat last night's work. We've lost the cover of night; it's all we can do." They spread out the natural colored canvas over the disturbed sand and sprinkled more sand over it so passing aircraft would not see signs of activity.

That day in the sun was the longest Juan Carlos had ever spent. If the Coast Guard or local authorities came by, they might want to search the boat in an excuse to curtail the drug trade. What would they do if a family went to the island to picnic, beachcomb, or skinny dip?

The duffels were nearly full with bars and placed by the catamaran's turn-turtle hatch in case they were inspected. They were willing to dump it in thirty feet of water rather than lose it. Shallower water could be disastrous, as the officials would be able to see the bags in the clear water.

The early, early flock of crows, those who had jobs that required an early start, moseyed in one-by-one. Nobody said anything about gunshots heard during the night, but only one of them was anchored near the hit man's boat. The second flight brought in three more who lived in the same part of the lagoon. Dirty did not ask if anyone had heard shots, as he would rather be involved as the second layer of information when he called the police. It was important to get the cops on the scene before the Frenchmen went out to look for Jorge.

Dirty got his wish in the second group. Dangerous Dan said to the guy next to him, "I think they're closing in on me. Did you hear those gunshots?"

"Nope," was a muffled reply from Zach Taylor, Dan's breakfast neighbor. Zach had an early flight to catch and was wolfing down a plate of Dirty Eggs. He was not interested in listening to any of Dan's bullshit that morning.

Dan had stripped a few gears over the years and swore that the CIA wanted to kill him, and he had good reason. As a marine biologist for the Navy, he had discovered that the CIA had been training pelicans to fly with tiny atomic bombs in their beak sack. With implants in the pelicans' brains, they could direct the birds to fly anywhere they wanted: into a politician's car for a sneaky assignation; into the side of an aircraft carrier, it did not matter where or what the target was. Dan had been talking about that, and only that, for well over ten years.

He was known as Dangerous Dan because he was literally dangerous to himself and to be around. He constantly scanned the sky for pelicans coming his way. Whenever he saw one, he panicked and hid under the nearest anything, from ladies' skirts to tabletops, and anything in his way was knocked aside.

Dirty walked over and asked, "Did you say you heard gunshots out in the lagoon?"

"Damn right. They're trying to flush me out. Good thing I keep changing my anchorage and painting my hull. They still can't catch me and you guys better hope they don't. They'll take this whole area out if they do. They won't leave witnesses to tell the press, believe me."

"I believe you, Dan. How many shots were fired?"

"Two."

"Do you know where they came from?"

"Of course. It had to be the stranger in the lagoon. He's one of them, you know. I can tell. There's something really sneaky about him."

"Why would he be shooting?"

"Practice."

"If he was going to dive an atomic pelican on you, why would he need to practice with a gun?"

"For two obvious reasons, Dirty. One, in case the pelican goes off course, he can shoot it before it hits an unwanted target. Or two, he has set up a different assault and plans to use the pelican as a decoy so he can shoot me."

Dirty was amused. “What about me; I know the CIA’s secret?”

“Oh, I’ve already warned everyone about that. Didn’t you get the message?”

“Guess I missed that one. What was it?”

“He’s going to blow you up. You really weren’t told, Dirty?”

“No. I guess none of the crows gives a shit if I am blown up. Don’t run off, Dan, the cops are going to want to talk to you.” As Dirty turned to call the police, he thought: *Too bad my witness has to be a paranoid screwball.*

Dangerous Dan stopped Dirty from using the island’s only means of communication, a VHF radio, when he said angrily, “Well, they were supposed to tell you, Dirty. I saw him planting one of the bombs under your boat!"

Dirty did not laugh as realization struck deep in his gut. Dan was screwy but he wouldn’t say anything he didn’t believe was true. *So. . . that’s why the hitter was so calm about dying; he knew he was going to take me with him. Son of a bitch! I am getting old.*

He smiled to appear that he was not taking Dan seriously and asked, “Where exactly did he place this bomb, Dan?”

Between big bites of greasy Spam and runny eggs, Dan mumbled, “Under the turn of the amidships bilge, starboard side.”

Dirty grabbed the VHF and called, “Police department, police department this is Dirty’s Joint.”

After a squawk, and some static, a voice said, “What do you want Dirty?”

“I’m reporting a shooting that took place in the lagoon. You need to send someone out to investigate.”

The dispatcher was trying very hard to stay awake as she took the information and said, “Someone will be there.”

Dirty sighed, knowing what was coming next, and asked, “How soon?”

Her disinterested answer was, “When they get there.” It was obvious that she, like so many other government workers, considered the lagoon area to be a white ghetto and preferred to keep her distance.

He waited a few minutes so nobody would think he took Dan seriously, and then grabbed one of the crows for bar duty. His boat was tied to the remains of a once-stout dock, which now consisted only of scattered pilings. One impaled his boat. He was in no hurry to cut it off; the piling kept him in one place so he did not need a full dock. His only concern was that another storm would come in and its surge would raise the boat high enough to float off the broken piling.

In the dinghy, he pulled himself to the midway point of the hull. He felt under the water for anything that was not a barnacle, sea squirt, or the long slimy green grass that hung from the boat’s undersides. It wasn’t a pleasant sensation and he hoped one of the giant barracuda didn’t mistake his fingers for something appetizing. An area that had been scraped clean was felt. In the middle was a metal box about a foot square and protruding six inches off the hull.

Dirty uttered, “It’s either an elaborate prank by the crows or it’s, as I thought, a going-away present from a dead man.”

He sat in the dinghy while wondering if it was preset to blow at a set time. He muttered, "No, he was a pro. He would have to see me aboard, then activate it. The son of a bitch, I shouldn't have been so good to him. Wonder if he had planned to do me last night? No matter, my luck is holding. One thing for sure, Dangerous Dan will never spend another dime in my joint." I owe him.

As he pulled himself aft, Dirty wished Tom were there. He had known about explosives and could have disarmed it easily. He thought aloud: *If I yank on the thing and it goes off, I'll never know it. Gamboilli's ghost will be cheated from his revenge. Fuck it, I'm pulling it off.... Whoa, Roberto, think.* He muttered, "The hitter needed my Hydra. How was he going to get it if I'm in pieces?" After a moment, he smiled. That fucker was going sneak in after I was asleep. Cut my throat, scalp me and blow everything up to cover the crime... Yeah, Abby, I owe you . . . unless —"

He pulled the dinghy forward and peeped around the bow to see if the crows were acting normal. The bar was empty. He smiled with a thought: *The fuckers are on the other side, waiting for me to come out screaming. If this is another gag . . . it's a damn good one. It had to be that fucking Zachary. He never comes for early breakfast and he's the only crow who could convince Dan that there was a bomb. I'm going to love getting that son of a bitch.*

Not so concerned about his safety, he eased himself down and reached under, and after getting the best grip possible, he pulled on the box. It did not move. He stuck both arms under the hull; his cheek was in the water and with every movement of the dinghy, saltwater got splashed into his eyes, nose, and mouth. It was firmly stuck, but with all of his strength, he began to move it. He closed his eyes in anticipation of the loud noise or a stink bomb explosion from an M80 rigged to go off in the metal box when the right thing happened.

He pulled it free with no special effects and was slightly disappointed. A great gag would have required something to happen. He positioned the bomb under his arm as if carrying a watermelon and pulled the dinghy with his other hand to the stern. The crows would be lined up in anticipation of his reaction. His plan was to throw it at them just as he rounded the stern and yell "catch" at the same instant. I'll see who gets the last laugh.

He prepared for the big show by getting the box in both hands so he could make a free throw pass with the phony bomb to the crowd. The wind pushed his boat to the stern; then, with his foot, he kicked off a piling to propel the dinghy past the stern.

He was stunned; no one was there, other than one atomic pelican taking a creamy dump on his transom. The dinghy glided on past and stopped abruptly when its bow struck another of the straggle-tooth pilings. The dingy stopped, but Dirty did not, and he and the bomb went overboard. When he surfaced, he still had the bomb, and was confused. "Where the hell are they?"

Then a terrible truth dawned on him: *Dan was telling the truth and everyone had evacuated the area. Suddenly the bomb became a BOMB! The last thing he was going to do was jar it.* He swam to the stern's diving platform and gently put it down. He hoisted his weight up on the platform, it creaked, and then he heard wood crack, and he wished he had kept it in better shape, fearing it would collapse.

His appearance, not the bomb, frightened the pelican away. Dirty carefully pulled himself on the transom until the palm of his hand landed squarely on the creamy and warm pelican dump; he slipped, falling into the aft deck. He was not having a good morning.

After a dash to the shower and a quick rinsing off of the slimy lagoon water, he put on a fresh set of his standard and permanently stained uniforms. He felt better in his somewhat white shorts, apron, T-shirt, and dry white painter's cap to hide his balding head and keep some of his sweat off the food. He grabbed his keys, a pistol, and a Coki canvas bag that he used to carry stuff when shopping. It was just the right size for the bomb.

When he went by the bar, he saw where all the crows had gone. They were watching Biddy chase the three Frenchmen around the boat yard. She was running as fast as her chicken run would allow, and every time she got close she kicked at them; sometimes it was a hit, but mostly she missed. The crows were delighted. The Frenchmen were not happy, but knew that if they popped the crazy little bitch, their surveillance days would be over. The scruffy looking sailors would be offended and a fight would ensue. Beloit did not like any attention drawn to him or his employees, so they ran. Maurice kept insisting they did not know anybody by that name and that it was impossible to get his telephone number. Biddy was deaf to his words.

As Dirty moved around behind the crows, he muttered to himself, "Keep kicking ass Biddy. Cops gotta find my boy before they can. Damn, but—"

Baer McNaasti walked up behind Dirty. "What's in the bag?"

Caught by surprise, Dirty answered, "Nothing. Pretty good show ain't it," he smiled.

Baer said, "Might ruin everyone's fun if that thing goes off. I watched you looking for something and noticed the way you were carrying it. You must not be on somebody's Christmas list anymore."

"Guess you're right. I don't understand it, though; always thought I was a cuddly little pushover. You know anything about bombs?"

"Just between you and me?" Dirty nodded, and led Baer to his Jeep. With their backs to the show, Baer took the case out, and looked closely at its entire exterior. As he put it back in the bag, he said, "It's sealed from water getting in, so it's controlled from a remote location. A timer doesn't need to be sealed."

Dirty smiled, and asked, "They taught you that in the fire department?"

"How'd you guess?"

"Any suggestions what to do with it?"

Baer smiled while he looked up at a monument on top of a mountain overlooking the sea. "I know what I'd do with it. Where's the actuator?"

Dirty smiled. "I think it'll be found in the next hour or so."

"That's enough time, want some help?"

"Sure."

Both men hastily drove away from Biddy's personal French revolution.

Emily, a pretty woman with cute freckles and rusty hair disembarked from the airliner. A light, colorful cotton shawl covered her shoulders to keep the airliner's cabin chill away. She wore a lightweight cotton oxford shirt with a button-down collar not buttoned. Neither were the top three buttons of her shirtfront, revealing white sloping breasts beneath her comfortable attire. The shirt was tucked into a wrinkled pair of khaki pants. She had hastily put on her Zora sandals when the aircraft began its approach. She had been anxiously eager to see the island, and started crying as soon she saw the destruction. She had weathered several hurricanes, including Marilyn, when eighty-percent of the buildings were rendered uninhabitable. This was much worse. Most buildings had no roofs; some trees still stood but had no limbs. The island was brown. She felt guilty that she had not been here during the storm; she should have stayed to face the difficulties her friends and neighbors had to endure.

As she stepped on the boarding ramp, the sun hit her face; she smelled the salt air: she was home. Stepping off the first step down from the open doorway, one of her loose sandal straps caught an edge of the ramp and held fast; she fell forward onto three burly men before her who were following an elegantly dressed woman. She knocked two of the three men down and scared the bloody hell out of the woman who shrieked in fear.

Fortunately, nobody was hurt. She apologized to the woman, who responded with a hateful look. Emily was struck speechless: The black-haired woman was beautiful; she was unnaturally pretty, her face, perfect. Her three companions, all big men, were very protective and made sure there would be no more collisions by keeping their bodies between the two women.

Emily waited for her luggage, still embarrassed about her fall, and upset at the rudeness of the woman and her companions. She waited, Cruzan style, with a dark rum and Diet Coke in hand. Pete had often asked why she mixed a diet drink with mostly alcohol. She did not care if it made sense, she liked it, and if it stopped only ten calories that she would not have to worry about later, it was even better.

She was eager to see Pete, and the first thing she was going to do was sock him in the stomach for not calling back. There was probably a good reason, but it was not good enough. He deserved a good sock for driving her crazy.

After her luggage was retrieved from the pile, she was surprised to find that two army buses had replaced the usual swarm of taxi vans. One was loaded for north side destinations, the other, for the south. The few remaining taxi vans were only being used at hotels. She was certain that her place was uninhabitable and told the driver to let her off at the boatyard. She fidgeted in her seat hoping Dirty would still be there. A thought relaxed her a little: *That damn bar has turned into some kind of shrine for those idiot Lagoonies. It had floated away before and they found it. It'll be okay.*

She was pleased to see the seventeenth century buildings on the waterfront had survived; the walls did, anyway. Most of the roofs were gone, and surely, the building's contents were strewn all over the Caribbean and Atlantic.

It was a struggle carrying her four leather bags across the boatyard's littered parking lot. Rocks, overturned boats, parts of boats, overturned cars, pieces of roofs from somewhere upwind, and just about everything else, covered the area. Only a narrow trail wide enough to get a truck through had been cleared. She was delighted to see the bar was there, but part of the kitchen was gone.

She hoped Dirty was all right. The memory of how afraid of him she used to be, until one day when he was very mean and made her cry, flooded over her. She smiled tenderly. That was the last time he ever picked on her, and she had magically become his surrogate daughter. Later, Dirty had told her that he had been rude because he was afraid that she was going to do the female thing and fuck up, err, pardon, mess up another free-spirited man's life. Then another problem developed; since under his wing, she was too good to hang out with a bum like Painter Pete.

Dirty returned to the boatyard and was disappointed that Biddy and the Frenchmen were not still going at it. He was suddenly excited, however, at seeing one of his adopted daughters struggling to carry her luggage. He stopped and said, "Okay girl, get your fanny in; I'll take you." They were only ten feet from Dirty's bar, and she would have responded with a wisecrack, but she was so happy to see him she dropped her bags, reached over and gave him a long, tearful hug.

Dirty wanted to ask about Pete, but was afraid that she expected to find him there. He decided not to ask. After her hug, she talked about all the damage and expounded on how happy she was that Dirty was okay and that the bar survived.

She asked if anyone had been lost or hurt. Dirty told Emily the names of those who didn't make it, those who were injured, those who lost everything, and those who had gone back to the States. Pete's name was not mentioned. She was shocked at all the people affected or dead. Some of whom she knew very well. Emily didn't ask about Pete, which to Dirty meant she had to know that he was okay. So he asked.

She put on a mock mad look and said, "He's got a major punch coming for worrying me to death. I didn't know he was okay until a couple of days ago. He finally called and was somewhere in South America. The *Gypsy Bitch* was lost to Bunny while in Martinique, and since then, he has been in Costa Rica. Pete's been a busy boy, I guess, and is supposed to be here in a couple of days. I suspect his major problem is, like always, he's broke. He told my mother that his phone call was going to be cut off, and it was, before I could talk to him."

Dirty was happy that Pete was still among the living. "Did he say anything about Tom and Grady?"

"No. I only got to say hello, then I started crying like a little baby. My mother got on the phone and wouldn't let me talk, but he's okay. I can't wait to find out how and why he's been gone for so long. I'm sorry he lost his boat, but he's okay. Isn't that great?"

"Yes it is,but you and I have to talk before you tell anyone else about Pete."

That produced a puzzled look on her face and he quickly put her bags in the Jeep, then said, "We'll leave them here until you can find a place to stay. Your place didn't make it. Most of it went to sea; all that remains is the cistern. I've got room on the boat for you and you're more than welcome to call it home. Or, there's a new girl on island; she's about your age, and has some nice digs. She'll be here pretty soon; maybe you two can team up. That would be a lot more comfortable for you."

"Thanks, Dirty. I kind of figured on staying with you until Pete gets here."

"Is he coming by boat or air?"

"I don't know. He said his boat was lost, but he's been to all those places. Either he has another boat or he's been flying."

"Let me tell you a quick story before we get to the bar. There are four Frenchmen looking for him. They think he has some kind of treasure that Tom found and stole from some rich guy in France."

She said, "That's ridiculous; Salvage Tom doesn't steal."

"I'm not so sure, but it doesn't matter. Tom was killed in a plane crash in Costa Rica." That news sent her in shock; she covered her mouth and slowly said in disbelief, "Salvage Tom's dead? In Costa Rica? That's where Pete was. He must have been in the crash, too. Is he hurt?"

"I don't know, Emily. I didn't even know that he was alive until you said he called. The men looking for him believe he's alive. Did you know he had been married before?"

"I don't know anything about it, other than he left her because she was such a bitch. Why?"

"Apparently she's looking for him with a vengeance. He did something that really pissed her off. It sounds like she's a powerful woman and always gets what she wants. If she can't get what she wants, she has some hired thugs who can. She was in Costa Rica looking for him. They say that she possesses an intoxicating beauty that makes all men melt, except Pete."

"The bitch better not let me catch her fucking around with him. I'll rip her a new one."

"Emily, where did you ever pick up that kind of language? I ought to turn you over my knee and give you a spanking. But instead, why don't I wash your mouth out with a cold beer and a cheeseburger?"

"Sounds great! Stupid airlines only served pretzels on the flight down. A $700 plane ticket, and they give you a lousy little bag of pretzels. They need some competition."

"Before we go inside, remember, you don't know where he is, and you only came here because you haven't heard from him. You don't know about the Frenchmen, or the beauty and the beast ex-wife, either. You can't even tell your best friends. Okay?"

"Okay, Dirty."

The gathering of crows were elated to see her, and Dirty didn't have to worry about her slipping up and saying something about Pete because she didn't have a chance to talk. Everyone, in turn, came to say how sorry each felt about Pete and his pals, and then had to relate their own stories of personal horror experienced during Big Eye. After the first story, she was grateful that she had not been there.

Dirty used the radio to call the police again, and was assured that an officer would respond as soon as possible. Dirty said, "Good thing I'm not being raped and murdered!" As he hung up the microphone, he heard the dispatcher laugh and say, "Who'd want to rape you, Dirty?"

That cemented his feelings for the island's police force. In his opinion, they were nothing more than a fat bunch of lazy slobs who had relatives in the administration. As each administration changed, more officers were hired. Once a cop, always a cop, and no one lost their job, but some would be placed on paid leave with phony disabilities to keep the numbers in line. It was nothing more than a tragic rip-off of the public's money. The school kids did not have books because the fat-cat do-nothings had all the money.

He asked about Biddy's assault on the Frenchmen. The crows said she had scared them away and she was out looking for them. His delight at hearing the story abruptly ended when he heard Emily choking on her cheeseburger. He moved to help, but she stopped him by putting her hand up and wagged her index finger side to side. She managed a swallow and took a big drink of beer, then without talking, she motioned him to come closer by wiggling her same finger again but this time in a forward motion.

She had a secret to tell. She cupped her hand around his offered ear and whispered, "I choked when I remembered something. I think I saw her, the bitch. She is the most beautiful woman I've ever seen. We were at the airport and there were three really huge men with her. When I tried to get close enough to talk to her, they moved in between us. They were nasty. Do you think it's her?"

It was Dirty's time. He cupped his hand around her ear and said, "How would I know?" He straightened himself out, smiled, and told the nearby crows, "Can you believe it, sweet little Emily has a crush on old Dirty?" They all laughed.

The possibility of the ex being on the island disturbed him. From Emily's description, it sounded like the woman and her henchmen. Jorge thought she didn't know about St. Thomas, but he had not been sure. Then an idea came to him and he smiled again.

Abby came in for her usual two o'clock breakfast, and she was introduced to Emily. They talked about everything in the world and refused to shut up, as they liked each other. That was good, except they ignored Dirty, which he didn't appreciate.

A while later, two Frenchmen came in and asked about their countryman. Dirty said, "Haven't seen him since the day before when he left with that other guy. Why don't you stick around; the man usually comes in a little later. What did you do to get away from the little woman?"

Maurice asked, "Why do you allow that woman to run free around here? She's obviously crazy. I've told your police department about her."

"What'd they say?"

With a smirk, Maurice said, "Told me that if it bothered me then to stay away from her. She has some crazy notion that I know her husband and that I know everyone in France and their phone numbers. She wants me to call someone in France to ask about him. It's not any easier for me to stand in the damn telephone line than it would be for her."

Dirty laughed and said, "It's not her fault. Her mother loved chickens, too. Some folks say that a big old Rhode Island Red is her father. So you guys are not part of the Frenchmen who took Roosterman fishing in Costa Rica?"

"No. I never met the man. We are here waiting for a yacht that is coming to pick us up for a month's sail. We don't know where it is; that's why we've been hanging out here."

"Well, this is the right place. It's the closest thing on the island that even resembles a marina. Have you tried raising them on a SSB radio?"

"Apparently the boat doesn't have one, we've tried. We'll just have to wait."

Dirty stood there wearing a sympathetic expression while thinking: *This son of a bitch is a great liar. Let's see how he reacts to this one.* He turned to face one of his trusted crows sitting nearby, and said, "Hey Murphy, maybe we're getting closer to finding out what happened to Pete. His ex-wife just landed on the island. I don't know if she knows about this place, but I've got some people looking for her. Let me know if you see a beautiful black-haired woman coming in."

Murphy was always looking for a woman. He couldn't hide his genuine reaction that a beautiful one was coming in; it was the highlight of his day.

He was not expecting the reaction his news generated. Maurice and the other man turned immediately and walked to their car. As they sped away, he smiled. That made it abundantly clear that they wanted nothing to do with that woman. He went back to the girls; they were still going at it, chattering away about shoes.

Finally, nine hours after his initial call, the police arrived. Dirty stood outside the bar with one foot propped up on a barstool and watched two fat policewomen try to get their masses out of the car. It would have been comical if it were not so sad. How could the police expect someone like that to give chase to the bad guys? The only thing they were good for was sitting on suspects to keep them from running off.

They waddled up to Dirty and, as usual, were in a foul mood. "What'cha call us for, Dirty? Dem be shoot'n gun all de time."

"Not in the lagoon, Cassandra. They say two shots came from a sailboat out there and nobody has seen the guy today."

"It be suicide, probably."

"Two shots, Cassandra?"

"Maybe he miss de firs' shot. You go out der an' see. If de man dead, call us back."

"No way. I have a business to run. It's your business to check out stuff like this. It's what I pay taxes for."

"Yo' expect me to go out der? You be a crazy white man, Dirty. I ain't go'n to get in one dem little boats 'n go out der. Shit mon, me don' swim."

"Well then, should I call your boss and tell him his guardians of our fair island are too afraid? Think he'll come here himself? Shit Cassandra, the body would deteriorate and turn to dust before he arrived."

"Dat's not me problem. I ain't go'n out der."

"Cassandra, you have to go. If there has been a suicide, then you are supposed to collect evidence, aren't you?"

"Depends."

"Depends on what?"

"On whether dat boat be out der in de ocean, or tied to de dock."

As usual, he was losing patience talking to the dependability-challenged police. "Tell you what. I'll get Tony to take you. He has a big flat-bottom boat. You'll be perfectly safe. How's that?"

Cassandra knew she could not wiggle out of going. Dirty was an asshole, and he would complain to the newspaper again if she did. She looked at her partner and asked, "Wha yo' t'ink?"

"Guess we haft to. Dis lazy muderfucker ain't going," she said, and both the blubber-bottom guardians of peace gave him the nasty look perfected before they even learned to speak. Many island people believe that mothers teach their daughters how to look mean before given their first milk bottle.

Cassandra said, "Well okay, but only if dat cheap ass muderfucker Tony be caught up on dat back chil' support. I don't have nut'n to do wid no law breaker."

The fat-ass pillars of the community got into a fight between themselves to see who was going. They agreed that both did not need to see what had happened, and each was adamant that it should be the other. Neither could swim, but they did not have to worry; with all that fat, they could not sink. Finally, the argument was settled; they both went.

Emily said to Abby, "Rub a dub, dub, two blubbers in a tub," and both giggled like little girls. Dirty was hoping Jorge had not revived enough to figure out what was going on and had swum away. A half-hour later, Tony and the cops had not returned, so the crows were sure the old boy had done himself in. When an ambulance pulled into the yard, their suspicions were confirmed. The medics came in the bar and ordered beers.

One of them asked, "Cassandra called; how the hell did you get her to go out there?"

Dirty sarcastically answered, "Community spirit drove her to overcome her fear of water."

"Bullshit. Her community spirit ends two seconds after opening her pay-check. She said there's a dead man out there and they've got another under arrest for murder." As the medic spoke, a police car squeezed into the lot. Officers Ortega and Washington entered the bar, sat next to the ambulance crew and joined them with more beer.

Ortega asked, "Who are those guys, Dirty?"

"Don't have a clue, Ortega; both were strangers around here. One owns the boat, and I guess the other is a Frenchman who has or had some friends here. Which one is dead?"

"Now Dirty, how the hell would I know? Give me another beer." After taking a big gulp he asked, "So, who are the Frenchman's friends? We may have to talk to them."

"I don't know them either. They're foreigners and have been coming in here for a few days while waiting on a boat to pick them up. Maybe they were waiting for the boat with the dead man on it. One of the Frenchman and the guy with the boat were pretty chummy."

Ortega looked at his partner and said, "Hey Washington, one of them is a Frenchman. Hope it's the guy who keeps bugging dispatch about Biddy." They laughed.

Dirty said, "It's probably his buddies. Biddy was chasing them all over the place this morning. She thinks they had something to do with her husband's disappearance. Maybe you should check them out."

"Rooster's missing? We'll check them out. Where're they staying?"

Abby answered, "At the Frenchmen's. They made me move out of my room to accommodate them."

Ortega looked at Dirty and said, "You've got two nice looking women in here, Dirty. You must be mellowing out. Why would they want to hang out in a dump like this? Are they taken?"

"They're my daughters and if I see you putting your Latin lover shit on 'em, I'm going to bust your Latin chops."

"You adopted a couple more, eh? Dirty, you are a dirty old man," and he laughed as he moved away to join the others. Just as Ortega sat down, there was a big explosion in the distance. Everyone turned to see the stone statute of past-Governor Franker, a master criminal and sleaze-extraordinaire, tumble down from its mountaintop home into the ocean. Franker had decided that the people would miss him after leaving office and had the statue made at great cost to the government. He was kind enough to donate the land that was in a place that all could see.

Everyone cheered at the eyesore's destruction, but Dirty laughed the hardest and for another reason. He had felt sure Cassandra would find the detonator and would not be able to resist playing with something she could not figure out.

The Windward Islands had returned to the way they were in the early twentieth century. Very few boats were left, and there were very few reasons for outsiders to sail into the area. The treasure hunters were not disturbed.

They all slept off and on all day; one man was awake to keep watch until the dusk finally arrived. During this time Tom and Juan Carlos discussed plans for legally declaring the gold. Juan Carlos planned to announce that the treasure site was found on his land. With all of his political friends, he would have no problem keeping the chests from being analyzed for soil type and location verification.

Tom told him how he had found the map and about his rationale that since the man's body, the map, and the briefcase were not in the sunken boat, or ever mentioned, they were not included in the salvage contract. That meant it was unclaimed and abandoned property. How was he to know whether the corpse came from the wreck, when the man could have fallen off any one of a dozen cruise ships?

Of course, Juan Carlos agreed with his way of thinking, and also agreed that since the man was never found, the Frenchman would surely think he had the map. Tom said, "Beloit will try to give you some trouble if he knows for certain that the treasure is the El Morro."

Juan Carlos said, "I'm not concerned. This treasure has been lost; people have looked for it for hundreds of years. He does not have the map or any proof whatsoever that he has any claim to it. The treasure could have been buried on my place as well as any Caribbean Island."

"Well, your property is pretty far off the coast to be a treasure sight. It might cause people to have doubts."

"I have land that extends to the Pacific Ocean and the Bay of Culebra. I also have property on the Caribbean side, and it's known that pirates used to hide in a bay there, and in fact, some treasure has been found. Everybody knows I'm a collector of Spanish relics. I'll tell them I was digging at a site for more and stumbled on it."

"What are you going to say if someone finds more gold on the mountain? That'll be hard to explain."

"I have sent a party to thoroughly search the entire area. When they come down, it will be clean."

"But what if someone found some of the ten bars we had before your party gets there? Pete said he's pretty sure his wife took some people up there. If Beloit gets his hands on just one bar, it could be enough to make a case against you."

"Maybe. I'll worry about that later."

As dusk slowly took over the sky, they made their way to the island and resumed their excavation. The second chest was just like the other; they were twice as rich. By midnight, the gold was loaded. The hole was covered for the last time.

They talked about sleeping and leaving at first light, but Pete did not want to press their luck. He took the boat out into the black waters while Juan Carlos bitterly complained that it was too risky. They could hit a shoal and sink, losing El Morro again.

Pete gave him a tired and irritable smile and pulled in the main sheet for more speed. He was tired, but he was a damn good seaman, and knew what he was doing. Then he realized that this was exactly why Emily hated to sail with him. He knew what he was doing, but others didn't. Therefore, he took time to explain it to Juan Carlos. "Tonight is going to be much easier than when we came in over the reef. The tide is a foot higher and the waves aren't breaking as much, they are just steeped up higher. I'm going to ride one wave laterally, like reverse surfing, over the reef, and with the additional tide, we should have four or five feet between the hard stuff and us.

Juan Carlos was disturbed. "Next time, Pete, don't explain. I felt better not knowing what you were going to do."

"Relax, get us both a cold beer."

The ride over the reef was exciting at moments, dreadful at others, but ultimately successful. In blue water, Pete set the course and Tom took over. Pete, who had done the most work, crashed on a cockpit cushion and was snoring in less than a minute, his beer half-full.

The crows were gone; the bar was closed, and Dirty was alone in the storeroom. He sloppily poured brandy into a dirty glass on a scarred old desk, leaving yet another stain. He occasionally took a sip while reflecting on the day's events. It had been a long day, but he had made progress. Biddy was hard on the Frenchmen's asses, the cops were bugging them, and the meanest woman they had ever known was on island. One had been arrested for murder and possession of an illegal substance.

Nothing was said about what caused the explosion and nothing ever would be. Tony told him Cassandra found the box, and when she realized what she had done, she tossed the little black box overboard. She threatened to put him in a world of shit if he ever told anybody.

He had successfully taken the hit man out without drawing any attention to himself, and he had just talked to his brother and learned Three Toes was toes up. Abby had taken Emily in and they were good company for each other. All the activity around the bar had been good for business; the crows drank and ate more. Now he had one more phone call to make. If his plan worked, then Pete should be in the clear with both the Frenchmen and his ex-wife.

He finished the brandy and looked up a number in his private address book. This man he did not worry about waking up; he rarely slept more than an hour at a time and only two or three times a day. He was a fellow Hydra, an *Associated Press* reporter, and he owed Roberto his life, several times over.

"Yeah. What'cha want?" the man impatiently said when he answered his office phone.

"Hi ya, Busy. Guess who."

"I'll be damned! You in town?"

"If I were, I'd be looking at your ugly face right now, not talking on the phone. Everything okay?"

"Too much fucking work, but things are good. How about you?"

"Good enough, but I need a favor."

"Just tell me. Don't ask, Roberto; you know that."

"Thanks. I need you to plant a story for me. A friend of mine has gotten himself between a couple of hard places. He's a good guy and needs an out. It could be resolved, if you'd send a release to several newspapers that unknown assailants killed him in a bar fight. It was gruesome and the murderers poured gasoline over him and watched him turn into cinders. Make it grisly."

"No problem. I'll copy his hometown TV and radio stations that one of their own has been killed; they love to get that kind of stuff."

"Sounds good. He lives in St. Thomas most of the time. That's where his problems are headed. He needs coverage in Costa Rica; the Tico Times would be a good paper. Run another in Houston; that ought to cover it."

"Which one of those places are you hiding in, Roberto?"

"I'm not in any. You don't think I'm stupid enough to give three locations where I might be, do you?"

"Yeah, Roberto, I do. I think you're tried of hiding. You ought to come back and talk to the Don. He'd understand what set it off. I'll damn sure back you. Most of the others will too, and that's making a hell of a strong statement that the Don can't ignore."

"You might be right. I'll think it over. Thanks for the favor, Busy. How soon will it be before the news hits the streets?"

"Too late to get it in tomorrow; it'll be the next morning."

The next day, the Frenchmen gathered in the Thirsty Conch's Lounge at the hotel. It was the only place to listen to a brief broadcast of the local news. They were hungry for news about Jorge.

Maurice, more than the others, was concerned at the news that Ann Blackburn was on the island. When he told Paul Pash, who had been watching the airport, Paul instantly said, "That's it! Damn it, I saw her, but I just caught a fast glance as she went past in a car. There were three burleys in the car, too. I didn't think it was Ann, because we didn't tell her where Pete was from, remember?"

Maurice put his head down, in shame, and said, "I told her just before she went to bathe. She had me so hot, I wasn't thinking of anything other than screwing her. We should have shot her to be sure she wasn't going to follow. She's treacherous. Wonder how she got down that mountain by herself?"

"Probably found a Sasquatch in the jungle and waved that pussy of hers at it." Jacque said with a grin. "As long as it's a male anything, it'll do her bidding."

Paul said, "I don't want her catching me off guard. She isn't going to torment me like she did those Kevin guys. If I see her coming, I'm going to put her down where she's standing."

Maurice said, "You can't do that, Paul, the cops would be all over us, and that'd blow our chance of locating Morgan and the goods. Then you'd have Beloit on our case, too, and there's no escaping his wrath."

"We need to find out where she's staying. I've already checked here; neither she nor anyone matching her description has checked in. There's not that many hotels open, so she could be staying with someone who still has a house standing. She may not know about Dirty's bar, but it won't take her long to find out. As soon as she does, she'll be asking about Pete and us. And that's when it'll hit the fan."

Jacque said, "I guess we know what happened to Jorge. She must have found him."

"I don't know, Jacque, there's still that guy he was friendly with on one of the boats."

Maurice said, "Wait a minute; that could be where Ann's staying. That boat . . . the stranger must have been one of her men. Shit! Let's get our guns and get out there."

The three men quickly departed, just as the broadcast started. They missed the report about Jorge's arrest for murder. As they left the room on their way out, two detectives were about to knock on their door. They had come to question them about the murder suspect, Jorge. One of the cops saw a bulge under Jacque's blue blazer. He felt it, and quickly pulled his own weapon.

The Frenchmen would not have to worry about Ann that night. It was illegal to have, and carry, weapons in the Virgin Islands. They were arrested and taken to the 300-year-old jail, where they were unable to make their one phone call. There were no working telephones. A local lawyer, Mr. Shys Gree, met with them to get the details of their arrest. He would try to make the call to Paris.

The police had refused to let Maurice speak to Jorge, since he was a suspect in the case. Shys Gree, however, was permitted and reported to Maurice that Jorge had no memory of ever talking to the murdered man other than a casual hello a couple of times. Jorge did not remember being on the boat, doing heroin, or tying the man up and shooting him in the head. The police report said otherwise, and gunpowder was on his right hand and forearm.

The thing that disturbed Maurice was that Jorge had a very fuzzy memory of being questioned by a New York man, and heard Ann in the background. Maurice was sure that Ann was behind this. He would not be surprised to find that she had found, and taken, the gold from their airplane.

The next morning, about an hour after the cow tongue sandwich was washed down with the world's worst coffee, Gree arrived with bad news. Their privileged way of life was now a catastrophe. When the police learned they had arrived in a private plane, they declared it a crime scene. It was being searched for weapons, contraband, and evidence that would further link Jorge to James Gugi, the murder victim. Maurice tried to get the lawyer to stop the search, but that was not going to happen. Gree was the arresting officer's uncle, and a big case against off-islanders would ensure a promotion for the cop and big bucks for the local lawyer. Several island authorities already had thoughts on seizing the airplane. That would put some money in all their pockets.

While his clients' best interests were not his own, the lawyer did make the call to their boss. The Parisian was not a reasonable man and promised heads would roll if Gree did not get them released immediately. Neither Beloit, nor his jailed employees, knew that they would never be bonded out. It was an opportunity for the police to strut. They had finally solved a crime. To make it worse, the island's politicians intended to share the limelight.

13

Taking Care of Business

A BRILLIANT RED DAWN WELCOMED PETE AS HE APPROACHED LAND. Tom and Juan Carlos had piloted the boat most of the forty hours under sail. With a steady wind and sea on their port beam, it wasn't much work. The catamaran had averaged fourteen miles per hour, and that was very timely. They were out of beer. Even Juan Carlos had taken up beer drinking while sailing, as Tom had said, "Beer drinking while at sea is obligatory. According to the ancient Vikings, it appeases the sea gods, and who the hell are we to break tradition?"

Being a traditional man, Juan Carlos was not going to defy tradition. Whether it was baloney or not, why tempt the gods? He was an extremely happy man, but Tom and Pete were apprehensive. All the gold was aboard and it was on its way to Juan's turf. If he had larceny in his heart and planned to take the gold without paying, there was little they could do about it. Juan Carlos's friend would have everything all set and the trap would spring as soon as they tied to his dock.

Not one person met them as the sailboat was tied to the little dock. Sanchez, Juan Carlos's friend, was supposed to be watching for their arrival and was to help unload their cargo. Juan Carlos shrugged off the no-show, suggesting that Sanchez's men had not seen the boat as it was going to be a heavy rain day and they might be moving the stock out of the lowlands.

Juan Carlos's only concern was that after the rain started, he wouldn't be able to take off from the soggy grass runway with a metric ton of gold aboard. He was in a hurry and taxied his plane to within thirty feet of the boat.

Juan cornered Pete and said, "It might be a good idea if you walk to Sanchez's compound to let him know we've arrived. Tom and I will get started loading the plane. I feel uncomfortable about this weather."

Something did not feel right to Pete about Juan Carlos's idea. Tom would not be much help; all he could do was sit in the plane and shuffle gold away from the doorway. Juan would have to do all the lugging. Juan's concern about soggy runways and weight was understandable, however, and Pete agreed to go. As he started the three mile slog down the jungle road, Pete could not stop thinking that Juan was trying to split them up. Walking on the narrow dirt road with jungle rising straight up on both sides gave him a creepy feeling. It was a perfect place for an ambush by greedy men, or hungry beast.

Maurice was revolted when their cold breakfast was delivered. Another tongue sandwich and it tasted worse than yesterday's. He expected action today, as Beloit had surely pulled the right chains.

When he heard multiple footsteps coming down the corridor, he was certain it was the worthless lawyer and his replacement that Beloit had surely sent. He was disappointed to see only the local-yokel Gree, the smug chief of police, another angry-looking man dressed in African attire, and a young man who appeared to be a photographer. All were dressed differently, but none wore smiles.

The chief motioned to the photographer to go to work. The young man clicked on a tape recorder and aimed the camera, waiting for the killers to get angry. The chief said, "I hope you Frenchies like it here. We searched your airplane yesterday and found an interesting array of weapons. Obviously, you're a bunch of hired killers sent here to hit poor Mr. Gugi. Your boss has been trying to get you sprung, but it didn't work. You people made a big mistake thinking you can come to my island and break the law. And your boss made a big error in judgment when he tried to pressure me into releasing you to roam freely among the good and honest citizens of our beloved community."

The chief gestured toward the man in African attire, and continued, "Our citizens have very responsible leaders who would never permit murderers to walk our streets. You foreigners think you can get away with anything. This man is Senator Bertram , one of our most seasoned and respected leaders."

The senator said, "You white people are all the same. I told your boss what he could do with his power. We are decent, peace-loving people who respect our laws. We cannot be bribed; you cannot buy justice on our island."

He pointed a finger at Maurice; the photographer was busy clicking away. The senator raised his voice. "We will not run in fear of the white man ever again! If you come into our country, you had better learn to respect the black man, our customs, and most of all, our laws. You're going to learn that you cannot come in my country and kill people. I've made sure there will be no bail for any of you. You are at the mercy of our judge and jury."

"We didn't kill anyone!" Maurice snapped angrily at the spiteful senator. The camera flashed. "Those guns were for hunting while we were in Costa Rica and—."

The chief interrupted him. "Costa Rica? So you are the men who took Rooster away! What did you do with him?" His eye squinted as he said. "Is he what you hunted?"

"Of course not. This is—."

The lousy lawyer interrupted Maurice. "You better tell them where they can find Rooster or they're going to charge you with murdering him, too. His wife is adamant about sending you to the hangman. Also, I've decided not to take your case. I will not hire out my good name to a gang of murderers."

Maurice was angry and was getting worried at how things were progressing. The photographer was delighted.

Paul whispered in Maurice's ear, "They didn't say anything about the gold." Maurice was unsure if Ann found it or if the cops had. Then he knew that's probably when the senator got involved. He asked the lawyer, "Were you present when they searched the plane?"

"Certainly."

"What happened to the gold bars?"

"What gold bars?" asked the lying lawyer with his big innocent eyes. Maurice wished he could get in one punch at Gree.

Things had certainly turned to shit and it got worse as the photographer kept taking pictures of the heroes of the island with their captured gangster murderers standing unhappily behind the rusty bars of justice.

Pete made it through the jungle without picking up any bullet holes or teeth marks on his hide and walked across an expansive sugar cane field. Twenty minutes later, he arrived at Sanchez's house. Several pick-up trucks were there but nobody was moving around. He knocked on the screen door's hardwood frame and the housekeeper appeared. She motioned him to enter and led him to the sitting room. It was full of men who were deeply engrossed in a televised soccer game, drinking beer, and smoking cigarettes. Venezuela was having a great deal of fun kicking the United States' ass. Sanchez looked up to see Pete; his polite distraction said why he had not seen them arrive; his mind and eyes had been glued to the television set. He apologized profusely, but still had trouble keeping his eyes off the tube.

Pete said, "Watch the game Sanchez. Do you mind if I place a couple of calls to the States?"

With his eyes on the scoring thrust of his team, he shouted, "Maria! Take Señor Pete to the telephone."

Pete's first call was to Emily; she wasn't home and it took almost five minutes to get her mother to hang up. Emily had gone to St. Thomas to meet him. That made him happy.

The second call was to Mongo. After telling him everything that had happened after they split at the hospital, he gave him the information needed to set up an offshore account. Before hanging up, Mongo happily accepted an all-paid trip to St. Thomas to go sailing. Pete was ready for some fun sailing, too. His only problem was getting Emily to go with him.

He declined help from the soccer fans, but used Sanchez's pick-up to get back to the boat. Hopefully, the plane was loaded and Juan Carlos would still be there. He wasn't disappointed; Tom and Juan were on the last bar as he parked near the airplane.

"Juan Carlos, I've got bad news for you. I talked to Mongo; he's setting up our account. He said the price of gold is going up. You sure your account can pay for this much gold?"

"I'm sure," he said with a smile. Then added, "You boys want to fix the gold price? Make it as of this time. If we leave it fluctuating, one of us is going to lose more money before the transaction is completed."

Pete and Tom agreed. Rain was threatening, but Juan still had to make the transaction by calling Mongo for wiring instructions. With the money going direct from Costa Rica to the international bank, Uncle Sam was not going to take half of their hard-earned cash. Tom guarded the airplane and its precious cargo, while Pete and Juan went to finish the transaction.

Juan made the call to Mongo; it was a done-deal. Juan called his bank in Costa Rica and gave them the okay to send the money. Fifteen minutes later Pete called his new bank. The millions were sitting there. Pete thought he could hear his money in the background. Each of the dollars chanted, "Spend me! Spend me first! No, spend me first!"

Juan Carlos said goodbye to Sanchez, although he would have loved to watch the soccer game, any soccer game. It was the Male-Latino's-Curse. They were now watching Mexico getting beat by Nevis.

Pete and Tom stood on deck of the catamaran and watched Juan Carlos taxi. The rain was only minutes away and it would be a heavy downpour. All three prayed that the plane was not too heavy. Juan Carlos had never tried flying with that much weight on board. The airplane shook with vibrations as the twin engines revved up to maximum power. Then it started to move slowly down the grass pasture as rain began sprinkling. Something appeared to be wrong; the engines were unnaturally loud for the speed of the plane. It got faster and the rainfall got heavier. Pete's nervousness turned to fear; he somehow knew the plane wasn't going to get up enough speed before hitting the trees at the pasture's end.

The soccer game must have ended as Sanchez, driving the flatbed truck loaded with his soccer friends, roared into view. Pete took his eyes off the struggling airplane to see what the truck was doing. When he looked back, the plane was off the ground and gaining altitude. Juan Carlos and the Lost Treasure of El Morro were safe. Pete and Tom both cheered in relief, and they waved goodbye to Sanchez and cast off from the little dock.

Pegleg stumped to the cockpit, jumped in, and landed on his good leg while reaching over to release the mainsheet. Pete waited for the bow to catch enough wind to pull her away from land, then sheeted in and turned out to sea. As they sailed away, Tom said, "Next stop, St. Thomas. Have you given any more thought as to what we are going to do to Grady?"

"Every time I think about him I get violent. I don't know. We'll just have to wait and see what he has to say." Tom agreed and stumped below. Pete heard a blood-curdling scream, "No!"

Startled, Pete ran to the companionway, looked inside, and asked, "What is it?"

"We forgot to get beer!"

As evening approached, Maurice's day had not improved. The incompetent lawyer returned to the cellblock. "Bad news, boys; I think you've just been fired. A jet just like yours landed. Two men got out and flew your plane out of here. It looks like your all-powerful boss has abandoned you. No sense in sinking good money after bad, I guess. I have more bad news. The senator is hopping mad that your boss would steal confiscated property so you're being charged for that theft, too."

Maurice snapped, "What's the matter? Your senator had designs on the plane himself, didn't he? He has our gold and figured he'd take the plane, too. Was it an even split between you guys?"

"Maurice! I'm shocked that you'd think such a dreadful thing," he said with a wicked smile.

Dirty and the crows didn't care about the Frenchmen or the murdered stranger. It was just another day in paradise where justice and injustice equally prevailed. For Dirty, his indifferent attitude was just an act. He was elated. His plan had worked better than he thought possible, because he had forgotten to consider two factors: government incompetence and greed. The way it had turned into a political and racial event, it got play from the racial mongers. It was a story with legs.

Dirty thanked God that Abby had mentioned the stranger and saved his life. Thanks to his brother, he was still safe from ambitious Mafioso headhunters. Thanks to the hit man, a ridiculous statue was destroyed. Thanks to Busy, maybe Pete would be off the hot seat. Emily seemed to have seen the light about being so hardheaded about sailing. If he could find the right man for Abby to fall in love with, Dirty would have had a damn good week.

Biddy had accepted that Rooster, like her children, the chickens, was gone and taken by the big Rooster in the sky. Dirty had told her that Jorge confessed and Rooster was killed instantly, feeling no fear or pain. She took the news commendably, and even invited him over to the Coop for dinner. He wasn't sure he should go; sure she was crazy, but her chickens were gone, and she had a hell of a body, great tits…and what was wrong with being crazy? Hell, everyone in the islands was crazy in one way or another.

The morning after Juan Carlos landed at his hacienda, the Spanish and English newspapers printed a release from the country's distinguished land baron and ally of the President.

> The fabled lost treasure of El Morro was found after 300 years of exhaustive searches from people from all countries. Señor Juan Carlos Gilli of Guanacaste found the treasure accidentally on his land while searching for Spanish artifacts. The treasure, all gold

> bars, is estimated to be worth twenty million dollars. The ancient gold is secured in Saint Joseph's Catholic Church vault and has been blessed by our Cardinal Valdez. It will be on display for the public for a small fee. For the complete history of the El Morro treasure, read next Sunday's edition.

Rudolf Calpino, Maurice's Costa Rican limo driver put the paper down and said. "Beloit is going to shit."

The next morning in Paris, Pierre Beloit sat at his breakfast table sipping tea and looking at two newspaper articles that had been faxed to him. It was a good thing an ocean separated him from Maurice, because he would have killed him. His treasure was lost. He had come so close, but Claude, his trusted employee, had gotten ambitious, and instead of following Beloit's orders and bringing him the map, had decided to find the treasure and bring it back instead. But he ended up running into a rock that stuck up in the middle of the Caribbean and sank the yacht. Three of the rescued crew had told him what had happened but they did not know what happened to Claude. Maybe he had jumped overboard and hoped to wreck the yacht in order to throw the trail off him; maybe he went down with the boat. No one knew, but he had not been found, neither had the map or the salvage diver.

After all those years, all he got out of the twenty million was nine lousy gold bars. Rudolf had made a notation on the bottom of the fax: "The treasure can be viewed by the public. Tourists must pay one dollar each. Costa Ricans pay ten cents. Private viewing by interested academics or collectors cost one thousand dollars a day." That upset him more. The bastard was going to make another ten million just showing the gold.

"That bastard! I will get my treasure back," Beloit yelled. Then he looked at the other fax. It was a picture of Maurice and his crew behind bars. Three fat black men were standing on the free side of the bars to claim the glory for capturing, as the headlines read, Notorious Murdering Smugglers Nailed by Promminent Virgin Islanders. He got even madder that the newspaper had even misspelled the headline. He looked up from the paper and angrily said, "Those stupid people will not get away with this."

The phone rang; he answered and listened as his anger grew. "You are positive the gold is not hidden in the plane?" He was so angry that he sent his fist crashing through the seventeenth century breakfast table's original glass. "Those island bastards have stolen my gold!"

He realized what his anger had just cost him, and was sickened at the smashed tabletop. He looked at his bleeding hand and reached for the brandy bottle on his desk.

The breakfast maid came running, saw the shattered glass and blood running freely down his hand and over the bottle of brandy and onto the expensive Prussian carpet. "Monsieur, you're hurt. The table, she is smashed, and you are bleeding on the carpet."

He looked at her and casually said, "C'est la fuck-it." After he had bandaged his hand and drank enough brandy to warm him sufficiently, he began thinking clearer. *With the treasure out in the open now, I'm sure the diver's friend will show up. Don't know what the Costa Rican collector paid him, but when he shows his face, I'll damn sure find out before I take pleasure in sending him to hell.* He picked up the telephone, while looking through his address book, and then dialed a long number.

Twenty-four hours after a phone call from France was answered in Washington D.C. by the head of the Justice Department, four Frenchmen in a dark, damp cell in St. Thomas were set free. A jet had been flown to the island to be used as bail for the Frenchmen and Beloit's property, including the gold bars.

The islander's arguments were futile; the woman in Washington had issued an order that was backed up with a promise of immediate firings and a full-scale investigation into the rumors of a corrupt justice system.

Senator Bertram went berserk at the news that a white woman in Washington could force his people to do anything. He was angry about the gold bars, too, but he was also afraid. Anyone who could pull heavy strings like that had to be someone not to trifle with. He had trifled by having the gold melted down and had planned to sell it to the jewelers of the Caribbean in small quantities. Shys Gree and the chief were his partners, and were just as worried.

With temporary freedom won, the four Frenchmen sat on the hotel's beach. Maurice said, "This is Beloit's plan: We are to grab Pete and anyone traveling with him, steal the plane, and haul ass to France. Obviously, we need to stay away from that crazy chicken woman while we look for Pete. After all the crap the paper said about us, and when she learns we're out, she may stop scratching the ground and start shooting."

Jacque said, "Don't forget, that raving-mad woman, Ann, knows we're here, too."

"Right. Therefore, we stay together and out of sight. After we get Pete, we are to talk to the fat cats about the gold. If those idiots melted it down, I'm afraid Beloit will be so mad that he'll try to get the American attorney general to drop an A-bomb on this dump."

"I hope he does," said Jorge. "Let's start our search for the gold with that weasel lawyer. I might just want to leave a Panamanian belly-pin with him."

Maurice asked, "What the hell is that?"

"The biggest knife blade I can find shoved all the way in through his navel and left as a decoration."

Maurice said, "Okay, Jorge, but I get the pleasure of teaching that big mouth, bigoted senator a few things about respect and decency."

The other two men did not care, as long as they could fuck up someone. Jacque asked, "What are we going to do with Ann?"

Maurice said, "If we see her, and can kill her without jeopardizing the mission, we will. If there are witnesses, we kill them too. I'm not going to walk around looking behind me like her husband has all those years."

Paul said, "What happened to that sailboat?"

"The fat cats impounded it. Turns out it was a stolen boat from Puerto Rico; the dead guy did not own it. I'm sure it was set up as a killing environment for us and Pete."

Jorge, "Wish I knew what I was doing there and what happened."

"I think they saw you, grabbed you to flush us out, but before it happened, you recovered enough to whack the guy."

Jorge shook his head in confusion. "I just cannot remember." He picked up a paper lying on the beach. It was the island's temporary two-page news sheet. Their release was not mentioned; however, it was devoted to a story about them being charged for blowing up the island's most prestigious statue. On the last page, he read something of great interest, an item by the *Associated Press*.

> LOCAL MAN MURDERED IN HOUSTON Peter Morgan from St. Thomas was brutally murdered in front of witnesses in a Houston, Texas tavern. For no apparent reason, two men attacked, and beat him senseless. The significantly injured man was then covered with lighter fluid and set on fire. Several bar patrons struggled to rescue him, but were held off by the murderers. The fire spread on the wooden floor, causing everyone to evacuate the burning building, while the attackers stood watching the victim's body vaporize in flames before they had to escape the inferno. The murderers disappeared into the crowd. No arrests have been made.

"Maurice! Our prayers have been answered. Look at this." Pete's death pleased them immensely, even though they had never seen him.

"Let's hope Ann did it. That way, she couldn't be here." All of them nodded in agreement.

The men left the beach to complete their tasks. After they found out who had the gold, they would take care of the bigoted senator, the Machiavellian lawyer, and then get the hell out of paradise. Beloit would have to find a fresh trail to the treasure.

The Frenchmen had gone through a lot since they had picked up Rooster. They were tired and wanted to go home; it was time for a friendly face and some loving. Moreover, the minute they took the airplane, they would be wanted men by the federal government.

In addition, it was a certainty that the local people would try them as absentees, and they would be guilty of every unsolved murder and rape in the territory.

Abby managed to get over to Dirty's earlier than usual, but only because Emily had heard the morning news and went into hysterics. Abby switched to her hysterical mode, too. They jumped into her car and arrived, both still in hysterics. The word was out, Pete had been murdered. Emily and Abby sat at the bar crying in anguish. The sympathetic crows paid their respects and drifted away from Dirty's bar; they could not deal with Emily's sorrow.

Dirty was confused; he asked Abby, "Why are you crying? You didn't even know him."

"Because Emily's so hurt. I hadn't met him, but I know all about him. She told me everything about Pete and Tom. It's so sad."

"Well, you two are hurting my business; don't you know men can't handle a crying woman? Now come on into my office; you'll feel better in there."

As he ushered them in, he said, "Old Dirty will give you just the right thing to make you feel better. I promise." He opened a pair of greenies, and told a crow, Cookie, to tend bar until he came back. He disappeared into the storeroom office.

The girls took the cold beers and sat on the cot. Both looked like shit; last night's mascara had run from the tears and neither had bothered to wash their faces or comb their hair before dashing off to Dirty's. In a way that pleased him; it felt good to be needed.

Maybe they would remember that feeling when he told them the truth. He had not warned Emily, as it was important for her reaction to be realistic; but she was taking it much harder than he had thought. He pulled up his chair so that he faced the girls. Male emotion made him want to hug and comfort, but he stopped himself. "Emily, you're going to hate me, but I have something to tell you."

"What?" she whined between sobs.

Dirty couldn't remember seeing a woman cry so much. Abby's emotions were inexplicable, but he had never been able to figure out women, anyway. Listen to me," he whispered. "The newspaper article is a lie." He had their attention.

Dirty continued, "I arranged to have that story sent out. It's pure fabrication." Both women looked at him as if he were Godzilla. "You cannot tell anybody, not the crows, not anybody. When the Frenchmen read it, and if they ever get out of jail, they won't be hanging around here looking for Pete Morgan. Also, that ex-wife will leave."

Abby was the first to speak. "You did that? How?"

"I may be an old, sweat-stained, greasy-spoon cook, but I wasn't always. You don't need any more of an answer than that."

Emily's tears rapidly slowed, she asked, "But why so mean? Those men standing over him, watching his body vaporize. That was so cruel. Why?"

Dirty smiled tenderly, and then said, "To remind Pete of what I'll do to him if he ever makes you cry again." Through her tears, she laughed, and then for the first time, ever, she saw emotion in Dirty's face, his eyes moist. It made her cry again; her hug was extra long with gratitude and love.

Young Carlos and JC sat in Juan Carlos Sr.'s office. The boys and their search team had returned from the wreck site. Both were still excited, even though disappointed. They had not found more gold; but it was obvious that someone else had been on the mountain.

They had found something else: three bodies. Two men, mostly eaten, and a woman with black hair, ripped apart by something big. Her arms and legs were torn off; her face was eaten away, and her torso had been chewed on by something with big teeth. It was agreed by all in the room that the legend of The Mountain of Lost Souls was true. The victims were not innocent at heart and the mountain claimed their lives in a most brutal way.

Juan Carlos firmly announced, "It's over. Whatever we found on that mountain must always remain our secret. The people who were killed, were killed by the mountain; it is none of our, or the police's, business. In fact we do not want to talk about the wreck ever again. It could affect our treasure."

"Chico, I told you that if we found more, I would pay you half the value of the gold. Well, I brought back the treasure and that would not have been possible without your courage to go to the mountain. I'm a man of my word. Do you know what that means?"

"No patrón."

"It means you are a very lucky and very rich young man. I have put your share into an investment with one of the kenaf gringos. It will be payable to you when you turn twenty-eight years old. It is set up, however, so you may withdraw money for schooling and living expenses while attending college. I'm not your father, but I'm interested in your welfare. You must leave your father's farm and start going to a good school. Your father has all of the money from the gold bar and can afford to hire workers. You are not needed to help him and now have more money than most people, including the gringos. So that demands that you be properly educated; you must be able to wisely handle your wealth."

Chico sat wide-eyed and asked, "Really? How much money do I have?"

"That is why I want you to be educated, so you never have to ask another person how much money you have, or anything else. When you learn how to figure it out, you can tell me. I want to come to your house on Sunday to speak to your parents about your future. I have some schools in mind, and if your parents agree with me, you will have to go now before you miss any more of the year."

Chico left Juan Carlos's house as happy as it was possible to be without being in heaven. He was excited at the prospect of going to school every day. He was rich, but had no idea what that meant, other than maybe he could buy some new clothes. That was all he needed, and maybe a big white hat.

Dirty had moved the girls back out to the bar. It was noon and the busiest time of day; the bar was full of crows. The moon was full, which meant absolutely nothing, but it seemed that on full moons they all ate and drank more than usual. As he relieved Cookie, the temporary bartender, everyone cheered and yelled for food.

"What's the matter with you shitheads? Can't you see grieving ladies are present? Get some fucking manners, and quit yelling and banging on the bar. You guys are just a bunch of shit-eating monkeys." Nevertheless, he loved them; the bunch of free-spirited boat-bums was his family. They were much better than his elite mob family in the States, and that was why he would never return.

Emily and Abby volunteered to help; it was better than just sitting around moping and drinking. Dirty declined, saying only one man in the world knew the secret of Dirty's burgers and he was not about to let that secret out to a couple of females. It was only plain hamburger meat straight from the package that he slapped and squashed flat on the dirty, greasy grill, which is probably why it tasted so good.

Instead of arguing, the girls served drinks and food while he cooked. It was the first time there had been more than one person working at Dirty's Beer Joint. He rather liked it. Things were going great until a crow came in and announced that the Frenchmen had made bail and were loose again. Dirty hoped they had read the news about Pete. Unfortunately, being on bail meant they could not leave the island, so he would have to keep Biddy hanging out at the bar.

Dirty was the first to notice a catamaran with full sails raised and racing in the channel between what was left of the dock and wrecked boats. They had the wind on their starboard quarter and were hauling ass. "Who the fuck is that?" He asked no one in particular.

The crows turned to look; everyone had something to say about the jerk sailing in.

"Shit, that guy's crazy."

"Doesn't he see this is a dead end?"

"Holy smoley!"

"He's fucking crazy or drunker than I am!"

"Look at that guy on the bow, he's dancing a jig. Hey! He has a fucking peg leg!"

"Who is that guy?"

Captain Murphy stood up and yelled at the speeding sailboat that was now only 100 yards away, "Hey, slow that thing down!"

The dancer did not stop his jig, but yelled back, "Can't slow down! We're in a hurry!"

Another crow yelled, "Are you nuts?"

The dancer yelled back, "No. Just thirsty! Been out of beer for five days!" The voice was familiar, but Dirty didn't know anybody with a wooden leg.

The girls were fascinated. As the boat closed to fifty yards, the dancer still danced, and the boat had not slowed. The crows began to get out off their barstools. If it kept coming, it was going to crash right into the bar. More crows yelled for the boat to stop. At thirty yards, the crows ran out of the speeding boat's path. They all intended to survive the crash so they could kick a couple of weirdoes' asses.

At twenty yards, Dirty knew his place was going to be wrecked and quickly ushered the girls out the side door. He took his shillelagh with him. Suddenly the catamaran's main sail went slack, then the jib. The main was quickly back winded, and then the jib; the boat slowed, and the dancing fool with his peg leg swinging wildly in the air did not care. He was in his own world.

The boat almost came to a stop before hitting the foot-wide beach, but Pete had miscalculated just slightly. Later he realized that his timing was off because, after being out in the open water for days, a sailor loses his sense of speed in relation to distance. The boat was only moving a mile per hour and Tom was ready to do his circus ending by turning to the crows, spreading his hands and doing the Daa Daaa thing, and then take a big bow.

Suddenly the bow caught bottom; the boat stopped instantly, but not Tom; he flew over the safety rail and landed on his back, his head slammed on the dirt floor of his favorite place on earth. He was jarred, dazed, but nothing was broken. It was good to be home. The first person to reach him was Abby. She feared the man had broken his back. She knelt over him.

Tom said, "I must be dead. I see an angel... You're such a beautiful angel. It's good to be dead. Now I know why *Lulu* was floating in the lagoon, this is heaven."

Dirty was the first to reach the boat with the club in hand: he was going to teach the reckless son of a bitch a couple of things about the proper way to pull into his place. He stopped, however, as the pilot came out of the cockpit and began walking toward him. The smiling face belonged to the man who had been causing all the trouble: *Pete was back.* Dirty felt like the son he never had had just returned from the dead.

Before he could say anything, a wild scream came from the row of crows; it was Emily. She ran forward, knocking other crows out of her way. As she dashed forward, she tripped over Tom's peg leg. She tumbled over and landed near him. As she was getting to her feet, she looked at the man with the wooden leg, who had his head cradled in Abby's lap. Her eyes widened to saucer size, and said, "Tom! . . . You're dead!"

"I know," he said; then dreamily added, "Hi, Emily, isn't it wonderful. I'm sorry you died, too. Did Big Eye get you?" Confused with Tom's response, Emily jumped up, and resumed her race to Pete.

Pete jumped off the bow, and they stood in ankle-deep water, as they grabbed each other and kissed. The crows cheered and applauded. Some were happy for Emily; others applauded Pete for his skill at bringing the boat in like that. It took more than skill though, it took guts, and most of them, at one point or another, had tried maneuvering into a dock while under sail. It was tricky business.

Dirty stood beside the loving couple for a minute to keep the crows away while Emily and Pete re-connected; but he was impatient, too. It was important to warn Pete about the Frenchmen and the possibility that his ex-wife was on island. When emotions cooled down between Pete and Emily, Dirty stepped in, and while shaking hands, he dryly said, "Good to have you back. Without your bar tab, I was having trouble paying my bills." Then Dirty remembered the dancing fool and went to see if it really was Tom. Pete and Emily followed him through the crowd. Tom was being cuddled by Abby, who was keeping the crows from stepping on him as they came by to ask about the leg and to learn where he had been. Everyone had a hundred questions.

The mother hen in Abby had come to the surface; she was protecting her own, the defenseless being in her lap. She reflected on all of the things that she had heard about Tom and his terrible luck. Now he had another missing body part, and he was deranged, too. Poor man thought he was dead, and had told all his pals that he was glad. She did not realize that he was only stunned by her beauty and something else, too, something that could not be explained or named, yet. Strangely, she had that same odd feeling.

It was great being home again with friends, and his loved one. Pete said, "I've been dry for five days now, so I've got a lot of catching up to do, Dirty." He looked around, waved at the crows, and asked, "Where's Grady?"

"Don't know. We thought he was with you."

"No. It's just Tom and me. Grady has been missing since the storm?"

Dirty said, "Yeah, but we'll go into that later. There're a few things you need to know, right now. And there're a few things we need to know. Where the hell have you been?"

"It's an incredible story and a long one. This one will outdo Zachary's craziest."

Dirty said, "I'm buying, but you're going have to do your drinking in the office while we have a chat."

Emily was still clinging to his arm, as they walked to the office. She said, "I was ready to go sailing with you until I watched you drive that boat in here. That really scared me." She smiled and added, "Maybe I was wrong?"

"Emily, I promise that was my last foolish act. I'm not going without you again."

None of the crowd was aware of a small jet that flew overhead about that time. On board were four Frenchmen and a heavy glob of melted down gold.

Getting the gold back had not been easy at first. Jorge with his newly-purchased knife and talent in killing was successful in getting the senator to show where it had been hidden in his house. At Jorge's insistence, the senator had called the lying lawyer and crooked cop and told them to come over under the guise that it was time to split up the booty. Beloit's lost treasure was to be avenged.

Maurice did not mind killing someone, but had no stomach for torture. Jorge had no feelings for killing or torture, both were only tools used in his trade. When they left the senator's house for the airport, the bigoted senator had been blinded by Jorge's new knife. That was the only way to keep him from differentiating between white and black. *C'est la ouch!* The lying lawyer would never lie again; his voice box was removed; unfortunately, the process proved impossible to do without killing him. *C'est la vie.* The police chief was treated the way any thief would have been in the Arabian world; both hands were cut off. *C'est la fuck-it.*

Pete and Tom were completely surprised to learn about the Frenchmen and planned to keep a very low profile by staying at Abby's place until they were ready to return the catamaran. Pete was terrified at the prospect that his ex-wife had followed him. He tried to leave immediately, but Emily had something to say about that. He was not going to run off again, he had promised.

Dirty showed him the newspaper article about his death in Houston, and said, "You won't have to hide very long. I'm sure the Frenchmen will leave the instant they have no reason to be here. They seemed to have gotten involved with the law here, and little Biddy. Believe me, those guys want no part of this place. I'm sure your ex-wife will want to leave, too. St. Thomas doesn't have much to offer tourists since Bunny hopped on us."

Emily suddenly said, "Oh my gosh!" She was horrified. "I'm so embarrassed, Dirty! I was mistaken when I told you about that woman. I saw her, and her bodyguards, in a *People* magazine that I found at Abby's place this morning. I forgot all about it when I heard about Pete. That woman was Carrie Burton, the actress."

Dirty smiled, chuckled, and said, "You little troublemaker." Pete wanted reassurance that it was not Ann, but that was impossible.

Tom was amazed that *Lulu* was still floating. Dirty said nothing, and Abby, angry that Dirty wouldn't tell anyone that he was a caring human being, finally entered the conversation by telling on Dirty.

Tom and Pete looked at Dirty in disbelief. Dirty was embarrassed, and said, "I figured it'd be cheaper than buying you food and booze for the next year. When are you going to get caught up with your bar tab?" Abby playfully punched Dirty in his stomach.

Tom smiled. "How about tomorrow?"

"Where are you going to get that kind of money? In fact, where'd you steal the cat?"

Pete and Tom smiled at each other and both said, "It's borrowed." They drank beer the rest of the afternoon and told Dirty most everything. They admitted to finding ten gold bars, the crash in Costa Rica, and the man who had bought the gold, and helped them get home.

Tom still couldn't believe that *Lulu* was floating. Abby asked what he intended to do with it. "Strip the paint off, and then replace all the wood, and then paint her. Then do the same inside. It's a lot of work."

"They say you're good with your hands. May I help; I'm pretty handy and have some money we can use to fix it up." That floored Tom. A beautiful woman with money was being nice to him? Then he was saddened with a thought: *If she's some kind of nympho, she's really going to be disappointed. What I wouldn't give for that transplant right now.*

"I don't think you know how much energy and money is needed here."

She still smiled at him and said, "I have plenty of both." Tom was all smiles when he finally understood it all: He really was in heaven.

14

Fun in the Caribbean Sun

THE CROWS HAD HEARD PETE AND TOM'S TALE MANY TIMES in the two days since they had returned. The story was that Mongo had paid for the hospital, and charter boat, and bought the gold bar they had found. The real treasure would remain a secret, or the Frenchmen would be back and the governments would want to collect their shares.

Being on the poorer side of the wealth scale, the crows appreciated the generous offer of a stranger to help their stranded friends. They immediately accepted Mongo and his wife Dallas, a first for anyone at Dirty's, other than unattached females. They had flown in to go sailing with the boys when they returned the chartered boat.

A couple of drinks after their arrival, the three couples boarded the catamaran. A few of the crows waded out and pushed the twin bows off the beach; the jib was back-winded until the bow swung around to face open water. Then both sails were set and the fast cat quickly accelerated to ten knots.

Everyone in the cockpit enjoyed the fast ride, except Emily, who was below and in the head taking a leak. She yelled, "Remember your promise, Pete!"

He slacked the main just enough so she would feel the slowdown, then slowly pulled it tight again. When she came out, she struggled to carry a heavy chest. "What in the world is this?"

Tom gave Pete a troubled look. Pete was supposed to hide the chest in Dirty's storeroom until they returned; but he and Emily had been so happy, he had forgotten.

"Sorry, Tom, I forgot, but I'll ship it back when we get there."

Emily still waited for an answer. Pete looked at Tom, asking with his eyes if they should tell their secret. Abby saw the look and understood; the boys had not been completely straightforward with them; there was more treasure than they had admitted to. She felt guilty for not being honest with Tom, and only fear of losing his friendship prevented her from telling him about Grady and Jerome's sinister plot.

Tom answered, "We haven't been honest about the gold. If people knew, there would be talk. That talk could end up in the wrong ears and cause trouble for us. That's one of the chests we found; we sold its contents."

"How much did you get?" Emily squealed with delight.

Both were quiet until Pete said, "Enough."

"Oh, come on. How much is enough?"

Tom said, "Enough to fix up *Lulu*."

"Wow! You found that much!" giggled Emily. Then she shook the chest, and said, "It's heavy, but feels empty. What was in it? There's no lid, how do you get into it?"

"All the gold is gone. You can pull off one of the planks to see inside."

She put it down on the cockpit floor and said to Abby, "Just imagine, this thing was made by hand over 300 years ago. Shoot, Tom, this is better than gold, any day. It'll make a neat magazine rack."

Then Abby added, "Oh yes, it would need some cleaning, though. Maybe put some brass parts, like handles on the sides, maybe brass corner guards, you know, just some things to make it look like an authentic pirate's chest." Then she and everyone else realized how silly her statement was. The brass-clad boxes were phonies. They had a genuine chest.

Emily pulled one of the top slats off and peered inside. She said, "What's this?" and pulled out an envelope addressed to Tonto and Pegleg. Neither Tom nor Pete had bothered to look inside since Juan Carlos gave them the chest. Both had agreed it would make a great beer cooler.

Tom opened the envelope to find a handwritten page from Juan Carlos.

Well boys, it has been an incredible journey for you two. It has been a fantastic experience for me. And we all came out winners. Who could ask for more? Even though you lost your leg, Tom, I'm sure you'll cherish these experiences enough to make your loss more bearable. In fact, your new leg is a hell of a lot more attractive than your good one.

The best thing about our venture is that we trusted each other. All mankind should have this trust but, unfortunately, when money or power comes into play, greed makes some people do terrible things to each other. That didn't happen to us. I'm glad you trusted me. Now that I know this, it is my turn to share something with you. If you are interested, you know where to find me. I have an authentic map. Due to the nature of the treasure, I can't be more specific, unless you guys want to try for it. The value should far exceed El Morro's. The reason I haven't gone for it myself is my lack of a couple of men with your talent, skills, and, most importantly, trust. There are a couple of problems, however, that we would have to deal with to be successful. The treasure site is an active volcano located within a remote mountain chain on the north coast of Colombia. It hasn't been much of a problem; however, I better warn you that some experts are saying the volcano may become active soon. But what the hell do they know? The other issue is the area is full of left-wing guerrillas who would kill their own mothers to get their hands on this treasure.

Your friend,
Juan Carlos

TO BE CONTINUED IN

LagOOnieville 2

Colombian Secrets

'A information can be obtained
'.ICGtesting.com
' the USA
'049260716

9 780977 086900